COME A LITTLE CLOSER

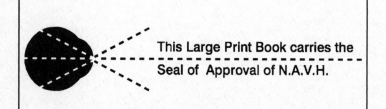

This Large Print Book carries the
Seal of Approval of N.A.V.H.

COME A LITTLE CLOSER

DOROTHY GARLOCK

THORNDIKE PRESS
A part of Gale, Cengage Learning

GALE
CENGAGE Learning®

Detroit • New York • San Francisco • New Haven, Conn • Waterville, Maine • London

GALE
CENGAGE Learning

LIBRARY OF CONGRESS CATALOGING-IN-PUBLICATION DATA

Garlock, Dorothy.
    Come a little closer / by Dorothy Garlock. — Large print ed.
      p. cm. — (Thorndike Press large print basic)
    ISBN-13: 978-1-4104-4406-6 (hardcover)
    ISBN-10: 1-4104-4406-6 (hardcover)
    1. Large type books. 2. Nurses—Wisconsin—Fiction. 3.
Self-actualization (Psychology) in women—Fiction. 4.
Wisconsin—History—20th century—Fiction. I. Title.
PS3557.A71645C66 2012
813'.54—dc23   2011043523

Published in 2011 by arrangement with Grand Central Publishing, a division of Hachette Books Group, Inc.

For Leo, the Apple of his father's eye

UNSPOKEN WORDS FROM THE BEEKEEPER

I send you love on the wings of a bee.
That jar of honey on your doorstep came
    from me.
It promises sweetness we both can
    share,
And maybe, just maybe, you can learn to
    share.

I bare my arm to the pain of stings
To claim the prize that my daring brings.
I'll give my heart just as eagerly
If one day you'll give yours to me.

                — F.S.I.

PROLOGUE

Carlson, Minnesota
August 1932

Christina Tucker gasped in fright as the jagged fork of lightning splintered across the darkening sky. Strong gusts of wind lashed the trees of the thick wood, bending boughs and violently rustling leaves. The fresh, strong scent of the storm enveloped her as if it were a blanket, overpowering. Heavy drops of rain suddenly began to fall, hammering against collapsed tree limbs and rocks, muddying the earth, and soaking her blouse to her skin. Thunder rolled toward her from close by, menacing. There was no chance to outrun the storm.

"Charlotte!" she shouted. "Charlotte! Where are you?"

Shivering from both cold and fear, Christina looked frantically for a sign of her older sister. Only moments earlier, Charlotte and their dog, Jasper, had been beside her as they hurried from one clearing to the next, racing between the massive evergreens and elms that surrounded Lake Washington, desperately trying to get home before the storm struck. She had only stopped for an instant to fix her shoe . . .

Now, she was completely alone.

"Charlotte!" she cried again in growing worry, her voice swallowed by the squall; there was still no answer.

Christina struggled to hold back her fears. She had no real sense of *where* she was. No matter what direction she turned, she saw only darkness, lit for a flickering instant by each flash of lightning. Though it was only late afternoon, the storm had brought heavy, dark clouds that shrouded the sky as black as night. Panicked, she could not remember what direction she had come from, or even where she had been headed. The lake might be in front of her or behind; if she *knew* where it was, she could have skirted its shore until she found town. But blindly stumbling into the brush would only make her more lost. *Who knew what could happen?* She could catch cold in the down-pouring rain, stumble into a deep hole, twist her ankle, wander so far out into the tall trees that she would never be found, or, even worse, encounter a wild animal.

If only I were older than eight, Christina thought. *Then I might know what to do . . .*

The rain began to fall harder; it pounded the forest so relentlessly that Christina couldn't hear any other sound. Every inch of her was drenched; raising her hand to shield her face couldn't keep the water from getting into her eyes or from soaking her dark hair.

She was scared, alone, and quickly growing cold; though the summer day had been hot and humid, a typical August afternoon in Minnesota, the rain had brought with it a chill that set her shivering.

She needed to get home, quickly.

Suddenly, the sound of rustling leaves behind her broke through the overwhelming din of the storm. Spinning on her heel, Christina searched for some sign of what had made the noise, but she could see nothing. She strained to listen, hoping with all her heart that it was Charlotte finally coming back for her, or that maybe Jasper was rooting around, his worn old nose somehow managing to find her scent and reunite them. But with every passing second, nothing, or no one, revealed itself. When she heard the sharp sound of a stick snapping somewhere off to her left, she let out an involuntary gasp, her nerves pulled tighter

11

than piano wire.

"Charlotte?" she asked. "Is that you?"

There was no answer.

BOOM! Thunder raced across the woods.

In that instant, in her mind, Christina heard the voice of her father as surely as if he were standing beside her. Over and over he had warned her about the dangers lurking in the woods around their home. Fox, wildcats, and even bears and wolves had been spotted, animals with sharp teeth and long claws, beasts capable of tearing her flesh from the bone. While there were beasts that walked on four legs, there were others who walked on two: men who were sick, who were desperate and depraved enough to hurt a little girl.

"Charlotte . . . ," her voice trailed, her eyes wide with fright.

When the leaves again began to rustle, Christina didn't wait to see if anything emerged from the brush. At the first sound, she was off running, blindly careening through chokeberry shrubs, plunging past ninebark bushes, and trampling baneberry flowers beneath her feet. Branches struck her face and arms as clinging nettles pulled at the fabric of her blouse and skirt, but still she kept going, her legs pumping furiously, desperate to get away from what was surely right behind her, breathing down her neck.

Ducking beneath a low-hanging branch, Christina bumped it, sending a cascade of water plunging down onto her head; she was so panicked that she ignored it, desperate to keep running. Her breath was ragged, her vision blurry with rainwater, and her arm ached from a long, thin cut sliced by a thorn, but nothing mattered except getting away as fast as she could.

BOOM! The storm continued relentlessly to pound the forest.

"Charlotte! Where are you? Charlotte?"

On and on Christina ran, never slowing, never looking back, just running, running. She had never been as resourceful or level-headed as Charlotte, never calm in a crisis; there was no way to keep Christina's emotions from running out of control. Thoughts rushed through her as fast as the trees she dashed past: horror at what was the source of the sounds that were closing quickly behind her; worry that she wasn't going in the right direction but running away from the safety she so desperately sought; the image of her mother, pacing before the window, wondering why her daughters weren't home . . .

Just as Christina was about to jump over a rotting tree stump, her feet suddenly flew out from under her and she crashed down onto the muddy ground. She fell hard, sliding on her front, the muck coating her clothes and face.

"Ooofff!" she gasped as the air was driven from her chest.

Desperately, she struggled to get back to her feet. Under the relentless driving rain, her hands grabbed fistfuls of the wet earth. Over and over she tried to gain purchase as her feet pushed, then slid, then pushed again before falling. No matter what, she refused to look back, to have to watch as what she had been running from finally caught up to her.

I won't let him catch me! I won't! I won't!

It was then, just as Christina was about to scream, that she heard a dog bark. The sound was close, cutting through the raging storm, and getting closer.

Jasper! And wherever he was, her sister was surely nearby.

Before Christina could call out either of their names, the bush beside her rustled and parted, revealing her sister. Soaking wet from the storm, Charlotte Tucker's blond curls cascaded down the front of her once-white blouse, now caked with streaks of dark mud. Her hands and arms were scratched and dirty, but from the broad smile on her face it was obvious that she didn't care in the slightest. Right behind her came Jasper, his tan coat wet and matted, his tongue lolling sideways out of his mouth. Panting without pause, he scurried over to where Christina lay and nuzzled his nose into the crook of her shoulder.

Even with the comfort of having been found, the fear did not leave Christina easily; she looked back over her shoulder to where she believed her pursuer to be, but there was no one there.

"Where in the world have you been?" Charlotte frowned, kneeling down beside her younger sister, the hem of her skirt flopping into the mud. "Jasper and I have been looking everywhere for you. It wasn't until Jasper heard you running around, crashing through the brush, that we knew where you were."

Jasper barked as if in agreement.

"I sto-stopped to tie . . . tie my shoe and you-you were gone!" Christina cried, struggling to contain the tremor in her voice. "You know how I ha-hate bein' in the woods by myself!"

"I didn't leave you —"

"Yes, you did!" Christina insisted.

BOOM! More lightning and thunder.

"What are you getting so worked up

about? We found you, didn't we? Nothing bad has happened to you, so stop your bellyaching."

Deep down in her heart, Christina knew that Charlotte was right; she *should* have been relieved, happy to be back with her sister. From the moment Christina found herself alone, all she had wanted was to find Charlotte. Listening to how childish Charlotte made her fear sound, Christina almost felt worse than when she believed she was being chased through the woods. It was humiliating. Charlotte was only six years older, but she always seemed so confident, so fearless, that no matter what Christina did, she always felt like a baby. She could no longer contain her tears. She had been as brave as she could be, but no more.

"If this is the way you're going to be," Charlotte huffed, "Jasper and I'll go on home without you," and she turned to leave.

"No, Charlotte!" Christina cried. "Don't leave me!"

Desperately, Christina tried to get to her feet but slipped back down to the muddy ground. The rain pelted her unmercifully. The thought of Charlotte leaving her behind was even more unbearable than the thought of being chased.

But just as her panic peaked, her sister

stopped, turned, and came back to her. Gone was the impatience and disgust for her young sibling. In its place was a spark of compassion.

"Get up out of the mud," Charlotte said as she helped Christina to her still-unsteady feet. "Our folks are used to me coming home looking like something the cat dragged in, but you being that way is going to turn their heads but good. More than likely, it'll just get me into more trouble."

"I'm sorry, Charlotte," Christina sobbed. "I was . . . I was so scared!"

"Just stop right there," Charlotte ordered, her voice sharp enough to bring a halt to her sister's emotional outburst. "There's something that you have to accept in life, Christina. No matter how much you want to believe otherwise, you will get lost again, you will be scared, you will be in danger, real or not, and I'll not always be there to help you."

"I know that . . . it's just —"

"No, you don't know. Everybody, no matter who they are, no matter how old they are, gets scared sometime."

"But you never do!"

"Yes, I do," Charlotte answered with a shake of her curls and a knowing smile. "But when it happens to me, I don't panic.

17

I don't invent things that go bump in the night. I keep my head and use it. When I do that, things have a way of working out."

"But I didn't invent anything!"

"You were running because you thought something was chasing you, right?"

Christina hesitated. "But . . . but there was!"

"Then where is it now?"

Confused, Christina looked around them; there was still no sign of whatever it was she believed had been chasing her. Even if it had been hiding, Jasper surely would have sensed it and growled. Maybe it *had* been her overactive imagination getting the better of her. Maybe she had been so frightened that she had created something out of thin air and she had run without *really* knowing the truth. When she looked back at Charlotte, she couldn't think of anything to say.

"You're going to have to learn not to turn tail and run away from what scares you," Charlotte explained.

"I . . . I know," Christina agreed. "But . . . but I'm still glad you found me."

"Me too." Her sister smiled as Jasper barked.

CHAPTER ONE

Longstock, Wisconsin
June 1946

Oak, elm, and evergreen trees whizzed past the open window of the Ford coupe as it raced wildly down the backcountry road, slipping on the loose dirt and gravel. The road twisted and turned, rose and then fell, but the car hurtled on faster and faster. Occasionally, Christina Tucker glimpsed an old, weathered house or a leaning barn, but she hadn't time to make out more than the color of paint before it was lost from sight.

She pressed her feet hard into the floorboard in a futile attempt to slow the car from the passenger's seat, one hand clenched tightly to the door frame, the other pressed flat against the dash. She felt sick to her stomach, certain she was about to meet a fiery end.

"Lord have mercy!" she gasped through clenched teeth.

"If there was one thing that was a given in this world, it was that someday Hugh Simmons was going to burn his house to the ground."

Dr. Samuel Barlow sat behind the Ford's wheel completely at ease, driving with one hand draped over the steering wheel, the other in his lap, rising only to shift. Gears ground as they were shifted, arguing loudly before jarring into place, a loud, screeching process. The wind rushing in through the window tousled Barlow's white, thinning hair. He talked with a slight accent unidentifiable to Christina, and when he wasn't speaking he had a habit of chewing the inside of his cheek. He was an older man who looked his age: his shoulders slumped slightly beneath his worn, rumpled dark coat, and his belly protruded in an obvious paunch. His eyes appeared large, behind the thick lenses of his glasses, and his face was a bit jowly, not the features of a particularly pleasant man. Still, although Christina found it easy to ignore the doctor's grumpiness, there was one thing about him that she simply could not ignore.

He was one heck of a poor driver.

"With the way Hugh always has one of those damn cigarettes clutched between his fingers," Dr. Barlow growled, "you'd think the fool had eleven digits instead of ten! Only a matter of time before he fell asleep, passed out drunk most likely, and burned his place to the ground."

While he spoke, the car drifted toward the shoulder, its wheels dipping over into the soft earth before he yanked them back to the center. Rocks pounded against the coupe's undercarriage, a noise made worse by the sirens and clanging bells of the fire truck and sheriff's cars racing down the road ahead of them. Christina fought the urge to cover her ears.

"Been out here so many times I could make the drive with my eyes closed." Barlow chuckled.

Christina caught a frantic glimpse of herself in the coupe's side mirror: wispy strands of her long, black hair swirled this way and that, dancing in front of her emerald green eyes, gliding over the bridge of her delicate nose, wrapping around her clenched jaw, before cascading across her white blouse. Beads of sweat flourished on her forehead. She didn't like what she saw; she looked ashen.

With his foot firmly planted on the accelerator, Dr. Barlow suddenly rocketed toward the sheriff's car directly in front of them with such speed that Christina was certain there would be a collision.

"Watch out for the — !" was all she had time to shout before fearfully closing her eyes, turning her head, and bracing herself for impact. Nothing happened. At the last possible moment, Barlow again swerved the car sharply, then braked so hard that the tires locked and skidded, shoving Christina's stomach into her throat, before again barreling forward. Through it all, he continued to chatter.

"I remember one time down at Marla's Diner," Dr. Barlow kept on, completely oblivious to how he was terrifying his passenger. "Hugh must've dozed off for a second while he was having breakfast, 'cause all of a sudden he leaped up out of his chair, yelling loud enough to wake the dead. You've got to be one hell of an imbecile to drop enough cigarette ash in your lap to burn a hole clean through your britches!"

It was almost impossible for Christina to believe that this was her first day in Longstock. She hadn't known what to expect on her arrival; on the train she had wondered if there would be a crowd, townspeople gathering to welcome her. She had not expected there to be a band or a parade as there had been when the men had returned from the war. But for there to be only Dr. Barlow, scuffing his shoes against the platform and doing nothing to stifle a yawn, was a bit disheartening.

Still, it hadn't done much to dim her excitement. This was to be the beginning of her new life, leaving behind her family in Minnesota and striking out on her own. She had long wondered what it would be like to experience such a moment, and no amount of disappointment was going to stand in the way of enjoying its beginning.

But just as Dr. Barlow was about to show her where she would be staying, the sheriff skidded his car to a halt beside them, its siren wailing, and frantically related what had happened. After Christina and Dr. Barlow had hastily wedged her trunk into the rear of the coupe, they all set off like a shot. Falling in behind the fire truck and sheriff, she and Dr. Barlow began the frenzied race to Hugh Simmons's home.

For as long as she could remember, all Christina had wanted was to help people. When her sister or friends skinned a knee or bloodied an arm or nose, she had faithfully tended to their wounds. She was fascinated by what it took to make a wrong thing right. Eventually, that interest had

23

blossomed into much more. Encouraged by her parents and grandmother, Christina had enrolled at a small nursing college in St. Paul. Her greatest inspiration had been her sister. When Charlotte Tucker graduated from school, she had moved to Oklahoma to become a teacher. She fell in love, got married, and began raising a family. Christina had worked hard, earned good grades, and thought her life would follow a similar trajectory.

But then the Japanese had bombed Pearl Harbor and her life, along with that of every other American citizen, had been changed forever. Instead of taking a position in a small town in the Midwest as she had long hoped, Christina found herself stationed at Fort Winger in Michigan. As a new member of the Army Nurse Corps, she was responsible for tending to soldiers sent home from the front lines with debilitating injuries. Every day, men arrived with missing limbs, some swathed head to toe in bandages, others burned nearly beyond recognition, all often on the brink of death or desolation. They came from every branch of the service, from all over the country, with backgrounds and accents unlike any she had met before. She cared for them as best she could; with a warm smile, an ear well suited to listening, while doing her best to hide the tears she could never completely seem to banish.

Years passed and the war raged on. When soldiers she knew were sent off to fight on the battlefields of Europe and the Pacific, men like Charlotte's husband, Owen, Christina feverishly prayed that they would not end up in her hospital; every time new soldiers arrived, she fought against the urge to search each of their faces, fearful she would see one who was familiar. Her prayers had been answered. However, she still saw more than her share of men whose lives were shattered, where rebuilding what once was would be painstakingly difficult, if not impossible.

Even after Germany and Japan surrendered, Christina's duty to those still leaving the battlefields showed no indication of stopping. Summer became fall, which then became winter, and still she worked with no end in sight.

But just as she began to wonder if things were ever going to change, salvation arrived in an unlikely form. One night during dinner, a fellow nurse read aloud a letter she had received from back home in Wisconsin; in it, among the usual recollections and gossip, was the offer of a nursing position. The girl to whom the offer had been made loudly declared she had no intention of returning to the life she had previously led; she wanted to find a job in New York City. Christina then surprised even herself by asking if *she* might inquire about the offer. A couple of letters and a lengthy phone call later, the job was hers.

In the days and weeks after, she'd been so excited she could barely sleep. She would have a chance to use what she had learned, in a happier place, not one filled with the results of the horrors of war. She took great pride in the comfort she had given to soldiers, but now she wanted to soothe children and care for the elderly. She wanted to help bring babies into the world, just as her grandmother and mother, midwives both, had done. She wanted to be a part of a community, to build a life that would take root. Longstock offered her just such an opportunity.

". . . taking his life in his own hands, which is just plain foolish!"

"Who's being foolish?" Christina asked, wondering if it could be possible that the doctor was talking about his own driving.

"Hugh is the fool, of course," he snorted. "If he had listened to what I've been telling him, he wouldn't be in the mess he's in today, by God!"

Dr. Barlow drove the car hard up a steep incline that soon veered sharply to the left. Not once did he step off the gas pedal; the engine strained, pressing Christina against the passenger's door. The coupe's rear end began to fishtail, shooting bits of gravel off the road and down into the ditch. Every terrifying instant, Christina expected the car to follow, plummeting over the edge and becoming a fiery, twisted mass of charred metal, but somehow they shot down the other bend of the curve in one piece. Still, they managed to clip a mailbox with the front fender, sending the box and splintered remains of the post hurtling over their hood and scattering behind them in the road.

"Shouldn't put the damn things so close to the road." Dr. Barlow frowned.

"How much farther is it?" Christina asked, more out of a mounting concern for her own safety.

"Just a short ways," Dr. Barlow answered. "Just up and down a few more hills and there it'll be on the river's side."

Even before she could see the dark, billowing plume of smoke rising from the burning Simmons home, Christina could smell it: an acrid penetrating odor drifting on the spring breeze, strong enough to make

27

her nose wrinkle. When the black spiraling smoke came into view, it looked angry.

"When we get there, grab my bag out of the back and follow close behind," Dr. Barlow explained. "Only the Good Lord knows how bad a mess that buffoon has made of things, so I don't know what I'll need and I don't want to be searching for my things or wondering where you might be."

"I understand."

"Then we'll get along just fine."

Now if we can only make it there in one piece.

The Ford coupe bumped and thudded over every pothole in Hugh Simmons's drive as it followed the fire truck and sheriff's car toward the house. Frustrated, Dr. Barlow whipped the car down into the tall grass and weeds of the lawn; the motion turned Christina's stomach while giving her a first glimpse of the fire's devastation.

The two-story house couldn't have been much to look at before the fire; items littered the yard and spilled over onto the drive. Christina spotted a cast-iron stove, an icebox missing two of its legs, a pair of sawhorses that had themselves been sawed in half, and an antique phonograph player,

28

its megaphone in tatters, rotted completely through. Rusted, empty food cans, bound stacks of newspapers, and discarded clothing filled in every available space, it resembled a garbage dump. A mangy old dog sat at the edge of the disaster, idly scratching at its ear.

Looming over it all was the house. Tongues of hungry red, orange, and yellow flames licked up and over every surface. Black smoke billowed from every broken window and doorway, pushed through gaping holes in the ramshackle roof, and soared skyward. Beams cracked and glass popped. The inside was undoubtedly packed full of refuse, more fuel to stoke the fire's insatiable hunger. Waves of intense heat washed over them, sucking the air from their lungs. Much of the house had already been consumed; it didn't look like it would be much longer before the whole thing collapsed.

"It was only a matter of time 'fore this happened." Dr. Barlow shook his head before setting the coupe's hand brake. He groaned as he got out of the car, then began striding toward the house. Christina grabbed his medical bag and hurried to follow.

All around them, men rushed to fight the fire. Members of the volunteer fire department pumped furiously at the well, feverishly filling buckets and passing them forward to douse the flames. Others soaked blankets beneath the pump faucet before flinging them, again and again, at the smoldering grass and bushes. One man took an axe off the side of the fire truck, its sharp blade gleaming in the sunlight, and began chopping at tree limbs that hung close to the side of the house, to prevent the fire from spreading. Over all the turmoil, the sheriff's voice could be heard, ordering the firefighters first one way and then another, all of them trying to do what they could so that the Simmonses didn't suffer a complete loss.

The Simmons family wasn't hard to find; Hugh, his wife, and their four children were sitting in the yard beside a gnarled elm tree in front of the house where a suspended tire twisted and turned in the scant breeze. They all appeared shocked and were streaked with soot and grime. One of the boys hacked with a persistent cough while the mother's tears cleared trails down her dirty face. Amazingly, Hugh Simmons held a lit cigarette between trembling fingers. He puffed on it furiously.

"This isn't the time for smoking," Dr. Barlow admonished, plucking the cigarette from Hugh's hand and grinding it out beneath his shoe.

Hugh gave no answer, staring silently into the fire and the rapidly diminishing sum of his life.

"We're . . . we're gonna lose everythin', ain't we?" his wife asked.

"Least you didn't lose your life," the doctor soothed.

Diligently, Dr. Barlow examined each member of the family for signs of injury. Hugh appeared to have suffered the worst of it; angry red burns ran up and down the lengths of his forearms and covered his hands; the first blisters had already appeared. Only small tufts of dark hair remained on his skin; the rest had been singed off; even his eyebrows and the hair at the crown of his head had vanished. Wrapping a cool, damp cloth around his head, the doctor carefully applied bandages to hold the cloth in place. Every time he asked for something, Christina gave it to him as quickly as she could. He was thorough, exact, and precise, never wasting any unnecessary sentiment on his patients, but not heartless; he reminded Christina of the military doctors she had served beside, men who were never rattled, as they dealt with the most horrific of wounds. Even with

Hugh, whom Dr. Barlow had reproached for being a fool with his cigarettes, he cared for the man with both compassion and concern, although he never answered the doctor's questions. Through it all, Hugh didn't so much as wince, his eyes fixed on the blaze.

The four children, three sandy-haired boys, each a year or so apart in age, and the youngest, a blond girl named Sally, had escaped the house soon after the fire had started. John, at ten the oldest boy, had followed his father back inside in a misguided attempt to fight the blaze and had suffered a touch of smoke inhalation for his troubles. Over and over he coughed up black phlegm, his eyes watering, his chest wheezing.

"Make sure he drinks plenty of water before you let him go running around too much," Dr. Barlow instructed John's mother. "He's a strong boy. Give him a bit of time and he'll be fine."

"What about the rest of us?" his mother asked. "When are we gonna be all right?"

To both of her questions, Dr. Barlow had no answers.

While the struggle to save the Simmons home continued, Christina wandered over to where Sally stood beside the elm tree, her back turned to all of the commotion. Absently, the girl scuffed at the dirt. When she had been approached by Dr. Barlow, she'd allowed herself to be examined with as much indifference as her father, although she nodded and shook her head when spoken to. Christina had brought a cup of water from the well, wondering if the girl might be thirsty.

"Would you like something to drink, Sally?" she asked.

Sally again made no answer, but when she looked back over her shoulder Christina could see tiny tears running down the girl's cheeks.

"What's the matter?" Christina asked, alarmed. "Are you hurt?"

In answer, Sally turned to face her, shaking her head. In her hands, extended toward Christina, was a tattered doll. It looked to be much loved; it was hand-sewn, red yarn for hair, missing one button for an eye, with clothes that were ragged and worn. Christina knew that *this* was the one possession Sally had saved from the fire.

"No . . . nobody asked if Charlotte wa-wa-was hurt," Sally sniffled.

"Your doll's name is Charlotte?" Christina asked, kneeling in front of the girl and brushing a strand of loose hair from her teary eyes.

"Uh-huh." Sally nodded.

"You sure picked a pretty name for her. Charlotte is my sister's name."

"Is . . . is my Charlotte burned?"

"Why don't you let me take a look at her," Christina said. Carefully, she took the doll out of the girl's hands; for a second, Sally seemed reluctant to let her companion go, but she finally relented. Although stained with food, hardened with saliva, and probably never having gone through the wash, the doll showed no burn damage.

"She looks just fine, sweetheart." Christina smiled.

"Are . . . are you sure?"

"Why don't we put a bandage on her just to be safe?"

When Sally Simmons's small face lit up brighter than the fire that was consuming her family's home, Christina *knew* that this, caring for others in their time of need, was what she was truly meant to do.

CHAPTER TWO

From the coupe's passenger seat, Christina watched the smoldering remains of the Simmons home as they burned away to nothing. Firemen continued to pour buckets of water onto the black, skeletal scraps, though there was clearly little left to save. The smoke still rising from the collapsed structure had changed from an angry black to a dishwater gray, lazily drifting up into the sky.

Dr. Barlow continued to speak with Hugh and his wife. While the parents remained traumatized by what had happened, the Simmons children had reverted to the lives they had known before the fire, playing on the tree swing, chasing one another around the yard, their laughter filling the air. From time to time, Hugh reached for his breast pocket and the cigarettes the doctor had already confiscated; every time he did, his wife smacked his hand.

Thank heaven no one had been killed.

Sweat ran down Christina's neck and soaked her clothes. The early summer sun, deepening an orange brighter than the fire's embers, had begun swinging down to the west. Night was still several hours away. The day's temperature only now was starting to cool, but Christina was exhausted, bone weary as much from travel as the stress of nursing. Nevertheless, she knew her job had been done well.

"Will they be all right?" she asked when Dr. Barlow slid behind the wheel, tossing his medical bag onto the backseat.

"About as well as can be expected, I imagine, given all that's happened. What'll eventually get them back on their feet is the realization that no one was killed. You can replace clothes and books, take new pictures and gather new mementos, but when life is gone, it stays that way forever."

"All I can think about is how much they've lost," Christina said, taking a long last look at the Simmons family. "What they once took for granted is all gone and will take years to replace. How will they care for their children? Where will they spend the night?"

"The church will provide for them as best they can. After that, it'll be on Hugh and Violet."

"I just wish we could do more."

"One of the hardest truths I've ever had to learn is that sometimes folks' lives get ruined, whether on account of their own selves or because of others," he explained while he turned the car's ignition key and the coupe's engine rumbled to life. "As a doctor, all I can do is treat their wounds as best I can. Any injuries to their spiritual selves or minds are best left in other hands."

"I still worry that it's not enough."

"Don't get me wrong," he grumbled. "I didn't say it sat well with me."

Christina was pleasantly surprised to find Dr. Barlow's driving better during the drive back into Longstock. Instead of his earlier reckless and terrifying madness, he now only *occasionally* drifted slightly over the centerline, and took curves at reasonable speeds.

The landscape that had been a blur a few hours earlier now readily revealed itself to Christina's eyes. Purple and white bellflowers flourished in the setting sunlight, billowing into the underbrush at the edge of the tall trees. A sudden, large break in the tree line revealed a broad river of fast, blue water rushing over smooth rocks. Just off the gravel road, two young deer raised their heads from where they had been eating berries to watch the coupe as it passed. It was all so similar to Minnesota that it was easy to imagine she was home.

"So I reckon this is the moment you tell me the reason why," Dr. Barlow said, interrupting her thoughts.

"Why . . . why what?" Christina asked, concerned that she had made some unknown mistake back at the Simmons home.

"Why you came to Longstock," he explained.

"Oh, well," Christina began, relieved, "there was a nurse back in Michigan who —"

"No, no, no, that's not what I'm talking about. I already know those particulars," he cut her off. "I may be getting on up there in years, but I'm not so far gone I can't recall letters and conversations from a few months back. What I'm asking is why you chose to become a nurse."

"Because it seemed natural for me to help people who needed it," she answered truthfully.

"There are lots of ways to do that." Dr. Barlow shrugged. "Like becoming a teacher or working through a church. That's providing for those in need. There are some folks who'd argue that standing behind the counter of a diner is the same, if those they're serving are hungry enough. So how is being a nurse better?"

"I'm not saying that it's better," Christina explained, "just different. When people are sick, injured, or suffering a pain they cannot bear, that's when they need someone who is trained to care for them. Being a nurse is the greatest career I could ever ask for." Catching herself, she added, "I suppose that sounds selfish."

"Not to these ears," he answered with a snort. "But if what satisfies you most is caring for those in need, medically speaking, why did you leave the Army? The way wars are always coming and going, there never will be a shortage of soldiers requiring care."

"That's why I left. Seeing all that carnage became too much to bear. Spending every day, without end, caring for men whose lives I know would never be the same became a constant that I couldn't ever completely let go. It was overwhelming and somehow futile. I know what I was doing was important, that I was serving my country, but . . . ," she faltered, remembering the difficult choice she had made to leave the Army Nurse Corps and return to chasing the dream of a life she had temporarily left behind. "But when I knew that I could no

39

longer stay, it didn't mean that I wanted to stop being a nurse, only that I needed to do it somewhere else. Explaining it like this, I still wonder if I . . ."

"Made the right choice?" Dr. Barlow finished.

Christina nodded.

"You did. If there's anyone who knows, it's me."

"What do you mean?"

"I understand your troubles because of the fact that, a long time ago, I was just where you are now," he explained. "There was a time when I had to make the same choice you did."

"You were in the Army?"

He nodded. "When I first got out of medical school, way back in '17, it was about the time the United States finally decided to get involved in the Great War. Everyone was so happy about it, all the parades and such, well, I got wrapped up along with the rest, and before I knew it I was on a steamer headed for France. I spent the next year up to my elbows in wrecked bodies and blood. I saw more devastation in that year than I reckon the Good Lord would've wanted me to see in my lifetime. I never could've imagined it. Still, like you, I knew I provided comfort and care, best I could. But when

40

the time came to walk away, for me it wasn't much of a choice to make."

"You served in France?"

"Somme River valley . . . some of the worst fighting of the lot."

"My father fought there," Christina said grimly. "He was badly burned by a shell that exploded close to him and had to spend months in a hospital. He bears the scars to this day. Who knows . . . you might have cared for him."

"I just might've. Seems like thousands of faces lay there beneath me on blood-soaked beds and tables. For a long while, after I'd come back home to Longstock, whenever I'd close my eyes to sleep, some of those boys would visit me. Chased me toward the bottle more than once, but it got easier to bear, day by day, till they were finally gone, back in the past where they belong and are resting in their graves."

"I'll never know how my father was able to go on." In Christina's view, Mason Tucker had succeeded in leaving his past behind to build a new, better life in the war's aftermath; she could only hope that every wounded soldier could do the same, though she knew it was wishful thinking.

"Seems like the battlefields of France have a way of ruining men, not just in my and

41

your father's war, but in this last one, too," Dr. Barlow said. "The same thing happened to me — ," he began, but stopped, suddenly.

"What did you say?"

The doctor's jaw flexed, his eyes blinking behind his glasses, before he answered, "Nothing . . . nothing at all. Now let's see about introducing you to your new home."

Longstock was visible to Christina from far to the north of the town; as the coupe sped down a decline, the thick canopy of elm trees parted and the valley below revealed itself. Houses were clustered around a curve in the Carville River, spreading outward for a bit until only a building or two dotted the few fields that led up to the woods. It looked quiet and quaint; except for the faint tendrils of wood smoke that rose from the occasional roof, it looked to Christina as if the town were sleeping.

"It's somethin' to look at from here, isn't it?" Dr. Barlow remarked.

"It certainly is."

"Just wait till you see it up close. It's not much in size, but it was the right place for me to put down my surgical bag and hang out a sign."

"I liked what I saw from the station." She smiled.

"The way we had to hurry out of town, you couldn't have seen much. Let's go down and give you a proper introduction."

As quickly as Longstock had appeared, it vanished, swallowed up by the woods. Having talked up the town, Dr. Barlow eased up on the accelerator, dropping the car to a lower speed. Winding steadily back and forth, the road dropped gradually before finally settling to run along the Carville River's banks.

As they approached town, Christina took a closer look at the fields outside of Longstock. Row after row of trees, all equally spaced from one another, dotted the land. Regimented like soldiers, they marched across flat ground, descended into shallow depressions, and rose up small hills. Some were large, with thick trunks, while others were little more than saplings, their small size supported by boards driven into the ground and tied straight with string. From each of the trees' branches hung apples, thousands of the fruit, meager for such an early time of season, their skins a soft shade of red.

"Look at all the trees!" she exclaimed.

"Tending to orchards is how most people in this area make a living," Dr. Barlow explained. "The land's too hilly and the soil too rocky to persuade another crop to sprout, and it's been more than twenty years since the last sawmill closed up and moved to more profitable grounds. Because of all that and the desire to make ends meet, the first apple tree was planted. Back then, no one knew they'd be so darn delicious. Just wait until you taste one. Come harvesttime, with practically everyone in town working in the orchards, there'll be more cider and apple pies than you could shake a stick at."

Between the rows of trees, Christina saw men walking back and forth, staring up into the trees' branches, pointing, and taking notes. Others pruned back wayward branches using long-bladed saws attached to long poles, while their companions picked up the refuse and tossed it in the back of a large truck. The whole operation seemed well practiced.

"Longstock is more than it looks at first glance," Dr. Barlow remarked. "Give it time and this town might become a place you won't ever want to leave; that's how it was with me."

"This was where you grew up?" Christina asked.

"All my life, until I went off to medical school." He smiled. "Before the war, I spent all of my time dreaming about getting away, about going to a big city full of skyscrapers and people packed together shoulder-to-shoulder. But after the fighting ended, after seeing nothing but death and destruction, the only thing I wanted was to get back to what I knew, back to a way of life that was simple and innocent, even if I no longer was."

"And you haven't regretted your decision?"

"Not a day, well, maybe once or twice over the years." Dr. Barlow chuckled. "But there's life and culture here, the sort you might not expect. Even in a town small as Longstock, people know about theater, music, politics, and there's even a passing knowledge of the game of baseball, though no one has a better grasp than myself, that's for certain."

"I've never liked it much myself." Christina frowned.

"And I guarantee you are a lesser person for it. Wait until I tell you about the time I got to meet Babe Ruth!"

Longstock's main street was nearly identical to the one on which Christina had grown up: dusty, dented cars and trucks parked outside of storefronts; a pair of older men sitting in front of the barbershop waiting

45

their turn in the chair, gossiping beside the signature red, white, and blue pole. The small theater's marquee advertised a new film starring John Wayne; a woman hurried from the grocer's, a sack of items balanced precariously in her arms as she tried to corral the two young boys who darted back and forth just out of reach.

Even now, almost a year after the war's end, American flags flew proudly from in front of nearly every door, crisp in the breeze, while bunting colored windowsills. A banner welcoming the return of Longstock's soldiers still flapped, hung across the street between two buildings.

Cheerful, friendly voices called back and forth, hailing neighbors. Dr. Barlow joined in the greeting, acknowledging people he met with a wave, a nod, and a good word.

"People here in Longstock are mostly the same as a doctor would find anywhere else," he explained. "Babies are born and old people die. They catch cold when winter arrives and break out in hives come spring. There are drunken brawls and accidents, fires and frostbite, drownings and car crashes, and there've even been a couple of murders in the twenty-five years I've been doctoring here. I've seen them at their worst and their best, changing from one day to the next, it seems, but all in all, it's home."

The doctor pulled the coupe into an empty space in front of the bakery. As she stepped from the car, Christina breathed in the sweet, savory aroma of fresh bread, cookies, and cakes that rolled out of the open front door; it made her stomach grumble loudly.

Wrestling her trunk free from the coupe's rear, they each grabbed a handle, and Dr. Barlow led the way up a flight of steps attached to the side of the bakery building. At the top, a landing led to the rooms Christina would be renting. Stopping to wipe the sweat from his brow, the doctor pointed to a building visible farther up Main Street and immediately around the nearest corner.

"There is our clinic," he wheezed. "Just . . . just a quick walk from here. I'll show it to you in the morning."

The apartment was small, but Christina hadn't expected, or wanted, much. There was a front room furnished with a patched-up couch and a lone table, an attached kitchen with a stove and icebox, a tiny bathroom, and a door that led down a short hallway to a bedroom. The main window faced west and the rays of the setting sun streamed inside, brightening the walls a pleasant shade. The little flat might have needed a fresh coat of paint or a picture or two hanging from the walls, but the sight of it brought a smile to her face.

"Now I know it isn't much," the doctor began.

"It will do just fine," she assured him.

Together, they hauled the trunk into the bedroom and dropped it on the floor beside the dresser with a loud thud; Christina frowned at the missing knobs on the drawers and deep gouges that chipped the paint on its surface, but quickly hid her unhappiness for fear that the doctor would see. After all, there was nothing wrong with it that she could not fix.

"One of the little-known perks of staying in this room is that you'll never need an alarm clock," Dr. Barlow said. "Every morning, the smell of whatever's coming out fresh from the oven will get you out of bed and down the stairs faster than any rooster could ever dream of doing."

The mention of food again set Christina's stomach to rumbling; it had been a long time since she had finished her small sandwich on the train.

"I am quite hungry," she said. "I suppose I should find something to eat."

"Well, then you're in luck," he crowed. "I'm inviting you to share a home-cooked meal, and before you even try to say that I shouldn't have gone to such trouble, I didn't. Tonight we're eating at my sister's home. There'll be roast chicken, mashed potatoes, more salads than will fit in your stomach, and of course an apple pie. So, if you've got any reservations about attending, you'll have to take them up with her, but I warn you, she's not above biting those who cross her."

Much to her stomach's joy, Christina readily accepted.

CHAPTER THREE

The sun was just setting over the edge of the western horizon, brilliant streams of burnt oranges and reds coloring the sky, when Dr. Barlow turned the coupe onto the street on which his sister, Clara Sutter, lived east of downtown. Elm trees had been planted between the street and sidewalk long ago, their lengthy branches spreading out over the street in a canopy that blocked out much of the sky. In the early evening hour, lightning bugs blinked in and out as the cicadas keened.

Clara Sutter's home was a modest two-story that was identical to most all of the others on her street. It was a bungalow style that had been popular for years, with a brick exterior framed by shutters that had been painted a warm shade of yellow. A low-pitched, gabled roof overhung a porch that ran the length of the front of the house; it was held up by brick supports, buttressed at the top by ornate, decorative braces. Big windows looked out at the street and a manicured walk led up to the front door.

"Just look at all of the beautiful flowers!" Christina exclaimed.

Bright red and pink blooms ran the length of the walk up to the porch and filled the stone planter boxes on both the façade and stairs. Potted ferns stood at either side of the bottom of the stairs, silent sentinels watching all comings and goings. Meticulously placed bushes sprouted beneath the side windows, all of the red, pink, and white flowers spread full, their petals soaking up the last of the sunlight.

"My sister started growing flowers just as her sons were shipped off to the war," Dr. Barlow explained. "Every day she could, she would tend to them, feed and fertilize them, dote over them like her life depended on it. It was her coping mechanism, the only way she could find to get herself through another day of worrying about what could happen to her boys."

"*Did* anything happen to them?"

"Now that . . . ," he muttered, "is one . . . difficult question to answer . . ."

Through the coupe's open windows, the piercing, rhythmic sound of metal banging against metal reached their ears. At the other end of the drive, a light shone through the windows of the detached garage. Over and over, the steady noise was carried over the evening air. When it was suddenly interrupted, a man's voice barked a harsh obscenity before the sound again resumed.

"That'll be my nephew, Tyler, working on his car," Dr. Barlow said with a weary shake of his head. "I just can't ever seem to get that boy's head out from under the hood of a car. Clara's afraid he's starting to like engines more than people."

Another, more colorful display of cursing came from the garage, as if in reply.

Just as Christina was shutting the car door behind her, footsteps sounded down the walk and she turned to find Clara Sutter hurrying toward them. Though much younger than her brother, she still shared a close resemblance; there were the same eyes and droopy face, but where Samuel Barlow's mood was sometimes sour, Clara's was as sunny as early morning. But as she wiped her hands on her flower print apron, Christina could see that, just behind Clara's warm exterior, there was a look of fatigue in her eyes and a tiredness around her edges.

"Oh, my dear, my dear!" Clara exclaimed, beaming broadly. "It's so very nice to meet you. Welcome to Longstock!"

"It's my pleasure," Christina answered, suddenly embarrassed by her lack of a bath and that she was still wearing dirty clothes; she wondered if she was as disheveled to look at as she felt. "I'm sorry that I'm not more presentable."

"Nonsense," Clara replied. "Just wait until you see the shape Tyler will arrive in. You'll look like a princess in comparison. Now, I'm just certain that after a long day cooped up on a train, then being dragged about by my brother, you must be starving!"

"Tending to people in need isn't the same as being dragged around," the doctor disagreed.

"Hush now, Samuel," she chided him. "The way you drive, it's something of a miracle that she's made it this far in one piece!"

"You talk as if your driving is any better!"

"Well, at least I have the good sense to know my limitations. Only the blindest of men go about in the darkness claiming that they can still see." Taking Christina gently by the arm, Clara asked, "Are you ready to eat?"

Without warning, Christina's stomach growled loudly. Embarrassed, she quickly said, "I hadn't realized just how hungry I was until we went to the apartment where

I'll be staying. The smells from the bakery were almost more than I could bear."

"Then you've certainly come to the right place. The roast chicken will be ready to come out of the oven any minute. Please, come."

"Making fun of my driving . . . well, I never . . . ," the doctor grumbled as they headed up the walk.

The inside of Clara Sutter's home was as attractive as the outside. The furniture wasn't showy but well lived-in and comfortable: a painting of a boat sailing across choppy waters caught the last sun through an open window; a vase of cut flowers added a splash of color; and a row of bookcases, filled with ornate volumes, lined one wall. The smell of cooking food wafted through the house. But what caught Christina's attention was the music. A record slowly turned on a player almost identical to the one lying discarded in the Simmons drive, needle dancing along its grooves, filling the room with classical music.

"You have such a beautiful home," she said.

"Thank you." Clara saw that her guest was especially interested in the phonograph. "Do you like music?"

"Very much. I grew up listening to my grandmother and mother playing the piano."

"I've found that listening to Brahms or Mozart as I work is the easiest way to make an unpleasant task go faster," Clara explained. "When I'm gardening, I especially like to entertain myself with a record, although once in a while I've had a neighbor ask if I might turn it down a bit." She laughed.

The dining room, just off the kitchen, was prepared for their meal; the table was covered in a pristine cloth, white china plates were framed by sparkling silverware, and goblets were filled with water. Unlit candles were set out between a bowl heaped high with mashed potatoes and a tray covered in steaming grilled vegetables. Five place settings had been prepared, each chair slid back for its occupant.

"I see you're still hoping that Holden will join us," Dr. Barlow said to his sister.

Clara looked nervously at their guest. "I told him that we were having someone over for dinner and that I expected him to join us."

"You know that'll get his dander up. He'll not come down —"

"I know perfectly well what works and

what does not work with my own son," Clara snapped, a sudden fiery look filling her eyes. "Just because you're the doctor in this family does not mean that I have to follow every bit of advice you so freely give. What Holden needs is the reminder that he's *still* welcome to join us."

"All I'm saying is —"

"Just hold your tongue." She glared. "I've already asked him, so there's no point in arguing it further."

Dr. Barlow looked as if he wanted to say more, but he glanced up to see Christina regarding them both uncomfortably, her eyes wide with surprise, and held his tongue.

An awkward silence filled the room. "I'm sorry, Christina," Clara finally said, her smile returning so easily that it looked practiced. "Holden, my oldest son, has a . . . it's just that he feels . . . well, instead of struggling to explain it to you, when he comes down and joins us for the meal I'm sure that you will understand."

"Well, I . . . ," Christina began, uncertain as to how to reply, but neither of them seemed to require an answer.

"Samuel," Clara said, turning her attention to other matters. "Why don't you call Tyler to the table and I'll fetch the chicken from the oven. In the meantime, Christina, make yourself at home."

And with that, they both left.

When she was alone in the dining room, Christina's sense of discomfort did not subside. She didn't know what Clara and Dr. Barlow were talking about, but the argument was one they seemed well accustomed to hashing out. Whatever problems Holden Sutter was facing, there had been two competing ideas for how to handle them. Christina hoped that, if Clara's son did join them, there would be no further confrontation.

Still, part of her wondered what *had* happened to Holden Sutter. That no one was willing to say it aloud unnerved her.

In the kitchen, she heard the sounds of the oven door being swung open and a heavy pan being set on a countertop.

"Tyler!" Dr. Barlow shouted out the kitchen window. "Get out from under that hood and come in here! It's time to eat!"

"Yeah, yeah!" a voice shouted in answer.

"The car will still be there when you've finished! You're not going to want to wait untill the chicken gets cold!"

"Hold your horses!"

"Don't make me come out there!"

"It might be the only way you'll get him

in here," Clara muttered.

Eager to avoid more bickering, Christina retreated farther into the living room, where she allowed her attention to be drawn to the top of a bureau. There she saw a photograph in a simple frame, which she picked up for a closer look; in the picture, two young boys stood directly in front of a man and woman, the latter of whom was easily recognizable as Clara Sutter. Squinting closer, Christina saw that it had been taken right in front of the house. From what she had heard, it was easy to assume that the two boys were Tyler and Holden, but she couldn't know for certain.

Suddenly, the back door in the kitchen slammed shut, startling her. She set the picture back down on the bureau in a clatter, nearly dropping it.

"You're lucky you came when you did, because I was about to come out there and drag you in," Dr. Barlow said.

"Quit lying," a man's voice joked loudly. "The way you love Mom's chicken, it would've been in your best interest to leave me out there until you helped yourself."

Christina stepped into the middle of the living room, giving her a slightly less obscured view into the kitchen. A man had joined Clara and Dr. Barlow, but the door frame prevented her from seeing him clearly. He was dressed simply; a grey work shirt was tucked haphazardly into brown work pants, all of his clothing smudged. She wanted to see more, but she couldn't bring herself to step out and be noticed.

"Go get cleaned up, Tyler," Clara scolded. "Being covered in grease stains is no way to meet our guest. You'll not make a good impression that way."

"Oh, that's right! I forgot we were having company!" Tyler complained. "Damn!"

"You just watch your mouth, young man!" his mother cried. "I will not tolerate that type of language under my roof! If your father were still with us, he wouldn't —"

"Yeah, yeah, yeah! All the nagging makes me wonder why I ever come out of the garage! Hell, she's probably from some backwater where dirt streaks are considered attractive! I bet she —"

As he talked, Tyler Sutter continued to move backward until, out of the corner of his eye, he got his first look at Christina Tucker.

As she sat down at the dinner table, there was much for Christina to enjoy: Clara Sutter's cooking was excellent, particularly her roast chicken, which practically fell from the bone. Dr. Barlow regaled them with funny anecdotes from his thirty years of medicine, laughing so hard that tears formed in his eyes; and the classical music had been replaced by a swinging big band, the sounds of trumpets and clarinets mixing with the clinking of silverware, the heaping of plates, and the filling of glasses.

But even as she helped herself to another serving of green beans, Christina was acutely aware of the awkwardness that had crept in at the edges of the room. Holden Sutter hadn't joined them, his empty chair sitting opposite his uncle's, his plate and utensils unused. While his absence was never acknowledged, Clara's gaze occasionally wandered over to the stairs, as if she expected him to appear at any minute. No verbal fireworks, though; this time, all held their tongues, at least so far.

And then there was Tyler Sutter.

Even though he now knew that Christina had heard every rude, despicable word he'd said in the kitchen, he showed no sign of embarrassment. Protesting every inch of the way, he had finally agreed to his mother's demand that he change into something more presentable, trading his dirty shirt for a white one; even now, sitting directly across from her, he fumbled at his collar, pulling it out and away from his skin. He rarely added anything to the conversation other than a snide comment or disdainful laugh. But through it all, Christina found it hard *not* to look at him.

Tyler Sutter was the sort of man whose appearance drew attention; he had a strong, firm jaw framing expressive features, particularly his eyes, the clear blue of a fresh April morning. His blond hair was cut short. Even in uncomfortable clothes, his broad shoulders and muscular arms were evident, straining against the fabric of his shirt. He had a habit of pursing his lips together, as if he was thinking over something important, which narrowed his gaze and made him look slightly mischievous, even dangerous.

The impression Tyler gave was one of detachment, as if he wanted to be anywhere other than the dinner table, probably back in his beloved garage, but through all of his posturing Christina noticed that his eyes remained alert, darting glances in her direction. She couldn't say much about his manners, but he *was* a handsome man.

". . . with three pigs underneath the trough!"

"No matter how many times you tell that story, Samuel," Clara gushed, "it still never fails to make me laugh!"

"Yeah," Tyler added sarcastically. "It's hilarious . . ."

Clara did her best to ignore her son. "So tell me, Christina, my dear." She smiled. "What do you think of Longstock so far?"

"I haven't had a chance to see much of it," she answered. "But what I've seen is certainly very nice. It reminds me of Carlson, the town I grew up in back in Minnesota."

"So it's boring there, too, huh?" Tyler smirked, his eyes devilish.

"Tyler!" his mother admonished.

"You look like you're about the same age as I am," he said, leaning his elbows on the table and fixing his stare on Christina, all the while ignoring the glares he was getting from his relatives. She felt a bit uneasy having him look at her in such a way. "With the war and all, I'd expect that to mean your nursing probably took you out of state, if not out of the country."

"I was in Michigan."

"Then that means you got to see more of the world than what you grew up around," he continued, leaning way back in his chair and folding his arms across his expansive chest. "Having experienced more than your own backyard, you should have developed a taste for something more, something better. Why would you ever consider settling for so little?"

Listening to Tyler Sutter speak to her in such a way irritated Christina. She'd never been the type of woman who would fly off the handle or angrily lash out, giving someone a piece of her mind, as Charlotte was more likely to do. But there was *something* about this man that riled her, and she found herself wanting to wipe the smirk off his face.

"If you're so set on running down anyone who would willingly return to small-town life, then why are *you* here?" she asked, growing bolder. "My grandmother used to say that anyone who talks from a pulpit should practice what they preach, so why don't you?"

Christina didn't know what reaction she expected; more than likely, she would have imagined Tyler would continue to talk wise, easily laughing off her barbs and proceeding with new ones of his own. Or that he might argue the point further, maybe even becoming crude with his comments. But what *did* happen surprised her; his mouth swung shut, his jaw clenched, and he stared at her with a barely suppressed anger. When he finally found his voice, it was through clenched teeth that he said, "It's Holden's fault."

"Watch what you're saying, boy," Dr. Barlow warned. "That's no way to talk about your brother."

"Would . . . would anyone like some pie?" Clara asked, anxious to move the conversation away from a topic that clearly unsettled her.

"Why is everyone in this family so damned afraid to admit to something we already know?" Tyler snapped, tossing his napkin into his plate. Veins stood out on his neck as he spoke, his voice rising. "Over and over we act as if nothing is the matter, setting a place at the table like he's going to come down those stairs and join us!"

"But it . . . it is possible," Clara said weakly.

"No, it's not!" Tyler barked. "It's been more than a year since he came home and it hasn't gotten any better! In fact, it's gotten worse. We all walk around worried that we'll say or do something wrong, but the fact is that Holden is never going to be the man he was. Expecting him to be so is just wishful thinking."

"He'll get better!" Clara protested.

"He's a grown man who doesn't want to leave the house!"

"Because of what happened to him during the war!"

"Why are you so set on defending him, Mother?" Tyler argued, a frustrated, ironic smile on his face. "The last time he sent you away in tears, didn't you say you were through trying to persuade him to leave the house? Didn't you swear that you'd done all you possibly could for him? Uncle Samuel." He turned and asked, "Didn't she say that she had had enough?"

Dr. Barlow gave no answer, a reply in itself.

"I can't give up on my son and send him back to the veterans hospital." Clara finally answered.

"Even if he's given up on himself?" When no one responded, Tyler snarled, "And you wonder why I spend so much damn time in the garage."

When the back door to the kitchen slammed hard enough to cause her to flinch, Christina wondered, not for the first time that day, if coming to Longstock had been a mistake.

CHAPTER FOUR

Christina picked up the last of the empty bowls from the dining room table and took them to the kitchen, still trying to understand all that had happened before her eyes. While her thoughts remained a jumbled mess, Dr. Barlow and his sister seemed unaffected by Tyler's outburst.

Clara hummed softly as she washed silverware, handing each piece to her brother to dry, neither saying a word about the earlier confrontation. Christina was amazed by the extent of their denial; even as Clara's son angrily slammed the back door and stomped off to the garage, she just smiled and asked if either of them was ready for a piece of pie; but Tyler Sutter had ruined Christina's appetite.

"Is that everything, dear?" Clara asked as Christina entered the kitchen.

"Only the platter with the rest of the chicken is left."

"Could you bring it to me?"

"Of course."

On the counter beside the sink was a plate on which Clara had placed some of every item that had been served at dinner: mashed potatoes, creamed corn, salad, as well as an enormous slice of apple pie. An empty spot remained. Christina did not believe that the food was being saved for the icebox; it was to be taken to Holden.

Though Tyler's older brother, Holden Sutter, had been thrust into the dinner conversation, he remained a mystery to Christina. All that she knew was that something terrible had happened to him and that his family strongly disagreed about how it should be handled. Eventually she *would* find out; someone would tell her in confidence or accidentally let it slip, but the thought of waiting was not appealing.

She wanted to know right there and then, but how?

One possibility was to approach Dr. Barlow and ask for the truth; given Tyler's tantrum, she doubted that her employer would deny her an explanation. But demanding things was not something she was comfortable doing; her sister, Charlotte, wouldn't have had any reservations, but she did. After all, she'd be working for Dr.

Barlow and didn't want to get off to a bad start.

Clara was putting the last of the clean dishes into a cupboard. Dr. Barlow sat at the small kitchen table; he pulled a well-worn pipe from the pocket of his coat and began filling it from a pouch; when it was lit, the sweet smell of tobacco filled the room. From outside came loud banging and clanging, the sounds of Tyler getting back to work on his car.

Clara placed a large piece of chicken on a platter next to the food she had already set aside, just as Christina had expected. She placed the plate and a large glass of milk on the tray and headed toward the stairs that led up to the second floor.

Christina took a deep breath, steeled herself, and proceeded with her plan.

"Are you taking that food to Holden?" she asked boldly.

Clara froze. ". . . I was," she replied, curious yet cautious.

"Then I would like to be the one to take it to him."

Clara didn't blink, even in surprise. Slowly, her jaw opened but no sound came out. Searchingly, she looked at her brother.

"I don't know if that's the best idea," Dr.

Barlow ventured.

"And why not?"

"Well . . . w-w-well, I j-j-just . . . it's that . . . ," he stammered, never managing to establish a solid footing for his argument.

"One of the reasons that you asked him to join us for dinner was to introduce him to me, wasn't it?" Christina asked, turning her attention back to Clara.

"Yes, it was." She nodded.

"Just because Holden chose not to come downstairs and join us at the table doesn't mean that we still couldn't meet," Christina explained patiently.

"Sometimes Holden can be . . . ," Clara said, "he can be . . . difficult . . ."

"I've spent the last couple years of my life dealing with people who were far more difficult than you could imagine."

"She's does have a point there," the doctor agreed.

Christina felt elated, even a bit triumphant that her reasoning was solid enough to earn an acknowledgment. Clearly, Clara was more skeptical, but she evidently could be swayed.

Truthfully, Christina didn't know why she wanted to meet Holden Sutter so badly. Maybe it was because everyone had acted so out of sorts about him. Tyler had reacted so intensely, had become so upset, that it only strengthened her desire, urging her to push on. Maybe it was because of how . . . *interesting* Tyler had proven to be that she just had to meet his brother. She knew that she was being forward, assertive, and even a bit presumptuous in making her request, but she'd already asked. There was no turning back.

"Just let me take him his supper," she pressed on. "Once Holden meets me, he may feel comfortable to join us next time."

"I don't think it's a matter of his being shy." The doctor frowned. "His reasons for staying in his room are complicated . . ."

"So tell me what they *are.*"

Dr. Barlow stared at her as smoke drifted lazily from his pipe up toward the ceiling, weighing her request. He glanced at his sister, but Clara only nervously chewed on her lip, keeping her thoughts to herself. Sighing deeply, he answered, "When Holden was serving with the Fifty-first Army Infantry in France, he . . . he . . . there was . . ."

Involuntarily, Christina held her breath, waiting.

Dr. Barlow swallowed and said, "Holden was caught in an —"

"Just let her take the plate up and she'll find out for herself," Clara suddenly inter-

rupted, her voice nearly cracking with emo-
tion; it was such a surprise that it made
Christina jump. "It wouldn't do any good
to explain something she'll have to see with
her own eyes."

"Are you sure?" Clara's brother asked.
"There's no telling if . . ."

Clara nodded.

Christina took the plate and glass from
her hands and moved to the stairs. Stopping, she looked back.

"It will be all right," she tried to soothe
them. "What's the worst thing that could
happen?"

Neither of them gave an answer, looking
at each other with concern.

Christina paused at the top of the stairs.

The hallway before her was short, with
two doors on either side. Each of the doors
stood open except for the one on the rear
right, the one she had been told was Holden's room. Starlight streamed through a
window at the other end of the hallway;
Christina could see only a sliver of the
moon at the bottom of the lowest pane, as
if it were a child peeking in from outside.

Well . . . this is what you wanted.

Suddenly, Christina found herself unable
to move forward. She wanted to forget her

71

ridiculous plan and go back to the kitchen and apologize for her rashness. Surely she would be forgiven. Eventually, she would learn what had happened to Holden Sutter and she would sympathize with his family's plight. Life would go on.

But it was then, just as Christina was about to give in to her fears and retreat, that she felt an overwhelming shame at her weakness, at her willingness to surrender. After being bold enough to ask to deliver Holden's meal, she had to see it all through to its conclusion; she just had to. Steeling herself, she pressed onward, tray in hand, determined not to turn back.

Slowly, Christina made her way down the hallway, wincing every time she caused a floorboard to squeak. Silently, she scolded herself for worrying about the noise; it wasn't as if she were trying to sneak up on Holden. Finally, she found herself standing before his door, light leaking out from beneath it. She took a deep breath, steadied the tray, and knocked.

"Just leave it outside," a man's voice said from behind the door.

Undaunted, Christina knocked again.

This time there was a longer pause, followed by the sound of a chair's legs scraping across the floor. Christina froze, bracing herself; she expected the door to the room to be swung open and to find herself face-to-face with the man she so desperately wanted to meet. But nothing happened.

"Just bring it in and set it on the night-stand, Mother," he said again, sounding annoyed.

Trying to keep her fingers from shaking, Christina felt for the knob and turned it, pushing the door open.

Holden Sutter's room would have been considered neatly furnished and orderly, in most respects. There was a bed, framed by a pair of outdated nightstands with matching lamps; a shelf over the bed crowded with handcarved figurines; a well-used dresser with one drawer missing an ivory knob; and a desk with an ornate hutch of beveled glass and birds carved into the wood. It *would* have been neat and welcoming if it were not for the hundreds of books that covered almost every surface. They were stacked in piles on the nightstands and desk, spread out across the bed, and lay open on the floor; they were even leaned up against the closet door in such a way that it looked as if they were a barricade meant to keep something inside. They came in all shapes and sizes, all colors and decoration of spine, spilling everywhere.

And there, standing in the middle of it, was Holden Sutter.

Before she had opened the door, Christina had attempted to steel herself for what she would see. With the way Holden's family had spoken, she expected to find him disfigured by fire, unmistakably scarred as her father had been, missing a limb, or suffering from some other form of trauma similar to those she had treated as a military nurse. No matter what she found, she knew she would not betray her emotions, that no shock would fall across her face.

She couldn't have been more wrong.

Holden Sutter was a strikingly handsome man. His hair was as black as coal, longer and curlier than most men wore, in stark contrast to his brother's. Stubble darkened Holden's square jaw. He wasn't as broad shouldered or thick of chest as Tyler, but Holden's wiry frame showed a clear strength. He was dressed smartly, wearing a button-down shirt and a pressed pair of trousers, hardly the ratty pajamas she would have expected. Past a pair of horn-rimmed glasses, Holden regarded her intently with his wide, dark eyes.

But what truly surprised Christina was that there seemed to be *nothing* physically wrong with him.

For a long moment Holden looked at her with a mix of surprise and confusion written across his face, but slowly his gaze narrowed, growing in annoyance.

"Who are you?" he asked with a deep, confident voice. "What are you doing here?"

"My name is Christina Tucker," she introduced herself with a pleasant smile. "I was invited to dinner by your uncle, Dr. Barlow. I've come to Longstock to be his new nurse. This is my first day here."

"You've only answered half of my question," Holden snapped, clearly unmoved by her attempt to disarm his displeasure. "What are you doing *here in my room?*"

"Your mother asked if I would bring you your dinner," Christina replied as she raised the tray. "Where would you like me to put it?"

"My mother did no such thing," Holden answered, shaking his head firmly and stepping out from behind the bed; when he did so, Christina saw that he did so without a limp or artificial limb, another sign he had no obvious handicap. "If there is one thing I have learned in the years I have spent under her roof, it is that my mother does not like to have *anything* interrupt her daily routine. Because of that, she is the only person who has brought me my dinner since the day I returned. Even when my brother or uncle has volunteered to do it for her, she's denied them, so pardon me if I don't believe your story."

Christina sighed. "I wasn't trying to lie to you," she admitted, "but because you didn't come down to dinner, I volunteered to bring it since I hadn't had a chance to meet you."

"I never come down to dinner."

"Why not?"

Though he was clearly surprised at the boldness of her question, Holden chose not to answer.

"Your mother invited you to join us," she pressed on.

"She invites me to every meal," he explained. "Breakfast, lunch, dinner, and every teatime in between."

"And yet you never accept."

"No, I don't."

"Well then, I suppose I shouldn't take your slight personally."

A whisper of a smile rose at the corners of Holden's mouth but quickly disappeared.

"Doesn't it get lonely eating every meal alone?" Christina asked, refusing to allow his silence to stifle the conversation. "In my family, getting together around the dinner table is the absolute best part of the day, talking, laughing, and catching up."

"Well, I choose not to have my mother hovering over my every bite."

"It can't be *that* bad."

"You're wrong," Holden said. "When she brings me my meals, she can't help prying. She asks if I'm all right, if I need something, if there's anything else she can bring me. Over and over, day after day, she never stops asking. It's gotten to where I can't stand to be in the same room with her."

"Which is why, when you thought that I was her, you asked me to set your dinner outside your door."

Again, Holden didn't answer, but Christina knew she was right.

Standing there, still holding the tray with his dinner, Christina found that there was so much more she wanted to know about Holden Sutter. If anything, having met him made him even *more* mysterious. No matter how hard she looked, she could see no outward signs of what afflicted him, of what kept him in his room and his family on edge. His bad manners and annoyance could be explained by many things, but Samuel Barlow had said that it was a result of something that had occurred while Holden had been with the Army in France.

There has to be a reason.

"Well then, now that you've brought me my dinner, it's time for you to go," Holden said abruptly.

"Where would you like me to put the tray?"

"Just hand it to me."

Christina tried to think of a reason to stay but couldn't come up with anything that wouldn't seem forced or contrived. It didn't help matters that Holden showed no desire to have a conversation; in fact, he seemed quite intent on getting rid of her. Resigned that her meeting with Holden would be brief, she handed him the tray.

"Thank you," he said without any gratitude. "I'd say that it was nice meeting you, Christina Tucker, but —"

Before Holden could utter another spiteful word, he began to shake violently, his hands clenching and unclenching the tray. It happened so suddenly, so unexpectedly, that Christina was shocked into inaction; she could only watch as the tremors raced throughout his body, spasming uncontrollably and jerking his torso first one way and then another. The tray that had held his meal flew from his grasp and crashed to the floor, shattering the plate and glass and tossing food and splashing milk over books and against the bedspread. Through it all,

Holden's face was a tortured mess, his teeth clenched in a grimace and his eyes wide and full of pain.

"Holden!" Christina shouted. "What's happening? Are you all right?"

A series of grunts and wheezes were his only response as Holden turned his back to Christina, who couldn't tell if it was involuntary, as he deliberately lowered himself to the edge of a chair filled with books. He managed to grab one of the arms, clenching it tightly, as if it were a life preserver in a raging sea. His shaking caused his glasses to slide off and clatter to the floor, where one of his shuddering feet kicked them farther away. Safely in the chair, cradling a shaking arm, he waited for the tremors to subside.

Christina stood beside him, unsure of what, if anything, she could do. She wondered if she shouldn't run to the stairs and shout for help; Holden's family would want to know what had happened, but because of all she had seen as a nurse, she felt certain that he wasn't in any significant danger; in fact, *leaving* him could be worse. She wanted to comfort him, to put a hand on his shoulder and help him through the worst of it, but because of how annoyed he had been with her entering his room she decided to keep her distance. In the end, she began picking up the broken pieces of glass and food that littered the floor, all the while keeping an eye on Holden's condition.

"Leave . . . leave it . . . leave it there . . . ," he managed when the worst of the tremors had ended.

"I'm almost finished," Christina said, wiping a smear of mashed potatoes off a tip-in plate image of George Washington. "Then I'll ask your mother to prepare another plate. You can —"

"No," Holden said defiantly. "Just . . . just leave it all . . . and go . . ."

"I need to pick up all of this glass first. You could hurt your —"

"Get out!" he shouted.

Christina leaned back on her haunches and looked at him. Holden still sat on the edge of his chair, holding his left arm in a way that reminded her of a wounded fox, trapped in a hunter's snare. She could see in his eyes that he was horrified that she had seen him in such a state, and that he regretted having ever allowed her into his room. But even then, she felt the strong urge to help him, just as she had already aided so many others.

The question was whether Holden would ever allow her that chance.

"*Is this* why you never leave your room?"

she asked.

"I want . . . you to leave . . . ," Holden said sharply, refusing to answer her.

"This was caused by something that happened to you in the war." It was a statement.

Silently, he stared at her, his eyes smoldering.

Christina had seen this response in many of the soldiers who had arrived at her hospital in Michigan. Whatever wounds they had suffered, both physical and mental, challenged them in such a way that they could not even bring themselves to acknowledge the wounds, choosing instead to ignore the problem. Even if there was a way to get better, they would rather accept the misery they knew than dare to try a different course with its own dangers. If Holden was the same, if his trauma had affected him in such a way that he refused to deal with it, then he would never get better and would remain trapped, both in his head and here, in his room.

"How often does this happen to you?" she pressed.

Again, Holden stood firm. "I told you . . . to get the hell out . . ."

Frustrated, Christina stood, holding the tray stacked high with fragments of glass

81

and ruined food. "You might ignore my questions," she admonished him, heading toward the door. "That's your choice to make. But while you stay in this room, acting like a stubborn ass, you're ruining the lives of your family. If you care about them at all, you'd do well to change while you still have the chance, because someday, when you've burned every bridge you have, *no one* is going to bring you your meals, and even your own mother won't give a damn what goes on behind this door."

With that, Christina left him, not willing to wait for an answer.

CHAPTER FIVE

Christina hurried down the front steps of the Sutters' home, refusing to slow down as she turned on the sidewalk and headed toward downtown Longstock and her new apartment above the bakery. Dark clouds bruised the bottom of the half-full moon, sliding off to the south on the light breeze. Thousands of stars watched silently. While the day had been pleasantly warm, the night was cooler; Christina shivered as her skin goose-bumped.

With every step, her heart raced, pounding in her chest. Ever since she had left Holden Sutter's room, it had been a struggle to contain her emotions; what began as confusion became anger, then disappointment, before turning into still something else, something she could not identify.

If Christina were to be truthful with herself, she was angry that she had become so upset. Back in the Army hospital in

Michigan, she had endured even worse verbal abuse. Once, an angry, wounded soldier had thrown a vase of flowers at her. Even in those difficult moments, she had managed to stay calm and detached, not allowing herself to take things personally.

But Holden had unnerved her.

She supposed it could have been because of the way he was treating his family. No matter what they did, he couldn't accept that they only wanted to help. Things had grown so bad that he could no longer stand listening to the constant barrage about his condition from his mother. Let alone listen to her worries.

The worst part is that I know I could help him.

Violent tremors such as Holden's were not that unusual; Christina had treated them before. The horrors of war caused many different reactions in the soldiers who experienced them. Men who were quiet, composed civilians could become hardened leaders under gunfire, while others, who previously had been loud and full of bravado, froze in the face of danger. Some hid the terrible events they had witnessed, pushing them down so far that they would never be talked of again, while yet others were overcome with fear. No man was the same.

Clearly, *something* terrible had happened to Holden.

When Christina had come down the stairs with the shattered remains of Holden's dinner, Clara Sutter's first assumption was that her son had become angry and hurled the tray.

"Oh, how could I have ever allowed you to go up there!" she wailed.

Even when Christina explained that the plate and glass had broken because Holden had suffered a tremor while holding the tray, tears continued to race down his mother's cheeks. Nothing Christina could say managed to calm her. Clara finally slumped in a chair at the kitchen table, buried her face in her hands, and sobbed.

"How was he?" Dr. Barlow asked once he had moved Christina out of earshot of his grieving sister.

"Stubborn, angry, difficult," Christina explained, recalling her first encounter with Holden. "You know that he suffers from tremors?"

"I've only seen them twice. Each time was very unpleasant."

"He won't let you treat him? But you were a military doctor; surely he knows that you could help him."

"Even if he'd let me try, I'm not sure I could do much for him," Dr. Barlow admitted. "My time in the United States Army was spent in a field hospital, cutting into soldiers who had already been punctured by bullets and shrapnel. Maybe if I knew what had happened to him . . ."

"He hasn't told you?"

"He hasn't told *anyone*. Not me, not his mother, not even Tyler. Once upon a time, back when they were boys, those two were as thick as thieves; now there isn't a word spoken between them."

Remembering Tyler's outburst during dinner, Christina wondered, if they had once been as close as Dr. Barlow described, how many times Holden had rebuffed his brother to reach this stage of isolation. Tyler must have been the first bridge destroyed. Listening to his mother's sobs, Christina had little doubt that more were coming.

"He'll never get better if he doesn't talk about it," she said.

"*You and I* know that, but don't say it too loudly around these parts," the doctor said with a glance at his sister. "There isn't anyone living under this roof who wants to hear it."

Eventually, Christina had excused herself, refusing a ride back to her apartment by explaining that she needed a breath of fresh air. At the end of the street, she stopped and looked back at the Sutter home.

Lights were on in one of the upstairs rooms. It was Holden's; she was sure of it. Even from far away, she could see his silhouette standing at the window, pulling back the curtain, watching her.

Christina turned and walked on.

Holden Sutter watched from the window as Christina Tucker stopped at the end of the street and turned to look back at the house. For an instant, he thought of ducking behind the curtain, out of sight. But by then it was too late; he felt certain that she had seen him. To hide now would be childish. Instead, he continued to look.

He saw her wipe a strand of dark hair from her face as the soft breeze stirred the fabric at the bottom of her skirt. He moved closer to the window, his hand pressing against the cool glass, fingers splayed; he wondered if she could see his movement, because of the light shining behind him, and imagine that he was waving to her.

When she turned once again to walk away, Holden finally released the curtain and returned to the solitary sanctuary of his room.

"Damn it all," he muttered to himself.

When she first walked into his room, Holden had been shocked and embarrassed. Certainly, he hadn't expected anyone other than his mother, so to find someone else standing before him had momentarily stopped him in his tracks. The embarrassment had come soon after; he knew that his room wasn't tidy, but in that moment he had seen what a mess he had allowed his life to become.

He was not prepared for someone young and beautiful.

Meeting Christina Tucker had set something stirring in Holden's chest, a longing he'd never expected to feel again. There had been a time when he had believed he would meet a woman, fall in love, marry, and have a family. Everything would have been perfect, but then he had gone off to war . . .

Since his return from France, Holden had been trying to convince himself that being alone was all right, that he could be happy without someone to share his days, but then *she* had opened his door, and in that moment he'd recognized the lies he had been telling himself. Her dark hair, sparkling green eyes, the warmth of her smile, even her scent, pulled at him, intoxicating him, making him that much more aware of what he still wanted but could never have.

Angrily, Holden kicked at a pile of books, spilling them.

Instantly, he regretted it. A slight twitch raced down one arm, causing his fingers to flex of their own accord. He'd found that his moods, particularly angry ones, triggered a spell of tremors. Most times, that first tingling was an unstoppable indicator of a full-blown episode, but there were other times he could hold it at bay, and he hoped that this one was containable. Patiently, he waited, every sense attuned to detecting another spasm. Seconds ticked by slowly, but eventually he felt certain he'd succeeded in not becoming a shaking mess.

Why did she have to see me that way?

Every time he suffered a shaking spell, Holden wished that he had died on that rainy day in France. He saw his tremors as a weakness, cowardice, a handicap. He could feel the leering eyes of everyone who saw him, their looks of pity, their offers of sympathy he did not want. In his worst moments, he still saw the woman on the train home . . .

But Christina hadn't reacted that way.

Picking his way through the piles of books that littered the floor, Holden looked at himself in the mirror that hung over his dresser. On most days, he couldn't recognize the man who now looked back at him. The man he remembered, the one he had once been, was hidden, lost, and all that remained were memories. Running a hand over his stubble, Holden wondered what it was Christina had seen before turning away in disgust. He was afraid that he knew the answer.

As she walked, Christina shivered. The wind seemed to pick up with her every step. Boughs bent and leaves whistled. Occasionally, a strong gust tugged insistently at the hem of her skirt. It was quite cold for June, as cold a night as any she could remember this time of year. She regretted not bringing a sweater.

To distract herself from her discomfort, Christina concentrated on her new surroundings. Lights shone in nearly every house she passed, revealing families sitting around their dinner tables, older couples reading silently, and young children laughing loudly as the sounds of that evening's radio program drifted out an open window.

Flower gardens were plentiful, though none as lovely as Clara Sutter's. Row after row of tulips, roses, and other varieties glistened in the moonlight. Occasionally, a dog barked at Christina until she was out of sight.

But try as she might, Christina's thoughts kept returning to Holden.

Over and over she replayed the things he had said to her, the way he had looked, searching for something she could have done differently, for a way in which she might have reached him, but nothing revealed itself. The whole encounter had been a disaster.

"Why did he have to be so resistant?" she asked aloud.

Thankfully, the day hadn't been a complete loss. Recalling the way she and Dr. Barlow had helped the Simmons family gave her a tremendous sense of accomplishment. She was concerned over whether, at that moment, they had a roof over their heads. In particular, she worried about little Sally. She hoped that the girl was warmer than she was.

Lost in her thoughts, Christina was startled by the sudden honk of a horn.

Quickly, she turned to see a car creeping along behind her. The glare of the headlights made it impossible to see clearly. She had no idea who was behind the wheel, or even if the driver was a man or woman. She'd been so distracted by her own thoughts that she hadn't heard it approach.

While she looked, there was another playful honk. The more she stared, the more certain Christina was that it wasn't the doctor's car.

Leave me alone! she insisted silently, turning away and hurrying her step. Over the clicking of her shoes on the sidewalk she could hear the car just behind, the driver increasing his speed to follow.

"Don't you want a ride?" a man's voice asked into the night.

"No!" Christina shouted, suddenly growing fearful. Her instincts were to run, heading either down the street or off into someone's yard. If she screamed, surely someone would hear her and come to her aid.

"Jeez!" The man chuckled. "Was I that big a jerk at dinner?"

Christina came to a sudden halt as the car slowly idled up to stop just beside her. Through the open passenger's window she recognized Tyler Sutter sitting behind the wheel, a mischievous grin on his face.

"I suppose you think you were being funny," she said, annoyed.

"What are you talking about?" he replied, wounded.

"Stop acting as if you don't know what I'm talking about, coming up behind me and honking like that! It scared me half to death! You're lucky I didn't start screaming for someone to call the police!"

"A lot of good that would have done you." Tyler laughed. "Most of the police in these parts can't catch a cold!"

At that, Christina had had enough. With the memory of how one of the Sutter brothers had treated her still fresh in her mind, she began walking, determined not to let herself be made sport of again.

Tyler pressed the gas pedal and was instantly beside her.

"Wait, wait, wait!" he pleaded. "You aren't really planning on walking the whole way back to your apartment, are you?"

"It's not that far," Christina said, never breaking stride.

"On most nights I'd agree with you, but a chilly one like this, a frail gal like yourself could catch her death of cold."

"I'm *not* frail," she snapped.

"Sure doesn't look that way," Tyler admitted while still matching her pace. "So how about if I admit that my coming after you is more than just concern for your well-being? What if I said your leaving so abruptly hurt my feelings?"

"Then I'd call you a liar," she answered, her chin held high.

"I've been a lot of things to every person I've ever met, but I can't imagine a one of them thinking I was being untruthful." He chuckled easily.

"I suppose that makes me the first, then."

"Maybe so, but the least you could have done was stop and say good-bye."

"After the way you left the dinner table, the last thing I would have expected you to want was company."

"Depends on whose company it was," Tyler said slyly.

"Well, I'm not the sort of woman who associates with strange men."

"Who's a stranger? I sat across from you at dinner! Besides, you'd never met my uncle before he picked you up at the train depot, and you got into his car."

"That's because he didn't act like a total jackass," Christina snapped.

"Just give him time, darlin'." Tyler laughed loudly. "Now listen, I just got the old girl fixed," he explained, slapping his palm down on the dashboard, "so why not hop in and share the first ride with me."

"What was it that fixed it? Your tools or your swearing?"

"A little bit of both, to be honest."

"I'm sure the whole neighborhood heard you. I wasn't raised to associate with uncouth men who cussed with every breath."

"Why do you have to be so darn difficult? I'm just offering you a ride home; it isn't like I'm asking you to go to bed with me."

The blatant suggestion stopped Christina cold, dropped her mouth open in shock, and flushed her cheeks a deep red with embarrassment. Never in her life had she been spoken to in such a way! Deep down, she wanted to scream at him, but she was so insulted that she couldn't even face him. Nothing Holden had said to her had struck so deeply. Without a word, she hurried away.

"What got under your skirt?" Tyler asked, revving the engine in order to keep up.

Christina tried her best to ignore him. The thought pained her, but she had to wonder if she could continue to work for Dr. Barlow; if she had to see the Sutter brothers regularly, her time in Longstock would become unbearable.

The sudden honk of the car's horn made her jump. "Didn't you hear what I said?" Tyler asked.

"Yes, I most certainly did!" She turned and shouted at him, no longer able to contain her mounting anger, her hands balled into tight fists, "And I cannot believe that you would speak to me in such a way! I didn't think it was possible for you to be any more disgusting than you were at dinner, but I gravely underestimated you, a mistake I will not make again!"

Instead of being shamed, Tyler widened his grin. "I suppose working yourself up into a lather is one way to stay warm. Keep it up and you'll need to start unbuttoning your blouse."

"Compared to you," Christina yelled through eyes growing wet with fury, "Holden is the nicest man I have ever met!"

Much faster than she would have thought possible, Tyler yanked back on the car's brake, threw open the door, and bounded across the headlight's beams to stand before her on the sidewalk.

"You talked to him?" he implored. "You talked to Holden?"

"I . . . I took him his meal," she answered, taken aback by the force of Tyler's insistence; where only seconds earlier she had wanted to confront him, she now found herself taking a step back, uncertain.

"And he let you into his room?"

"He thought that I was your mother. If he'd known otherwise, he would have left me out in the hall; I'm sure of it."

"What did he say to you?"

Christina stared into Tyler's eyes and did not like what she saw. Gone was the jovial,

good-natured prankster she had been introduced to. His gaze was maniacal. He had
moved so close that he towered above her,
his broad frame a little threatening. She
feared that he was capable of an outburst
that would put what happened at the dinner table to shame.

"He . . . he wasn't happy that I was
there . . . ," she answered vaguely. "He
wanted me to leave . . ."

"What did he *say* to you? Tell me everything!" Before Christina could say a word,
Tyler grabbed her by the arm. Startled, she
tried to squirm away, but it only caused his
grip to tighten.

"You're . . . hurting me . . . ," she complained.

"Did he have an episode? Did he show
you why he never leaves that damn room of
his?" Tyler kept hammering her with questions, unwilling or unable to hear her protests.

Desperately, Christina fought to free
herself. With every twitch and pull, Tyler's
grip continued to tighten; she was more
scared now than when she hadn't known
who was following her in the car. Finally,
she kicked him in the shin, the point of her
shoe cracking into bone. The sudden pain
cleared Tyler's muddled thoughts. Releasing

her, he stepped back, looking down at his own hands as if he hadn't known what they were doing.

"Christina . . . I . . . I'm-m-m . . . ," he was surprised to find himself stuttering.

"Stay away from me!" she shouted as a tear streaked down her cheek. "Just stay far away from me!"

Running down the sidewalk toward the heart of town, Christina was surprised to find that, for the first time since she had met him, Tyler Sutter didn't have a comeback.

CHAPTER SIX

Luther Rickert cursed the sun as he rolled over, clawing his way up from a restless sleep. Even with his eyes closed, he could feel the warmth of the sunlight streaming through the open window, falling across his back and legs. The inside of his mouth felt like mud and tasted worse, while his lips were sticky with dried spittle. Blindly, his hand reached out and touched a bottle, sending it skittering away. He knew that he wasn't lying in his bed, but where he *was,* was anybody's best guess; he didn't have the strength or desire to open his eyes and find out for certain. Even as he remained as still as he could, his world spun dizzily.

And it ain't no one's damn fault but my own . . .

The previous night had started like most of his evenings: drinking in a bar. Luther had been at Colton's, Longstock's bottom-of-the-barrel tavern, making another go at drowning his sorrows. As usual, he'd failed. A bottle of beer, followed by a shot of whiskey and then another beer, before eventually ending with Lord-knows-what, had finally left him where he now lay. Try as he might, he hadn't the slightest idea how he had gotten there.

Only snippets of the night swam up in his booze-addled memory, as if they were fish in a muddy river, barely visible. Luther remembered ordering a round of drinks, being challenged to a game of pool, making an ass of himself while he was winning, someone shouting at him about a woman he had been looking at for too long, and then it all got hazy . . . Faintly, he recalled harsh words, an angry shove, and then a punch. Gingerly, he raised a hand to his face, wincing as he touched a mess of bruising around his mouth and along his jawline. He could only hope that he had given as good as he'd *obviously* got.

A sudden uncomfortable tossing in his stomach told Luther that he wasn't getting any more sleep. Somehow, he was going to have to get to his feet. With considerable effort, he opened his eyes, cursing at the brightness; everything before him swam, refusing to come into focus, making his head throb from the effort.

"Where in the hell am I?" he mumbled, but it was a question he already knew the answer to.

He *was* in hell.

Standing on the back porch of the home his father had built with his own hands, Luther puked over the railing. When he was certain his stomach had settled, he urinated into the bushes, absently running a hand through his dark, unruly hair; he'd had to go so bad that it was a miracle he hadn't pissed his pants while he slept.

The day was too bright; even though he shaded his eyes, the relentless glare eventually forced him to look away. From where the sun stood in the sky, he guessed that it was sometime in the early afternoon.

"Goddamn it all," he spat.

For the last three months, Luther had been working for Amos Worthington, laboring in the old man's orchards to the west of town. Luther wasn't trusted to do much, trimming branches, digging holes for new saplings, and other simple handyman work around the barns, but it had put money in his pocket and, just maybe, did something to rehabilitate the mess he had made of his family's name. Luther hadn't been the best worker, but he hadn't been the worst, either.

But lately, things had been going to hell in a handbasket. He'd started having a few problems with his fellow workers, an argument here and there, one of which had nearly led to a fight. Then there'd been the matter of some missing tools, which, ironically, he *hadn't* taken but for which he had been suspected, although never openly accused. Finally, he'd been late a couple of mornings on account of his drinking. The last time it had happened, the warning had been clear: do it again and don't bother coming back.

And then he'd gone and gotten good and drunk again.

"You stupid son of a bitch . . . ," he cursed himself.

Luther knew he was weak; over the course of thirty-two years, he'd never met a vice he hadn't taken at least a passing shine to. While he did his share of gambling, cursing, fighting, smoking, and sleeping with any loose woman foolish enough to share her bed with him, he was especially tempted by alcohol. He loved it all, from the cheapest swill to the finest whiskey. Where his love of drinking had come from he couldn't say for certain. His parents had been teetotalers of the staunchest kind; the only exception they ever made was for communion wine.

Luther had once broken into a church to get drunk on that, too.

Every chance he got, Luther headed for the nearest bottle and settled down for a lengthy stay. Nearly every dime he managed to scrape up was soon drunk away. He'd long ago lost count of how many times Sheriff Keller had picked him up for public drunkenness outside the tavern; he'd slept off a hangover in the town's lockup so often that his jailers jokingly referred to his cell as "the Rickert Suite." After he'd been temporarily banned from the bar, he'd become so desperate that he tried making his own booze in a still out in the hills. That had worked fine for a while, until the day he'd blown it up, badly burning his forearms when he'd tried to keep the resulting fire from spreading to the woods. Still, his appetite kept on unabated.

He'd stolen money, ruined friendships, wrecked jobs, and broken bones. Drinking had even kept him from fighting against the damned Nazis; he'd spent most of the war in a stockade for offenses ranging from insubordination to striking an officer, all because he couldn't be bothered to stay sober.

In the years before his parents had been killed in an automobile accident, they had been so embarrassed by their elder son that they wouldn't even acknowledge him in passing on the street.

But through it all, the worst thing he had ever done was . . .

Luther shook his head; it was too damn early in his day to start feeling sorry for what had happened.

After all, it hadn't been his fault.

Stumbling back inside, Luther caught a glimpse of himself in the cracked glass of the front door. With his coal black hair matted down in places and sticking straight up in others, a lighter stubble peppering his jawline, a nose broken so many times that it leaned first one way and then another, Luther was certainly a mess to behold.

Even his clothing was unkempt; the faded blue shirt he wore was torn in several places and filthy, especially around the collar. While the lingering smell of alcohol still clung to him, a matter made significantly worse by the vomit dribbled down his chest, the odor of dried urine rose from his boots.

The bruises on his face had already blossomed into a kaleidoscope of ugly colors: black, red, and purple. He was lean of build, wiry, with a strength not easily seen but quickly felt by anyone choosing to cross him. He looked mean, like a dog who growled at the slightest provocation. No wonder he had no friends, no woman, and no family.

Narrowing his dishwater grey eyes, now bloodshot with color, he was struck by how much he despised the face that looked back at him.

Luther started toward the kitchen, but a new wave of nausea washed over him, sickening his gut and making his knees quiver. He slumped heavily against the wall to keep from pitching over on his face.

"Stay upright," he told himself. "You sure as shit don't wanna die here . . ."

The home in which Christian and Celia Rickert had raised him now hardly resembled the place Luther had inherited. Gone were his mother's crocheted doilies and painstakingly stitched pillows, his father's bird-watching books, and the family's heirloom King James Bible. In their place was a mess beggaring description: filthy clothes caked with grime and sweat were strewn over the furniture; dirty dishes and plates littered the floor, many of them growing moldy; and old newspapers, most sprinkled with mouse droppings, filled in every remaining crevice. Every photograph had been turned facedown, save one. The roof leaked water in the lightest of rains. A floorboard in the kitchen had rotted clean through. Outside, the place was in desperate need of a new coat of paint. The house, much like the life of its lone remaining occupant, was falling apart.

And I don't give a good goddamn.

In the kitchen, Luther leaned over a faucet for water that he gulped down thirstily; he had to have something in his gut for when he vomited. He needed to eat but was disappointed, although hardly surprised, to find the inside of the icebox and cupboards empty. Fishing through his pockets, he produced a couple of coins, maybe enough for a sandwich at the diner. Now, having lost yet another job, he had to wonder where his next meal would come from.

It was hard for Luther alone in his kitchen, to believe that he'd once considered himself to be rich.

Standing in the pouring rain at his parents' funeral, staring down into the hole that had been dug for their coffins, Luther had struggled to suppress a smile. At the reading of their will, he had been shocked to discover that, though they had extricated him from their lives while alive, his folks had left him the entirety of their estate. Just imagining all of the money made his mouth water. It had come with but one condition: that Luther care and provide for his younger brother, Donnie.

Even as Luther had chased the last grieving guest from his parents' house, practically bursting with excitement to begin tearing the place apart in search of valuable items to sell, he had meant to keep that promise.

But fate had another idea.

Donnie Rickert was seven years younger than his brother; Luther always wondered if the boy was an accident; he'd just assumed that his parents were afraid that they'd have another child as rotten as he was. From the beginning, their worries seemed to be well-founded. In everything Luther did Donnie wanted to be involved, and no amount of persuasion could convince him otherwise; their mother often lamented that Donnie was young enough to idolize his brother but not wise enough to know better.

"You should watch it," Luther warned his brother. "Pa's gonna think you'll end up just as bad as me."

"Maybe I'll be worse." Luther's kid brother winked.

When Luther robbed a gas station in Hampton in the middle of the night, Donnie had been his lookout. The time Luther had stolen a car from the train depot, Donnie had whooped it up beside him in the passenger's seat. When he'd been badly burned when his still exploded, Donnie was the one who bandaged Luther up the best he could before taking him home. Luther had introduced his brother to his first drink, lit his first smoke, and taught him how to fight and curse. Whenever Luther was up to any mischief, Donnie was by his side.

And so it was on the night that Luther's life had been changed forever.

For two months after his parents' deaths, Luther had lived like a king. He had indulged in every want he could dream of, gambling until dawn one night, buying a woman the next, and drinking every step of the way. It was the greatest time of his life. But eventually he had begun to run out of money.

Everything of any value in the house had already been sold, his inheritance squandered down to the dregs, so in order to keep the good times coming Luther had decided to return to something he knew a great deal about: crime.

One night, well-lubricated with whiskey, Luther decided to commit a robbery in Longstock in order to steal money or, at the least, something he could sell. To his addled mind, he'd made his choice well. With no planning, not a shred of worry, and Donnie at his side, he somehow managed to drive them the short distance from his parents' home.

It didn't take long for things to start falling apart. Luther had insisted on bringing the bottle of whiskey along; he never stopped drinking from it, even as the dark alcohol spilled down the front of his shirt. He'd assumed he could jimmy open the lock to the back door, but, in such an inebriated state, he soon grew too frustrated to continue, eventually resorting to slamming his body into the door in an attempt to knock it off its hinges. When that didn't work, he punched a hole through a window, slicing his hand. Once inside, Luther made no attempt to be quiet, rooting through drawers, knocking over chairs, tossing things on the floor, and shining his flashlight all around without a care in the world.

"If you keep doin' that, we're gonna get caught!" Donnie hissed at him.

"Quit whinin' like a woman," Luther answered, then took another slug of the whiskey.

Donnie's concerns proved to be well-founded; they hadn't been in the building three minutes before he noticed a police car slowly driving past. He immediately threw himself to the floor but was horrified to find Luther still standing in front of the window, glaring out into the street.

"What in the hell do you think you're doin'?" Donnie shouted at his brother.

"They ain't . . . they ain't gonna get me . . ."

Somehow, Donnie managed to drag his brother toward the back door, Luther protesting every step of the way. Before they made it outside, the sounds of a car door slamming and the voices of the lawmen broke through the silence that blanketed Longstock. Stumbling, the brothers reached the car.

"Gimme the keys!" Donnie pleaded.

"Go . . . go to hell . . . ," Luther slurred, taking another swig; somehow through all that had happened he'd managed to hold on to his precious bottle.

"You ain't in no shape to drive!"

"Slide over and shut your yap!"

By the time Luther managed to get the keys into the ignition, the cops rounded the corner, shouting as they drew their guns. Even in his drunken state, Luther knew he and Donnie needed to get away as quickly as they could. Tromping down on the gas pedal, Luther sped the car off like a bullet, past the sheriff's deputies and roaring out of town. Faster and faster they went, gaining speed as Donnie nervously peered out the rear window, the sound of sirens wailing behind them.

"We're . . . we're gonna get away . . . ," Luther rejoiced.

But even as he crowed over escaping yet again, Luther was too drunk to remember that the road suddenly, sharply turned to the right. By the time he understood what was happening, it was far too late. With the tires screeching, the steering wheel useless in his hands, and Donnie screaming beside him, Luther drove them over an incline and down into the orchard beyond.

In the months that followed, he couldn't recall being afraid in those moments, the feeling of weightlessness as the car's wheels left the ground, or even the impact of the car smashing into an apple tree. When the blackness finally released him and Luther clawed his way back into consciousness, what he found was something that he could never forget.

Wiping blood from his eyes, through a haze of booze mixed with pain Luther saw Donnie. He was wedged into a space between what remained of the door and dashboard. Donnie's body resembled the destruction of the car; mixed among the twisted metal and shattered glass of the automobile were pools of blood, broken bones that protruded through skin, and a low, insistent sobbing.

"Donnie?" Luther asked, instantly more sober than he had been in years. "Oh, Jesus, Donnie!"

By the time the sheriff arrived, Luther had struggled out of the shattered driver's window and was sobbing, his hands shaking uncontrollably. Eventually, with the help of the fire department, Donnie was freed and rushed back to Longstock, clinging to life . . .

He died a few hours later, just as the sun rose over the eastern horizon.

Luther had no idea how the whiskey bottle had gotten into his hand. The last thing he remembered was standing in the kitchen before the empty icebox, thinking about the night Donnie had died, and then . . . After all of the years that liquor had been his closest companion, he was surprised to find that now, suddenly and surprisingly, he was disgusted by the sight of it; it was as if he were holding a poisonous snake, a serpent that coiled around his arm, its fangs sunk deep into his flesh, refusing to release him from its grasp. With a shudder, he threw the bottle, shattering it against the wall.

It was then, just as the last fragments of glass fell to the floor, that Luther understood how wrong he had been: he had been wrong to spend so much of his life drunk, wasting years he could never get back; he had been wrong to agree to let Donnie come along that fateful night; but worst of all, he had been wrong to accept the blame for what had happened, to believe that Donnie's tragic death had somehow been his fault.

Hurrying into the living room, Luther swiped at the rubbish that littered the fireplace's mantel, sending most of it crashing to the floor. The only object that was spared his wrath was a photograph, his dearest possession. In it, Donnie was perched on the hood of a car, the very same automobile they had crashed. He was much younger, but Luther could still easily recognize his brother's easy smile, the tuft of his brown hair that never seemed to want to lie down, and the mischievousness in his stare. In the photograph, Donnie had so much to look forward to, so much to *live* for, that it nearly broke what little remained of Luther's heart.

"And it was all taken away from you . . . ," he mumbled, tears welling in his eyes.

There was no denying that the accident had caused Donnie's injuries and, for that, Luther was undeniably to blame. But when the sheriff had taken Luther's brother from the wreck, Donnie *had been alive.* In the end, the final responsibility for what had happened lay in Longstock, with the man who had been trusted with saving Luther's brother, with the man who had failed in his duty.

The man to blame for Donnie Rickert's death was Dr. Samuel Barlow.

And he's gonna pay for what he did to Donnie.

CHAPTER SEVEN

Christina awoke with a start. Blinking rapidly, she shielded her eyes from the bright rays of light that streamed into her room as the sun began to peek over the horizon. For a brief moment, she was unsure of where she was; absolutely nothing looked familiar, but it was then that she remembered her new home, her new career, her new life.

And that new beginning has already brought me unexpected problems . . .

It had taken her hours to fall asleep. She had run the rest of the way back to her apartment and begun pacing the floors, back and forth, over and over, trying to put her talks with Tyler and Holden Sutter out of her mind. Unfortunately, that had proven easier said than done; even as she paced, she had rubbed her forearm where Tyler had grabbed her. Finally, sometime just after two o'clock in the morning, she had drifted off, still dressed in her clothes. Now, she felt exhausted, bone weary, but she knew that she had no choice but to rise and go about her day.

"Charlotte would call you a baby if you did otherwise," she told herself.

From below, the smells of the bakery rose to greet her: the sweet, unmistakable aroma of freshly made bread, rolls, and pastries. Faintly, Christina could hear the sound of someone whistling. On any other morning, Dr. Barlow would certainly have been right about one thing; her apartment's location was better than any alarm clock.

Occasionally stifling a yawn, Christina washed and dressed. The lure of the bakery eventually proved to be too much; back at her kitchen table, she ate a delicious blueberry muffin still warm from the oven, washing it all down with a cup of the black coffee the bakery sold. When she had finished washing her dishes, she stood before her dresser mirror and took a long look at herself.

"You've definitely looked better, but you *have* looked worse . . ."

With her black hair pulled back and wearing just a touch of makeup, she wondered if her fatigue was evident; she hoped the bags under her eyes weren't *too* obvious. Still, she *was* excited. Tilting her head to the side, Christina smiled. While yesterday had introduced her to many new things, both good *and* bad, this early morning felt like yet another start, one she desperately wanted to make the most of.

Because she had set out a bit early, Christina decided to take a closer look at Longstock before walking the short distance from her apartment to Dr. Barlow's office. Strolling beneath the flapping red, white, and blue American flags that flew from almost every building, she glanced into store windows, nodded to the friendly men and women she met, and listened intently to the sounds of activity and conversation that filled the morning.

"We just got in that saw you wanted, Raymond!"

". . . never had a pie that good in my whole life, I swear to you . . ."

". . . and then the poor little fella fell asleep in my arms. It was the cutest thing I've ever seen!"

For a moment, everyone was so pleasant and welcoming, so *homey,* that Christina felt as at ease as she did back in Minnesota.

Rounding the corner at Main Street, Christina took her first good look at Dr.

Barlow's medical office. The building was older, a squat single-story that had been built of weathered brick. It was pleasant on the eye, both clean and well kept. A single, large window looked onto the street, with the doctor's name painted in large, white script on the glass. Two pots of geraniums sat on the brick ledge that jutted out from beneath the window, basking in the morning sun. Loud, off-key singing floated out of the open door of the shoe-repair shop next door, a man's tenor occasionally punctuated by the pounding of a hammer.

This was the place where Christina would work as a nurse. Taking a deep breath, she pushed open the door.

The inside of Dr. Barlow's clinic was nearly as bright as it was outside; sunlight streamed into the small waiting room, washing over the chairs lined up against one wall. Potted plants added a touch of color. Posters, one an advertisement for the virtues of vaccinations, hung on the walls. Just opposite the door was a worn, oak desk; sitting behind it was a middle-aged black woman who smiled broadly at Christina as she entered.

"I'm sorry, darlin'," the woman said with a slight southern accent, "but Dr. Barlow isn't here just yet. Until he arrives, why don't you tell me what's botherin' you?"

"No, I'm not . . . I'm here because . . . ," she answered, stumbling out of nervousness. "My name is Christina Tucker. I'm Dr. Barlow's new nurse."

"Oh, my goodness gracious!" the woman exclaimed, coming from behind the desk and hurrying across the waiting room.

Even as she was taken by the arms and greeted with a broad smile, Christina would not have been able to say what had surprised her more, being mistaken for a patient on her first day in the office or meeting a black woman in almost all-white small-town Wisconsin.

The woman introduced herself as Callie Davis. She had been working for Dr. Barlow for almost seven years, ever since she and her husband, Abraham, had come north from Alabama in search of work. They certainly hadn't intended upon staying in Longstock, but one day became two, which became a month, then a year, and so on; Callie understood it to mean that the Lord had had a plan for them all along, and who was she to contradict His instructions?

"I should'a known better the moment you walked through that door!" Callie laughed; it was so infectious that Christina couldn't help smiling. "The doctor told me I should expect you this mornin', but I must not a'been as awake as I should a'been."

"But how could you have known?"

"Honey, the chances of someone steppin' through that door that I don't know by name are 'bout the same as a pig goin' next door to Mr. Gabrielson and askin' him to cobble together a pair of shoes!"

Even if Christina were deaf, she would have immediately understood that Callie Davis was a chatterbox. *She never stopped talking!* Though her hair was a salt-and-pepper that leaned more toward white than black and she had crow's-feet that creased the corners of her eyes, Callie had an exuberance about her that made her seem far younger than her years.

Christina took an instant liking to her.

"Now be honest with me." Callie smiled. "Wasn't yo surprised to come in that door and find a colored woman sittin' here?"

Christina reddened a little but nodded. "It wasn't what I expected," she admitted, but quickly added, "I hope you don't think that I —"

"You don't have to worry." Callie smiled, placing her hand on Christina's arm. "It only takes one look at yo to realize there isn't a hateful bone in yore body. I can't say the same 'bout some people livin' here in

Longstock."

"Is it *that* bad here?" Christina asked, knowing that the trouble Callie faced was very different from what she had experienced with the Sutter brothers.

"It was much worse in the beginnin', back in the days after the good doctor saw fit to hire me. Grown men would step back out the front door of this place to take another long look at the writin' on the window, in case they'd made a mistake and walked in the wrong place. Made me wish there was a photographer beside my desk just so I could remember all those shocked faces. One time the doctor was stopped comin' out of church and asked to let me go, but he's a stubborn one and he told me to sit tight. Through it all, I just kept smilin'. Things were easier for Abraham, workin' as he does for John Marston makin' furniture, because there weren't many people who *had* to see him. For me it's different. Folks get sick no matter what color they are. But by and by, as the years went along, most people got used to me bein' here. However, some of the folks that call for Dr. Barlow to come visit *them* when they're sick do so just so they don't have to deal with me."

"But that's terrible!"

"What's worse is that they'd rather lie

there sicker than a dog than let go of the prejudice they've held on to for so long."

"Anyone who feels that way gets exactly what they deserve."

"Even though I'm the object of their scorn, I try not to hold it against them. I pray for them and hope they someday realize we are all God's creatures, black or white," Callie said.

Listening to Callie speak of the hardships she had faced reminded Christina of the men she had cared for at the Army hospital. On the inside, past whatever color their skin happened to be, they were *all* flesh and blood, fragile enough to have been broken. Each of them faced a choice: to try to be whole again or to give up and wallow in his pain and suffering. Whichever road they took was their own decision. Memories of Holden Sutter's anger returned and she found herself wanting to talk to him again, to battle his stubbornness as Callie had battled the racism she faced, and to beat it back with kindness.

"I wish I knew how to change people's minds," Christina said.

"If you ever figure it out, make sure and tell me, hear?"

While they waited for Dr. Barlow to arrive,

Christina was pleasantly surprised when Callie began to sing. In the beginning it wasn't much, little more than whispering, but as the song continued, her voice kept growing stronger until it had filled up the waiting room. It was a rich, delicate melody about a gypsy whose wanderings had never brought her to a place she could call home. But what amazed Christina was that Callie was so at ease, so natural, that it seemed she wasn't even aware of what she was doing.

"That was truly beautiful," Christina said when Callie finished.

"Thank you, darlin'."

"And it was certainly better than anything I've heard in a long time."

Callie nodded, a faraway look crossing her face, before she suddenly asked, "Do you have a man?"

Completely taken aback, Christina stammered, "I . . . I d-d-on't . . . Why do y-you . . . ?" all the while turning beet red with embarrassment.

"I bet you think I'm bein' nosey." Callie laughed.

"I thought we were talking about singing."

"Singin' gives me joy." She smiled. "I was taught by my momma, just as she'd been taught by hers. I sing when I wake up in the

123

mornin' and right before I go to sleep at night, when I'm walkin' to work and even when I'm settin' food on the dinner table. There's only one thin' I love more than singin'."

"What's that?"

"Abraham." Callie beamed, her smile as bright as the sun. "From the first moment I laid eyes on that man, I knew he was goin' to be mine. He's hardworking, kind, and willin' to do his share of the cookin'. Unfortunately, there is one thin' he is not."

"He's not a good singer?" Christina asked.

"You're close." Callie sighed. "If my Abraham had the voice of a brayin' mule that'd just stepped on a nail, I would be understandin'."

"Then what's wrong?"

"The problem is that Abraham *will not* sing."

"Never?" Christina asked.

"Not once."

"Even if you ask him to join you?"

"If I were to get down on my hands and knees and beg him for one note, I swear that man would not let out a squeak."

"That's . . . that's just . . ."

"Strange is what it is," Callie said. "But what's *truly* odd is that he *likes* music. He listens to records and to the radio. He'll whistle; he'll snap his fingers; he'll cluck his tongue. Whenever *I* start singin', Abraham stops what he's doin' to listen. But the man *will not sing!*"

"Is it because he's shy?"

"That man doesn't have a shy bone in his body." Callie laughed.

"It looks to me like you have a mystery on your hands."

"The reason I asked you if you had a man was that, if you did, maybe you might've had some idea what I could try, some way to persuade him."

Romantic involvement had never been something Christina had been particularly good at. She'd had flirts and crushes, pursuits that had come to nothing and others she later wished hadn't. There were dates to the movies and dances, occasionally a chaste kiss, but what there had *never* been was the possibility of something *more.*

It pained Christina to admit it, but when Charlotte had first met her future husband she had felt a slight sting of envy. When she left for nursing college and later headed off to the Army hospital, she hoped to meet the man of her dreams, but here she was, in Longstock, still waiting for him to appear. So far, the only eligible men she'd encountered were Holden and Tyler Sutter, and neither of them seemed suitable to be *any-one's* husband.

"I'm afraid I wouldn't be much help," Christina replied.

"Well, when you do meet a nice man," Callie winked, "find out if he can sing before you give him yore heart."

When Dr. Barlow arrived at the office, he looked as if he had just rolled out of bed. His hair was a rat's nest of curls and tangles, his glasses were a bit off-center, whiskers peppered his cheeks, and there were bags under his eyes. His clothing was equally sloppy, with his jacket slung over a wrinkled shirt that was missing a button. One hand clutched his medical bag as the other brought a cup of coffee up to his lips. "I'm not late, am I?" he asked, but when he turned his wrist to look at his watch he spilled some of his drink on his shoes. "Damn it all!"

"You've still got a couple of minutes to spare," Callie told him.

"I was early," Christina explained.

"There's absolutely nothing wrong with getting a head start," the doctor explained as he shook coffee from his shoe. "Come back to my office and we can get started."

Dr. Barlow led the way past Callie's desk

and down a narrow hallway to the rear of the building. Doors lined both sides of the hall; through one, Christina observed an examination room, with a table, several chairs, and a bureau full of medical instruments and jars, housed behind glass doors.

At the end of the hallway, the doctor opened the door to his office and turned on the light. Christina stifled a gasp of surprise; the inside of the room was a near-exact copy of Holden's. Stacks of medical tomes were piled on the floor, cluttered up chairs, and leaned against walls. Open books, folders, and half-scribbled notes were scattered over every remaining surface; some had even been tacked to a lampshade on his desk. With a quickness surely the result of much practice, Dr. Barlow weaved his way among the stacks, skipped over a column that had slid into his path, and dropped into his desk chair. With a frown, he quickly slammed shut one of the desk drawers while trying to find a place for his coffee.

"I've been meaning to tidy this up a bit," he explained, "but a doctor's work never seems to leave enough time."

Christina didn't know what to say or where she should go; in the end, she decided that the safest course was to say nothing and stay still. Somewhere back down the hall, the telephone rang.

"Most mornings aren't particularly busy, but you never can tell when one will buck the trend," Dr. Barlow said. "I'll have you follow along beside me. If I request something, get it for me as best you can. If you don't know where something is, just ask. Hopefully, we won't have any emergencies like that fire yesterday. Now then —"

But before the doctor could say another word, they were interrupted by the sound of Callie racing down the hallway and throwing open the door. "Dr. Barlow! Dr. Barlow!" she exclaimed breathlessly. "That was Eunice Hester on the telephone!"

"Oh, no!" the doctor groaned. "What now?"

"She said that you had to come quick! She said she's dying!"

CHAPTER EIGHT

As they drove through the heart of Long-stock, taking Main Street south and out of town, Christina was shocked by Dr. Barlow's lack of urgency. Ever since he'd received the news that Eunice Hester was dying, the doctor hadn't appeared to be in the slightest hurry; before they'd left the clinic, he'd calmly packed his medical bag, given Callie a few instructions should anyone come in during their absence, and sauntered out the door to his car, finishing his cup of coffee. His behavior certainly didn't reflect that of a physician whose services were desperately needed.

While Christina still didn't feel safe with Dr. Barlow behind the wheel, an unmistakable change in his driving had occurred. The trip to the Simmons home had been fraught with peril, full of near-collisions, screeching tires, and honking horns, but now he drove as if they were out for a leisurely Sunday excursion. Though they occasionally drifted back and forth across the median and once in a while Dr. Barlow tromped roughly on the brakes, Christina didn't feel as if her life was in imminent danger.

"Don't you think that we should be going a little faster?" Christina asked, not quite believing she could say such a thing.

"We're not in any rush." He shrugged.

"But what about the telephone call?" she asked, more confused than ever. "Callie said that a woman was dying. She said you had to come quickly."

"If I had a nickel for every time Eunice Hester called to say she was knocking on death's door, I'd have enough spare change to afford one heck of a nice lunch!"

"Wait . . . you . . . you mean that . . . that she's *not* dying?"

"Oh, heck no, she most certainly is not!" Dr. Barlow exclaimed, letting go of the wheel to gesture with both of his hands, sending the car drifting across the centerline. "You see, Eunice knows that if she squawks loud and long enough, I'll come. I won't come running, but I *will* come nonetheless. She knows darn well that I was planning on driving out to her place the day after tomorrow, just as we had agreed during my last visit, but that doesn't mean a thing when measured against a bridge game or a lunch or any other such nonsense!"

"But that means that she's lying to you."

"It's not that she's fibbing, but more that she likes to get a fella's goat. She's a prankster, a tease. She's always going on about some new cockamamie idea, whatever has her fancy on that particular day. Half the time I'm there, all we manage to do is argue back and forth. After all of these years, it just chaps my hide the way she expects me to drop everything at a moment's notice."

"Then why not stay back at the clinic?" Christina suggested. "If you're so upset, just ignore her call."

"If I were to do that, that old bat would die just to spite my stubbornness! Probably spend the rest of my life being haunted!"

For the rest of the drive to Eunice Hester's home, the doctor recalled all the times he had butted heads with Eunice, going on and on with no end in sight. After a while, Christina just stared out the window.

Is there such a thing as a normal day in Longstock?

Eunice Hester's home was well off the beaten path, several miles outside of Longstock. Following a long, winding drive from the main road, passing through a thick stand of enormous oak, elm, and evergreen trees, the doctor brought the car to a stop in front of a home that would have looked less out of place in a bigger city, somewhere like St. Paul or Milwaukee.

Standing two stories tall, with a bit more squeezed into an attic, Eunice Hester's home was impressive. A gabled roof, tiled with wooden shingles, covered a house that seemed big enough for at least a dozen occupants. The morning sunlight that managed to penetrate the trees shone off beveled windows. On the long porch held up by a row of sturdy columns, an arrangement of chairs was set around an antique coffee table. From the top of the stairs, a white-and-orange-striped cat paused in mid-step to stare at them, before bounding off into a bush and disappearing from sight. But what most caught Christina's attention were the two stone gargoyles that looked down at them from the corners of the roof, their faces chiseled into menacing grimaces, a pair of silent sentinels watching all who approached.

"Those look a bit . . . peculiar . . . ," she said, pointing.

"Aren't they, though," the doctor agreed. "Eunice had them sent over on a steamer all the way from Europe, said that when she saw them hanging off a castle in Spain she couldn't possibly live without them. When they arrived, it took over a dozen men to get the danged things off the train to where they now sit. They creep the hell out of me, they do."

"I agree . . ."

They got out of the car and headed up the walk toward the house. Christina was surprised to find that the lawn wasn't in the same immaculate condition as the home; weeds sprouted through the long grass and poked up between the stones of the walk, while clumps of rotting leaves, undoubtedly left over from the previous fall, crowded up against the bottom of the steps and porch. She couldn't imagine how much time had passed since the hedges had last been trimmed. She wondered why things were in such disarray. Still, her attention kept returning to the gargoyles; as she walked, she imagined that their eyes were following her.

"You don't know how many times I've trudged up these damn steps," the doctor grumbled.

When Dr. Barlow rapped on the door, striking a bronze knocker cast in the shape of a lion's head, the sound echoed sharply across the woods, but no reply came from inside the house.

"She drags me out into the woods and then leaves me standing at the door," he complained. "The least she could do is answer."

Dr. Barlow knocked again, harder and longer than the first time, but still there was no reply.

"Do you suppose she could have left?" Christina asked.

"She's never done it before," he answered, rubbing his whiskered chin, "but with that woman, there's a first time for *everything*."

"Should we keep knocking?"

"If Eunice didn't answer the first two times, I don't reckon that a third is going to convince her to come to the door." The doctor frowned. He turned and started heading back toward the car.

"But what if she really is in trouble?" Christina said, growing concerned that they were making a mistake in leaving.

"She isn't," Dr. Barlow said over his shoulder.

"But you said that she's never done *this* before," Christina said, refusing to let go of her sliver of doubt. "It couldn't hurt to check around the house more closely, could it?"

The doctor stopped in his tracks, let out a deep sigh, nodded his head a couple of times, and turned back toward the house. "No, I reckon it couldn't," he acknowledged, "even if it is for that old bag."

They agreed to split up and check the property for any sign of Eunice. Dr. Barlow would continue to knock on the door and look into the windows along the front of the house. Christina would follow a stone path that led around the side of the home toward the rear of the property.

At the back of the house there was another, smaller porch. Christina climbed up a short set of stairs and knocked on the door that opened onto the kitchen. Over and over she rapped, but there was no answer. Everything was silent, save for a pair of squirrels chattering away at each other in the trees and a woodpecker diligently hammering away on a branch.

Where could she have gone . . . ?

Christina peered into the windows from the rear porch. At first she saw nothing but a deep, dark gloom. Thick shadows cloaked the interior of the house, making what she managed to see, an enormous chair, some reading lamps, and a vase full of flowers, seem as if they were sitting under the night sky.

Moving from one window to the next, Christina looked into the house until she stood before the last one. Just as she was about to turn away, something caught her eye. There, in the deepest shadows, looking down a hallway that led toward the front of the house, she saw a pair of feet. It wasn't much, no more than the middle of a calf down, the feet lying flat on their heels, with one shoe, clearly a woman's, having fallen to the floor, but the sight of it sent a tremor of fear racing through her.

Maybe Eunice Hester *had* been telling the truth when she called . . . maybe she was dead . . .

Christina's first instinct was to shout for help; she and Dr. Barlow had each agreed to let the other know if they found any sign of Eunice Hester, but the sound remained in her throat. It wasn't because she was panic-stricken but rather that her training as a nurse told her that shouting out would be a waste of time if someone's life was in danger.

Something more direct was needed. Without hesitation, she ran to the rear door, tried the knob, and was grateful to find that it was unlocked. But just before she rushed inside, there on the threshold, she hesitated.

What if Eunice Hester had been attacked?
What if whoever had done it was still inside?

Christina had never considered herself brave. Whenever she became frightened, she was much more likely to give in to it than confront the dark or the unknown. Charlotte had chided her mercilessly when they were children, desperately trying to break her of her cowardice, but there was no way that Christina would ever become the risk taker that her sister was.

"Don't be afraid . . . don't give in to your fears . . . someone needs you . . . ," Christina told herself.

Taking a deep breath, Christina stepped over the threshold, moved through the kitchen, and entered a darkened study, her eyes adjusting to the murky gloom. The faint smell of tobacco lingered in the air, surprising her, but she ignored it, hurrying around the table and chairs and down the hallway. There, just as she had seen through the window, she found a pair of unmoving feet.

She knew she was looking at Eunice Hester. The woman was old; her deep wrinkles were clear even in the dim light of the hallway. Thin as a bird, she had hair white as untouched snow. Her clothes were a bit out-of-date, although a touch flamboyant; her pleated, fire-engine red blouse was fastened at the collar and held in place by an ornate, sapphire-bejeweled brooch. She was flat on her back, one arm thrown across her chest, while the other lay at her side; gaudy rings decorated many of her fingers. If it were not for the small trickle of blood spilling from the gash at her temple into a growing pool on the floor beside her head, it would seem that she was merely sleeping.

Christina jumped as a strange, sudden sound rose up from the darkness that enveloped the house. For a moment she remained perfectly still, listening, wondering whether someone else lurked just out of sight, the person responsible for Eunice's condition, watching Christina, waiting for the opportune moment to strike, but the only sounds that she could discern were the steady ticking of a grandfather clock and the creaking of the old house. Shaking her head, she reminded herself to stay focused.

Turn on a light! Do it quickly!

Eunice lay near the bottom of a steep, carpeted staircase that disappeared up into the darkness above. Christina looked around, straining to see clearly, and discovered that she was in a small foyer. Beside the stairs stood an elaborately carved table, decorated with a pair of photographs, a vase full of cut flowers, and a lamp, which she immediately turned on.

In its glow, Christina marveled at what she saw: a towering elephant tusk stood upright on the other side of the table, its ivory festooned with beads and a deep red satin cloth; wooden masks, crudely carved and painted in a rainbow of bright colors, leered down at her from the walls; an enormous painting of a giraffe, its long neck craned back over its body, was affixed to the space above the stairs; a stuffed penguin sat on top of another table, looking ready to take a swim in frigid ocean waters. Overlooking it all was a lavish chandelier, its finely cut glass reflecting light up and across the high ceiling. It was as if she had wandered into a museum rather than someone's home.

It was clear that Eunice Hester's eccentricities did *not* stop with her stone gargoyles.

"Mrs. Hester?" Christina said, turning her attention back to the unconscious, bleeding woman; when she spoke, her voice echoed, sounding undersized in such a large space. "Can you hear me?" There was still no reply.

A tremor of fear raced through Christina; until that moment, she hadn't stopped to imagine that Eunice wasn't sleeping as she appeared, but rather that she was dead.

"Mrs. Hester?" she repeated. "Please answer me . . ."

Then, in the faint light, Christina noticed Eunice's chest rising and falling, although it did so weakly. Flooded with relief, Christina could not stifle a sigh. Grasping her patient by the wrist, Christina rejoiced at finding a pulse. Though Eunice Hester had been battered and bloodied, she was still alive.

But what in heaven's name had happened to her . . . ?

CHAPTER NINE

"You're nothing more than a damn fool, old woman! A damn fool!"

Dr. Barlow taped the last of the large bandage to the side of Eunice Hester's bruised and bloodied forehead and then threw the roll into his medical bag in disgust. His anger was obvious.

"Maybe so, but I didn't get to be such an old woman by accident, you know." Eunice smiled, throwing a wink to Christina, clearly enjoying the outburst her injury had caused. "I can't be *too* much of a fool to have made it this far."

"Keep this up and I guarantee that you won't be getting any older!"

"One of these days, you'll get your wish!"

"How can you treat this like it was some kind of game!"

Dr. Barlow and Eunice Hester had been at each other's throats from the moment the older woman regained consciousness.

Christina was shocked, listening to it all, surprised that two adults could speak in such a way.

Once Christina had determined that Eunice wasn't in any immediate danger, she'd raced for the front door, unlocking it so that the doctor could get inside. It had taken them some time to wake Eunice and even longer to get her into a chair in the study. Dr. Barlow had thundered and ranted the whole time, demanding that Eunice explain how she had ended up bleeding at the bottom of the stairs. But as furious as he had been up until that point, learning *the truth* made it much, much worse.

Eunice had, just as the doctor had supposed during the drive, fibbed when she had told Callie Davis that she was dying; of course, that didn't mean that Eunice saw it in quite the same terms.

"It wasn't as if I were *really* lying," she offered in her own defense. "If you think about it, all of us *are* dying, some just more quickly than others."

What she couldn't deny was that her reason for bending the truth was selfish; an old friend had surprised her, calling to say that she'd be coming to town for a visit later that afternoon. Eunice had concluded that she should clear her calendar by hook or by crook. And so she'd called Callie and lied in order to get him to come before the scheduled time. Pleased with herself for pulling another fast one over on the doctor, Eunice had decided to celebrate with a cigarette; her mistake had been in lighting it while she was descending the staircase. Distracted while striking a match, she had missed a step and tumbled more than a dozen feet to the floor, striking her head hard enough to knock herself unconscious.

"Do you not realize that you're almost ninety years old?" Dr. Barlow bellowed. "How can you possibly believe that it's still a good idea to go tromping up and down those stairs like a woman half your age? It's a miracle this hasn't happened before!"

"Who says it hasn't?" Eunice chuckled.

"Laugh all you want now, but you'll see how funny it is tomorrow morning when you're too sore to get out of bed!"

"If I am, I'll have the good sense not to bother *you* with it!"

"Thank heaven for small favors!"

"Poor Samuel," she said with mock concern. "Wouldn't the world be a better place if everyone just did as you told them?"

"I might as well wish for all of the apples in town to turn to solid gold!"

Never in all of her time as a nurse had

Christina heard a doctor speak to a patient as rudely as Samuel Barlow now fumed at Eunice. Christina couldn't have been more shocked. It was both unprofessional and unbecoming.

However, though Dr. Barlow's words were rougher than tree bark and his bedside manner resembled that of a grizzly bear, there was *something* in the way he cared for Eunice that made Christina wonder if much of his bluster was for show.

When he had first looked upon Eunice's bloodied, unmoving body, Dr. Barlow had rushed to her, his expression one of grave alarm, and held her hand in his own with the kind of tenderness often reserved for a child. He had been quiet, only softly, insistently repeating her name until her eyes finally fluttered open; his relief had been instantaneous, even if it had been immediately replaced by harsh words. Even now, as he continued to lecture her, it was obvious that he was concerned.

Christina understood *why* he cared; her own first impression of Eunice Hester was that she was easily likeable. Though her skin was mottled with age spots and her face deeply marked by wrinkles, her green eyes still held a vitality and mischievousness that was impossible to miss. Her quick smile and warm laugh, even in the face of the doctor's scolding, as well as the winks she kept sending Christina's way, made it feel as if they were fellow conspirators in a game Eunice was intent on playing. Even with the bruise blossoming across her forehead, she seemed ready to commit more tomfoolery.

"When did you plan on telling me about the cigarette?" Dr. Barlow asked.

"What about it?" Eunice replied, looking away.

"I've been your doctor for more than twenty-five years. I've treated you for more things than I can remember, but not once can I remember you mentioning that you were a smoker."

Eunice rolled her eyes; for an instant, she looked like a child caught sneaking a hand into the cookie jar before dinner. "You said it yourself earlier, Samuel." She sighed, lifting her hands in a pose of surrender. "I'm almost ninety years old. Since I don't have a whole lot of time left, I thought that it might be fun to take up some of the habits I've spent my whole life avoiding."

"You must be joking!"

"If I was, I don't think we'd be having this ridiculous conversation."

"*This* might be the craziest thing you've done yet!"

"What better time to start than when there aren't enough years left for it to do me much harm? Seems quite smart to me . . ."

"It *would* to a woman as crazy as you are!"

"Do you know what I'm thinking about trying next?" she asked, but didn't wait for an answer. "Bullfighting!" Eunice exclaimed happily. "The last time I was in Mexico I went to a match and, to be perfectly honest with you, it didn't seem to be all that difficult. All you do is stand there, while everyone in the arena cheers, twirling a red cape about, waiting for the bull to charge so you can just step aside and plunge your sticker into its side. Why, anyone could do that!"

"I think that it's a lot harder than it looks," Christina said, finally feeling as if she could join in the conversation.

"Don't bother trying to talk her out of it," the doctor cautioned. "Even if *we* both know that she's likely to be trampled underfoot, once *Eunice* has made up her mind, you would have better luck pulling the moon from the night sky than getting her to change it."

"Oh, hush now, Samuel," Eunice chided him. With a wicked smile, she turned to Christina and asked, "Why do you think I shouldn't become a bullfighter?"

"I don't know," Christina answered, playing the role of innocent, aware that Eunice was teasing. "It seems awfully dangerous . . ."

"Would you like to know a secret?" the older woman whispered.

"I suppose . . ."

Eunice's smile softened as her eyes lost their playfulness, narrowing and becoming serious. "The most foolish thing that you could ever do would be never taking a chance. When I remember all of the things I've done, all of the people I've met, and all of the places I've been, it reminds me that each of the risks I took was worth it." Eunice grinned, as if she were imagining herself in a bullfighting ring, a sword in her hand. "If I'd never taken those risks, why, I'd be nothing more than another old woman waiting for death to come knocking. So when your own opportunity presents itself, whenever love and adventure introduce themselves, you'd be worse than a fool not to take them by the hand."

Christina acknowledged the advice with a smile, thinking to herself that Eunice, unknowingly, had hit upon the hesitancy that often governed her decisions.

■ ■ ■ ■

While Dr. Barlow packed up the last of his things, Christina moved out of the study and back to the foyer where she had first found Eunice. Remembering her worries upon entering the house, her fear that there was someone lurking in the shadows, and her panic at the thought that Eunice Hester was dead embarrassed her now. Even the mysterious smell of tobacco had an easy explanation.

Christina was relieved that she hadn't said a word about any of her fears; she could only imagine how it would have looked to Dr. Barlow. Considering the harsh way he'd spoken to Eunice, Christina could only imagine what a lecture he might have given her.

Running her fingertips along the top of the table beside the stairs, Christina touched one of the picture frames and paused. In the chaos of her first moments inside the house, she hadn't noticed what images they held. The first was of a woman, standing before an open tent, desert sand all around, a dark-skinned handler holding the reins of a one-humped camel; even with the passage of years, it was easy for Christina to see that the woman was Eunice Hester. The other photograph was equally exotic. In it, Eunice stood beside a well-dressed man, both of them surrounded by dozens of children; Christina couldn't be certain, but she thought that they must be Chinese. They were all gathered in front of a school.

"That handsome man beside me was my husband," a voice spoke from behind Christina. Startled, she turned to find Eunice standing in the hallway. The older woman, with her forehead bandaged and her bruise growing uglier, looked to be every one of her nearly ninety years.

"You should be sitting down," Christina told her.

"My dear, if you don't watch yourself, you'll end up sounding just like Samuel," Eunice answered with a smile.

"There's a part of me that takes that as a compliment."

"You should, but don't worry, I am fine, I assure you," Eunice replied, dismissing Christina's concerns with a wave of her hand. Carefully, she shuffled across the floor to stand beside the table, holding on to it for support.

"I hope that you don't think I was snooping through your things."

"The thought never crossed my mind."

"Where was this picture taken?" Christina asked, showing Eunice the photograph with all of the children.

"We were in Shanghai," she explained, as a twinkle of memory lit in her eyes. "Those were the days before the Boxer Rebellion, back before the country went a bit wild. There were all types of foreigners there, people from all over the world. You couldn't walk down the street without hearing half a dozen languages being spoken. Albert and I took donations from back home in the States and used them to build schools, erect dams, fix old roads, anything that would help. We used to have dinner with Herbert Hoover and his wife. It was all so long ago."

"It seems so exciting. When I think of all of the places you must have been," Christina said, sweeping her hand around the foyer at all of the mementos on the walls.

"Albert and I *did* travel to a lot of wonderful places," Eunice admitted. "But not a one of them would have meant a thing to me if he hadn't been there by my side every exhilarating step of the way. For every strange new language I heard, every exotic food that I was brave enough to taste, every wild animal I saw, and every local custom that I somehow managed not to offend." She laughed. "All of them were adventures because Albert was there, experiencing them with me. When I was with him, the whole world was my oyster."

"He sounds like a remarkable man."

"He was," she answered, her voice growing wistful. "He's been gone now for almost fifteen years."

"I'm very sorry to hear that," Christina said respectfully.

"That's nice of you to say, my dear," Eunice answered, her smile returning, "but it's just like I told Samuel earlier. Every one of us is meant to pass on from this life. Unfortunately, we often don't get to stay as long as our loved ones would like. When Albert died, it took me quite a while to get my feet back under me. But in the end, I suppose I realized that he was still beside me in his own way, watching down from above."

"Then I'm sure he would agree with me that you should take it easy."

"Oh, hush!" she said, laughing.

Christina followed as Eunice led her around the foyer, pointing from one object to the next and telling her a story for every item; it was like having a guide in a museum. When they stopped in front of another photograph, showing Eunice and her late husband in a carved-out boat on a jungle river, she paused before turning to Christina.

"Have you given your heart to some lucky young man?" she asked.

For the second time that morning, Christina found herself surprised that she would be asked such a thing. But just as she had when Callie Davis had inquired, Christina took no offense from Eunice's question; it wasn't that she was being judged, but rather that Eunice was genuinely interested.

"I haven't met that man yet," Christina answered.

"You will," Eunice said confidently, "and when you do, even if you were to decide to settle here in Longstock and *never* leave, with that special man at your side, adventures you will, most certainly, have. Shanghai is nice, but it doesn't hold a candle to celebrating a child's birthday or waking up beside your husband every morning."

"I reckon that you would know what you're talking about."

"I do." She nodded. "I truly do."

Much as Christina wanted to agree with Eunice, another part of her thought that if all of the men in Longstock were made from the same mold as Holden and Tyler Sutter, she wouldn't find a husband until *she* was ninety years old.

■ ■ ■ ■

For the rest of the late morning and into the early afternoon, Christina accompanied Dr. Barlow as he visited patients who lived far from Longstock's center. They checked in on Eugene Sanford, a farmer who had been in a machinery accident, so the doctor could be certain that the cast he had placed on the man's leg had hardened properly. They stopped to see the Apitz family, whose newborn daughter the doctor had recently delivered. Christina took great pleasure in holding little Emily in her arms as the baby cooed and tugged at her finger. Finally, at the home of Margaret Gilles, an elderly woman Dr. Barlow believed was suffering from dementia, Christina took a bite of an offered piece of blueberry pie that seemed to have had its sugar substituted by salt.

"It's all that I could do to swallow it," she explained after they left.

"You did fine," the doctor assured her. "As far as Margaret is concerned, it was the best darn pie you ever tasted."

With every stop, Christina began to feel more comfortable and confident. After the drama of finding Eunice bloodied and in a heap at the bottom of the stairs, tending to run-of-the-mill occurrences such as broken bones and new babies reassured Christina that every day in Longstock wouldn't be as crazy as her first. She went about her work with a smile.

Still, Eunice's words about the joys of having a man to share her life nagged at her from time to time, especially when she was at the Apitz home. There was no point in denying that she wanted to have a family someday; reading Charlotte's letters left little doubt how wonderful it was. But right then, as Christina sped along the back roads of Wisconsin, it all seemed so very far away, almost unattainable. Even as exciting as her day had been, she couldn't help but wonder if it wouldn't be *even better* if there were someone special waiting for her at home, someone she could tell all about it.

By the time they neared Longstock, the afternoon sun was high in the sky, baking the road before them. Absently, Christina wiped away a bead of sweat that had begun running down her cheek. The first thing she was going to do once they were back at the doctor's clinic was drink a tall glass of water.

"I reckon we're going to have to stop for gas." Dr. Barlow frowned as he peered at the coupe's fuel gauge. "If we don't, I'm afraid we'll have to *push* it the rest of the way back."

Pulling off of the road at the end of Main Street, the doctor guided the automobile into the parking lot of a service station. He brought the coupe to a sliding halt just before the fuel pump. While the engine was still ticking, an attendant rushed out to help them, smiling as he unlatched the hood and began checking the fluids. Another began filling their nearly empty tank as the pump's meter clicked noisily.

"You might as well get out and stretch your legs," Dr. Barlow suggested. "I know my old bones sure could stand to get out from behind that wheel."

"That sounds like a good idea," she agreed.

But just as she was about to open the door, she saw something that stopped her cold. There, standing in the open bay of the filling station's garage, wiping his grease-stained hands on a soiled rag, was Tyler Sutter. He was watching her intently; a sly smile spread across his face as he tucked the dirty rag into his back pocket.

Christina didn't know what she should do; her fingers tightened around the door's handle, but she made no move to open it. Maybe she could just ignore him by staying in the car and waiting for the doctor to return.

But it was then that the decision was made for her.

Tyler began walking toward the car.

CHAPTER TEN

"I see my uncle's got you out traipsin' through the woods on one of the hottest damn days of the year," Tyler said as he leaned his forearm against the roof of the car, peering down through the window, bringing with him the pungent aroma of oil mixed with sweat. "I reckon if it gets any warmer I'll be able to fry myself up a mess of bacon and eggs on the sidewalk."

Christina didn't comment, setting her jaw as defiantly as she could manage, and kept staring out the coupe's windshield, even if all she had to see was the top of the raised hood.

It didn't take long for Tyler to understand her intentions. "Oh, I see how it's gonna be." He chuckled. "I'll just stand here talking away while you give me the silent treatment. I guess you haven't gotten over our little run-in last night." Running a hand through his short hair, he added, "I figured you weren't the sort of woman who'd be so skittish over something as harmless as a honking horn."

"Following along behind me in your car was the *least* of the things you did wrong last night," Christina snapped, instantly upset with herself that he had goaded her into breaking her vow of silence so easily. "If I were to start talking about all of the things you did to make me have a horrible impression of you, I don't know *when* I would finish!"

"I get it." He nodded. "Now you're gonna play hard to get."

"Excuse me?" she asked, incredulous.

Tyler grinned. "Isn't that just the way it is with you ladies these days? When it's obvious that you're developing feelings for a man, you go out of your way to make him feel so worthless and unwanted that he tries all the harder to win you over, just like in the movies or in all of those magazines you're always reading. Well, darlin', that's where I'm one step ahead of you. I *know* that you're smitten with me, so why don't we just skip all of that courtship nonsense and get down to what really matters, especially with the kissing and then to somewhere . . . well, you might call it romantic, I guess."

Christina simply *could not believe* the words that were coming out of Tyler Sutter's mouth. Never in her wildest dreams could she have imagined having to listen to such inappropriate advances. With her heart pounding in her chest, she decided that she had no choice but to tell him how offensive he was.

But when she turned to him, determined to give him a piece of her mind, to tell him in no uncertain terms that she never wanted to hear such talk again, she stopped; Tyler's face was twisted up into an outrageous expression, like a dam struggling to hold back water, finally giving way as he burst into huge bellyfuls of laughter.

"Oh, that's rich!" He laughed, slapping a hand against the coupe's top. "I can't believe you bought that junk! You thought that I was being serious; admit it! Boy, they must not have much that passes for humor back in . . . Minnesota, wasn't it?"

Christina flushed a bright red, angry that she was the butt of Tyler's joke, and turned back to face front; the last thing she wanted was to give him the satisfaction of knowing he had gotten to her.

"You did, didn't you?" he kept prodding. "You actually believed I was serious with all that!"

"If you think you're being funny," she managed, "you're not . . ."

"I tell you one thing." Tyler chuckled. "If there's something we need to work on, it's the fact that you take everything so damn seriously!"

"*We* don't need to work on anything!"

"If I don't help you, who will? My uncle? He might be skilled as a doctor, but he's as humorless as a tree stump!"

Bantering back and forth with Tyler was quickly becoming exhausting. Christina desperately wanted it to end and for him to leave her alone. Craning her neck to look around, she saw no sign of Dr. Barlow; she wondered if she shouldn't get out of the car and look for him so that they could leave the filling station, but she had doubts as to whether Tyler would allow her to pass.

Frustrated, unsure of herself, and more than a little bit fearful of what might happen, Christina began to get emotional. Tears sprang to her eyes. Beads of sweat dotted her brow. She couldn't help remembering how Tyler had violently grabbed her by the arm the night before, his fingers digging into her flesh, a crazed look dancing in his eyes when he learned about her meeting with Holden. Involuntarily, she rubbed the spot where Tyler had held her, wincing from both the physical discomfort of the bruise and the memory of how she had received it.

It was then, while Christina was struggling with her recollections of Tyler's outburst, that he did something completely unexpected . . .

He touched her again.

Reaching through the open window, Tyler gently took Christina's hand in his own. Although her first, panicked instinct was to pull her hand away, she found herself doing nothing of the sort. Tenderly, his fingers traced a slow arc across hers; despite the roughness of his skin and the streaks of oil and grease that dirtied the back of his hand, she found his touch affectionate, warm, and even inviting. The way that he managed to surprise her was becoming something of a habit.

"Christina," he said, his voice losing all of the annoying playfulness with which he'd almost always spoken to her; at the sound of her name, she couldn't resist looking at him. What she found in his eyes held her as firmly as he had the previous night, though this time she didn't struggle to break free. "Apologizing isn't something that I'm particularly good at, but I wanted to tell you that I was sorry for the way I acted last night. Sometimes . . . I act before I think things through all the way. I shouldn't have behaved as I did."

"You frightened me . . . ," she admitted.

"And that's why I'm telling you this," he said, as a wisp of a smile curled at the corners of his mouth. "I hate thinking that, on your first day in town, you might have felt as if you'd made a mistake in coming here."

"It wasn't like that," Christina protested.

Tyler looked at her closely for a moment. "Looks to me like we're going to have to work on your lying, too."

Christina couldn't help but laugh. Looking at him, she was suddenly struck by the realization that Tyler Sutter was a very handsome man, much more than she had previously noticed. With his broad shoulders, close-cropped hair, and easygoing manner, he was someone who could easily catch a woman's eye.

"Now how about letting me make last night up to you," he said.

"What . . . what do you . . ." But before she could even finish asking her question, he had opened the car door and gently, but insistently, helped her up and to her feet.

"Hey! Uncle Samuel!" he hollered.

Christina followed his gaze to where Dr. Barlow stood beneath the filling station's awning, drinking a bottle of Coca-Cola. Startled by his nephew's shouting, he sputtered, spilling some of the liquid down the front of his shirt. Annoyed, he began wiping it off with his hand.

"What is it?" the doctor asked, frowning.

"I'm going to borrow Miss Tucker here for a little while," Tyler said as he began pulling Christina toward the side of the garage and away from his uncle. "When we're finished, I'll bring her on back to your office."

"Now just a second there," Dr. Barlow began to protest, still preoccupied by the soda that had stained his clothing. "We only stopped for gas and our day's already been a mess so —"

"I really need to —" Christina began.

"That's settled then!" Tyler exclaimed, allowing neither of them to finish their complaints. "You won't even know she's gone!"

Without another word, Tyler hurried toward the side of the building, practically dragging Christina along behind him, weaving between the empty oil barrels that littered the ground and plunging between the posts of a broken fence and into the dense overgrowth that lined a stand of trees.

Behind them, Christina heard the unmistakable, yet fading, sounds of the doctor's protests.

Once they had passed through the first dense bushes, Christina struggling to keep nettles from becoming twisted in her hair, they stumbled out into a small clearing. Splotches of sunlight dotted the ground, shifting with the faint movement of the thick canopy of leaves far above. A pair of squirrels, startled by their unexpected arrival, scurried out of sight in a crescendo of chattering complaints. Christina hardly had time to identify the faint trail that wound up a small rise and away from the garage before Tyler began leading her down it.

"Where . . . where are you taking me?" she asked, trying to maintain her footing among the rocks and exposed tree roots that littered the path.

"It's a surprise." He smiled over his shoulder.

A part of Christina found Tyler's evasion of her question charming, even a bit mysterious. Undoubtedly, it would be much easier to just accept his mischievous ways and go along with his game, seeing it through to the end. But she knew that she could *not* allow that to happen.

Far too often in her life, Christina had allowed herself to be led somewhere she didn't necessarily want to go. Often, she would do what someone else wanted simply because it was harder to disagree, all because she didn't want to rock the boat.

From the first moment that she had met Tyler, he always seemed to have the upper hand, laughing at a joke given at her expense and making her seem foolish. It was a feeling she did not appreciate. She knew that the only way to put an end to it, to keep it from becoming a habit, was to dig in her heels and let him know that enough was enough.

"Just stop, Tyler!" she shouted. Pulling her hand free from his grasp, she stood stock-still.

Tyler's momentum carried him a bit farther along the trail and, when he finally came to a halt, he looked back at her as if confused, not quite able to understand why she was no longer beside him.

"Now why do you have to be so difficult?" he said.

Christina took a slow, deep breath. "I know that you're excited to show me something, but you can't just expect me to be dragged along behind you without knowing where we're going. That's just not fair to me. Besides, I really shouldn't be gone from my job for very long."

"Don't worry about my uncle," Tyler reassured her. "We'll be back before he gets too bent out of shape."

"What about your boss? Isn't he going to be upset that one of his employees just took off in the middle of the afternoon?"

"Raymond spends every day sitting in his office, drinking whiskey and listening to the baseball games on the radio." Tyler laughed. "Hell, even if I didn't show up one morning, I doubt he'd notice."

"I still want to know where it is you're taking me."

"I told you that it was a surprise."

"And I just told you that explanation wasn't good enough."

For a long moment, Tyler remained silent, staring at her. Christina wondered if he wasn't contemplating grabbing her arm and resuming their mad dash through the woods. Clearly, he was a forceful man accustomed to getting his way.

"I know I haven't given you a whole lot of reasons to trust me," he finally said, making his way back to where she stood with her arms folded defiantly across her chest, "but couldn't you just give me the benefit of the doubt?"

"I don't know you well enough to do that, and what I *do know* of you . . ."

"Doesn't my apology for last night mean anything?"

"It . . . it does . . . ," Christina answered truthfully. "But what if I were to get lost? I don't know my way around these woods."

"Why do you think I was holding on to your hand so tightly?"

"Because you know that there was no way you could get me out here willingly."

"You say that like you don't want to be here."

"The thought *had* crossed my mind."

"Look," Tyler said, holding his hands up in mock surrender. "I know I'm asking a lot for you to take me at my word, but I *really* wish you would. The place I want to take you is special to me, that's all. There's no way that you'll get lost, absolutely no wild animals this close to town, and I'll even have you back to work before my uncle fires you, okay?"

"Maybe it's not wild animals that I should be afraid of," Christina suggested, the meaning of her words clear to the man she spoke them to.

"Perhaps I should ask you where you *think* I'm taking you," he said as a slow, sly smile spread across his rugged face. "Are you wondering if I'm *that* bad a man, the danger-ous sort who's dug a hole in the middle of nowhere where he stashes all of his unsuspecting victims?" When Christina visibly recoiled at his words, he immediately dropped all pretense and sighed. "You know, I meant what I said earlier about working on your sense of humor. Do you suppose it would help if I told you I was telling a joke *before* I said it?"

Christina knew that her reaction had been silly, but if there was one thing that amazed her about Tyler Sutter, it was that he never failed to surprise her. Though it didn't come easily, she resigned herself to giving him the trust he had requested. Reaching out, she placed her hand in his and said, "Show me what it is that's got you so darn excited."

Tyler led the way as they walked down the path that had been worn through the underbrush. Up and down gentle rises, beside the gurgling waters of a small stream, and among the birds, squirrels, rabbits, and other wildlife that watched their passing, they walked on, neither of them saying a word. Christina had no idea how long it had been since they had left the garage, but just as she was about to ask how much farther they had to go, Tyler came to a stop as the path opened into a clearing.

"We're here," he said.

Stepping out of the break in the trees, Christina found her breath taken away by the beauty of the scene before her. It was obvious to her that the clearing had, many years before, been a farmer's field. While there was no sign of what crops had been grown there, furrowed rows marked its boundaries, now almost completely over-grown with weeds. A small, dilapidated building stood at one end of the clearing, its weathered boards and roof somehow managing to remain intact. Beside it, an old tractor rusted under the open sky. The land sloped gently away from them, allowing plenty of early summer sunlight to brighten all that she could see.

"It's beautiful." She smiled.

"I guess so." Tyler shrugged as if this was the first time he had ever given the matter any thought.

"This was what you wanted to show me? The clearing?"

"Sort of," he answered. Taking her gently by the shoulders, he turned her toward a corner of the field opposite from them and pointed. Following his direction, Christina could barely make out three white boxes ar-ranged closely together; in the glare of the sun, they were almost invisible to the eye. From so far away, she imagined that they were chests of drawers.

"Do you know what they are?" Tyler asked.

"No, I don't," Christina admitted.

"Those are my beehives."

As if Tyler were a magician who had drawn back the stage curtain to reveal his newest sleight of hand, Christina immediately became aware of things she hadn't seen only moments before. Bees buzzed in the air all around them, landing on the wildflowers along the edge of the tree line, their tiny bodies heavy on the petals, the stems bowing, before righting themselves to collect nectar. From one flower to the next, the bees proceeded about their work. The air hummed softly with their activity. One landed on Christina's wrist; she quickly shook it off.

"How . . . how many bees are there?" she asked nervously.

"Thousands, for sure." Tyler beamed with pride. "There's no way of knowing exactly, since I don't reckon they'd hold still long enough for me to count them."

"Aren't you afraid of being stung?"

"Not anymore." He shrugged. "The first couple of times it happened, it hurt like holy hell, but after a while I managed to get used to it. Nowadays, it's not much of a bother.

Besides, it's not as if I just mosey on over to the hives dressed like this."

"What *do* you wear?"

"Let me show you."

Tyler led the way to the corner of the clearing that was closest to the hives but opposite. Nervously, Christina watched as bees buzzed all around them, flitting from one flower to the next, paying little attention to their new visitors.

A metal footlocker lay in the tall grass, a sprung padlock hanging loose from a clasp. Tyler threw back the lid with his foot and revealed the trunk's contents. A wadded pile of white cloth and meshing half-covered a strange metal contraption that resembled a coffeepot.

"What's all of this?" she asked.

"This is what I wear when I *do* want to get near those hives," he explained as he pulled the cloth out of the trunk and held it up for her to see. It was a full-body suit of heavy fabric that would cover almost every inch of its wearer. Attached to the neck of the suit was a bit of fine mesh, topped with a brimmed hat.

"And that's enough for you to keep from being stung?"

Tyler chuckled as he shook his head. "Even if I wore a suit of armor, a couple of those little buggers would manage to get through. They can be quite persistent when they want to be. Even when I'm wearing this," he explained, rustling the suit, "I always get nailed once or twice, mostly on account of the fact that I never use gloves."

"Why not?" Christina exclaimed, nearly shivering at the thought of exposing her own skin to a swarm of insects. "You're just asking to get stung!"

"I need to have my hands free so that I can work with the hives," Tyler said. "Farming honey takes a nimble hand. It isn't the sort of thing that can be done wearing gloves. Besides, when I get stung, it's just a matter of scraping the barb out with my fingernail before it starts hurting too much.

"But that doesn't mean that I'm not a cautious fella. I make sure they're as docile as possible before I go rustling around in their homes."

"How do you do that?"

"With this," he said, pulling the odd metal device out of the trunk. Up close, it appeared even stranger than at first glance. A metal cylinder was surrounded by rough wire mesh and topped with a retractable cap; it really *did* appear to have been made out of a coffeepot. Where the handle would be a metal glove had been welded to the side; inside was a metal wire that ran to the pot's lid.

"Do you brew them something to drink?" Christina joked.

"Very funny," Tyler replied sarcastically. "This is a smoker. All you need to do is fill it with dry pine needles, maybe a length of old twine, anything that will produce a lot of smoke, and set it on fire."

"And that confuses them?"

"Strange as it may sound, it actually calms them down," he explained. "Once they've gotten a good dose of the smoke, they all abandon the hive and start feeding. I don't really understand the science of it all, but that's what they do. Then, while they're flying about, gathering pollen, that's when I extract the honey from the hives."

"But you still get stung, even with the smoke?"

"That's just part of the job, I guess."

"It seems . . . complicated . . ."

"It is and it isn't." He shrugged.

"Even if I were wearing that suit," Christina said, running her fingers against the fabric, "and using the smoke, I don't think I'd feel safe."

"You're only in danger if you *believe* you are."

Christina turned to look at Tyler; he was

staring at the beehives, but there was something in the way he'd spoken that made her wonder if he was talking about the trauma she'd witnessed in his family. Memories returned of the aggressive way he had grabbed her, along with the way he'd stormed from the dinner table.

Does he think that Holden's problems are all in his head?

"Maybe you could help me sometime," he suddenly said, pulling her from her thoughts.

"Oh . . . oh, no . . . there's no way that I could . . . it would . . . ," she mumbled.

"Why the heck not? Rustling together another suit wouldn't be all that difficult. Heck, I'd even make sure it had a pair of gloves." Tyler chuckled warmly. "If you were too frightened, you could always stand a ways back from the beehives, but then you wouldn't see the honeycomb when it's first pulled out. Missing that would be a shame."

From the moment she had met him, it had been clear to Christina that Tyler Sutter was a man of contradictions. He had been charming, loud, and brash at his mother's dinner table. When following Christina in his car, he had been a prankster, obnoxious, and finally aggressive. Back at the garage, he'd been disarming, annoying, yet apologetic. Even now, standing among the buzzing bees in the middle of the clearing, he demonstrated a curiosity about the living world that made her rethink how she looked at him. When she had gone to bed the night before, she had never wanted to see Tyler again, even wondered if she had made the right choice in coming to Longstock, but now she had begun to feel more at ease, even a bit comfortable in her new home. Gone was the desire to distance herself from Tyler. Instead, she wondered what side of himself he might show her next.

"I . . . I suppose I could think about it . . . ," she said.

"That's good enough for me," he answered, "for now."

"You know, I never would have imagined that a guy like you would be interested in something like this."

"That's only because you don't know me very well."

"I suppose not."

"We'll just add that to the list of things we need to work on."

Christina was surprised to find that now, unlike in most all of her other conversations with Tyler, she didn't feel the need to disagree. She was happy and at ease, completely unaware that they were being watched.

CHAPTER ELEVEN

Annette Wilson could *not* believe what she had seen.

Walking back toward Longstock beneath the thick canopy of trees, she couldn't get the image of Tyler Sutter talking with some strange woman . . . some *whore,* out of her mind. She had seen him smiling at her, laughing at something she'd said, had watched helplessly as the two of them held hands as if they were lovers.

Turmoil and torment gnawed at Annette's stomach, and she had to fight the urge to vomit into a bush.

And it had been such a wonderful day . . .

Only an hour earlier, Annette had been bursting with excitement at the possibilities before her. Hurrying down the street under a gloriously clear sky, a picnic basket swinging in her hand, she had hoped to make it to the garage before Tyler left for lunch. She'd thought that a surprise might cheer him up a little. The last time she'd spoken to him, he'd told her that he never wanted to see her again for the rest of his life, but she'd known he didn't really mean it. *Everyone* in Longstock knew how great a burden Holden had placed upon his family, so she had felt certain that Tyler was under such stress that he couldn't be held responsible for everything he said. He just needed to spend some more time with her to realize he shouldn't *ever* be without her.

Just as Annette had rounded the corner, Tyler stepped from the garage; seeing his face filled her heart with love, so intense that it nearly burst. She raised her arm, beginning to wave, and nearly wept when he'd returned the gesture with a smile, but immediately she had known that something was wrong, that he hadn't seen her, but rather that he had been happy to see someone *else.*

Since that moment, Annette had felt as if she were sleepwalking. Under the glare of the summer sun, she'd watched while Tyler directed his attention toward the woman in the car, eventually helping her from the car and leading her behind the garage and into the woods. Feeling as if he had taken *her* by the hand, Annette began to follow them, somehow managing to put one foot in front

178

of the other.

Watching them from a distance, trying to stay both out of sight and close enough to peer at them between the branches and leaves, listening to them as they talked with an intimacy that shocked her, Annette could not comprehend how Tyler could do such a thing to her.

After all, they were to be married.

If Annette were to admit it to herself, the truth was that things between them were delicate and they always had been. Tyler Sutter had never *told* her that he understood the special nature of their relationship, but Annette knew that he was aware nevertheless.

From the very first moment she had looked into Tyler's blue eyes, Annette had *known* that they were destined to spend their lives together. They'd only been schoolchildren, but even as a boy he had mesmerized her with his handsomeness, the way he spoke, and his charming personality. It was undeniably love at first sight. She had excitedly embraced the idea that he was the man she would grow old beside. Immediately, she had made the decision to stay as close to him as possible, always to be by his side, certain that he would return her feelings and they would live happily ever after.

But on the day she had first told him how she felt, Tyler's response was to push her down into a mud puddle.

That first setback was only the beginning; he pulled her hair, called her terrible names, and one time spat at her feet. Try as she might, he remained stubborn, behaving horribly toward her. Her older sister assured her that this was the way *boys* were, but as they became men things would change; his taunts and expressions of disgust would turn to a tender courtship and professions of love practically overnight. At this point in their lives, Tyler was *clearly* still a boy.

"Hold on to what you know in your heart is true," she told herself.

The worst part was that Tyler became more and more handsome as he got older, drawing the attention of almost every woman in town. Annette suffered as she watched girls blush as they handed him love letters, saw him holding hands with one hussy after another, and sat with each in the back of the Odeon, Longstock's movie theater, her imagination running wild at what Tyler was doing in the darkness with his date only a couple of rows ahead of her. Though humiliated, Annette remained undeterred, determined not to allow her love for him to waver.

But then, one snowy winter afternoon when they were seventeen, Annette had watched Tyler and Caroline Satterly share a kiss behind the school. Every embarrassment, every slight Annette had ever received from Tyler, seemed to be nothing in the face of this betrayal. At first, she had been furious at the man to whom she had willingly given her heart. But no sooner had the thought entered her mind than the *truth* revealed itself to her; it was the fault of all of those young girls, those promiscuous *whores* who were trying to tempt her beloved into doing things that would keep him from the life he was destined to have. And so, with hatred in her heart, she had decided to take matters into her own hands.

She would never allow a girl to come between Tyler and her!

Caroline Satterly and her family lived on an apple farm on the remote, far northern edge of town, reached only by a winding dirt road. Even in the cold winter months, Caroline's parents were often busy making preparations for the upcoming season, leaving their daughter to walk home most nights. Without any neighbors, she was alone for miles.

One cold evening, beneath a gently falling

snow, Annette waited in the bushes just off the road, concealed by the blanketing darkness of night. Her gloved hand held an imposing length of metal pipe. Though her exposed skin felt the harsh bite of winter and she had to stamp her feet from time to time to ensure she could still feel her extremities, she was infused with a burning hatred, a desire for revenge that could overcome any obstacle put before her.

Finally, Caroline trudged into view.

Annette couldn't remember much of what followed. Her memories were a confusing jumble of images: the sight of her arm frantically swinging the pipe over and over into Caroline's legs, the girl lying defenseless on the frozen ground, her piercing screams going unanswered. But even as Annette gulped deep gasps of the frigid air into her burning lungs, the pipe falling from her hand to clatter at her feet, she knew that she wasn't finished.

Grabbing a fistful of Caroline's blond hair, Annette told her rival for Tyler's affections that if she didn't break off their relationship immediately, the beating she had just received would be nothing in comparison to what would come next. Furthermore, if she told even a single soul anything about Annette Wilson attacking her, she wouldn't live to see another day. Immediately, pleadingly, Caroline had nodded her tear-streaked face in agreement and Annette had left her sobbing in the middle of the road.

Caroline had ended her romance with Tyler the next day.

But Tyler still hadn't come around.

Try as she might to fight her growing discouragement, Annette wondered when Tyler would finally accept her love. Over and over she tried to show him the depth of her affections. Every time she wrote him a letter, he threw it away unread. When she suggested that they go to the movies together, he laughed in her face and walked away. If she called him on the telephone, he hung up as soon as he heard her voice.

Annette knew she wasn't a beauty in the sense that Lana Turner and Rita Hayworth were. When Annette looked at herself in a mirror, lamenting her hazel eyes that were set too close together, her slightly hooked nose, and an unavoidable overbite, she wavered in her conviction that she was attractive enough for a man as handsome as Tyler Sutter. It didn't help matters that she hardly came up to the middle of his chest and was a bit dumpy on top of everything else. But whenever she felt depressed about her appearance, she remembered how her father had always told her that his younger daughter was drop-dead gorgeous on the *inside* and that was all that truly mattered. She would always remain a dutiful wife, a woman who would be proud to cook, clean, and raise children in a loving home. How could Tyler *not* see that?

And so she had persisted.

When Tyler and the rest of the young men of Longstock had gone off to fight in the war, Annette had waited for him to return as if they had already been married. Every Sunday, she had gone to church, sitting in the pews with the other women, mothers, wives, daughters, and sisters, praying with all of her might that Tyler would be returned to her safe and sound.

As the war with Germany and Japan dragged on, Annette's father eventually suggested that she take another man as a husband; he knew an older apple grower whose wife had passed away a couple of years earlier and who was now interested in remarrying. By Longstock's standards, he was wealthy; Annette would have had a comfortable life. But she steadfastly held her ground. What was the point in accepting a man's hand in marriage if her heart belonged to another?

She was determined to be Mrs. Tyler Sutter.

But now the war had been over for nearly a year and Tyler *still* refused her overtures. She had been at the depot the day the train carrying many of Longstock's returning soldiers had pulled in; she'd dreamed of a tearful reunion that would signal the start of their life together. But when she finally ran to him on the platform, he walked right past her without a word; she might as well have been one of the depot's lampposts for all the attention he paid to her.

Over and over she had tried to speak with him; she waited outside the garage where he worked, outside his mother's home, even stood along the road on which she knew he often drove, but all to no avail. She called him on the phone, wrote him letters, even baked him cakes that she left outside his door. But every time he saw her he was as dismissive as ever, often in a rude enough way to make her blush.

But I still love him and I always will!

Rushing down the trail back toward the garage, Annette was suddenly surprised to realize that she still clutched the picnic basket in her hand so tightly that her fingers were bone white. She flung it into the woods and it smashed against a tree trunk, spilling sandwiches, potato salad, and a couple of slices of apple pie onto the ground.

Tears welled in Annette's eyes. They were not tears of sadness that her special day with Tyler had been completely ruined but tears of anger at the interloping slut who had stuck her nose where it didn't belong. In a heartbeat, Annette knew that Tyler's rejection of her wasn't due to any shortcoming on her part but rather because someone, some *bitch,* was distracting him.

Annette had been through this before; memories of the beating she had given Caroline Satterly sprang into her mind. What she had done that dark, snowy night had squelched that romance and that was ultimately best for Tyler whether he chose to admit it or not.

"I'll do whatever it takes to keep that tramp away from my Tyler," Annette fumed, "even if it means that I'll have to kill her."

Luther Rickert stepped into the deeper, darker shadows of an empty garage across the alley from Samuel Barlow's office just as the doctor slammed on the brakes, bringing his car to a sudden, screeching stop. When Barlow got out of the car, the old man took a wheezing breath as he wiped sweat from his brow with the back of his hand. Just the sight of the bastard who'd murdered his brother made bile rise in Luther's throat and he had to restrain himself from going after the son of a bitch right then and there.

For the last couple of days, Luther had been watching every move Barlow made; he had waited outside the doctor's house, followed as he walked the short distance to work, and even stood outside his bedroom window when Barlow shut his light off for the night. Luther was always in the shadows, always watching. Only hours earlier, he'd even been there as Barlow had driven off with that pretty new nurse of his.

If there was one thing that Luther had learned in the time he'd been following the doctor who, as a result of his own neglect, had allowed Luther's brother to die, it was that he would have no trouble murdering Barlow.

". . . gonna have to kill somebody . . . ," he said to himself.

Luther rubbed his thumb against the cold metal trigger of the pistol shoved into his waistband. Touching it made him feel powerful, as if he were capable of doing anything he wanted, that he couldn't be stopped. Even now, it would be simple for him to

walk into Barlow's clinic, kick down whatever door the old man chose to hide behind,
and put a bullet in the middle of his forehead, all in broad daylight. There was no
one who would stand in Luther's way. It
would be as easy as snapping his fingers.

But that was *too* damn easy . . .

From the first moment that Luther had
sworn off alcohol, there had been a clarity
to his thoughts that he hadn't felt for years.
This wasn't to say there weren't problems;
his craving for booze gnawed at his gut
every second of the day, whispering to him
to give in to his urges, even making his
limbs shake from time to time, a cold sweat
dotting his forehead. But he somehow managed to keep his demon at bay. He had no
choice; there was a job to do.

The simple answer to his problems would
be to kill Samuel Barlow. After all, he was
responsible for what had happened to
Donnie, for taking from Luther's life the
only thing that truly mattered. It would be
an eye for an eye, a fair trade. But regardless of how much satisfaction he might gain
from watching Barlow plead for his life, killing him wouldn't bring Luther's brother
back.

It also meant that Luther would go to
prison for the rest of his life.

Luther had never given a damn about what he had done to his life up until that point and didn't see much of a reason in starting now. A part of him expected to spend some of his life behind bars. Still, in exchange for so many excruciatingly long years locked up he reckoned that he should get something in return worth such a steep price. Just taking Barlow's life would be too simple, not rewarding enough. What Luther really wanted was for the man to suffer just as much as he had, as much as he *still* did, to wake up every morning with a longing ache for what had been taken from him and he could never have again.

It wasn't that Luther had any reservations about killing Samuel Barlow. If necessary, he would spill the man's blood without a moment's hesitation; Luther had been in enough drunken brawls, plenty of bar fights where pool cues and rickety chairs were weapons used to bash a man's brains in, that he was no stranger to violence. His father had always preached *turning the other cheek,* but Luther was rather partial to the idea of *splitting a man's lip* instead.

There was no doubt in Luther's mind that Barlow deserved to die for what he had done; any man in his position would feel the same way. He *could* kill Barlow if it came to that.

But even though Luther's instincts, on that first morning of sobriety when he'd puked his guts out, *screamed* at him for vengeance, they had given way to something different . . . Now he wanted Barlow broken, utterly hopeless, desperate, and struggling.

Just like I am!

Standing there, watching the doctor's office, Luther realized that Donnie's revenge was going to take longer than he had first expected. He would continue watching, he would keep following Barlow, until he found the answer to his puzzle. He would find what the old doctor treasured the most, maybe his widowed sister or a special patient with whom he always shared a laugh. Hell, even murdering the bastard's pastor was an option. But just then, Luther was struck with an even more enticing thought; he should do to Barlow *exactly* what was done to him.

Barlow had two nephews, Tyler and Holden Sutter, who'd both been put on a goddamn pedestal by the people of Longstock. Luther's memory was a bit hazy on the details, but one was supposed to be smart enough to become a senator or president, while the other was handsome enough to turn the head of every woman who laid eyes on him. Either of them would've been more likely to spit on Donnie or Luther Rickert than give him the time of day. They were successes where Luther remained an utter and complete failure. Where there was hope for their futures, his was as bleak as a desert in July. But it was because of all of those things that they had value. What if something was to happen to one of them?

When Luther took his hand off the gun and turned on his heel to walk away from the doctor's office, he was filled with a purpose, one that would bring him satisfaction.

Chapter Twelve

Christina slammed shut the passenger's door to Tyler's car and hurried as quickly as she could up the short walk to Dr. Barlow's office. Worry gnawed at her that the trip to Tyler's beehives had taken too much time and that the doctor would be angry with her; nearly two hours had passed since she allowed herself to be led from the coupe and into the woods. Tyler had volunteered to smooth things over, but Christina didn't want him making excuses for her behavior. If she had *wanted* to leave Tyler's company, she would have demanded he take her back sooner.

Behind her, Tyler loudly revved his car's engine and sped off back to the garage, the tires screeching, followed by a playful blast of the horn. Christina wondered if he'd had the misfortune to inherit his uncle's reckless driving habits.

Christina rushed into the doctor's office.

She was surprised to find that not a single chair in the waiting room was occupied. The whole building was oddly quiet; the only sound was the faint whirring of the fan on Callie's desk.

"Is anyone here?" Christina called, her voice loud in the otherwise deep stillness.

Then she heard footsteps moving toward her from the rear hallway. "I'm sorry, but I'm afraid we're closin' up for the — ," Callie began as she came into view, stopping only when she realized to whom she was talking. "Goodness gracious, honey! I didn't know it was you!"

"Where is everyone? Why are we closing so early?" Christina asked, more than a little confused.

"Dr. Barlow said that we should call it a day," Callie shrugged, "so I'm doin' as he told me. I was just getting ready to lock the door."

"But what if someone needs help?"

"This isn't quite the same as what I reckon you're used to with that military hospital, darlin'. Back there I suppose there'd never be a day where somebody wasn't in need, but here in Longstock things run at a different speed." As she talked, Callie went around the office lowering window shades, switching off fans and lights, settling business until the next day. "Some days it's real busy around here with runny noses, aches and pains, and even a broken bone to spice up the goin's-on, a never-endin' stream of folks. But then there are other days when nothin' happens."

"And today is one of *those* days," Christina said.

"Maybe not as slow as *that,* but the doctor seemed intent on shuttin' the door, so that's what I'm doin'."

Listening to Callie explain what had happened, Christina worried that she was the reason for Dr. Barlow's decision. She remembered how he had protested Tyler's intention to take her with him and even recalled hearing the doctor complain just before they were out of earshot. She imagined him coming back to his office and waiting for her, growing more impatient and angry with every passing minute, until he finally became so incensed that he stormed out of the office, ordering Callie to lock the door behind him.

"Did Dr. Barlow seem upset to you when he left?" Christina asked.

"I know you haven't been in town long, but I'm sure you noticed how moody he can be," Callie answered, oblivious to Christina's reason for asking. "That frown of his can come out at the most unexpected times."

"Are you sure that he wasn't angry —"

"Why are you askin'?"

Christina told Callie everything: about how Tyler had shanghaied her from the doctor's car and taken her off into the woods; Callie's eyes narrowed occasionally at some of the more exciting elements of her story, but she never went so far as to tell Christina what she was thinking.

"I don't think that was the reason Dr. Barlow closed for the day," she said when Christina finished.

"But what if it is? I've only been in town for two days. The last thing I want to do is upset the man I just started working for."

Callie thought about it for a long moment before finally shrugging. "Then I suppose the best thin' to do is go over to his place and ask him. That way, you'll set yore mind to rest."

"He wouldn't mind if I stopped by?"

"Honey, if he's already mad at you, throwin' a little more gas on the fire isn't gonna hurt," Callie said, laughing even though she saw the distress on Christina's face.

Christina couldn't help but think that maybe Tyler had been right; maybe she *did* need to work on her sense of humor.

Once Callie had given the directions to Dr. Barlow's home, she let Christina out the front door. But just as Callie stuck her key in the lock, she stopped.

"Did you give any thought to my Abraham?" she called out to Christina. "About how I'm goin' to get him to sing?"

Despite all the things that had happened that day, an idea had occurred to Christina while she had been talking with Eunice Hester.

"What about suggesting that the two of you sing a duet?" Christina proposed. "Find a song that was specifically written for two and each of you take a part. That way, he would *have* to join in."

Callie was already shaking her head. "It *is* a good idea," she said. "But I already tried that."

"Why didn't it work?"

"When I first suggested it, Abraham didn't say no. We sat down at the piano and I started to play," Callie explained. "The first part was mine, but then when it came Abraham's turn it proved to be just another disappointment."

"In what way?" Christina asked.

"Instead of singin' the words, he just

196

hummed along to the melody." Callie chuckled. "I thought for *sure* that was gonna work! I darn near slammed my fist into those piano keys!"

At that, Christina joined Callie in laughing. "I guess I'll have to keep working on it then."

"You do that! I'll get my Abraham to sing yet!"

Samuel Barlow's home was a short distance from his office. Following the directions she had been given by Callie, Christina walked back to Main Street and followed it away from the center of town for a couple of blocks. Though she passed a few stores she hadn't looked into yet, she was far too distracted to window-shop. Finally, she turned down a residential street, with homes along both sides of the broad, tree-lined boulevard.

Dr. Barlow's house sat on the opposite corner of the first intersection she reached. Unlike his sister's area, this part of Longstock seemed to have been built a long time ago. Grand Victorians rose all around Christina among towering trees that had to be hundreds of years old. Most of the houses were in pristine condition, with crisply painted columns that supported long porches; beveled glass on the windows; and well-manicured lawns.

The doctor's house was not as well maintained as those belonging to his neighbors: the front of his porch sagged a bit where one of the supports seemed to have rotted; tall weeds sprouted from spidery cracks in the walk; the whole house looked a little worn and weathered and appeared to need a new coat of paint. But to Christina's eyes it looked to be more well lived-in than decrepit.

Taking a deep breath, Christina went to the front door and knocked. There was no answer. Though she strained her ears to listen, she heard no sounds from inside. Christina knocked again, much harder and more insistently than before, but still there was no reply.

"Where could he be?" she wondered.

Suddenly, Christina was struck by a truly frightening thought; maybe he'd fallen down like Eunice Hester had or suffered a heart attack. Maybe he was unconscious and in dire need of medical attention. Maybe it was something worse.

Desperately trying to suppress the fear that had begun to constrict her chest, Christina pounded on the door hard enough to make her hand hurt. But nothing stirred.

Frantically, she turned the knob but found it locked tight.

"Dr. Barlow!" she shouted; her voice sounded faint to her own ears, swallowed up by the rustling leaves and chirping birds. Still, she had to make herself heard. "Are you in there?"

Convinced that something horrible had happened, Christina was determined to gain entry to Samuel Barlow's home. Quickly, she raced down the front stairs, crossed the lawn toward the driveway, and skirted a particularly unkempt row of bushes. Sitting at the back of the drive and just before the open doors of the garage was the doctor's coupe. Seeing the car erased any chance that this was a simple misunderstanding or that Samuel Barlow had stepped out for a moment; he *was* home.

Hurrying up the drive, Christina found what she had been hoping for. On the side of the house, just before the walk that led to the backyard, there was a side door; she imagined that when the house was first built it was used as a servants' entrance. But just as Christina was about to reach for the knob, she heard something that stopped her cold.

From the backyard came the sound of shattering glass.

Christina was frozen in place. When she'd first noticed Eunice Hester's feet lying in the hallway of her home, Christina's imagination had created an intruder, someone who had done the older woman harm. While *those* fears had proven to be unfounded, they now returned tenfold; there was little chance that Christina had misheard; *someone was here.*

But Christina did not run. Not because she was paralyzed with fear but rather because her concern for Dr. Barlow was so great that she could not bring herself to abandon him, not if he was in need of her help. She suddenly found herself wishing that Tyler were there with her.

While she continued to listen, there came the sound of slurred speech, peppered with cursing, followed by a long groan.

Christina headed toward the back of the house. With every step, she fought the tremors that rose within her. Her hope was that, if confronted by an assailant, she would still have time to run away.

The inside of the garage was dark and foreboding. Christina peered intently into its depths but couldn't make out anything no matter how hard she tried. She fearfully expected someone to jump out from the shadows and grab her by the wrist, dragging her back into the garage to a fate she couldn't bear to imagine. But even as she waited for it, there was a sudden, loud commotion, as if something had been knocked over, but instead of the garage, it sounded as if it was coming from the backyard.

Still unwilling to commit herself too far in case she could no longer escape, Christina decided to take a quick look around the corner and gasped at what she saw.

Samuel Barlow wobbled unsteadily near the tall fence at the rear of his property. While Christina watched, the doctor tried to take a step but immediately lost his balance; he would have fallen on his face if his hand hadn't managed to find a fence post to support him. As near as Christina could tell, he appeared to be talking to himself.

What . . . ? Is he . . . drunk . . . ?

Christina simply *could not believe* what she was seeing. Though she'd only known the doctor for a couple of days, he'd never struck her as the sort of man who would get drunk in the middle of the afternoon. He certainly had his share of flaws, he'd been stubborn at times and his driving was undeniably erratic, but there was little doubt that he took his responsibilities as Longstock's lone doctor seriously; at least she had thought so, until now . . .

She never could have imagined *this.*

But just as Christina had begun condemning the doctor for his drunkenness, she began to notice things that painted a different picture. For one thing, he wasn't as unsteady as might've been expected; growing up with her uncle Otis, Christina was well accustomed to the teetering and tottering of someone who had been drinking. She also noticed that one sleeve of Dr. Barlow's shirt had been unbuttoned at the cuff and rolled up past his elbow.

Wait . . . he couldn't be . . .

". . . did all I could, but . . . ," drifted across the distance between them, the doctor lazily punctuating his words with his hands.

Even as Christina tried to make sense of Dr. Barlow's ramblings, she discovered the shocking truth. Several medical instruments she was quite familiar with lay on top of a weathered table beside the doctor: a length of leather with a buckle on one end, a small brown bottle, and a depressed syringe. Though she was much too far away to read the label on the bottle, there was little doubt in her mind as to what it contained.

He had taken morphine.

Looking at Dr. Barlow, Christina now saw his behavior for exactly what it was: that of someone on drugs.

Even if she had wanted to try, Christina couldn't believe that Dr. Barlow's actions were the result of her afternoon with Tyler. He clearly hadn't liked having his new assistant taken away, but it couldn't possibly have angered him so much that he sought solace by injecting morphine.

Then why had he done it? . . .

The question that Christina now faced was whether she should reveal herself to the doctor. She was certain he hadn't noticed her; she wondered if it wouldn't be better to just walk away and let him sleep it off. But in the end, she knew that there wasn't any choice to make; if she were to leave him and something happened, if he hurt himself, she'd never be able to live with her shame. Taking a deep breath, she stepped around the corner of the house.

"Dr. Barlow," Christina said forcefully, announcing herself as she strode to where he wobbled unsteadily.

"What's that . . . ?" the doctor mumbled, turning to look at her; Christina noticed how he peered intently, his eyes drowsily fluttering, as if he was trying to stay awake. It wasn't until she was standing before him that she saw a spark of recognition. "Ahh, my dear girl," he cotton-mouthed. "Come to . . . join me . . . perhaps . . . ?"

Without answering, Christina snatched the hand with the rolled-up sleeve and pulled it toward her. Just as she'd expected, there was a fresh needle puncture in the crook of his elbow, the mark red on his pale skin. What she *hadn't* anticipated were all of the other, older tracks that were dotted around the newest one. Somehow, she stifled her gasp.

"What are you . . . ?" Dr. Barlow asked, trying to pull his hand free from Christina's grasp, but she held firm. Looking down dreamily at it, he seemed momentarily surprised by the markings of what he had done. "I suppose you're wondering how in the hell that happened . . . ?"

"We need to get you inside so we can get you cleaned up," Christina said determinedly, taking him by the elbow and insistently leading him back toward the house.

"I don't think that's necessary . . ."

"Come with me," she ordered.

Once Dr. Barlow got moving, he leaned almost all of his considerable weight against Christina, forcing her to struggle to keep him upright. Though it was a strain, she never allowed him to slow down, keeping their pace steady. While they walked, he kept on complaining.

"Hold on, hold on, hold on," he repeated. "We're forgetting my instruments. They shouldn't be . . . shouldn't be left outside where someone . . . someone . . . ," but he couldn't speak further.

"I'll get them later," she reassured him.

"Can't let anyone know . . ."

Will I ever *have a normal day in Longstock?* Christina thought.

From a pot on the stove Christina poured another steaming cup of black coffee and placed it on the kitchen table in front of Dr. Barlow. He was hunched over, clutching his throbbing head between his hands, his elbows on the tabletop. Slowly, he picked up the cup and took a careful sip.

"Drink as much of that as you can," Christina said. "It's about the only thing besides time that will make you feel better."

The only response she got was a groan.

Several long hours had passed since Christina had managed to lead Dr. Barlow from his backyard and into the house. After dropping hard into a chair just inside the side door, he'd kept trying to get back to his feet, but every time he only wobbled for a second before collapsing, the morphine's hold on him strong. When she'd returned from fetching his leather strap, syringe, and mostly empty bottle of morphine, he'd watched her with hooded eyes, his mouth partly open; at first, she wondered if he hadn't fallen asleep, but when she poured the morphine down the sink drain he'd moaned, mumbling an incoherent complaint.

Christina knew how powerful of an addiction morphine could be. During her time at the Army hospital, she'd met several soldiers who had been unable to resist its lure. It was a powerful drug, alleviating all of its user's troubles in a haze of bliss. But using it over and over made its taker dependent, and it required more and more morphine to produce the same effect. If the body didn't get what it craved, the side effects could be debilitating; cramps, shaking, diarrhea, and vomiting were just some of the symptoms. She'd seen men who were addicts, normally the kindest of people, attack doctors just to get their hands on more. She was determined to find out just how big an addiction Dr. Barlow had.

After several cups of coffee, he'd eventually begun to regain his senses, but along with an improvement in clarity had come a splitting headache. Moaning and groaning, he'd shockingly uttered a few curses; he'd even apologized for a couple of them. All the while, Christina had wondered why he'd do such a thing to himself, especially because he was a doctor and should know better.

"Are you going to tell me why you were injecting yourself with morphine?" Christina asked.

The doctor was silent.

From the moment they'd entered the house, Christina had been repeating the same question, but she had yet to receive anything like a real answer; occasionally, he'd made a sound, but never anything she could understand. In the beginning, she'd assumed that he was too far under the morphine's influence to reply clearly, but now she knew that he was purposefully ignoring her.

"I know that it's not any of my business," Christina began, careful not to overstep her place, "but I'm surprised to have found you this way."

"It's not." Dr. Barlow coughed.

"Excuse me?"

"It's not any of your business," he repeated.

Frustration and anger raced through Christina at his harsh words. Everything she had been through was because she'd been worried about him. To be unappreciated, to be spoken to in such a way, was more than she could bear. Turning on her heel, she stalked toward the door, determined to leave him to his misery, but just as she was about to leave he called to her.

"Christina, wait." Dr. Barlow tried to rise from his chair, but a wave of wobbliness washed over him, sending him back onto his rump in a hurry. "Understand that I didn't mean for it to come out that harshly, it's just . . . it's hard for me to . . . aw, hell, there're just some things that are too hard for me to explain. My reason for . . . for what I did this afternoon is one of them."

Christina looked at him for a long while, the only sound the ticking of a clock in another room. She remembered the way he had looked that morning when he'd arrived at work, his clothing a disheveled mess; it was possible that he had fallen asleep after a night of shooting up morphine. How big a problem was she facing? "Is this something that you make a habit of?"

"This is the first time I've ever been found out," he groaned miserably.

"I'm talking about your taking morphine," she answered, unable to see any humor in what had happened.

Shame crept into his features. "It usually

isn't this bad . . . ," he said sheepishly.

Christina remembered the number of needle marks spotting his arm and winced. "It isn't something that you should be doing at all," she corrected him. "You should know much better. You're a doctor!"

"I know, I know," he groaned.

"You need to stop this right here and now," she kept on, "because I don't think that I could work for someone who made a habit of doing what you did today, especially someone responsible for the care of so many others."

"You're right, you're right . . ."

"People in this town are depending on you." She refused to let up. "They have to know that you'll be there, and are sober, when they need you. Imagine what would happen if there was an emergency. If there were an accident where a doctor was needed, then —"

"I said you were right, damn it!" he shouted, the loudness of his own voice causing him to wince in pain. Immediately, he tempered his tone: "You're right, Christina. There's no excuse for my behavior."

"Then why did you do it?" she asked yet again.

For a moment, Christina thought that he might open up whatever it was he was holding inside, but his eyes fell to the table, where they remained fixated on his shaking hands.

This time, when she got up to leave, he didn't say anything to stop her.

Christina trudged up the steps to her apartment under the watchful gaze of the early moon as it rose in the eastern sky. Cicadas buzzed insistently and she glimpsed bats swooping for unwary insects in the fading light. She was exhausted, both physically and mentally, but happy that she was at the end of yet *another* eventful day in Longstock.

Dealing with Samuel Barlow had rattled her. The doctor had seemed so dependable, someone she could count on to be stable in an otherwise unstable place. But after the shock of seeing him under the influence of morphine, she knew that she would never look at him the same way. Her uncle Otis's drunkenness had been one thing, but he hadn't had any responsibilities to speak of, certainly not that of caring for an entire town. She could only hope that it would not affect their working relationship so badly that they could no longer do their jobs. Only time would tell. For now, she just needed to sleep.

At the top of the stairs, just in front of her door, Christina saw something sitting on the landing. Coming closer, she saw that it was a small bottle, about half the size of a canning jar. It was filled with something, a liquid.

"And just what might you be?" she said.

Picking up the jar, Christina held it up to the fading light of the sun. About all that she could tell was that it was golden in color and that when she tipped the bottle to the side it scarcely moved. When her curiosity finally got the better of her, she opened it and immediately knew what it contained by its smell.

It was honey.

Without a doubt, she knew that Tyler had left it for her as a gift. Looking around, she expected to see him watching her, but there was no one to be seen in the twilight. Butterflies filled her stomach at the thought that he had brought her a gift, especially one that she knew was so close to his heart.

"Maybe this place isn't so bad after all . . ."

CHAPTER THIRTEEN

Christina was wakened by a creaking on her staircase. The sound had interrupted a pleasant dream of a summer day back home in Minnesota, of her mother's delicious apple pie and the whistling of the wind through the reeds that ringed Lake Washington. Christina had been just about to step into the cool water when something intruded, pulling her awake. Blinking the sleep from her eyes, she lay completely still in her bed, listening. At first there was only silence, but then she heard it again, clearly, a weight on the stairs, an unmistakable sound.

And I bet I know just who it is . . .

Christina had no idea what time of night it was, the sky outside her window was pitch-black except for a sprinkling of stars, but in her heart she knew that there was only one possible explanation for what she was hearing.

It was Tyler.

After the surprise of finding the jar of honey, it had taken several hours for her to calm down enough to sleep. Even though she'd been utterly exhausted by the ordeal at Dr. Barlow's, she couldn't help replaying her afternoon with Tyler over and over in her mind. She saw his smile, his laugh, and heard the words he had spoken. She was embarrassed by the way that she'd mis-judged him. By the time they'd parted at the doctor's office, she had understood that there was much more to Tyler Sutter than she'd originally thought; his gesture of a gift was more proof of that.

And now he's come back . . .

Dressing quickly without turning on a light, Christina hurried to the door, pushed a few loose strands of hair from her eyes, and turned the knob.

Outside, the night air was cooler than she'd expected, immediately raising goose bumps on her arms. Crickets chirped their odd melody; the sound was steady, as rhythmic as the beating of her heart.

Christina was surprised to find that the landing and stairs were empty all the way down to the bakery. There was no one, not a sound, nothing.

For an instant, Christina wondered if

she'd imagined the whole thing; maybe it had been a figment of her dream that had followed her into consciousness. But then she remembered how clear the sound on the stairs had been, how it had set her heart to beating.

"There was someone here," she whispered. "I'm sure of it."

Leaning against the railing of the landing, Christina looked out over the sleeping town. If whoever had been on the stairs *was* still around, perhaps she could still see him.

Only a couple of lights shone behind closed windows, but Christina was afforded a clear view of downtown by the soft glow of the heavens above. Main Street was empty except for a mangy dog wandering in search of a meal, companionship, or both. Certain that she was not alone, she surveyed the rooftops, finally stopping in front of Dr. Barlow's office, and it was there that she saw *something*.

It wasn't much, little more than a flutter of clothing or the passage of starlight over bare skin. But as Christina looked closer, she realized that someone was standing in the deep shadows beside the shoe-repair shop. She couldn't be sure, but it looked as if it was a man. Regardless, the person was looking right at her; when he saw that she was just as intent in watching him, he stepped farther back until he was almost lost to sight.

"Tyler?" she muttered softly. "Is that you?"

Christina raised her hand and waved, but her gesture seemed to have the opposite effect from what she'd intended; now that the man had been noticed, he stepped back out onto the walk and hurried quickly away, his head down.

Beyond a shadow of doubt, Christina knew that the man had been the source of the noise on her steps. For whatever reason, he had been watching her. Stubbornly, she clung to the hope that it was Tyler; maybe he was rushing away because he hadn't intended to wake her. Still, doubts nagged at her.

There was only one way to know the truth.

Christina knew that what she was considering was reckless, possibly even dangerous if she was wrong about the man's identity; the safer decision was to go back inside and get some sleep. Instead, she found herself hurrying down the stairs and into the night.

Standing beneath the awning of the shoe-repair shop, Christina took a moment to get her bearings. Only a minute before, the man whose steps had been creaking upon her stairs had stood in this very spot. Looking up, she saw that the location offered a perfect view of her apartment; with the landing bathed in starlight, he would have had no trouble seeing her every move.

But now he was nowhere to be seen.

Rushing down the block in the direction he'd headed, Christina paused at the first street corner she reached. Up and down both roads she saw nothing. She'd hurried down the stairs as quickly as she could; surely he hadn't had time to leave the street.

"Come on, come on," she muttered. "Show yourself."

It was a sound that finally grabbed her attention. From somewhere a block to the south came the clattering of a trash can. Without any hesitation, Christina raced in that direction; she would feel pretty silly if she were to find an alley cat digging through the trash in search of a midnight snack.

Halfway up the block, she stopped. There, down an alleyway that ran between two rows of houses, Christina saw a man running away.

Tyler's name nearly burst from her lips, but she squelched the urge to shout, instead determined to catch him and find out why he had been watching her.

You're not getting away from me that *easily.*

Hurrying down the alleyway, Christina desperately sought to cut the distance between them. Racing past cars, telephone poles, and even a startled orange cat, Christina leaped a fallen garbage can lying in the middle of her path; it had to have been the source of the sound that had alerted her. The clicking of her heels hitting the ground echoed off the surrounding buildings. On and on, she ran as fast as she could.

Ahead of her, the man looked back over his shoulder and, upon seeing her, increased his efforts to get away; he seemed as afraid of having his identity discovered as she was intent upon learning it. When he reached the end of the alley, he didn't hesitate, crossing the street without pause and disappearing around the corner, out of sight. Christina followed, relentless.

For many long blocks, she managed to keep pace. Even when her legs began to burn from the strain and she pulled huge gulps of air into her heaving lungs, she refused to give up. Slowly but surely, the gap between them began to narrow. More and more often, the man looked back over his shoulder.

Why does he want so badly to get away from me?

Finally, Christina came so close that she

knew the man wouldn't be able to escape her. They were both slowing down, but his decline was clearly greater. For the first time, a question rose in her mind: *What happens when I do catch him? . . . What then?*

"Stop!" she shouted breathlessly. "Stop running!"

Amazingly, the man did as she commanded, coming to an awkward, skidding stop in the middle of a block. Christina did the same. Both were completely exhausted, breathing hard and dripping sweat, standing only a couple of feet apart. Still, the man kept his back to her.

"Why . . . why were you . . . running away . . . from me . . . ?" she asked.

The man did not answer, his hands on his knees.

"Who . . . who are you . . . ?"

Slowly, the man straightened, squaring his shoulders and taking a long, deep breath; it was as if he was settling his nerves, resigning himself for what came next. When he turned around, revealing himself, Christina gasped, her heart nearly leaping from her chest in surprise.

It was Holden Sutter.

Never in the furthest reaches of her imagination would Christina have thought that the man she had been chasing down the streets of Longstock in the middle of the night was Tyler's older brother. It was unbelievable! She had assumed that she had been following Tyler or, at the worst, a Peeping Tom who had been watching her for his own perverse entertainment. The truth proved far more shocking.

"Why . . . why are you here?" she asked breathlessly.

Holden made no response, choosing to stare at her, his chest heaving.

"Answer me!"

Still, he didn't reply, though his eyes never left her.

Christina began to experience the same feelings she'd had in Holden's room; there he had done everything he could to make her feel uncomfortable, out of place, as if she didn't belong. It had been an infuriating, humiliating experience and had caused her to question whether she should remain in Longstock. But *that night,* they had been in *his* room, a sanctuary that she had been led to believe he never left.

Now was different.

"They told me . . . that you never left your room," she pressed, growing more impatient with every word by his failure to respond. "They said that you'd been there ever since returning from the war . . ."

Holden's mouth opened, but no sound came out.

"Tell me!" Christina exploded, stepping toward him angrily. "I haven't chased you all over town for nothing! I deserve an answer!"

Her words finally broke Holden's silence, but not in a way she would have ever expected; instead of appearing chastised by what she'd said, he reacted furiously, exploding in anger. "How could you have been so foolish!" he shouted.

"Me?! What . . . what are you talking about?" she replied, completely taken aback by his outburst.

"What woman in her right mind follows a stranger through darkened streets? It's the middle of the night! There's no one around to help you if you needed it!"

"Why should I be afraid of someone who was running away from me?" Christina blurted, amazed by what Holden was saying.

"What if it had all been a plan to get you alone? What if I had led you down that alley and hidden, waiting for you to come by so that I could have my way with you? There's nothing you could have done to stop it! Nothing!"

"I . . . I was just . . . ," she began, confused.

"It's a good thing that you were never on a battlefield. With what passes for your common sense, you wouldn't have lasted five minutes!"

On the evening that Christina had walked away from the Sutters' home, she had been upset at the horrible things that Holden had said to her, but they were nothing in comparison to what he was saying to her now. He was the one who had started all of this. He was the one who had been watching her apartment in the middle of the night. He was the one who had led her on their ridiculous race through town. And now he was the one trying to make her feel bad about it.

"Now wait a minute!" she shouted at Holden, just as he was about to accuse her of another imaginary offense; he stopped suddenly, as if she'd struck him in the chest. "How dare you try to turn this on me! This isn't *my* fault! *You* were the one lurking outside my room! *You* were the one who chose to run away from me! Don't try to turn this against me just because you got caught!"

"That's not what I —"

"And another thing," she interrupted him, refusing to give him another opportunity to

221

change the subject. "You haven't answered my questions! I want to know why you're out here tonight, out of the room that I had been told you never left, and I want to know right now! No more lying! No more changing the subject! Tell me the truth!"

Holden fell silent in the face of her outburst. For a long while, they stared at each other, neither of them saying a word. Because of the way she'd yelled at him, Christina expected there to be lights coming on in the houses around them, but she refused to look away from Holden.

Slowly, the tension that had filled him from the moment he'd stopped running began to leave him; his fists unclenched, his shoulders slumped, and the big crease that had furrowed his brow relaxed. In its place was a look of embarrassment at how he'd spoken to her.

Finally, Holden broke their silence. "I'm sorry . . . that I yelled at you the way I did," he muttered.

"You should be," she said, though her own anger was also lessened.

Christina was surprised by the breadth of change in Holden; though they'd only met twice, both times had been full of turmoil. As he was now, he was totally different.

"When I knew you'd seen me," he explained, "I panicked. I didn't want you to know who it was."

"But *how* could it be you?" Christina asked. "Your uncle told me that you *never* leave your room."

"That's because no one knows I do this," he finally said, his eyes finding hers and holding on with such intensity that she couldn't have looked away even if she'd wanted to. "I've kept it a secret from everyone."

"But why would you do such a thing? They'd be happy for you!"

"The last thing I want to do is give them false hope," Holden said, gesturing wildly with his hands. "The more they believe I could get better, the greater disappointment when I fail in the end. I can at least spare them that."

"If that's what you truly believe, then you've failed before you even started," Christina argued.

"It's the truth!"

"Only because you *choose* to fail, not because of what's truly inside you!"

"And I suppose you know what that is," he said, annoyed.

"Do you want to know what I think?" she asked, stepping so close to him that he couldn't help backing up. "I think that you *want* to return to the life you had. Long-stock is still your home, just as it was before the war. You could have everything you've always wanted, but you won't do the work, so instead you come out here to feel sorry for yourself, to feel *pity,* but that's only because you don't have the guts to fight for it!"

"That's not it!" Holden shouted. "That's not it at all!"

Christina didn't truly believe what she was saying to Holden, not all of it. What she hoped was that he would be so shamed, so infuriated by what she said, that he would fight to throw off the shackles that bound him.

"Then why are you here?" she asked.

"Because if I spent the rest of my life in that room at my mother's house I'd go crazy!" he said. "But I can't go back to my old life! I just can't!"

"You *won't* do it." Christina shook her head. "It's bad enough that you're lying to your family about never leaving your room, but it's worse that you insist on lying to *yourself* about the reasons why."

"This," Holden snapped, holding up his left arm, the one that had shaken with tremors when she'd been in his room, "is why I can't!"

224

"You can get better!"

"No, I can't!"

"It only takes time. Trust me, it can be done."

"Not for me."

"If that's what you believe, then you've failed before you've even started."

During her time at the Army hospital, Christina had met soldiers who made the same arguments as Holden. Unfortunately, some of them never managed to escape the crippling fears brought on by their injuries. Others were able to break through their depression on their own, while still others needed a push.

She hoped Holden was one of those who needed just a little help.

"I can't go back to my old life. With my . . . with my . . . *tremors* . . . ," he said as if the word was a curse on his lips, "I don't know when I'll be overcome. It could happen anytime, anywhere. I . . . I don't . . . I *can't* let anyone see . . ."

"*I* saw them," Christina said.

Holden nodded grimly. "You did," he said, "but I wish you hadn't."

"I don't think any less of you for having seen them. They're not a sign of weakness."

"That's because you never knew me before," Holden explained.

"Then move away from here," Christina suggested. "Go someplace where no one would know you and start again."

"I could never do that . . ."

"Tell me why."

Holden gave no answer.

Christina refused to let her argument rest. "If you choose not to go somewhere you won't be known, then your choice *has* to be to stay here and get over what has happened to you. You said it yourself: the alternative would drive you crazy."

For a long while, Holden still didn't reply, but Christina could see that he was thinking about what she'd said. When he finally spoke, his voice was as soft as a whisper. "How . . . how would . . . I even begin . . . ?"

"You need to tell someone what happened," she said. "You need to unburden yourself by talking about what happened to you during the war."

"Who would listen?"

"You could tell your brother," Christina suggested. "Tyler would listen to anything you had to say."

At the mention of his brother's name, Holden stiffened. He looked away, his face a mask of confusion. "I . . . I couldn't . . ."

"You *could*," she encouraged him, stepping closer, wanting to place her hand on his shoulder but not daring to, not yet. "Back when I worked at the Army hospital, many of the servicemen I cared for were encouraged to confide in someone. That way, by letting out what they held inside, they'd no longer carry their burdens alone. Tyler could be that person for you. From what he's told me about your relationship as brothers, he'd be willing to do *whatever it took* to help you, I'm certain of it. You just have to give him a chance."

The whole time she had been talking, Holden had looked away, but now, when he finally returned her gaze, the look in his eyes was pleading and intense.

"I would rather confide in you," he said.

Christina gasped. Until that moment, Holden Sutter had largely been unfriendly, unquestionably rude, and spiteful enough to make her never want to see his face ever again. That he could say such a thing to her was a shock that she struggled to absorb. Replying seemed impossible.

"You would want . . . to tell *me* . . . ," she finally managed.

"If . . . *if* I decided I wanted to talk," he answered, "I would . . ."

"Why me?"

"Because you're used to dealing with this

sort of thing," Holden explained. "You're also not a member of my family and you would never tiptoe around me like my mother does. Besides, I think that you're —" But he immediately fell silent.

"I'm what?" Christina asked.

Holden turned away from her, looking even more uncomfortable. Suddenly, unexpectedly, he turned back and stepped close, taking her hands in his own and looking down into her eyes with so much intensity that it was now Christina's turn to look away briefly, then back to the man looming over her.

Instantly, she thought of how Tyler had rushed forward and grabbed her the night he'd followed her in his car. She'd been bruised by how forcefully he'd held her; Holden's tenderness was just the opposite. At that moment, beneath a streetlight, in the middle of the night, Christina noticed not for the first time that Holden was a handsome man in his own right; though undeniably different in appearance from his brother and more than a bit disheveled, he *was* attractive; with his longer hair, piercing dark eyes, and rugged features she knew that there had undoubtedly been a time when he'd turned women's heads.

And that he could do so again.

"Promise me one thing," he said softly.

"What?" she answered breathlessly.

"Don't tell anyone in my family about having seen me tonight. If I'm going to do this . . . if *we're* going to do this, it should remain between us."

"I'll agree if you answer one question."

"Just ask."

"Why were you outside my apartment in the middle of the night?"

Holden suddenly released her hands.

She saw the tremor start to shake up the length of Holden's arm; it started at his wrist, running to his elbow and then to his shoulder. A look of panic immediately filled his eyes. Before she could say a word, could offer whatever help she could give, Holden turned and ran, his feet pounding on the sidewalk, and soon he disappeared into the night.

This time, she didn't follow.

CHAPTER FOURTEEN

"Morning," Dr. Barlow growled when he finally arrived at the clinic, almost half an hour later than expected. Most of the seats in the waiting room were already filled with patients, many of whom looked up when he came in the door; Christina saw several frown at the sight of him.

Samuel Barlow was a mess. While his clothing wasn't as untidy as it had been the previous morning, it wasn't particularly presentable, either; a dark stain dribbled down one leg of his wrinkled pants, and he'd missed a button on his shirt when dressing. In one hand he held a mug of coffee, while the other shielded his eyes from the morning sunlight.

But it was his face that truly spoke of his poor condition. Dark circles underlined his bloodshot eyes. His skin was ashen in color, a particularly sickly pall. Tufts of his hair stood up at odd angles, as if he'd had a rough night of sleep, or had tried to pull it out in fistfuls. Christina knew that *she* didn't look her best that morning, after chasing Holden around town in the middle of the night, but she looked like a peach in comparison; only a blind man wouldn't have noticed that the doctor was hungover.

"Are you feelin' all right, Dr. Barlow?" Callie asked; Christina couldn't tell if Callie was asking because she had *no idea* of the cause of his suffering or because she knew *exactly* what was wrong.

"I'll be fine," he muttered as he went through the waiting room and down the hallway to his private office.

"Give us a moment before we get started with the patients," Christina told Callie as she hurried after him.

Reaching the doorway to his office, Christina saw evidence that Dr. Barlow must not be entirely steady on his feet; just inside the door, several stacks of his books had been tipped over, cascading all over the floor. Somehow, he had managed to make it behind his desk and into his chair. The light had been left off, so Christina purposefully flipped it on.

"Please turn that off." The doctor winced, still shielding his eyes.

"If you're not in any shape to see patients,

231

then you shouldn't be here," she snapped, angry that he would show up to work in such a sorry state. "I may not be capable of treating everyone, but I could —"

"I said that I'll be fine and I meant it," Dr. Barlow cut her off. "Let me finish my coffee and then we can begin."

Christina took a deep breath. "I know that I'm new here and that it's not my place to say anything, but I *cannot believe* that you would inject yourself again *after* I'd left. Hadn't you had enough?"

"I swear to you, Christina, I did no such thing," he protested, weakly raising his eyes to look at her; dark circles underlined his bloodshot eyes, making it obvious that he wasn't feeling well. "But sometimes I go too damn far . . . take too much . . . I was up half the night, woke up a mess."

Though she was still skeptical, Christina had to grudgingly admit that she didn't know what the aftermath of a morphine binge really was. Her memories of the soldiers she'd cared for who had gone into withdrawal were few, made up mostly of ashen faces and sweaty brows. But for someone who'd taken the drug for as long as Dr. Barlow seemed to have done, imagining the consequences of stopping was much more difficult. As for herself, she'd never had the urge to so much as drink, having only the occasional sip with friends. Understanding what he was going through was difficult.

"If you're not feeling well, then you shouldn't be here," she repeated in a tone that wasn't as confrontational.

"Poppycock," Dr. Barlow groused. "There are people that need me."

"But they need you with your wits about you."

"I have them, don't you worry. Besides," he smiled weakly, "if I'm here, then I won't have the chance to do anything as stupid as I did yesterday, will I?"

Christina had no answer.

"Give me a minute to get myself together and then have Callie send Mrs. Hutchinson into the examination room."

"Are you sure?"

"Don't give up on me just yet."

Against her better judgment, Christina did as she was told.

Most of the morning was spent treating patients. True to his word, Dr. Barlow saw every one of them; thankfully, nearly all of their ailments required routine assistance. The doctor lanced the boil of a housewife who was so frightened by the instruments he was using on her foot that she covered her eyes for fear of fainting. He changed the dressing on a burn that a mechanic for one of the orchards had received from an unruly truck engine. Dr. Barlow even listened patiently as an elderly man described the way his arthritis made it next to impossible for him to open his mail.

The only real trouble came when Margaret Madison brought her uncontrollable twin sons, Jimmy and John, to receive their immunization shots. The two boys, age five, were *far* from cooperative. From the moment they arrived, the office was filled with one hysterical crying fit after another. The very second that one of them finally calmed down, the other started up; the unfortunate result was utter chaos.

"Jimmy, stop hitting your brother," Mrs. Madison ordered.

In response, Jimmy did as he was told, choosing to *pinch* John instead, starting his brother screaming so loud that it seemed to shake the rafters.

Christina could see the effect all of the commotion was having on Dr. Barlow; listening to the boys was like having an air-raid siren pressed against his ear. It was all he could do to get the needles in.

The instant he had depressed the final

plunger, he turned to Christina and said, "I'll let you finish up," and was out the door, retreating to his office.

Left to fend for herself, Christina came to the quick conclusion that bribery was her best defense. "All right, boys," she said, giving the Madison twins her biggest, brightest smile. "Let's play a game, shall we? Whoever can stay quiet for the longest is going to get a lollipop when we're finished. Now, who's interested?" Immediately, all of the tears dried up and the whimpering came to an end, allowing her to apply their bandages in peace and quiet.

When lunchtime rolled around, Christina went to ask Dr. Barlow if he'd like to come with her to the diner, but she found him with the light to his office off and his head down on his desk, snoring loudly.

"Should I wake him?" she asked Callie back in the waiting room.

"With how he looked when he come through that door this mornin'," she smiled, "I'd say that he needs as much sleep as he can get."

Christina wasn't sure how to reply. There was no telling if Callie suspected that Dr. Barlow was using morphine; Christina had already chosen not to say anything about yesterday when she'd arrived that morning.

The last thing she wanted was to cause problems between the doctor and Callie, but Christina couldn't stop thinking about the responsibilities they had to their patients. The more she thought about it, the less she felt there was a choice to make.

"Does he . . . does Dr. Barlow often come to work . . . sick . . . ?" she asked tentatively.

"Are you askin' me 'bout his takin' morphine?" Callie answered.

Christina relaxed, but only a little; clearly, Callie knew *exactly* what was going on, which was, in itself, unsettling. "Is it something that happens often?"

"Usually it ain't this big a deal," she explained. "Days like today come few and far between. Most times it strikes me as bein' harmless. He manages to pull himself together and ain't quite as grouchy as he is today, but occasionally there're times when he takes a bit too much. Yesterday must have been one of *those,* but I reckon you already know that . . ."

"I'm afraid so," Christina said.

Because she no longer had to tiptoe around the issue of Dr. Barlow's drug problem, Christina decided to tell Callie everything that'd happened when she'd gone to his home. Through it all, she was careful to keep her voice down in case the doctor revived enough to hear what was being said. Callie nodded often.

"That seems about right." Callie shrugged.

"You don't sound all that concerned," Christina said, surprised.

"Don't think that I ain't worried about him," Callie explained, "because I most certainly am; it's just that he's usually not this bad, and on those rare occasions when he is, there ain't never been any real problem come of it."

"But that doesn't mean that one *won't*."

"I know, but —"

"What happens when someone walks through that door who really needs his help and he can't provide it?" Christina argued, her passion rising. "If something terrible were to happen, could you live with that?"

"I don't want any such thing," Callie said, "but after all that the doctor has done for me and mine, it ain't my business to get involved. Besides, he *is* a good man. He's a regular at church, kind to most everyone who walks through that door, and ain't never passed judgment on the folks of this town. Nothin' more could be expected."

"A doctor shouldn't be taking morphine."

"I agree, but whatever reason he has, well, that's *his* burden to carry."

237

"I don't know if I can stay silent," Christina admitted.

"Then that will be 'tween the two of you."

Toward the middle of the afternoon, an older man entered the clinic in rough condition. Alone, he managed to stumble inside with the help of a cane and immediately plopped into a chair beside the door. Wet coughs rose from his chest as he hacked into a handkerchief, causing the loose jowls of his face to jiggle. Age spots darkened his hands, his thinning white hair was combed over his mostly bald head, and enormous wrinkles cragged the corners of his eyes. When he finished hacking, he looked around, his eyes filled with tears. Christina noticed that both his cheeks and nose were covered in a wide spider's web of cracked blood vessels, staining his skin a red so bright that it was as if he had been outside in the freezing cold of winter.

"Betcha didn't think I'd manage to live to make another doctor's visit, did ya?" the man coughed as he laughed.

"Now, Mr. Felton," Callie said with friendly affection, "we both know that you're too stubborn to leave us that easily."

"Too *ornery*," he corrected her. "And call me Archie, sweetheart."

"You weren't so ornery that you walked the whole way here, now were you?"

"With the way my feet are all swelled up, I couldn't walk all the way downtown if my appointment was scheduled for next year!"

Callie turned to Christina and said, "Gettin' a straight answer out of him is harder than pullin' teeth!"

"My son brought me," Archie said with a shrug, pointing toward the front window and out to the street. "But he's so goddamn mad at me for everything I've done he wouldn't even help me to the door. Said he'd wait in the car till I was finished."

"Then why don't I help you on back to the examination room?" Christina offered. "That way he won't have to wait for long."

"Who could say no to a pretty woman like you?" Archie cackled.

After Callie went to get Dr. Barlow, Christina had a few moments alone with Archie Felton in the examination room. Glancing over the medical chart that Callie had handed her before she left, Christina was surprised to learn that Archie was only sixty-two years old; with his poor physical health and, in particular, the deep wrinkles that lined his face and hands, she would've thought him to be much older. Still, there was little doubt that his heart remained young.

"I suppose this is where you help me get undressed." He winked at her with a mischievous smile.

"Why don't we wait for the doctor to arrive?" Christina smiled right back; it was certainly not the first time that a patient had made an inappropriate advance toward her. Besides, she found Archie's flirting to be harmless, even a little charming.

"Now where's the fun in that?!"

"In the meantime, why don't you tell me what's bothering you?"

"The same thing that's *always* bothering me, sweetie," Archie replied. "I'm a worthless fool who doesn't have the common sense to quit drinking himself into an early grave."

Christina couldn't hide her surprise. Once he'd told her, she knew that it should've been obvious; almost all of his physical problems were those of someone suffering from alcoholism. She was a little bit embarrassed that she hadn't seen it sooner.

One of the things that she found so likeable about Archie Felton was that he reminded her of her uncle Otis; he, too, had been a gregarious man with his share of problems but whose personality made it easy to look past them. Otis had died an early death; if he'd lived longer, Christina supposed that he would have looked an awful lot like Archie. Just as she was thinking of asking him more about his drinking, Dr. Barlow knocked on the door and entered the room.

"How are you feeling, Archie?" he asked, his eyes never leaving the folder clutched in his hands. Christina could see that his nap had done him good; a bit of color had returned to his skin and he seemed more alert.

"Same as always, Sam," Archie answered. "Still shitty as a rainy day." Turning to Christina, he added, "Sorry for the language, darlin'."

"It's nothing that I haven't heard before," she answered.

"Now isn't it a damn shame that someone as beautiful as you knows language as ugly as mine?!"

"I know we've had this talk a dozen times before, but I don't suppose you've given up the drinking?" Dr. Barlow asked.

"Oh, I've *tried*," Archie said, "but I never quite try hard enough, I reckon."

"That liquor you're so fond of is going to kill you."

"It's taken most everything else from my

241

life, so I figure it might as well have my last breath, too." Again looking over at Christina, he said to the doctor, "I assume this here's the new nurse you were talking about on my last visit."

Dr. Barlow nodded. "This is Miss Tucker. She's just arrived."

"You seem like a nice young woman," Archie said with a smile just as warm as any she ever got from her uncle, "so I'm going to give you a bit of advice. Treat alcohol as if it were poison."

"I'm not much of a drinker," Christina said.

"You should keep it that way. If I would've, only the Good Lord knows how different my miserable life would be. I'd have my health, all of the money I've wasted, and so much in between. Who knows, maybe my son wouldn't be so ashamed to be seen with his old man that he would be sitting out in the car right now. Even my beloved Agnes would still be by my side."

"Agnes died from a stroke, Archie," Dr. Barlow interjected.

"That was no doubt caused by having to live with a fall-down, worthless bum who pissed away every cent he had on drink," he said wistfully, "money that would've been better spent caring for the woman who'd been foolish enough to love him. To this very day, I'm still so damn embarrassed that I can't visit her grave."

Listening to Archie, Christina was reminded of her talk with Eunice Hester. She, too, had given Christina advice about how to live her life, about the choices she might someday be confronted with, although Eunice's had a much more positive outlook. Still, Christina found herself rapt with attention, listening to the life lessons Archie was giving her, knowing that she would be a fool to disregard the warnings he'd chosen to ignore.

"Booze has ruined my whole life," he said, "so don't let it ruin yours."

"I won't," Christina promised.

"That's just what I wanted to hear."

"You're not dead yet, Archie," Dr. Barlow said. "All you have to do is quit drinking."

"You're one to talk, Sam," Archie shot back, looking deep into the doctor's bloodshot eyes. "Just because I'm half-blind from drinkin' doesn't mean I can't see the state *you're* in. Whatever it is you're doin' to yourself, if you're not careful you're gonna end up in your grave every bit as fast as I'm gonna."

Christina glanced at Dr. Barlow's face and could see that Archie's words had struck close to home; his face was immediately crestfallen and flushed, ashamed. The doctor quickly turned away from both of them.

"We're talking about *your* health," he said defensively.

"No, what we're *really* talking about is the both of us," Archie corrected him. " 'Cause we both know that getting addicted to something is like a rabid dog; once it sinks its fangs into you, it's harder than hell to get 'em back out."

Once the last patient had been treated, the floor swept, and the lights turned off for the day, Christina went in search of the doctor. She'd watched closely to make certain that he hadn't gone out through the front door, but when she looked in his office she was surprised to find that he wasn't there, either. The same was true of every other room. Finally, she saw that the back door had been propped open, so she stepped outside.

Dr. Barlow leaned his back against the hood of the coupe, smoking a cigarette as he stared off into the distance. Though he looked better than when the day began, he still appeared tired and, like Archie Felton, older than his years. She had hoped that they might have a chance to talk, but seeing him in such a deep, introspective state made her think that it could wait. Then, just as she was about to retreat inside the clinic, he glanced up and saw her.

"I'm sorry that I was . . . such a mess today," he said as he dropped the cigarette, extinguishing its burning ember with the toe of his shoe.

"I thought you did quite well," she replied, "given the circumstances."

"That I'm going to end up just like Archie Felton?"

"I wouldn't say *that*."

"Not yet, anyway."

When Archie had left the clinic, hobbling out to the car, his son refused to get out and open the door for his father. Christina had noticed that Dr. Barlow was watching. Though Archie was pleasant enough while sober, there was no reason to doubt that he had allowed alcohol to destroy his life, just as he'd said. Christina wondered if, when Dr. Barlow watched the other man, he feared he was looking at his own future, a life consumed by addiction.

She couldn't imagine that such a view would be pleasant: poor health, alienation from everyone he'd ever loved, barely making ends meet because he couldn't escape the cruel grasp of his drug. Surely Dr. Barlow didn't believe that it would happen to him, but Christina doubted Archie had ever imagined he'd find himself in such an unforgiving place.

The other thing that Christina realized was that Samuel Barlow's situation wasn't all that different from his nephew's; Holden Sutter had his own demons to contend with. If left untreated, they would ruin his life as surely as Archie Felton's had ruined his.

"Why do you do it?" she asked.

"You asked me that yesterday," Dr. Barlow answered.

"I'm still waiting for an answer."

Dr. Barlow nodded grimly, checked the packet of cigarettes in his front shirt pocket, and, when he found it empty, wadded it up and threw it on the ground. "Having to explain myself isn't something I'm used to."

"You shouldn't think about it as giving an answer to *me* but more that you're doing it for yourself," Christina said. "If you tried to deal with the problem by acknowledging it, maybe you'd find a solution."

Sighing deeply, he said, "I don't want to end up like Archie . . ."

"Then start changing your life by telling me why you inject yourself with morphine."

Christina hoped that she was reaching him. If he could just break through the wall he had built around himself, there might be a way for him to avoid the future Archie represented.

"I know that what you're suggesting might be what's best," Dr. Barlow said, "but I . . . I just can't. Not yet . . . not now." He paused, looking her in the eyes. "But if I *did* decide differently . . . I suppose that you might be someone I would be willing to let listen . . ."

"I'd do whatever it took to make things better," she answered honestly.

"If I ever change my mind, I'll hold you to that."

"I'd be honored."

Once she had left the clinic, walking home to her apartment, Christina was filled with the desire to reach out to someone else, to stop that person from meandering to the same rough place that Archie had found himself, where Dr. Barlow was unfortunately headed, albeit by taking a different path.

Now it was time for her to help Holden.

CHAPTER FIFTEEN

You can do it . . . just raise your hand and knock.

Christina stood outside Holden's bedroom door, unsure of what to do. She had been in this situation before; on the night she'd first met the Sutter brothers, she had carried Holden's tray to this very spot, thinking that she would just knock on the door, introduce herself, and maybe make a friend in her new town. Thinking about how *that* had turned out nearly made her laugh.

But today, she desperately wanted things to turn out differently . . .

Though she hadn't been able to achieve the breakthrough she'd hoped for with Dr. Barlow, Christina felt more strongly than ever that she needed to reach out to Holden. After their breathtaking chase through the darkened streets of Longstock, she was convinced that he needed to unburden himself of the demons he carried.

To that end, she felt she needed a reason to see him.

Returning home from work, she had telephoned Clara Sutter in the hope that she might be invited to dinner the following night; Christina had no doubt that her grandmother would have been appalled at such forward behavior, but she'd felt as if she had little choice. She'd considered asking Tyler, but he would have wanted to know why and she didn't think telling him the *truth* was an option; she remembered the way he'd overreacted to her speaking with his brother; he would have to find out later.

Fortunately, Clara had been happy to hear from Christina and immediately asked her to come for dinner. So, with a freshly baked loaf of bread tucked under her arm, she'd headed to the Sutter home, arriving early so that she might find some time to be with Holden.

"Are you sure you want to go up there again?" Clara asked when Christina told her of her intention. Clara's face pinched up uncomfortably, as if she had bitten into a lemon. "The last time didn't go well for *anyone.*"

"I'm sure it will be fine," Christina tried to reassure her, but from the worried crease in Clara's forehead it didn't seem to work.

Now Christina stood before Holden's door, hesitant.

In the end, it was remembering how he had hurried to her, putting his hand on her arm with a surprising gentleness, that convinced her. As she thought of that moment, it was impossible to believe he would be as bad tempered as the last time she entered his room.

Taking a deep breath, Christina knocked.

Holden was surprised by the sudden sound at his door. He glanced toward the clock, but doing so only increased his confusion; his mother wouldn't be bringing his dinner for more than an hour. Maybe he'd just imagined it, a popping or groaning of the house that only sounded like someone rapping at his door, but no sooner had he created such a fantasy than it was dispelled by another, more insistent knock.

"Who is it?" he asked, more than a little curious.

"It's Christina. I was wondering if we could talk."

When he heard her voice, Holden's heart began pounding so hard in his chest that he worried it might start a tremor in his arm. Ever since she had doggedly chased him through the streets of Longstock, he'd been unable to get Christina Tucker out of his mind. Hell, from the first time he had met her forgetting her *wasn't* possible. That was why he had been standing outside her window in the middle of the night, why he'd made the mistake of walking up the stairs to her apartment, and why he was now frozen in place.

His bedroom was in the same state it had been on her first visit, with tall stacks of books spread everywhere. Once his books had been a comforting sight, a barrier against the world outside his door, but looking at them now embarrassed him. But he also knew that he couldn't make Christina go away, he didn't *want* her to go away, and she'd be stubborn enough to stand there for hours. Besides, she'd seen it before. Nervously, he went to the door, took a deep breath, and opened it.

"Hello," she said simply, paralyzing him.

"He-hello, yourself," he managed to reply.

Every time Holden had been around Christina, he'd found himself dumbstruck by her looks. Today was no exception. With her long black hair cascading over her shoulders, a smile that lit up her eyes as surely as if they were stars in the sky, and the gentle curve of her cheek, he wanted to drink her in, to revel in her as if she were a painting in a museum.

The problem was that this work of art *spoke* to him.

"May I come in?" she asked.

"Of . . . of course."

Holden stepped aside to let Christina enter, shutting the door behind her. For a moment, he rested his head against the door, trying to compose himself. He was so nervous that beads of sweat dotted his forehead.

What in the hell's the matter with me?

Holden had been around other women before, gone on dates where he'd been charming, funny, the life of the party. Then, it had been natural, easy. But now, he was cotton-mouthed and tongue-tied, both at the same time.

If you don't pull yourself together, she'll leave . . .

Christina moved a small stack of books and sat on a corner of the bed, her hands in her lap. After almost dropping a couple of volumes of encyclopedias, Holden freed up a chair opposite her.

"I've done a lot of thinking about the other night," she began. "Especially about the things you said before . . . before you left . . ."

"I'm sorry that I left so abruptly," he said.

"I understand why you did." Christina smiled, gently reaching over and placing her hand upon his, on his *left* hand; Holden marveled at how comforting her touch felt, about how he never would have allowed anyone else to touch him in such a way.

"I hope I didn't frighten you," he said.

"You didn't. Well, *maybe* a little . . ."

"It wasn't my intention," Holden replied truthfully; in fact, it was the absolute last thing he would've wanted.

Christina gave his hand a soft squeeze. "Though I have to admit that I was surprised to find you lurking around my apartment in the middle of the night," she said, her eyes narrowing teasingly, "there's a part of me that's glad you were there."

"There is?"

"Of course," she answered, "because now we've got an opportunity for a discussion. We have the chance to help you get off your chest what's bothering you, so you can begin the return to the life you clearly still want."

Though it truly pained him to do so, Holden removed his hand from Christina's. "You want me to talk about what happened." He frowned deeply. "You want me to tell you about what happened during the war . . ."

"You said that you'd be willing to talk about it."

"I said that I *might* want to," he disagreed. "I didn't mean *now*. I meant someday in the future."

Christina frowned deeply. "Holden," she began, "the only way things are ever going to get better is if you let go of the burden you're carrying. Your tremors will never improve if you stay in this room. You have to stop turning your back on every offer of help. You have to *let it go*."

Holden wanted to trust her; he hadn't been lying when he'd said that she was the one person he could see himself telling. But *actually* letting it out was proving to be a different matter. No one else knew what he had seen that day, not a doctor, not his fellow soldiers, not his family, no one.

"I . . . I don't know if I'm ready." He looked away.

"I don't believe that." She shook her head, contradicting him. "The reason you leave this room and walk around town in the middle of the night is because you *want* to return to the life you're keeping at arm's length. You need to take a chance, Holden. You need to let it all out."

"I'm . . . I'm afraid to . . . ," he answered,

the shame of his fear coloring his cheeks.

"Talking about it will finally set you free."

"I don't want you to think that I'm weak . . ."

"I would *never* think that about you," she said emphatically. "All that I'm asking is that you trust in me. I promise that if you stop holding it inside of you, things *will* get better."

"Do you really believe that?"

"With all of my heart."

And so, Holden did as she asked.

Normandy, France
June 24, 1944

Holden Sutter smoked the last of his cigarette, savoring the burn of tobacco in his lungs, before crushing the butt beneath his booted foot. Tugging his rifle closer against his shoulder, he struggled to keep his eyes open. The hours before dawn were the most difficult of guard duty; he was at his most exhausted, while it was simultaneously the best opportunity for the Germans to attack. Thankfully, so far the only thing he'd heard was the faint chirping of the few birds stubborn enough to still live in the unforgiving midst of war.

June in northern France was far chillier than he'd expected. Bruise-colored clouds drizzled rain at all times of day, blotting out the sun and the meager warmth it provided. Thick droplets of dew clung to the tramped-down grass of what had once been a cow pasture, the animals long since eaten. His feet felt as if they were encased in blocks of ice. A persistent wind chilled his bones, making him long to be inside near the fire.

Holden looked back at the enormous country manor his unit had occupied during their pursuit of the retreating Nazi forces. The home carried the same name as the town in which it sat, La Boissière, a fact that Holden found quite strange. Three stories tall, it had been built in the middle of the eighteenth century, the consolation property of a nobleman whose love of a common woman had caused him to fall from standing. It had more rooms than Holden could have ever imagined necessary, two kitchens, and a huge great room warmed by a fireplace large enough for a man to stand upright inside; he fervently wished that he was before it now.

From the outside, La Boissière was impressive to behold. Its grounds stretched far and wide, full of ponds, pastures, and forests. Beside the house were two long rows of trees, their canopies thick enough to prevent detection from the air; the Germans had placed their military beneath them during the D-day invasions, and now the Americans did the same.

They had learned how the Germans had used the property, as well as its remarkable history, from the woman who owned it. Yvonne Duval hadn't left when the Nazis arrived, coming at midnight to take claim of the home that had been in her family for nearly two hundred years. In her mid-forties, she had been aged dramatically by the war. Her long brown hair was streaked with grey, but now, with her family's freedom finally restored, she'd gone about welcoming their American liberators with a smile and no shortage of gratitude.

One day, Yvonne had approached Holden as he stood in front of the house.

"Est-ce que vous voulez manger?" she'd said.

"I'm . . . I'm sorry, but I don't understand . . ."

When she'd made the motion of eating, Holden had followed her into the kitchen, where she'd prepared what little food she and her family had left. His unit had taken an instant liking to her.

Still, Holden couldn't wait for the war to end.

The weeks leading up to the invasion of

Normandy had been ones of great stress, but they had also been filled with the desire to finally start doing what his nation had gone to war for: driving the Nazis from Europe.

Finally, the time had arrived.

Holden's unit had been in the third wave that came ashore at Omaha Beach; it had been a struggle not to vomit on the wave-tossed ride across the English Channel. The carnage he had seen that day would stay with him for the rest of his life: watching men make the ultimate sacrifice by giving their lives, bleeding to death upon the rocky beaches of a nation that was not their own. Holden had fought hard that day, protecting his fellow soldiers, taking the lives of the enemy, and was proud of what he had done.

But that didn't stop him from longing to return to the life he'd left behind.

For as long as Holden could remember, he'd wanted to be a teacher, to stand in front of a classroom of children and fill their minds with knowledge, with curiosity, with virtues they would carry with them for the rest of their lives. He wanted to paint, to carve figures out of wood, and, most important, to meet someone he could love.

Only the Good Lord knew what his brother, Tyler, wanted out of life, but as for himself, he knew *exactly* where he was headed.

Looking back at La Boissière, Holden could see no lights; blackout rules were in effect. There was no sense in giving the Germans a target.

Digging into his pocket, Holden found that his last Army-issued pack of cigarettes was empty. Before the war he hadn't been a smoker, had believed smoking to be a bad habit, but nowadays he could not deny that cigarettes calmed his rattled nerves. Right then he needed a smoke to help keep him awake.

The only thing left to him was a pack of German cigarettes he'd found in La Boissière. They'd been sitting on the fireplace mantel when the Americans had arrived, as if someone had just set them down for an instant, intending to come back for them later. Holden didn't know why he had done it, but he'd pocketed them. They'd been with him for the three days he had been stationed here, but he hadn't gotten around to smoking any of them; something about lighting one felt like treason. Still, he hadn't thrown them away, either.

Why in the hell not? he thought to himself.

But just as Holden was about to strike a match, careful to cup it so that no one could see the flickering of the flame, he heard the crack of a stick behind him. Immediately dropping the smoke, he yanked his rifle free and aimed it where he'd heard the sound.

"Who's there?" he hissed.

"Keep your shorts on, Sutter," a voice answered him as a soldier stepped out of the brush and into the scant light of the early morning.

Vinnie Burretti was as typically a New Yorker as Holden imagined one would be, especially since he'd never been to the famous city and really only knew about them from the movies. Vinnie's greased-back jet-black hair, the wild way he gestured with his hands whenever he got excited, and the way he never stopped talking recalled his Italian neighborhood back home. His accent, his slang-filled vocabulary, and his constant joking all helped him become an instant favorite among the other men, except when it came to playing cards; to get involved in a poker game against Vinnie was to be soon parted with your hard-earned money.

"Since I'm about ready to pitch over on my face," Vinnie chuckled, "I figured I oughta bum a smoke offa you before I do it."

"They're German," Holden told him.

"As long as they ain't wet, I don't give a damn if they're Chinese."

The men lit each other's cigarettes and were content to smoke for a while in silence, watching as the sun began to peek over the horizon.

"Damn, that hits the spot!" Vinnie said after taking a long drag. "Maybe those Germans know how to do somethin' right, after all!"

"Say," Holden asked, "If you're over here, who's guarding the other side of the pasture?"

"Don't worry about it. The Nazis are fifty miles east of here by now and gettin' farther by the minute. Besides, ain't havin' somebody to talk to a helluva lot betta than pacin' back and forth, dreamin' 'bout sittin' in fronta that fire? Lucky stiffs! It's so cold out here a fella could freeze his meatballs off if he wasn't careful!"

Holden couldn't help but laugh. And Vinnie did have a point; company on a morning like this sure beat standing alone.

"I ever tell you 'bout my cousin Sal and the two Sicilian broads he was supposed to pick up at the docks?" Vinnie asked, but he didn't wait for an answer before starting in. "Sal's always drivin' that taxi of his, though everyone knows he got the job 'cause his deaf uncle on his mother's side knew this one guy who imports bananas who called in a favor. Anyways, he . . ."

Even though Holden and every other guy in the unit had heard this particular story, along with all the other ones Vinnie was so fond of telling, he had no desire to interrupt. But just as he started to chuckle to himself, recalling how the tale of Vinnie's cousin ended, a faint sound pulled at his attention.

"Hang on, Vinnie," he said, listening intently. "Do you hear that?"

Carried on the wind, barely audible over the slowly stirring birds, was a steady droning, a noise not unlike the rhythmic buzzing of bees; the sound sent a shiver running down Holden's spine.

"Airplanes." Vinnie nodded.

"But whose?"

"There ain't no way German planes are still flyin' round these parts." He chuckled. "I told you, they're *miles* from here. So anyway . . ."

Holden's unease wasn't so easily calmed. He scanned the skies above, straining to find the source, but it was hard to localize the sound and the closeness of the trees didn't allow for much visibility. The noise grew steadily louder and ever closer. Vinnie was probably right; it was probably a squadron of American Mustangs or British Spitfires, nothing for them to worry about. But Holden couldn't shake the nagging feeling that something was wrong —

Suddenly, they were nearly startled out of their boots by a pair of planes roaring over the edge of the forest, their wings scarcely clearing the treetops, hurtling past the field in which the men stood, dumbfounded, before banking over La Boissière. As they turned, their insignia were visible in the morning sunlight.

"Germans," Holden said, his mouth going dry. "Those are German planes."

"Aw, shit," Vinnie muttered.

Though the aircraft had thundered past them at tremendous speed, they were already making a turn. Holden had no way of knowing what the pilots had seen, if it had been him and Vinnie standing in the pasture or if they'd somehow noticed the vehicles sheltered beneath the trees, but there was no doubt that they were coming back for a reason.

"Run, damn it! Run!" Holden shouted, pulling Vinnie with him.

La Boissière stood nearly two hundred yards away; Holden knew there wasn't much chance of reaching it before the German planes caught them, but the possibility of safety was enough to get him moving. The ground was uneven, a mess of furrows and holes, causing him to stumble, nearly going down, but he somehow managed to stay on his feet, desperate to get away.

"We're gonna make it," Vinnie huffed beside him. "We've gotta!"

Holden felt as if his legs were submerged in molasses, as if time were standing still, but only for him and Vinnie. He didn't dare look back over his shoulder, understanding that death was pursuing them.

Halfway there, Holden heard the unmistakable sound of the airplane's machine guns roaring to life, spitting out bullets that chewed up the earth all around them. Holden and Vinnie both dived to the ground, their hands over their heads, their helmets pushed down around their ears. The sound was deafening. At any moment Holden expected a bullet to pierce him, ripping into his flesh and taking his life, but by some miracle it didn't happen. Instead, the planes raced over him and away. For an instant, he felt a tremor of hope.

But then he heard the whistling . . .

Holden had been a soldier long enough to become familiar with that noise; it was the sound of a bomb plummeting to earth.

Paralyzed with fear, Holden saw his life flash before his eyes; images of his family, of Longstock, of the future he'd so desperately sought, all shot past him, tantalizingly out of reach. Once the bomb struck, everything he had built toward, everything he'd ever wanted, would be taken from him.

"Move, damn it all!" Vinnie shouted, yanking Holden's arm so hard that it was nearly pulled from the socket. "Move!"

Though Holden managed to make it to his feet, he couldn't find the strength to go forward, tottering unsteadily, as Vinnie continued on without him. Holden's ears were filled with the shrill sound of the bomb's descent. In the face of such overwhelming fear, a part of him had already given up.

When the bomb exploded, Holden saw everything clearly: how the German pilots had understood the greater strategic importance of the huge manor house, how firing their machine guns at him and Vinnie was likely an afterthought on their approach, and that by running to La Boissière he and Vinnie weren't rushing to safety but to their doom.

The worst was what happened to Vinnie; Holden was looking right at his friend when the bomb exploded short of the house, tearing him limb from limb. Flesh, bone, and blood rained down on Holden, while Vinnie's helmet was hurled over Holden's shoulder and back into the pasture behind. In an instant, Vinnie was gone.

When the other soldiers in his unit raced out of La Boissière, their shouts tinny in the deafening aftermath of the explosion, Holden hadn't moved an inch, his eyes wide and his voice gone, covered in the gruesome remains of Vinnie Burretti, frozen shock still, except for the violent tremors racing down the length of his left arm. Crushed in his palm was a pack of German cigarettes.

For Holden Sutter, one fight had ended, but another had just begun . . .

When Holden finished telling Christina what had happened to him in France, he was surprised to discover that she had been correct about one thing; unburdening himself *did* make him feel a bit better, as if a tremendous weight had been taken from his shoulders. Dredging up the memories of that fateful morning, remembering a day that had haunted him ever since, had been difficult, but he understood that he'd taken a huge step forward, one that might someday lead to his recovery, and it was all because of Christina.

"I . . . I don't know how to thank you," he said.

"But I didn't do anything," Christina protested, wiping tears from the corners of her eyes. "It was you. You've unlocked the door to your memories."

Holden shook his head. "I may have been the one speaking, but if it wasn't for your coming here," he explained, looking at her, trying not to lose himself in her remarkable beauty, on both the inside and out, "I would never have told another soul . . . never . . ."

"You would have talked about it eventually," she disagreed. "Someday, you would've told Tyler or your mother. Maybe you would have shared it with your uncle. But I'm still glad you decided to tell me. I'm honored."

Holden knew that Christina was mistaken in her belief that he would've eventually opened up to someone else, but the last thing that he wanted, right then, was to argue with her. From the first moment he'd met her, he'd known Christina was *special,* different from any other woman he'd ever encountered, and nothing that'd happened since had caused him to question that belief. He even allowed himself to think that maybe she was right; maybe there was a chance he could get back the life he'd thought lost . . .

"So what do I do now?" he asked.

"You just took a huge step." She smiled, making his heart beat faster. "Now you need to figure out what the next one will be, and then the next, and then the next, until you're right where you want to be."

"But I . . . I thought that . . . you would just tell me . . . ," Holden answered, momentarily confused.

"Only *you* know the answers."

"But I *don't!*"

"Yes, you do," Christina said, rising from the bed and carefully making her way toward the door.

"Where are you going?" he asked.

"To dinner. That's why I'm here. Your mother invited me."

"But I wanted to talk."

"Then come with me."

Holden was surprised by how easily she suggested it, as if it were as simple to do as breathing or writing one's name. But he knew that he couldn't do it, he just *couldn't,* not yet, not so soon. He opened his mouth to protest, to argue that she was asking too much, but suddenly stopped short.

Christina had already gone, leaving open the door to the hall.

CHAPTER SIXTEEN

When Christina came down the stairs from Holden's room, she found Tyler talking with his mother in the kitchen. He was giving her a hug, the door open behind him, as if he'd just arrived. He looked up and smiled, his features instantly brighter.

"My mother says you're joining us for dinner," he said. "I suppose enough time's passed for you to forget how horrible it is to sit across from me."

"This time, I expect you'll be on better behavior," she answered. "I wouldn't bet on it."

"He will be," Clara added, "or he'll spend the night in the garage!"

Christina was undeniably happy to see Tyler; a couple days had passed since he'd taken her to visit his beehives and she hadn't realized how much she missed spending time with him. Still, she doubted that he had any idea that she'd come to speak with Holden; either Clara had chosen not to tell him or there hadn't been time. Something between the two brothers had been broken; Christina hoped that there was still time for it to be fixed.

"I haven't had a chance to thank you for my gift," she said to Tyler once Clara had left the room.

"What gift?" he replied, narrowing his eyes slightly.

"Who else would have brought me honey? Did the bees enjoy my visit so much they flew a jar all the way across town?"

"I thought you should enjoy the fruits of my labor," Tyler admitted.

"*Your* labor? Don't the bees do all the work?"

"Hey now!" he answered in mock indignation. Pulling up the right sleeve of his oil-stained work shirt, he showed the underside of his forearm; angry welts reddened his elbow. "They might *make* the honey," he chuckled, "but it isn't easy getting it out!"

Christina laughed; she was really beginning to enjoy what was growing between them. Though Tyler was still a rascal, it was easy to spend time with him, to laugh at his jokes. One moment was comforting, the next exciting. It also didn't distract from her pleasure that Tyler was as handsome a man as she'd ever met.

Still, Christina kept thinking about Holden. Listening to what had happened to him during the war weighed heavily on her heart. His having witnessed the harsh, brutal death of his fellow soldier and his continuing fear that danger was everywhere were partially the cause of his tremors. Recovering from such a trauma was hard, but it *wasn't* impossible. Christina believed what she'd told him; the only way he was ever going to get better was to talk about it. Together, they'd taken the first step, but there was still a long way to go.

Christina had been sincere when she'd invited him to come down for dinner; she doubted he'd accept her offer but had extended it just the same. She *wanted* to help Holden any way that she could. Though she'd unquestionably started off on the wrong foot with Holden, just as she had with Tyler, she found their odd relationship growing stronger.

Who knew where it could go?

Just like the first time she'd come for dinner, Christina found Clara's table to be a smorgasbord of plenty. Another thing that remained the same was that a place was set at the table for Holden; a plate, silverware, a glass, and a napkin were arranged in expectation; Christina hoped that they might be used someday soon. After saying a blessing, Clara encouraged them to dig in.

Christina loved everything on her plate; she hoped that she'd eventually be as good a cook as Clara. It was turning out to be a wonderful evening and Christina was happy that she'd been invited, even if she'd gone about it a bit underhandedly. While Tyler wasn't as obnoxious as he'd been during the first dinner, he was still feisty.

"So where's Uncle Samuel tonight?" he asked between chews. "It isn't like him to miss a free meal."

"I invited him, but he said that he couldn't make it," Clara explained. "He said something about not feeling well."

"He looked a little drawn at the clinic," Christina agreed.

"I just *bet* he's been under the weather," Tyler mumbled. "He probably gave himself too big a shot."

"Tyler!" Clara shushed him. "You shouldn't say such a thing!"

"Why not?" He shrugged. "It's not like I'm lying!"

"Don't talk like that in front of company," she scolded, glancing quickly over at Christina.

"You think she doesn't know yet?" He

chuckled. "Heck, she's spent every day since she got to town with him. Trust me, she knows."

Christina had wondered whether Dr. Barlow's family was aware of his morphine problem; obviously, they knew. She'd contemplated saying something to Tyler in the hope that he might have some advice, but now she understood that all he would've given was ridicule.

"I'm sorry about this," Clara said to Christina, clearly upset.

"That's all right," she answered. "Tyler is right, though. I *have* noticed . . . things . . ."

"See?" Tyler jumped in before forking another bite into his mouth, not knowing when to quit.

"Actually," Christina continued, ignoring him, "I'd hoped that we could talk about his problem. The other day —"

Before she could say another word, Christina fell suddenly silent; what had stopped her, what seemed to snatch the air out of her lungs, was the sound of footsteps.

Holden stopped halfway down the stairs, his heart pounding in his chest. Beads of sweat dotted his forehead and his nerves felt frayed. At any moment, he expected his left arm to start shaking; carefully, he

273

steadied himself by placing it on the wood banister and taking a deep breath.

You're almost there . . . hold yourself together . . .

He wasn't anxious because he'd left his room. Almost every night, Holden unlatched his bedroom window, carefully sneaked across the porch's roof, and shimmied down a trestle to roam Longstock's streets. But this was the first time he'd allowed others to see him. He could only imagine what his mother's reaction would be. Tyler's, too. But in the end, there was only one person whose response *really* mattered.

Christina.

Holden couldn't believe the impact she'd had on him; it was hard to imagine that he'd met her only a couple of days earlier. Regardless, he found himself wanting to please her, to show her that he'd listened to what she'd said. Because of her, he knew he had to change and had started to *believe* that he could.

Even the fear of his arm trying to shake itself loose from its socket no longer paralyzed him. He knew that he wasn't cured, that at any moment he could lose control of his own body, but now that he'd unburdened himself *everything* suddenly felt possible, including returning to the life he'd once so desperately wanted.

Holden felt he looked like a wreck. Before he'd left his room, he'd tried to make himself more presentable, putting on a different shirt and combing his hair. Still, he hadn't been able to look at himself in the mirror for very long; he didn't much like the man who looked back.

Well . . . here goes everything . . .

Holden slowly made his way down the rest of the stairs and, with his heart twisting itself into a knot, stepped into the dining room.

Because she'd heard him coming, Christina was looking at the doorway to the dining room when Holden entered. Immediately, tears sprang to her eyes. He appeared tired, his heart and body exhausted from his telling her about what happened during the war, but when his gaze met hers he gave her a smile that brightened his whole face.

"Is there room for one more at dinner?" he asked.

Hearing her son's voice, Clara gasped, dropped her silverware with a clatter, and nearly leaped from her chair. Seeing Holden in the doorway, smiling faintly, sent tears coursing down her cheeks; for a long while she didn't say anything, her mouth open, wondering if what she was seeing was real or a cruel dream.

"Ho . . . Holden . . . ," she managed. "Am I . . . are you . . . ?"

"Yes, Mother," he replied.

"Oh, my boy!" Clara cried, rushing to embrace him tightly.

With her arms around Holden, her face pressed to his chest, Clara finally set her emotions free from the shackles she'd placed on them, shaking and sobbing so hard that when she spoke no one could understand a word. Incapable of moving, Holden instead tried to comfort his mother, placing his hand on her back and trying to hush her hysterics, but it did no good.

"I see that there's still a place set for me," he said, looking over her shoulder at the table.

His words managed to break through Clara's tears. "I knew . . . I *always* knew that you'd get better! I knew it!"

"There's still a long way to go, but today," Holden said, looking over at Christina, "someone helped me take the first step."

Clara followed Holden's gaze and, when she understood that he was looking at Christina, her face glowed as brightly as a Christmas tree. "This is all because of you!"

she gushed, wiping the tears from her face. "I don't know how, but you've given me my son back! Thank you, oh, thank you!"

"I . . . I didn't do anything, really," Christina answered, a bit self-conscious.

"Don't be so modest, dear! Of course you did!"

Christina was embarrassed by Clara's praise. She knew how hard it'd been for Holden to talk about the war; because of that, *he* deserved all of Clara's congratulations. Still, Christina took some pride in getting him to join them. Clearly, he *wanted* to recover; the fact that Holden was standing in the dining room was proof of that. Thrilled by what was happening, she turned to Tyler, ready to share in the joy he must be feeling at having his brother back.

But when she looked, she found that Tyler was staring at *her*, not Holden, and that his eyes held a simmering anger.

Tyler looked at her for a moment longer, the edges of his mouth turning up into a vicious sneer, before turning to look at his brother.

"You're nothing but a coward," Tyler spat, wadding up his napkin and throwing it down on his plate.

"Tyler!" Christina shouted sharply in surprise. "What are you doing?"

"Ever since they shipped you home, you just stay in that damn room of yours and make our family the butt of every joke in Longstock!" Tyler kept on, his voice growing louder with every word. "You've refused everything we've done to help you! You have no idea how many nights I've had to listen to Mother cry because of how you've treated her! And now we're just supposed to forget everything you've done, all because," he added, glancing at Christina, "someone's told you you're better? You're pathetic!"

Holden received his brother's hateful words in silence; Christina didn't know if the reason he didn't defend himself was because he agreed with Tyler or if he didn't want to upset his mother. But neither did he bow his shoulders under the weight of Tyler's accusations. Instead, Holden stood taller, listening to every word, unblinking and unwavering.

Clara could no longer bear to hear one of her sons speak so viciously. "How can you say such things, Tyler?" she wailed, her tears returning with a vengeance, no longer full of joy and relief but confusion and pain. "He's your brother! Your family!"

"No, he's not!" Tyler growled back, standing up so quickly that his chair clattered to the floor behind him. "To me, he's dead!"

Before anyone could say a word, Tyler stalked from the room, slamming the kitchen door behind him so loudly that it sounded like a gunshot, leaving everyone left behind dumbfounded.

Banging the door shut as hard as he could, Tyler leaped down the short stairs, skidding to a halt in the tall, dew-laden grass of the backyard. Anger constricted his chest and his hands were balled into fists. He thought about screaming or finding something hard to hit but instead stared up into the cloudless sky, wondering if his rage would subside if he counted the countless stars; he doubted if even *that* would help.

"Damn you, Holden," he muttered. "Damn you . . ."

Seeing him appear in the doorway had almost stopped Tyler's heart. He'd been struck speechless. It'd been so long since he'd even tried to reach out to Holden, so long since Tyler had even *seen* him, that it was as if he'd somehow forgotten who he was. But then Tyler had followed Holden's eyes, finding where they'd gone, listening to what his mother said, that Christina had encouraged him.

Christina Tucker had mesmerized Tyler. Remembering the afternoon he'd taken her to see his beehives had dominated his thoughts for the last couple of days. She was so *different:* challenging, intoxicating, nothing like any of the other women he'd ever met. He liked that she didn't take his guff but gave it back instead. When she looked at him, he saw someone he wanted to get to know better, whom he wanted to allow to see the real him.

But now Holden was interfering.

Fearful that if he looked over his shoulder, Christina would be staring back, Tyler chose to walk away. When he'd learned that Christina would be coming to dinner, he would never have imagined that it would end as badly as the first time, but here he was, retreating to the garage after again making an ass of himself.

Damn you, Holden.

For the second time since she'd come to Longstock, Christina sat at Clara Sutter's dining room table, amazed that a family could behave in such a crazy way. Christina's ears still rang with the sound of the kitchen door slamming shut, as she struggled to accept that Tyler had *again* made a scene. She found herself unable to say a word, her voice lost.

"Why does he have to be that way?" Clara

wailed. "How could he say such terrible things to his own brother?"

Christina had no answer. She and her sister, Charlotte, were certainly different from the Sutter brothers. Their bond of family was unshakeable; even when they'd been children, Christina could never remember their saying such hurtful things. It was almost unbelievable, though she'd heard every word.

Her eyes couldn't leave the door; she held on to a sliver of hope that Tyler would reappear, explaining that it was all a terrible joke and rejoicing at his brother's recovery. But with every passing second, she understood that Tyler had meant every word . . .

But as bad as she felt, Christina could only imagine how much worse it was for Holden, how angry he must be.

Finally turning, she found him doing his best to console his mother, but Christina was surprised to see that he didn't look angry; on the contrary, he looked disappointed. His eyes held hers.

"Go after him," he said simply.

"Holden, I don't think that —"

"When he's upset like this," Holden cut her off, "what he needs is someone to talk to so that it doesn't get worse."

Christina frowned. "Maybe he just needs

some time alone . . ."

"Tyler may not want to admit it right now, but I'm still his brother," Holden said with a weak smile. "No matter what he thinks about me, I care about what happens to him. Right now, he needs someone."

Christina didn't relish the idea of fulfilling Holden's request, but she felt as if she had no choice but to do as he asked. It was clear to her that, no matter how horribly Tyler had treated him, Holden genuinely cared for his younger brother. If trying to speak to Tyler would make Holden feel better, she should try. After all, he'd come so far in only a day's time that she didn't want anything to set him back. Besides, if there was anyone Tyler might explain himself to, it was she. She owed it to everyone to try.

"I'll talk to him," she said.

"Thank you, Christina," Holden said, looking at her with an intensity that made her heart beat faster.

Worried that she wouldn't find Tyler, Christina set off looking for him.

CHAPTER SEVENTEEN

Tyler's favorite place in the world was beneath the hood of a car. Ever since he had been a little boy, working on things with his hands had given him comfort. First disassembling something, then putting it back together, gave his life a sense of order, especially when life seemed anything but orderly. Tuning a fussy engine, replacing a cracked hose, changing the fluids, doing whatever it took to make things right, *that* was what made him happy.

So, of course, now that he'd once again made a mess of his life, the place where he chose to retreat was the garage.

Hoisting the hood of his Ford Tudor, Tyler smiled. Ever since he'd bought it, he'd done his best to keep it in pristine condition, doing the routine maintenance to prevent any problems from cropping up. Even now, when he knew the car was running fine, he began checking all of the hose clamps, looking at the cylinder heads, and then examining the transmission. Slowly, his tension began to ebb as he lost himself in the nuts and bolts of his beloved car.

When the side door to the garage creaked open, he had no idea how much time had passed since he'd stormed out of the house. Though he knew someone was standing there, he kept on working.

"Tyler?"

The sound of Christina's voice shook him; she was the last person he'd expected to come after him. Remembering how he'd glared at her after Holden's unexpected arrival, then the way he'd spoken, saying terrible things, had led him to believe that she wouldn't want to speak to him for a long time. But here she was. Ignoring her would only make things worse.

"Yeah," he said, still underneath the hood.

"Are you all right?"

"I'm fine," he answered gruffly, reaching for his wrench and getting back to work. "What are you doing out here?"

"Shouldn't I be asking you that question?" Christina replied.

"I'm working on my car."

"I thought it was running fine. There didn't seem to be anything wrong when you brought me back from your beehives."

"It's . . . I'm just . . . fine-tuning it, is all," Tyler mumbled.

Christina stepped around the front of the car and stood beside him. Looking at her, Tyler was momentarily stunned by her beauty; even in the sparse light of the garage, he marveled at her long hair and the curve of her cheek. But even as he felt attraction toward her, he was struck by the realization that, with as much as he'd messed up, he couldn't possibly deserve a woman as wonderful as she was.

"That looks complicated," she said, pointing at the engine.

"It's no different than anything else." He shrugged. "Once you get the hang of it, it seems like the most natural thing in the world."

"Have you always been interested in cars?"

Tyler nodded. "My father taught me," he explained. "He wasn't the most mechanical guy in the world, the type who was more at home with a book in his hands than grease underneath his fingernails, but one of the things he couldn't stand was not knowing the answer to something. When he bought his first car, he resented the fact that he didn't understand how it worked, so most nights he'd come out here and start digging around beneath the hood. Sometimes he did more harm than good. I was always at his elbow, taking it in right alongside him. Somehow, we learned together."

"It was the same for me when my mother learned how to sew," Christina said. "When I look back on it now, those were some of the happiest days of my life."

"I know exactly what you mean."

One of the reasons that Tyler was growing so fond of Christina was because she was willing to listen and try to understand. Anyone else would have stormed into the garage and demanded to know what in the hell was wrong with him, but she chose a different tack. Eventually, he expected her to raise the subject, but he appreciated the fact that she allowed the explanation to take its time. Right then, however, he didn't feel like waiting.

"I suppose you're back to thinking I'm an ass again," he began.

"Again?" She smiled. "That would mean that there was a time I *didn't* think that way about you."

"Ha-ha," Tyler said sarcastically. "Very funny."

Slowly, the smile faded from Christina's face, her eyes filling with concern. "But I do wonder why you behaved that way," she said. "All of us are more than a little concerned."

"You talked with Holden about the war?" Tyler asked.

"I did."

"Then why didn't you tell me?"

This was the question that was rolling around in his guts, churning up bile and making him feel miserable. Something about it felt like betrayal, as if she had purposefully withheld it from him.

"Because I spoke with him only this evening," Christina explained. "I was coming down from his room when you arrived. But," she added, "even if I had done it days earlier, that doesn't mean that I have an obligation to tell you. What happened was between Holden and me, no one else."

"He's my brother," Tyler argued. "I have a *right* to know."

"Then you should ask *him*."

Tyler knew that, in some regard, Christina was right; it wasn't fair for him to expect her to tell him everything that went on between her and Holden. Still, Tyler had been more than a bit surprised and, though a part of him was ashamed to admit it, he didn't like the idea of their spending time together. He didn't want to call it jealousy, but he didn't know what other description would fit. There was nothing that said she was his, but still . . .

"What happened between the two of you?" Christina asked, stepping closer and putting her hand on his arm. At her touch, Tyler felt as if he'd grabbed hold of a live wire. "What caused you to behave so boorishly?"

Tyler looked around the garage. Surrounded by such familiar things, by his family, he knew that he couldn't tell Christina the truth. Not here.

"Come with me," he said. "Let's get in the car and go for a drive. Maybe then I can tell you what you want to know."

He could see from the look on her face that she was distrustful, as she'd been back at the gas station. "It's nothing like before," he tried to reassure her. "I just can't talk about it here. Trust me."

Christina was still hesitant, but he could see her slowly warming to the idea. Finally, she nodded her head in agreement.

Slamming down the hood, Tyler pulled out his keys. "Let's go."

Christina shivered slightly as the cool night breeze rushed through the open window of Tyler's car, teasing at her long hair. Though she was colder than she would've liked, the noise prevented them from talking, leaving her with plenty of opportunity to wonder where they were going.

Tyler drove the Tudor south and so far out of town that they were soon surrounded by fields of apple trees. Crickets chirped, their conversations faint over the crunching of the car's tires on gravel. Eventually, they crossed the river at a rickety bridge before taking a looping turn and heading back toward Longstock.

"It isn't far now," Tyler said.

At a rusted gate, its lock hanging open and limp at the latch, Tyler left the road and headed up a weed-choked drive. Up they climbed, back and forth along a switchback path. The going was rough, full of rocks and potholes, and Christina held on to the door as they bounced and shook. Finally, the ground leveled out, revealing a field filled with row after row of abandoned apple trees. They all stood ghostly and silent. Tyler brought the car to a stop and shut off the lights, the engine ticking as it began to cool.

"It's a ways out of town, but I think the view's worth it," he said.

Christina couldn't have agreed more. With the cloudless sky and a nearly full moon, there was plenty of light to see how utterly magnificent the valley looked. Situated high above the winding road and river below, she could see for miles in either direction. Undulating forested hills adjoined the orchards to form a living chessboard. Far to the north, the outlying lights of Longstock twinkled.

"It's beautiful," she declared. When she looked back at Tyler, she found that he wasn't looking out the window but rather staring directly at her; caught, he quickly turned away.

For a few moments, they sat together in silence. Finally, after what seemed like hours, Tyler began to speak.

"I should've said it earlier, but I'm sorry for how I acted. You shouldn't have had to see that."

"I'm not the one you have to apologize to," she replied. "Holden deserves to hear it."

"Holden." Tyler winced as if the word had pricked his tongue. "You have no idea what it's been like to spend my whole life in his shadow. Uncomfortable as hell."

Christina didn't answer. The truth was that she understood much better than Tyler imagined. While she and Charlotte had no obvious sibling rivalry, it wasn't particularly easy being her little sister. But she had felt little resentment, had never tried to follow in Charlotte's footsteps. Though Christina could've said something, she waited for Tyler to talk, to unburden himself, just as Holden had.

"Ever since we were little boys, *everything* that Holden did got noticed," Tyler finally began, his voice soft, his words carefully chosen. "I can't remember a time he wasn't considered the fastest, smartest, funniest, most popular kid in Longstock. Everyone was drawn to him, happy to just be around him. My parents worshiped the damn ground he walked on," Tyler spat. "That's why it was such a disappointment when I came along."

Christina could hear the hurt in Tyler's voice.

"They wanted another son like Holden, someone they could hang their hopes on and brag about," he said, looking off into the distance. "When they figured out that I was *nothing* like him, they rode me mercilessly. They tried everything they could think of to change me. But the harder they tried, the more I fought back. After a while, they just quit and centered all of their attention on Holden. They didn't give a damn about me."

"How can you say that?" Christina asked, shocked. "Your mother loves you every bit as much as she does your brother! It's as plain as day!"

Tyler shook his head. "Holden's *special*," he disagreed. "Why do you think she lets him speak to her so disrespectfully? Night after night I have to listen to her crying, upset that he won't talk to her or has slammed the door in her face. I tell her he needs to go back to the hospital, but she shakes her head and says that I don't understand what he's going through. So back she goes, over and over, no matter what he does! If *I* acted that way, my mother wouldn't do any more than she absolutely had to for me."

"I don't believe that for a minute!"

"That doesn't mean it isn't true."

Since her first visit to the Sutter house, Christina had wondered what she would do if she were in Clara's position. Confronted by the suffering of a child, Christina imagined that she would go to any lengths necessary to make things better, no matter what it took. But what if that help was rejected? What if she had to listen to Holden's insults? In the end, she knew that it wouldn't have mattered; no matter what, she couldn't have turned her back.

And that's why Tyler's wrong . . .

"If only my father were still alive," Tyler

said wishfully. "Things would be different. He wouldn't have allowed Holden to be this way."

"Your father . . . ?" Christina asked. "I don't mean to pry, but . . ."

"He died when I was fourteen," Tyler said. "He had a heart attack while he was working in the yard. Uncle Samuel always said that it happened just like that," he explained, snapping his fingers, "that he never felt a thing, but he was still gone."

"I'm sorry," Christina offered.

"Things seemed to get worse after he died. Holden was a bit older, more responsible, so he was the one my mother turned to for support. We managed to get by, but it wasn't easy, especially not for me. My father was the only person in the family who seemed to understand me. He was disappointed I wasn't more like Holden, but he could see I was trying to be my own person.

"I'm nothing like my brother. Where Holden's polite and well-spoken, I'm a smart-ass." Tyler gestured with first one hand, then the other. "While he has his nose in a book, I'm under the hood of a car. Holden's the fella that most fathers hope their daughters will marry, while I'm the one they warn them to stay away from."

"You say all of this as if you're a terrible

person."

"Compared to Holden, I am."

Christina hesitated, but only for an instant. "I don't think you are."

Tyler turned toward her in the moonlight, the intensity of his gaze enough to make her heart pound hard in her chest; what she'd said was forward, but it *was* the honest truth.

"There is one other person who doesn't think badly about me," he finally said, breaking their stare.

"Who?" she asked.

"Holden," Tyler answered with a laugh. "Even after everything that I've said and done, *he* was always the first one to defend me. He never let anyone say something bad about me, not even our parents. He always encouraged anything I wanted to do, tried to cheer me up when I was down, never let me feel sorry for myself," he explained, shaking his head. "All our lives we've been compared, but he already knows I don't measure up."

"It's not like that," Christina argued. "I'm sure of it . . ."

"The only moment Holden and I were treated as equals was when we went off to war," Tyler explained, ignoring her. "While he went to France, I spent nearly three years hopping from island to island in the Pacific, fighting the Japs. It was the hardest thing I've ever done, but I'm proud of it. When I found out Holden had been hurt, I felt terrible. Sure, we've had our troubles, but I would never have wanted *that*. I tried to help him, but he never gave me the chance, never gave anyone in the family a chance.

"So to see him come marching down the stairs . . . it makes me sick. After all the hardships he's caused, everyone else will see fit to forgive him, but not me. Seeing him smile, watching him be hugged by our mother, made me hate him more than ever before!"

"But why?" Christina asked.

"Because now," Tyler said slowly, holding her eyes with his own, "now he wants the same thing that I want. He wants you."

Christina was dumbstruck. This had to be something out of Tyler's wild imagination, of his simmering hatred for his brother. But there was something even *more* shocking in what Tyler had said. It wasn't just that he was suggesting Holden had a romantic interest in her, but rather that he was upset because it interfered with *his own.*

Just a few days earlier, Christina's dislike of the Sutter brothers was so great that she had wondered if she should leave Longstock. Now, they were vying for her affections. But what truly amazed her was that Tyler's admission didn't upset her.

"You're . . . y-y-ou're im-m-m-agining things . . . ," she stammered. "Holden doesn't . . ."

"Am I, really?" Tyler laughed humorlessly. "I saw how he was looking at you, and I'm sure you saw it, too."

Christina knew in her heart that Tyler was right; when Holden had appeared at the bottom of the stairs and had been embraced by his mother, he'd looked over Clara's shoulder, right at Christina. In his eyes she'd noticed something; there'd been an intensity that had unnerved her, a look of longing a part of her had recognized.

"If what you're saying is true," Christina said, "that doesn't mean I return his feelings."

"It doesn't mean you deny them, either," Tyler countered.

Answering him would've been as hard as plucking one of the thousands of stars above from the sky, so Christina chose to remain quiet. Ever since she'd discovered Holden walking Longstock's darkened streets, she hadn't been able to look at him quite the same. Learning what had happened to him in France had further changed her view.

Only a trace remained of the person he'd once been, a confident man who was loved by all, but she could still see it.

On the other hand, Tyler was also intriguing. Her first impression of him had been so far off the mark that she was almost ashamed of herself. When he'd talked about his beehives, he revealed a different person, someone she wanted to get to know better, handsome, cocky, and headstrong. She had felt something growing between them, even if she couldn't have said what it was; now, clearly, he'd admitted the same.

"Do you hate me?" he asked, his voice oddly soft.

"How could you ask such a thing?"

"Do you?" he persisted.

"No . . . not at all."

"Then why are you sitting so far away from me?" Tyler asked, putting his hand on the space between them. "Why don't you come a little closer . . . ?"

Christina knew what Tyler wanted; she wasn't *so* inexperienced with men not to know what he was suggesting. But accepting his offer would undoubtedly make things more complicated between the two of them, as well as between her and Holden. Still, there was a part of her that stirred at Tyler's advances, a yearning that was uncomfortable and exciting, all at the same time. In the end, whatever reservations she had weren't enough to hold her back.

Tenderly, Christina reached over and placed her hand on his, their fingers immediately intertwining. Slowly, she slid toward him, her heart skipping a beat as he moved to meet her. The warmth of their bodies touching sent shivers of excitement racing across her skin. Suddenly a bit nervous, she marveled at how boldly she was acting. Uncertain about what she should do next, Christina waited for Tyler to lead.

"Isn't this better?" he asked.

His hand found her chin, lifting her face toward his. Outside the Tudor, an owl hooted, an insistent call, but Christina paid it no attention, her mind spinning at how she'd gotten herself in such a situation but hardly regretting it.

"You know," Tyler said, his lips close, his breath on her face. "I'm not as bad as everyone likes to think. I wouldn't —"

"Hush," Christina quieted him, placing a finger on his lips, a gesture that made him smile.

When Tyler leaned down, she rose to meet him, closing her eyes, curious, *excited* about where this was all headed. Gone were her worries about why Tyler hated his brother, about the possibility of Holden having feelings for her; all that mattered was that instant, however long it would last.

As his lips touched hers, Christina let her hand move to Tyler's chest, steadily drifting until she squeezed his biceps, yearning for his touch. His kiss was softer than she would've expected, tender, as if he was being careful not to allow his passion to race out of control. But she marveled at his strength, at how strong his skin felt beneath her touch, at how closely he held her to him. She wondered if he worried she'd try to get away; he needn't have.

There was nowhere else she would rather have been.

CHAPTER EIGHTEEN

Christina stared down at her plate of untouched eggs and hash. Lazily, she stirred her fork in the food, loosening the yolk. She'd taken only a sip of her coffee. Everything smelled wonderful, and while she assumed that it probably *tasted* just as delicious, her thoughts were such a swirl of new, incredible emotions that she couldn't bring herself to find out.

Marla's Diner was packed with people. From where Christina sat in a booth at the front window, she could see that nearly every table was full, with a handful of customers still waiting near the front door. Back in the kitchen, a sweaty cook feverishly tried to keep up with the piling orders, slapping a bell whenever a plate was ready. Wafting around the room were the rich smells of pancakes and coffee, the clinking of silverware and glasses, and bits of conversation.

". . . darn worms will get into everything if we're not careful . . ."

"Gimme a couple of eggs, hard, with a side of bacon, and a glass of . . ."

". . . so then I said to him, 'I don't know if we can keep . . .' "

Across from her, Dr. Barlow had his nose buried in the newspaper held up in front of him. He'd been that way ever since they'd arrived, occasionally nibbling on his food but not saying much. Christina could see the morning's headline: AMERICAN ATOMIC ENERGY PLAN SUBMITTED TO UNITED NATIONS. Apparently, it was much more interesting than talking with her.

Not that I mind . . . especially not after what happened last night . . .

Long after Tyler had taken her home, Christina lay in her bed, staring at the ceiling, remembering the feel of his lips touching hers. Nothing untoward had happened between them, he'd remained a true gentleman, but Christina found herself shocked at how forward *she* had been. Kissing Tyler had stirred something inside her, like the winding of a grandfather clock. Still, she also thought about Holden, wondering if Tyler hadn't been right about his brother being attracted to her. Though she hadn't slept much, she felt energized, as if she were walking on air, even if that meant her head was in the clouds.

Arriving at the doctor's office, Christina had struggled through the morning, walking around in a daze, her thoughts drifting back to Tyler. Thankfully, she hadn't been as absentminded around the doctor, helping him tend to their patients; there didn't need to be *another* reason for their relationship to be further complicated. When he suggested they go to lunch, Christina had readily accepted.

Now she wondered why he chose to ignore her.

The only thing that had penetrated her daydreaming was Dr. Barlow's improved condition. Though he was as grouchy as ever, he no longer looked quite so rough around the edges; there were no dark bags under his eyes, his hair was neatly combed, and he'd even taken the time to shave. He was as presentable as he'd been the day they'd met at the train station. Now if she could only do something about his attitude . . .

"I suppose Tommy Williams won't be climbing tall trees anytime soon," Christina began; the young boy had been brought in by his mother after falling from an apple tree and breaking his arm. Dr. Barlow had reset the arm that morning, encasing it in a plaster cast.

The doctor gave no answer, turning a page of his newspaper.

"As upset as his mother was," Christina continued, "I doubt that she'll let him out of her sight long enough to get into mischief again."

Dr. Barlow still gave no reply, not even a grunt or a nod of his head.

Christina frowned; she'd had about enough. The first time, she could assume that he hadn't heard her, but now she was convinced he was ignoring her. Dropping her fork with a loud clatter, she gruffly snapped, "If reading a newspaper is what you wanted to do, I don't know why you bothered to invite me along!" With that, she rose to leave.

"Christina, wait," he said before she could get to her feet. "Just . . . just sit back down and we can talk . . ."

Christina paused, reluctant to give in so easily.

Several people sitting around them had obviously noticed how they'd spoken to each other. Dr. Barlow gave each of them an easy smile and nod, which seemed to satisfy their curiosity.

"Please," he said.

Sighing, Christina sat down again. She looked at him warily as he folded his newspaper, setting it aside. For a long moment, he remained silent, rubbing his thumb along the edge of his watch, refusing to look up at her. Finally, he spoke.

"Ever since you left my house that afternoon, I've tried as hard as I could to act as if nothing had happened between us," Dr. Barlow began, his voice low to keep from being overheard, "but every time I open my damn mouth to speak, all I can think about is the sorry state I was in."

"I don't judge you for that," Christina said. "Every one of us has problems. Some are just worse than others."

"I don't reckon there are many as bad as mine."

"Holden would disagree with you."

Dr. Barlow nodded his head. "You're right about that," he agreed, "but that doesn't mean my problem doesn't embarrass the hell out of me. Someone of my standing isn't supposed to behave that way.

"But the worst was seeing Archie Felton. It was a reminder of what I could someday become. That thought scares me so much that I haven't had any morphine since; I swear." As if to plead his innocence, the doctor put his hands out in front of him, then clasped them together; entwined, they shook slightly; Christina didn't know if it was because of nervousness or withdrawal.

"I don't think you're as bad as Archie," she said.

"But I could be, don't you see," he argued, his voice growing a bit louder and more strained. "If I keep going the way I have, then someday everyone I care about is going to shun me the same way Archie's family does him."

"All you need to do is stop."

"That's easier said than done." Dr. Barlow frowned, shaking his head. "Even though I've managed to quit every once in a while, who knows when the day's going to come where I can't resist anymore, where the enticement's too great to ignore?"

"Then you have to get help," Christina explained. "You need to confront the reasons *why* you abuse yourself the way you do."

For a moment, she thought he was going to let it out right there, in the middle of the diner, but suddenly the front door swung violently open, starting an unexpected commotion.

Archie Felton stumbled inside, almost falling on his face, already drunk as a skunk in the early hours of the afternoon. His clothing was a mess, his shirttails untucked and filthy, his shirt stained so badly she would've had a hard time guessing its true color. His face was flushed a bright red, his eyes wet, and his jaw slacked open. Christina couldn't believe what she was seeing; it was as if he'd been waiting outside for a cue to make his grand entrance.

"Careful now, Archie," the woman behind the lunch counter said as she quickly moved to where he wobbled, steering him unsteadily toward a nearby seat. "You look like you could use a cup of coffee." Clearly, his drunkenness was something people in the diner were used to.

Seeing him in such a sorry state, Christina was reminded of how bad off Dr. Barlow had been when she'd found him; wondering if he could see what she was thinking made her flush with embarrassment.

She needn't have bothered; clearly, he *was* thinking the exact same thing.

"Come on," he said gruffly, throwing some bills on the table he left. "I've suddenly lost what was left of my appetite."

Outside, Christina hurried to catch up to Dr. Barlow as he walked briskly down the sidewalk. All around her, life appeared to move at a leisurely pace; clouds ambled across the sky, birds glided on the scant breeze, and what few people shared the street with her and Dr. Barlow seemed to be in no hurry to get where they were going, just another easygoing summer afternoon.

Christina, however, saw everything in her life rocketing along, moving far faster than she either wanted or expected. Her recent arrival in Longstock, her relationship with Tyler, discovering Holden wandering the streets in the middle of the night, and finding Dr. Barlow under the influence of morphine all fell right on top of one another. It was enough to make her dizzy.

"Dr. Barlow, wait!" she called to him. "Just wait a minute!"

Finally, the doctor stopped near a street corner, wiping sweat from his brow with the back of his hand, his face twisted up in exasperation.

"Of all the days to see Archie like that," he muttered. "Just when I thought I couldn't feel any worse!"

"It's just bad luck, is all," Christina offered.

"Everyone in town *knows* Archie is a drunk," Dr. Barlow explained. "Everyone!

You saw the way Patty came out to help him into a chair! Dealing with him is old hat by now!"

"No one seemed upset."

"Not to his face, they weren't! But believe me, there isn't a soul in Longstock who feels any pity for him." The doctor frowned. "Not after what all he's done to his family. He was right, you know, back in the clinic, about how his drinking put his wife in an early grave. Somehow, she managed to put up with him for twenty years, but paid for it with her life. I'm amazed his son agreed to drive him anywhere! He doesn't deserve an ounce of pity!"

Christina wanted to contradict him, she felt sympathy for what Archie Felton had done to himself, but held her tongue.

"I can only imagine what people think when they see me walk past," Dr. Barlow fretted, growing more and more agitated. "I'd be a fool to think that I do much better hiding my own demons! How many people shake their heads when I walk by, thinking, 'There goes the sad, old drug addict'!"

Before Christina could reply, before she could argue that he was jumping to conclusions, the doctor suddenly, shockingly, lurched forward, slamming into her. The force of the collision nearly lifted her from the ground and was strong enough that she couldn't keep from falling. Her backside hit the sidewalk hard, sending shivers of pain racing up her spine. While her purse skittered away, thrown as she fell, Christina cried out in hurt and surprise.

Dr. Barlow tottered above her, looking as if he would fall to the ground beside her, but somehow he managed to stay upright. His newspaper flew out of his windmilling hands, flapping down like a bird shot from the sky. His face flushed an angry red.

"What in the hell?" he asked furiously.

A man walked past them, one hand stuffed into his pocket, the other lifting a cigarette; once he'd taken a deep drag, Christina thought that she heard him chuckle. His clothing was unkempt, worn through with holes and soiled. She hadn't gotten a look at his features; not once did he bother glancing in their direction, choosing instead to keep walking away, slowly at first, but then steadily faster.

"You! You there!" Dr. Barlow shouted, striding purposefully to catch the stranger. "Wait just a minute!"

The man paid the doctor no mind, walking along as if he didn't have a care in the world.

"What do you think you're doing?" the

doctor asked, his face twisted in consternation and outrage. Grabbing the man by the shoulder, he spun him around. "Didn't you see what you caused back there?" But the rest of his words remained unspoken.

Now that the stranger was facing her, Christina got her first good look at him. Dark, greasy hair hung low over his forehead, framing a pinched-up face as worn as his clothing. Stubble peppered his sunken cheeks, making him look even more disheveled; with his wiry build, he reminded her of a rodent. It was difficult to tell how old he was; though youngish-looking, he appeared to have led a hard life. But it was his eyes that truly unnerved her; narrow and cold, they regarded the doctor with a flat, menacing gaze, even as a trace of a smile curled the corners of his mouth. Christina had the unpleasant feeling she and the doctor were in some kind of danger; she looked around, but there was no one who could possibly help them.

The change in the doctor's demeanor was both immediate and unexpected. The anger that had fueled him down the street in search of an apology drained from him in an instant. He let go of the other man's shoulder as quickly as if he'd been bitten, while his knees looked more unsteady than when he'd collided with her.

"You . . . it can't . . . it can't be you . . . ," he muttered, awkwardly stepping away from the stranger.

Menacingly, the man stepped close to Dr. Barlow so fast that Christina thought he was going to strike him. The doctor must have felt it, too, because he raised his trembling hands in a feeble gesture of self-defense. Instead, the man leaned close to Dr. Barlow's ear, whispering something that set the older man's shoulders shaking, before patting him hard on the cheek, giving Christina a wink, and again walking away. This time, the doctor made no move to go after him.

For a long moment, the doctor remained frozen in place, watching the man disappear around the nearest corner. Then, as if someone had snapped his fingers in front of his face, the doctor suddenly stirred, frantically looking around. Seeing Christina still lying on the sidewalk, he rushed back and helped her to her feet.

"Are you all right?" he asked, his eyes darting back over his shoulder.

"I'm okay," Christina answered. "Who was that man?"

"No one . . . he was no one," Dr. Barlow answered nervously.

"But it looked like you knew him, like he knew you. Why did he run into you like that?"

"It was just an honest accident." He tried to smile reassuringly but failed miserably. "It's nothing to worry about. But we should get back to the office. Callie will be wondering what happened to us." Without giving Christine a chance to respond, he took off at a trot, rushing away quickly.

Christina knew Dr. Barlow wasn't telling her the truth about the stranger. What had occurred looked completely intentional. But just like his morphine abuse, she knew he wouldn't talk about it, even if she asked. For now, it would have to remain a mystery.

With a frown, she once again hurried to catch up.

Luther knew he shouldn't have taken the risk of letting Samuel Barlow see him, but he hadn't been able to help himself. Days had passed since he'd begun shadowing the bastard, but no matter how carelessly Luther watched, the man never seemed to notice. Standing outside the diner, Luther had decided that he might as well remind Donnie's murderer he was still alive. Besides, there was nothing quite as satisfying as giving someone a good scare.

"Goddamn son of a bitch," Luther growled.

He'd had no idea what Barlow was talking about with that pretty, young nurse of his, but it was clear he was getting worked up over it; he was so utterly oblivious to everything around him, Luther knew he could have killed Barlow in that moment, but it was becoming a game to him, a game he enjoyed playing. Instead, he'd decided to give the doctor a playful nudge. Luther hadn't intended to hit him hard enough to barrel into the woman, but he was happy with the outcome nevertheless.

The whole thing was so damn funny he couldn't help but laugh.

Listening to Barlow shout, working up a full head of steam, Luther knew that risking everything was worth the opportunity to see the man's face once he discovered who was messing with him. Sure enough, when Barlow grabbed him, turning Luther around, the look on the bastard's face had been priceless; it looked like someone had grabbed him by the pecker and squeezed.

But now, only a few minutes after he'd walked away, Luther felt empty inside. This *wasn't* a game. This *wasn't* something he should be laughing about. No matter how much fun he was having, Barlow had taken his brother away, had let Donnie die. For the thousandth time since the crash, Luther imagined what had happened after his brother had been brought back to Longstock from the car crash, Donnie lying on Barlow's examination table, his body broken but savable, his life ebbing away, while that son of a bitch stood there and refused to lift a finger to help.

The only thing that mattered now was getting his revenge. No matter what it took, regardless of how difficult it was to resist the desire to have a drink, Luther would make Barlow suffer as badly as he had. If he didn't kill one of the doctor's precious nephews, maybe he'd have to consider the nurse. She'd looked a bit insulted when he'd winked at her. Luther liked that kind of spunk; maybe he'd have a little bit of fun with her first. It wasn't too hard to imagine that *that* would hurt Barlow but good.

What put a smile back on Luther's face was remembering what he had said to Barlow when he'd leaned in, the man nearly speechless at seeing who was interfering in his life.

I'm comin' for you, and there ain't a damn thing you can do about it . . .

Annette Wilson smiled to herself. Standing

in the shadows of the alleyway across the street from the hardware store, she watched as the whore who was fooling around with *her* Tyler got knocked to the ground. That the deed had been done by a worthless piece of trash like Luther Rickert made it all the better. From where she stood, it didn't look as if it had been an accident. Who knew what the circumstances were, but they pleased her nonetheless.

After all, the enemy of my enemy is my friend . . .

When she'd first seen Tyler showing an interest in the new girl in town, Annette had no idea who she was. Carefully, Annette had started asking around, talking to people who'd met her. To a person, not a bad word had been said, but Annette knew it was because no one had seen her for the bitch she *truly* was. Just remembering her beside Tyler in the pasture was almost more than Annette could bear.

Still, she'd managed to learn a few things about Christina: that she was originally from Minnesota, that she'd been a nurse in the Army, but most important, where she was staying in Longstock.

Annette had stood outside the bakery the night before, watching silently as Christina had walked the long blocks to the Sutter home. The indignation had only gotten worse when, later in the evening, Annette had seen Tyler driving off with the tramp in the passenger's seat.

That was the last straw! If I wait much longer, it'll be too late . . .

It was going to be much harder to get to Christina Tucker than it'd been to attack Caroline Satterly. Caroline's family lived along a deserted stretch of road. She was set upon in the middle of the night. There was no one to see anything or hear her cries for help. But the whore's apartment was in the middle of Main Street. There was no telling who might see, who might hear.

To Annette, it was worth the risk of being caught, if only to ensure that Tyler would no longer be in that slut's clutches, that he would then be *hers.*

Moving deeper into the alleyway, Annette watched as Dr. Barlow helped Christina to her feet. *She looks worried . . . just as she should be.* When the doctor hurried away, she lingered, looking around, as if she knew danger was nearby, not knowing how real those worries were.

I'm coming for you, whore, and there's not a thing you can do about it . . .

CHAPTER NINETEEN

For the second time in a matter of days, Christina was wakened by the sound of creaking on her stairs. The noise was clear and unmistakable. It was followed by a knock on her door.

Outside her bedroom window, the sky was an inky black with a light scattering of stars. Christina had gone to bed early, tired from a trying day, and had no idea what time it was. Dawn was undoubtedly hours away. Lying in bed, slowly trying to get her bearings, she was startled when the knocking came again, this time a bit louder and more insistent.

Her first thought was that it was Tyler. She'd been wrong to make this assumption before, but it didn't seem so farfetched now that things between them had significantly changed; with the way they'd kissed, the passion that had blossomed between them, it seemed possible that he'd want to spend more time together.

But why did he have to come in the middle of the night?

Christina rose from bed and put on her robe. Stopping in front of the mirror, she tried to manage her hair, but it was too wild and unruly from sleep and wouldn't do what she wanted. Whatever Tyler might've expected, he would have to take her as she was; next time, he'd have to come at an earlier hour if he wanted her to be more presentable.

But just as she was about to turn the knob, Christina stopped. Just like the last time she'd stepped out onto her landing in the middle of the night, she had no guarantee that her visitor would be who she expected.

If it's not Tyler, then who . . . ?

Though it unsettled her, the first person who leaped to mind was the strange man who'd bumped into Dr. Barlow that afternoon. Though the doctor spent the rest of the day acting as if nothing had happened, Christina could see that something was weighing on his mind. She had no doubt that he knew the stranger, but for whatever reason, he chose to keep the truth to himself. Whoever the man was, he wasn't the sort she wanted to encounter, especially not in the middle of the night.

Christina knew the stranger was capable of violence. She'd seen it in his narrow eyes, the way he'd approached the doctor, even in the way he'd winked at her. He hadn't done anything other than run into Dr. Barlow, but that didn't mean that he wasn't capable of much worse.

Christina's thoughts were interrupted by yet another knock at her door. The sound startled her so badly that she jumped.

Nervous as she was, she simply couldn't imagine that, if the person on the other side of the door meant to do her harm, he'd be stupid enough to announce his presence by knocking.

With a deep breath, Christina opened the door.

"I'm sorry to wake you, but I really wanted to see you."

Holden Sutter stood on Christina's landing, smiling sheepishly. She felt foolish that she hadn't considered it could be he, especially after the way he'd looked at her the last time they'd been together. He looked the *exact* opposite of how she felt; while she stood in her robe, her head still groggy with sleep, he was both well dressed and alert, as

fresh as if it were the middle of the afternoon.

"I wondered if you wouldn't like to go for
a walk with me," he said.

"What time is it?" she asked, stifling a
yawn.

"Somewhere around four." Holden
frowned, suddenly aware of how odd it was
for him to be standing in front of her door
in the middle of the night. "I shouldn't have
wakened you," he said, turning to leave.
"That was inconsiderate of me. I'll let you
get back to sleep."

"No, it's all right, really," Christina said
quickly, stopping him before he'd made his
way down only a couple of stairs. "It'll just
take me a minute to shake out the cobwebs."

"We can do this some other time."

"Let me get dressed and I'll be right out."

Back inside her apartment, Christina took
more time wrestling with her conflicted
thoughts than she did putting on her
clothes. Try as she might, she couldn't stop
herself from wondering if Tyler wasn't right,
that Holden had a romantic interest in her.
She hoped that he wanted to talk about his
tremors, about the war, and about the steps
he could take to get better, but she had her
doubts.

But walking with Holden would also give

her an opportunity to learn more about the rift between the brothers. She'd heard Tyler's side of the story, but her mother had taught her that there were always *two* sides to every tale.

"Are you sure you're up for this?" Holden asked when she reappeared on the landing.

"Let's go," she answered.

Walking beneath the moon as it descended to the west, Christina listened intently as Holden told her about Longstock. Peering into darkened storefronts along Main Street, marveling at incredible houses along the river, and pointing in every direction, he regaled her with stories of the people he knew, of the hijinks he used to get into when he was younger, of happier times. Listening to Holden laugh, Christina could see more of the man he'd once been, before the tremors.

Even physically, he looked changed, more put together. But Christina saw the greatest difference was in his eyes. When Holden spoke, they reminded her of jewels, sparkling with life, laughter, and wonder, deep and powerful, the sort that a woman could find herself lost in . . .

"It sounds like you and Tyler used to do a lot of things together," she said.

"We did," Holden agreed. "When we were little boys, things between us weren't so complicated . . ."

Christina didn't know how to answer. The thought of telling Holden what Tyler had said in the car made her feel as if she'd be betraying him in some way. He'd confided in her, extending to her a trust she wanted to respect, and that meant remaining silent. Thankfully, Holden needed no prompting to keep speaking.

"It was hard for Tyler when we were growing up," he explained, his brow furrowed. "My parents had such high expectations for him. But where things came easily for me, my brother struggled. He was smart in his own way, doing things with his hands, things that I'd have no idea how to do, but no one ever acknowledged him for what he was.

"I stood up for him as best I could, tried to make my mother and father understand that they weren't being fair to him, that Tyler was his *own* person, but I don't think it made much difference. The older we got, the more Tyler started resenting me."

"He feels as if you were put on a pedestal," Christina offered carefully.

"He's right," Holden agreed. "I never wanted the attention, but when you're a kid it's hard to make yourself heard. In the end,

322

it was easier to go along with it than try to make a change. Of course, that's why I'm such an embarrassment to everyone now."

Christina thought about arguing against what he'd said, to tell him that he was wrong, but instead she decided to change the subject.

"I'm sorry about what happened last night."

"I suppose I should've expected it." Holden shrugged.

"If I'd known that he would act that way, I never would've suggested you come down to dinner."

"Whenever I would've chosen to leave my room, Tyler's response would have been the same."

"I'm still happy you came downstairs."

"Me too," Holden said, giving her a pleasant smile. "After you made the offer, I kept thinking about how much better I felt for having talked about what happened in France. For the first time since Vinnie died, I felt like taking a chance. Even with what Tyler said, I still hope we can fix things."

"You just need to talk to him."

"I don't know if he wants to hear what I have to say."

"He'd listen if you gave him a chance."

"Is this what he told you when you drove

off together?" Holden asked; his question caught Christina so completely off-guard that she had to look away.

"We . . . we didn't talk about you . . . ," she lied.

Holden nodded as he kept walking. "Even if you had, it's really none of my business. You've been right all along." He smiled at her, his eyes sparkling in the night. "If I want to know how Tyler feels, I'm just going to have to ask him myself."

"Even though I got a lot of attention when I was younger," Holden said, stopping on the sidewalk and directing her gaze toward the house across the street, "that doesn't mean Tyler didn't have his share of admirers."

Christina couldn't help but marvel at the opulence of the home. Recessed from the iron fence that ran the length of the sidewalk, the house looked to be twice the size of any of its neighbors. With decorative stained-glass windows, perfectly manicured bushes that fronted an enormous porch, and a walkway lit up every couple of feet with ornate lampposts, it was certainly impressive. Even in the murky light preceding the dawn, Christina sensed that nothing was out of place, not even a lone weed sprouting in the lawn. It was fancy enough to put Eunice Hester's grand, eccentric house to shame.

"Who lives there?" she asked.

"It belongs to Charles Wilson, the richest man in Longstock," Holden explained. "His family was one of the first to settle in these parts. They had the good sense to buy up every bit of land they could get their hands on. When newcomers arrived, they sold acreage back at a huge profit. Charles lives comfortably off those spoils."

"What does this have to do with Tyler?"

"Charles has a daughter, Annette, who's always been a bit obsessive about my brother. Ever since we were kids, Annette wouldn't let Tyler out of her sight. She followed him around like a puppy, wrote him love letters, and baked him cookies, all in the hope that he'd love her as much as she did him. Any time a girl showed too much interest in him, Annette would chase her off. That Tyler never returned her affections didn't seem to matter in the slightest. She just kept right on pining after him."

"So what happened?" Christina asked, a little uneasy.

"Nothing happened." Holden shrugged. "I'm sure Annette's in there right now, dreaming of a life where she and Tyler are happily married."

"That all sounds a bit . . . creepy . . ."

"She's just confused," he explained. "She always struck me as the sort of person who was not exactly all there in the brain department."

Christina couldn't take her eyes off Annette Wilson's home. Something about what Holden said unsettled her; it was like the frightening stories Charlotte had told her about walking on someone's grave. With a shiver, she told herself that she was imagining things.

Longstock's school sat to the east of town, built at the base of the valley, with thick stands of trees rising to the crest of the hill, and was framed in by the groves of apple trees that were the town's lifeblood. Three stories tall, it'd been built of brick so dark that it looked foreboding in the gathering light of morning. It stood still and silent, except for the sound of the steel clip that occasionally clattered against the flagpole.

The school appeared old; a marker at one cornerstone read: "1905," but changes appeared to be coming; a new addition was being constructed off to one side, with sawhorses at the ready, as well as piles of bricks to be mortared into new walls, hallways, and classrooms.

Holden stopped and looked up at the school. "Somehow, every time I go out for a walk, I always end up here." He sighed.

"This is where you wanted to teach?"

He nodded. "Ever since I first sat in one of its classrooms, this building has always been special to me," he explained. "I thought being a schoolteacher meant you were one of the smartest people in the whole world. Mrs. Binghampton, my first teacher, sure seemed that way. There wasn't anything she didn't know. To be like her seemed the greatest thing I could ever hope for."

"My sister would love to hear you say that." Christina smiled.

"She's a teacher?"

"In a small town in Oklahoma. But I don't think that she's been fond of the profession for quite as long as you. If I remember correctly, she wasn't particularly happy going to school."

"Boy, I sure was." Holden smiled broadly. "It didn't matter what the subject was; arithmetic, writing, you name it, I was always excited to learn something new. If I wasn't covered in chalk dust at the end of the day, I was upset. The only time I was more disappointed was when it snowed so much school was canceled!"

"Is that why you always come here? To remember those times?"

"That's part of the reason, I suppose." He shrugged. "But most of it is because I thought I'd still be here, now, teaching children just as I'd been taught. It's the only thing I ever wanted to do."

"Then why don't you?"

"Not with this I can't," Holden answered, raising his left hand.

"But you can get better!"

"I feel good about coming down to dinner," Holden shook his head, "but rejoining my family is one thing. Standing in front of a roomful of children is another. What if I started having a tremor in front of them? How would I ever be able to explain it? How could I handle the embarrassment?"

"Just days ago you thought that you'd never be able to sit down to dinner with your family," she argued passionately. "Why are you so willing to assume that anything is impossible anymore?"

"My tremors aren't going to go away."

"Only if you choose not to do anything to get better. Talking about what happened was only the first step back to the life you want." Pointing toward the school, Christina said, "The only thing that will hold you back is your own stubbornness."

"I wish it was that easy . . ."

"*I* believe in you."

Christina's words seemed to light a fire within him; Holden's face brightened. But just as she hoped that he would begin to believe in himself, that he would take another step in his recovery, his face suddenly drained of color and his eyes grew wide with fright.

"Holden?" she asked in concern. "What's wrong?"

Even as she spoke, Christina knew the answer; just like the last time he'd come to her apartment in the dark of night, Holden was suffering a tremor. Fearfully she looked at his left arm; he'd pulled it close against his chest, but she could see it begin to twitch, an uncontrollable movement that shook his fingers, wrist, and forearm. The last time this had happened, he'd run off in shame.

Christina was determined that *this time* things would be different. In desperation, she grabbed Holden by his right arm; immediately, she felt him try to pull away, but she held firm, straining to keep him in front of her.

"Holden, look at me," she said as calmly as she could, wanting him to fixate on her instead of his arm. When he still wouldn't do as she asked, fighting against her, she repeated herself, a bit louder: "Look at me!"

Holden's eyes were as skittish as those of a cornered animal whose only thought was to flee as fast as it could. But somehow, the harshness of her voice cut through his fear and he focused on her, just as she'd asked.

"I want you to do as I tell you," Christina said softly.

"But-but I-I-I can-can't —"

"Don't say 'can't,' " she quieted him. "Don't say a word. Listen to the sound of my voice. If you can do that, I swear everything will be all right."

At the same time Christina was trying to project herself as confident, inside she was struggling to control her emotions. None of the various treatments she'd witnessed at the Army hospital seemed exactly the right course of action; she knew Holden would only be reachable for an instant and that she had to help him as quickly as she could.

"Don't think about your arm," she kept talking. "Just concentrate on me, nothing else."

Though he was obviously struggling, it was clear Holden was trying his best to do as she asked.

"Take deep breaths," Christina encouraged him. "Breathe in, then let it out slowly, slowly; relax; don't think about it." She did it along with him, breathing in unison. With every breath, Holden was improving, the tension easing from his shoulders, and the shaking of his arm subsided. Finally, all was as it had been, the two of them smiling at each other, thrilled that a crisis had been averted.

"I . . . I've . . . never been able to stop one before," he marveled.

"I knew that you could do it!"

"It's all . . . all because of you . . ."

Christina laughed. "All I did was show you the way," she smiled, "but you were the one who did all of the work."

"Maybe . . . maybe you're right . . ." He smiled, his eyes as bright as the rising sun. "Maybe I *can* get better . . ."

Listening to Holden, Christina was so happy for him that tears sprang to her eyes. This was the breakthrough she'd been hoping for; she *knew* it was! While there was still much work to be done, he now knew that he could overcome whatever obstacles remained.

"I'm happy for you. You can beat this thing."

Before Christina could say another word, Holden leaned forward and kissed her; she was so surprised that she gasped. Though she tried to move backward, his hand found her hip and held her close. But what happened next shocked her more than she thought possible; she stopped trying to resist. For a moment, she allowed herself to melt into Holden's arms, returning his passionate kiss.

But then, just as quickly as Christina had given in to her impulses, the feeling passed and she thought of Tyler; she could only imagine how upset he would be if he could see what she was doing with his brother.

Putting her hands against Holden's chest, Christina firmly pushed herself away. He looked down at her imploringly; she knew he wanted nothing more than to return to their embrace, to their kiss. For her part, all Christina could do was cry.

Tyler had been right all along.

"Christina," Holden said, holding out his hand to her. "I didn't mean to upset you . . . I would never want to cause you any pain . . ."

"Just . . . just don't . . . ," she sobbed.

"All I wanted was to thank you for all you've done, to let you know how much you mean to me."

But Christina couldn't bear to hear another word. She'd made such a mistake, such a terrible mistake.

This time, it was her turn to run away.

Chapter Twenty

Christina walked in a daze. She felt dizzy, sick to her stomach, and weak in the knees all at the same time. For a while, she'd considered calling the doctor and lying, telling him she was sick and wouldn't be coming to work, but she'd changed her mind; hiding in her apartment wasn't going to make *anything* better.

From the moment she'd raced away from Holden, just as the morning sun was coloring the eastern horizon in brilliant shades of pink and purple, she'd been unable to think of anything other than the moment they'd kissed. Up until then, she'd been so excited that he'd suppressed his tremors, so happy he was finally getting better, that she would never have expected him to do something as brazen as kiss her.

But he had, and that had upset her whole life . . .

At the same time, Christina knew it wasn't

fair to place all the blame on Holden. She *had* kissed him back. It hadn't been for long, but there was no denying she'd given in to her urges, meeting his passion with her own. For a brief moment, she'd enjoyed it.

But why . . . why did I do it . . . ?

There was no denying she found Holden attractive. He was smart, interesting, and could make her laugh. She also felt close to him because he'd confided in her the reason for his tremors. Given time, she was sure the bond between them would grow.

What stood in the way was Tyler. Christina's attraction to him had led to their kiss beneath the stars, something she definitely didn't regret. While he had his share of flaws, there was more to him than she had expected. That he'd opened himself up to her, sharing both his beehives and his feelings toward Holden, made her wonder what other things Tyler would reveal to her. They were building a relationship, something to be treasured, not betrayed.

She was caught between two brothers.

Christina arrived at the clinic without any answers to her problems. There was no choice but to put her worry aside until later; she had responsibilities that wouldn't wait. She could only hope the day would be without turmoil. But just inside the door, she realized her hopes were about to be dashed.

Dr. Barlow raced down the hallway from his office and into the waiting room. He was clearly distressed. Out of breath, he was stuffing things into his medical bag.

"Come on!" he shouted to her. "We have to go!"

Without waiting, Dr. Barlow ran back down the hall, banging open the door to the alley. Moments later, Christina heard the coupe's engine roar to life.

"What's going on?" she asked Callie as she headed after him, confused.

"Oh, sweetie," Callie answered. "I'm afraid it's Eunice Hester. We just got a call. It doesn't look good . . ."

"Couldn't . . . couldn't it be the same as before . . . ?"

Callie's eyes grew wet. "Not this time," she answered solemnly.

Christina stood beside Dr. Barlow in Eunice Hester's bedroom. Neither of them said a word. Eunice lay peacefully on the bed before them, almost certainly having died in her sleep. Her hands had been crossed at her chest, a sheet pulled up to her elbows. Out in the hallway, a woman sat in a chair and sobbed without interruption, mourning her loss. Occasionally, Christina wiped her own eyes.

There hadn't been anything they could've done; by the time they'd arrived, Eunice had been dead for hours. Her grieving friend had discovered Eunice when she hadn't come down for breakfast. She didn't appear to have suffered. If Christina looked closely, she could almost see a smile at the corners of the older woman's mouth. Once she had left this life, there was little reason to doubt that she was happy in the next, once again at the side of her beloved husband.

But she'd left a void behind.

Even Christina, who hadn't had the pleasure of knowing Eunice for long, missed her. Though she'd been eccentric and had enjoyed provoking those she cared for, Eunice embodied many of the attributes Christina wanted for herself. Fiercely independent, possessed of a sharp wit, ready to travel the world at a moment's notice, Eunice had been a woman who ardently went after what she wanted, including love.

Christina wondered what Eunice would've thought of the mess she now found herself in.

For Dr. Barlow, the loss seemed particularly strong. Though he'd driven recklessly out of Longstock like a man possessed and then dashed up the stairs of Eunice's house so quickly that it left him wheezing at the effort, he now stood frozen in place, his face pained. He'd undoubtedly seen hundreds of bodies in his time in the Army and even over the decades as a small-town doctor, but it wasn't always as personal for him as it was now.

"Are you all right?" Christina asked him.

"We may've enjoyed giving each other a hard time," he answered without looking at her, "but I really cared for that old bird."

Christina smiled. "I'm sure she knew it."

"I reckon that over the dozens of times I came out here for one illness or another I somehow convinced myself Eunice would *never* pass, that she'd be around longer than those damn gargoyles."

"She was almost ninety years old."

"You'd think that'd make it easier," Dr. Barlow glanced at her, "but somehow I don't feel any better." Frowning, he fished a pack of cigarettes out of his shirt pocket. "They say a doctor shouldn't get emotionally involved with his patients, that it only complicates things."

"We both know that's easier said than done."

He nodded gravely, appreciating that she agreed with him. He stuck a cigarette in his mouth and was just about to strike a match when he suddenly stopped.

"I need to smoke this in the worst way," the doctor explained, "but if I were to do it in her house, I know Eunice's ghost would haunt me for the rest of my days. If I go out on the porch, I imagine she'd appreciate my thoughtfulness. That way, I could keep an eye out for the sheriff and the hearse that'll take her body back to town. Would you care to join me?"

Christina nodded toward the woman still sobbing in the hall. "Will she be okay alone?"

"She's upset, but I don't think it's anything to worry about," Dr. Barlow explained. "Besides, I think it's time we talked about some things." Glancing over where Eunice lay, he added, "Before it's too late."

Dr. Barlow took a deep drag of his cigarette, blowing the smoke off the porch, watching as it slowly drifted across Eunice's yard. Christina sat on a chair beside an ornate coffee table, its dark wood scoured in strange carvings, waiting for him to say something.

Though there were things about the doctor that Christina desperately wanted to know, she felt she didn't need any more drama in her life. Just trying to come to grips with what had happened with Holden was nearly enough to make her want to lock herself in her apartment. But Dr. Barlow's problems intrigued her. From the moment she'd first discovered him under the effects of morphine, her assumptions about his normal life had been irreversibly shattered. On top of that, there'd been the encounter with the dangerous-looking stranger in town.

Is it possible that these two things, two secrets, *are related?*

"You told me you wanted to know why I took morphine," Dr. Barlow began.

"I do," she answered.

The doctor nodded. "My problem goes back to the Great War," he explained, choosing his words carefully. "When I went off to fight, I had so many expectations. I was excited and frightened out of my wits, often at the same time. It didn't take too long for me to understand that the only important thing was that I came home alive. What I never would've expected was that *living* with what I'd witnessed would be worse than being buried in all that mud."

Dr. Barlow held his hands out before him,

palms raised upwards, staring down at them as if they were still covered in blood. "These goddamn hands of mine have seen so much suffering." He sighed. "Even if I was out on my feet, so tired I could barely keep my eyes open, another stretcher would be laid in front of me, carrying another boy who'd never get to see his sweetheart again, who'd never walk or was screaming in pain while I tried everything I could to keep him alive."

Christina understood the stress he'd been under. Though she'd never experienced combat, she'd spoken to plenty of doctors and nurses who'd returned stateside from the battlefields and had listened as they described the exhaustion, the never-ending wounded, and how they'd struggled to cope. Her own father, Mason Tucker, had told her about the hospital where he'd convalesced, about the countless beds filled with the casualties of war.

"When I was in France," Dr. Barlow continued, "even during the few hours I managed to get any sleep I'd dream I was still in surgery, a scalpel in my hand, blood staining my fingers, splattered on my clothing. Every once in a while, I'd look down and discover that the soldier I was about to cut into had my face. To escape all of that . . . I started taking morphine."

"Did that make it any better?" Christina asked.

"It did." He nodded. "Once I gave myself a shot, I could sleep. I'd still wake up to the same nightmares, but for a brief while it was worth whatever withdrawal I suffered through. My mistake was assuming once I got back home to Longstock things would go back to the way they were before the war. I hadn't counted on the damn dreams taking the boat with me.

"The first time I had one back home, I didn't worry too much. The second time, I was shaken up pretty bad. The third time, I started keeping a syringe and a bottle of morphine in my bedside table. There hasn't been a week in the last twenty-five years I haven't had a nightmare."

"Have you tried to get help?"

"There isn't anyone around here that could make me forget those broken-up bodies, those faces I see in the night."

Christina couldn't help but draw a connection between what Dr. Barlow was telling her and Holden's experiences. Like his nephew, the doctor had suffered a trauma he'd been unable to avoid. But rather than try to unburden himself, he'd chosen to keep it inside, allowing it to fester until it had defined him. Every time he sought sanctuary in morphine, he was refusing to confront his demons.

But as she had with Holden, Christina now saw an opportunity for Dr. Barlow to get better, to take back his life.

"That first night that I went up to Holden's room, you agreed with me that the only way he was ever going to get better was to talk about his problem," she said.

"I did," he agreed.

"Then why are you willing to give your nephew advice that you aren't applying to yourself? Holden has made such great strides! If you'd give yourself the same opportunity, then —"

"Because the only person I ever considered telling the truth to just passed away in her sleep," Dr. Barlow cut her off.

"Eunice?" Christina gasped.

"Maybe that's why I enjoyed her company so much," he said with a sad smile. "She used to spend her days crossing the world and experiencing everything under the sun, cherishing those memories as she got older. But for me, the one time I crossed the ocean turned me into an addict. I hope she wouldn't mind my saying this, but I suppose I was jealous."

"It's not too late. If you'd let it out, things could get better."

Dr. Barlow shook his head. "Maybe when I was younger there'd have been a chance, but now I'm just an old man whose life has gone to hell in a handcart."

While Christina understood that he was upset about Eunice's sudden death, she wondered if his gloomy outlook wasn't partly the result of his run-in with the strange man.

But before she could ask, the sheriff's car pulled into Eunice's drive, followed by a long, black hearse.

"I hope you don't think less of me because of what I've told you," Dr. Barlow said as he crushed his cigarette beneath his shoe.

"Not at all," she answered.

The doctor nodded. "I suppose we should get back to work."

Christina had a hard time concealing her disappointment. While she'd received some answers to her questions, she hadn't received all of them, and the chance to ask looked to have passed; there was no way of knowing when, if ever, she'd get another opportunity.

The rest of the day was spent dealing with Eunice Hester's death. The sheriff made note of what had happened, talking at length with Eunice's still-distraught friend;

though she wasn't privy to what was being said, Christina thought he looked sympathetic, with his hat in his hands. Dr. Barlow took great care in preparing Eunice's body for transportation to town. On one occasion, Christina noticed him wipe a tear from his eye. Arrangements were made to notify Eunice's next of kin, a cousin living in Madison, and then they were finished.

Neither of them said much during the drive back to Longstock. Christina's thoughts careened around her head as if they were caught in the grasp of a tornado: Eunice lying unconscious at the bottom of the stairs, the feeling of Tyler's lips against hers, and Dr. Barlow's explanation for his taking morphine were whirling there, but her attention settled again and again on what had happened with Holden.

In the end, Christina knew she had to take a measure of responsibility for allowing their kiss to linger. If she'd truly wanted it to stop, she would've resisted when it began, but instead, she'd met his affection with her own. Ultimately, the blame was hers.

What truly worried her was what that kiss would do to Tyler. How could she begin to tell him about what'd happened between her and his brother? She was so ashamed, so embarrassed, that she couldn't imagine facing Tyler. Still, Christina knew that when she eventually did, she'd have to tell him the truth. Given how strained things were between him and Holden, there was no telling what the repercussions might be.

How did I manage to make such a mess of things . . . ?

As soon as Christina had that thought, Dr. Barlow turned the coupe down the alleyway behind the clinic, and she saw Tyler leaning against the side of the building. He was out of the sun, but she could still see the smile creasing his features when he saw them drive up. Bending down, he picked up a tattered box at his feet.

"Howdy, Uncle Samuel," Tyler said as they got out of the car. "I hope you don't mind my having a word with your new nurse. This time, I promise I won't kidnap her."

"I'd appreciate that." Dr. Barlow nodded. "I'll be inside when you're done, Christina." Without another word, he headed inside.

"Boy, he's in a sour mood today." Tyler frowned.

"It's because Eunice Hester died," Christina explained. From the moment she'd gotten out of the car, she'd been unable to meet Tyler's eyes, instead keeping them at her feet.

"That's too bad. Although I reckon even she knew she was living on borrowed time."

"I should probably go and see if he's okay," Christina said quickly, shuffling her feet toward the door. She knew that the longer she spent with Tyler, the greater the chance she'd have to come clean, and right then she just wasn't ready to face his probable reaction.

"Now hold your horses for a moment," Tyler replied, gently but firmly taking Christina by the arm. "I hoofed it all the way from the garage to show you the gift I made, so the least you can do is take a look."

"Gift?"

"Here." He handed her the box. Inside, she found the same mesh and cloth outfit he'd shown her when he'd taken her to see his beehives.

"It's a beekeeper's clothes," Christina said.

"Right as rain."

"I don't understand. You've already shown me this."

Tyler shook his head. "This isn't the same one," he explained. "What you're holding is the one I made for you. It took me a bit longer than I'd expected, but now you can join me, that is, if you still want to."

The thoughtfulness of Tyler's gift was enough to overwhelm the last remaining defenses Christina had built around her shame. No matter what she might've wanted, it would've been impossible to stop the downpour of tears that came gushing from her eyes.

"What's the matter?" Tyler asked with concern, undoubtedly surprised to find that instead of the gratitude he might've expected, he got tears. "If you've decided against harvesting the h-h-h-ives with me, that's f-f-ine," he stammered, utterly confused. "I just thought . . . because of what you said . . ."

Christina knew she had no choice; she couldn't be around Tyler, not now, not after what she'd done.

Dropping the box onto the ground, she yanked her arm free of his grasp and dashed toward the back door of the clinic.

"Christina!" Tyler shouted. "Wait!"

But she was already inside, leaning her weight against the door, hoping that he wouldn't come after her and demand an explanation for how upset she'd been. Long seconds ticked by, but nothing happened. Finally, Christina opened the door to check, certain that he would be just on the other side, waiting her out.

But Tyler wasn't there, leaving Christina alone with her misery.

It seemed that she was making a habit out of running away from the Sutter brothers.

CHAPTER TWENTY-ONE

For the third time in nearly as many days, Christina heard sounds on the stairs that led to her apartment. She lay in bed, hardly stirring, when there was a sharp knock on the door, and wondered if she should answer.

What I really need now is to be left alone.

Christina's evening had been quiet. She'd come home from work exhausted, both physically and mentally. After a simple dinner, she'd tried to do some reading, thought about going for a walk, but her mind was such a state that she'd decided the best course was to go to bed early, get a good night's sleep, and start again in the morning. She'd even had the irrational hope that maybe a solution to her problems would come to her in a dream.

Lying in bed, she found sleep as elusive as a slippery fish struggling to get back to its watery home. No matter how much she tossed and turned, she couldn't get her dilemma with Tyler and Holden out of her mind. So instead, she'd stared at the ceiling as the hours drifted by.

But now she had a visitor.

Which of the Sutter brothers stood outside her door? After what had occurred in front of the school, Holden had plenty to apologize for. On the other hand, Tyler was undoubtedly confused by what had happened that afternoon. Maybe he'd come for an explanation, one she still didn't want to give.

The knock came again.

Christina sighed deeply.

There seemed little chance she could just lie in her bed and pretend she wasn't home. Regardless of which brother was out there, he'd probably become so worried he'd knock her door down. There was no choice but to get up and face the consequences.

Putting on her robe, Christina turned on a light in the living room and went to the door. Her hope had been to put this moment off, if only for a little while longer. She turned the knob and opened the door.

Before she could see who stood on her landing, something struck her out of the night, flooding her arm with excruciating pain. The agony was so great, so unexpected, that she screamed as much out of surprise as hurt. But even as she grasped her arm, she was struck again and again.

The only way for Christina to get away was to fall onto her back and desperately try to wiggle away. It was then, scuttling on the palms of her hands, trying to elude the vicious assault, that she finally got a look at her attacker.

The person on the other side of the door hadn't been Tyler or Holden.

It was a woman.

The moment Christina Tucker opened her door, the instant Annette saw her face, the rage she'd struggled to keep inside of her exploded. Gritting her teeth, she swung the steel pipe as hard as she could. The feel of it striking Christina's arm was ecstasy. Blinded by anger, Annette swung over and over, hitting her rival for Tyler's affections, hoping to break her bones into tiny pieces, all with the grim determination to go back to the way things used to be, back before she'd interfered with the future Annette so desperately wanted.

If I have to, I'll kill you. Tyler is mine!

After days of watching Christina strut around Longstock as if she were the prettiest girl at the church dance, Annette had decided to act. Watching Luther Rickert knock Christina to the ground had been satisfying, but Annette knew it would take *much* stronger measures to send the message that Tyler Sutter was off-limits.

That evening, Annette had followed Christina on the short walk from the doctor's office to her apartment and then waited in the shadows across the street, hoping the bitch wouldn't have any company. Hours had slowly passed. Eventually, Christina had shut off her light, but Annette still didn't move. She'd wanted to be certain her rival had gone to sleep; if she was groggy when finally confronted, she'd be far less capable of fighting back. Once midnight had come and gone, Annette knew the time had come. Squeezing her steel pipe so hard that her hand hurt, she'd made her way up the staircase. After a simple knock on the door, she'd waited, certain that this night would be better, more satisfying, than when she'd shown Caroline Satterly the error of her ways.

"Stay away from him!" Annette shouted, stalking after Christina as she scuttled away in terror. "You're not good enough! Only I am! Me!"

"Who-who are you?" Christina asked, her voice panicked, her eyes wide with shock and pain.

Annette answered with her pipe, swinging it hard against Christina's knee; the sound of her scream was sweet music to Annette's ears.

"Why is he interested in a whore like you?" Annette screamed so hard that her throat hurt. "You must've lied to him! Deceived him! Why else would he show you his bees?"

For the first time since Annette burst through her door, Christina appeared to have some idea of why she was being attacked. "T-Tyler?" she stammered. "This is about Tyler . . . ?"

Listening to the slut saying Annette's beloved's name drove her over the edge. With a snarl, Annette again swung the pipe at Christina's legs, but this time she must've been too obvious; quickly the wounded woman slid to the side, and the pipe struck nothing but the wooden floor below; the weapon hit the ground so hard it sent sharp needles of pain racing up the length of Annette's arms.

"Don't you dare say his name!" Annette bellowed.

Christina tried to roll over onto her side, struggling to get to her feet, but the effort seemed too great for her. While she was on

354

her knees, Annette kicked Christina in the rear, sending her sprawling onto her face with a thud. Wisps of a smile curled at the corners of Annette's mouth when she saw how helpless Christina truly was, but it wasn't enough to quell the boiling rage seething inside her.

"Everything was fine before you came here!" Annette shouted. "We were going to be married! I just needed more time, but then you came along and ruined everything!"

"Wait!" Christina yelled. "Wait!"

"Everything will go back to the way it should once you're gone!" Annette yelled, shouting over Christina's protests. "I'll be the one who marries him! I'll be the one sharing his bed! Not you!"

Deciding to end things once and for all, Annette raised the pipe and prepared to strike. It'd be so simple: just drive the steel rod into the back of Christina's head. If she died, no one would discover who'd done it. With her gone, Tyler would need someone to help him through his grief, someone who'd give him whatever he needed.

But just as Annette swung the pipe downward, Christina desperately kicked out, striking her just below the knee; it was enough to unbalance her, making her legs wobble before she tumbled to the floor, landing awkwardly on her shoulder. The metal pipe flew from her hand, skittering off into the corner.

Annette was not hurt, wasn't frightened that Christina had managed to defend herself; she even wasn't surprised that it'd happened. All she felt was anger.

If it's the last thing I do, I'm going to kill this whore!

Christina knew she had to get away. Whoever this woman was, she was absolutely crazy. Even though Christina had managed to knock her off her feet and separate her from the iron pipe that had inflicted bruises on her arms, hands, and knee, she was far from safe. Her attacker still lay between her and the door, so Christina glanced toward the windows; it might be worth trying to reach them, but as hurt as she was, there was little chance to get one open before she was again assaulted.

Even as Christina struggled about what to do, she wondered about the woman's identity. From what she'd been shouting, it was clear she was infatuated with Tyler. He'd never mentioned another woman.

So who is she?

Suddenly, Christina remembered the

enormous house Holden had stopped before the night he'd kissed her. He'd spoken about a girl who was in love with Tyler, who'd been obsessed with him ever since they'd been children. Was this the *same* woman?

"Annette?" she asked softly, the name rising through the fog of memory.

Though the crazed woman didn't reply, Christina knew from her reaction that she'd been right; Annette's eyes grew wide and her jaw clenched tightly. Immediately she scrambled to her feet, so Christina did the same.

Christina's knee throbbed so badly that she could barely put any weight on it; the moment the pipe had struck, she'd feared it might be broken. But now that she was upright, she tried to put the pain out of her mind and focus on getting away.

But Annette had a different idea.

Christina had hoped her attacker would go after the pipe, looking away long enough for her to burst past and out onto the landing. Instead, Annette charged her with the viciousness of a starving wolf, the taste of blood on its muzzle.

Annette bowled into Christina so hard she couldn't stay on her feet. The two of them crashed to the floor in a tangle of arms and legs. Christina landed on her back, the air driven from her lungs; her head struck the floor so hard that she saw stars blinking before her eyes. Before she could react, Annette grabbed two fistfuls of her hair, yanking with all her might.

"You won't have him!" she cried, tears streaking her cheeks. "I won't let you come between us!"

Filled with a furious anger, Annette pulled Christina's hair one way and then the other. With surprising strength, Annette drove her victim's head down to the floor; desperately, Christina tried to keep the blackness crowding the edges of her vision from overcoming her. The pain was incredible as her eyes filled with tears.

Frantically, Christina mustered what little strength remained to her, certain that if she didn't, Annette was going to kill her. Balling up her fist, she punched as hard as she could, striking the crazed woman in the stomach. The blow wounded Annette; air whooshed from between her snarled lips, and, while her hands remained tangled in Christina's hair, her grip relaxed. Again and again, Christina punched, sensing an opportunity to get free. For a moment, it looked as if it might work; Annette tottered unsteadily above her, but then Christina was slapped so hard she saw more stars and her hope faded.

Fear raced through Christina. Only minutes had passed since she'd opened her door, but it felt as if she'd spent hours fending off Annette's attack. Christina's whole body hurt from being struck by the pipe, wrestled to the floor, and now pummeled in the head. Though she was fighting back as best as she could, she knew it wouldn't be enough, that soon she'd be defenseless.

But just as Christina was about to give up hope, Annette was lifted off her as easily as if she were a child's doll. All Christina could see were Annette's two kicking feet before she was flung toward the door.

"What in the hell are you doing?"

Blinking through tears, Christina saw Tyler standing above her, his face a mask of confusion and anger. He was looking at Annette, who'd already scrambled back to her feet and was again going after Christina. Tyler grabbed Annette, holding her in place, but she was so desperate to get at Christina, straining so hard, that he was forced to lift her from the floor.

"I won't let her come between us!" Annette yelled, her voice shrill, full of violence and insanity.

"Stop it, Annette!" Tyler shouted. "Stop

359

fighting me!"

Though he was the object of her infatuation, Tyler's words seemed to enrage Annette further. Christina was shocked to see her clawing madly at his arm, desperate to break free.

"Let me go!" she hollered. "Let go, damn you! I'll kill her! I'll —"

With his free hand, Tyler slapped Annette hard across her face. The sound was like the cracking of a whip, filling the apartment. The blow was solid; immediately Annette's cheek flushed a bright red. Her eyes grew wide with shock, filling with tears, as she crumpled to the floor at his feet.

Christina wanted to get up, run to him, and bury herself in his arms so that she could feel safe. But the wave of darkness that had threatened her finally crested, crashing down and pulling her under.

She saw Tyler bending down toward her, his mouth moving, and then everything went black.

Sitting on the examination table in the doctor's office, Christina winced as Dr. Barlow poked and probed around her knee. Every touch felt as if a thousand needles were being jabbed into her skin. Her knuckles were white from gripping the table beneath her. Biting down on her lower lip, she tried to squelch the scream welling in her throat. She tried to focus on the wall opposite her, but the effort made her vision swim.

"I don't think anything's broken," the doctor said once he'd finished. "But I reckon you're going to be black-and-blue come morning. You're lucky it wasn't worse."

"She meant to kill me," Christina said, shivering at the memory.

"Don't worry. Annette won't be a danger to anyone now."

In the aftermath of Annette's assault, Tyler had first phoned his uncle and then called the sheriff. Annette Wilson now sat in one of Longstock's jail cells. Once her father had been notified of what happened, he'd ranted and raged, demanding that his daughter be set free, but nothing would be getting her out for a long time. Since she'd been slapped Annette hadn't said a single word but had only cried, her head in her hands, her blond hair shaking with each sob.

"That girl was always a bit odd," Dr. Barlow said. "All those years pining for someone who didn't want her must've sent her over the edge."

Christina looked over at Tyler. He stood

in the doorway, his arms folded sternly across his chest, his eyes never leaving her. Usually, his look was easygoing, carefree, a smile only a joke away. Now, there was no humor to be seen in his frown of concern.

"All that matters now is Christina," Tyler said. "She took a heck of a beating before I got there."

"She checks out all right."

"I'm more worried about her head. With the way she blacked out, something could be wrong that you can't see."

"I'm fine," Christina tried to reassure him, but even as the words left her mouth she was again submerged beneath a wave of dizziness and had to steady herself on the table. When her vision cleared, she found that he'd moved to stand beside her, his fingers gently touching her own.

"Don't tell me *that* was nothing," he said.

Christina shook her head carefully.

"It might be a concussion," Dr. Barlow said. "Given what happened tonight, I don't think she should be alone. Someone should keep an eye on her in case things take a turn for the worse. I'll call Callie and see if —"

"She can stay with me," Tyler said firmly.

"It might be best if Callie were to care for her. After all, she's had some training. If things were to worsen . . ."

Tyler shook his head. "If there's a change, I'll call you immediately," he said. "I'll make certain that someone stays by her bed at all times. I'll do it myself if I have to."

Dr. Barlow sighed; Christina could see he understood arguing it further would be pointless. "I'd best call Clara so that she knows what to expect," he said before leaving the room, closing the door behind him.

Now that she was alone with Tyler, Christina was surprised to find that she felt worse. After Annette's attack had ended, all Christina had wanted was the safety of his arms, but now she was reminded of what had happened between her and Holden and how she'd run from Tyler earlier in the day.

"I'm . . . I'm so thankful . . . that you were there . . . ," she mumbled, her eyes moist with tears of both gratitude and shame.

"I couldn't sleep," he explained. "After this afternoon, I lay in bed wondering what it was I'd done wrong. I suppose I should've waited until morning, but I reckon both of us are glad I didn't."

"You deserve an answer."

"Not now," Tyler whispered, patting her hand. "Whatever it was can wait. You need to rest and get your feet back under you. Until then, it doesn't matter."

But Christina knew he was wrong; it *did*

matter, maybe now more than ever. If Tyler knew she'd betrayed him, would he still be willing to spend the night watching over her? In her heart, Christina knew she couldn't allow him to make such an offer without knowing the truth.

But just as she was about to say something, he leaned down toward her and she knew he wanted to kiss her; it wouldn't have been as passionate as what they'd shared under the stars, probably nothing more than a tender kiss on her cheek, but she turned away and started crying.

"Are you all right?" Tyler worriedly asked. "Should I go get my uncle?"

"Stop!" Christina sobbed. "Just stop!"

Though it seemed even harder than struggling with Annette, Christina pushed herself to be honest, even if the consequences broke both their hearts.

"I know that you . . . you only want to help," she struggled to say, "but there's something you need to know . . ."

"What?" he asked.

Looking Tyler straight in the eye, Christina said, "I . . . I kissed Holden . . ."

CHAPTER TWENTY-TWO

Sitting in the small, enclosed space of the examination room, Christina listened intently to the few sounds that reached her. There was the steady, rhythmic ticking of the clock hanging on the wall, the faint sound of Dr. Barlow's voice as he spoke on the phone with his sister, and the frenzied pounding of her own heart. But it was the noise she *didn't* hear that truly unnerved her, the silence of the man standing before her.

Tyler stared at her uncertainly, as if he couldn't believe what he'd heard, as if she'd spoken to him in a foreign language.

"What . . . what did you say . . . ?" he finally managed, his voice a growl.

Christina swallowed hard; it'd been hard enough for her to say such words the first time, but she knew that now that the cork was out of the bottle, it would be impossible to put it back again.

"I . . . I kissed your brother . . ."

This time, she knew that he had heard her; the effect of her words was noticeable. Tyler stiffened and then wobbled, as if he'd been punched in the gut. His lips pursed in a tight grimace as his breathing became ragged, his shoulders heaving in time to his chest. He'd been looking straight into Christina's eyes but now immediately looked away.

"What . . . w-w-hat in the hell are you t-t-alking about?" he stammered.

"I didn't mean for anything to happen," she argued pleadingly. "I swear that I didn't! Holden came to my apartment in the middle of the night. He asked me to go for a walk with him, and after what had just happened I thought I would be providing encourage-ment."

"By kissing him," Tyler spat angrily.

"That's not what I mean! When I came to your mother's house for dinner, he ex-plained what had happened to him during the war. He told me about the cause of his tremors! I thought that he was making another step of progress by finally leaving his room, so I went with him. Everything was fine until . . ." But then she faltered, recalling that fateful night.

"Until what?" Tyler prompted, demanding an answer.

Christina took a deep breath, steeling herself. "We were standing in front of the school," she began, already ashamed for what she was about to say. "Holden explained how disappointed he was that he was never going to be a teacher. All of a sudden, he started having a seizure. We were both panicked, but somehow we managed to calm him until it passed, but then . . ."

"Then what? You decided to kiss him in celebration?!" Tyler snapped dismissively, throwing his hands into the air. His voice was so loud that Christina was certain that Dr. Barlow would've heard every word.

"No! That's not what happened! *He* kissed *me!* I didn't want him to, but he leaned forward and kissed me!"

Tyler hesitated. "Did he force himself on you?" he asked, his question full of accusation. "Did he *make* you do something you didn't want?"

Christina blanched, remembering how she had met Holden's passion, allowing him to pull her close, letting herself go, and rejoicing in his touch. "No . . . no, he didn't . . . but I . . . I wasn't expecting him to . . . well, I . . . ," she struggled, trying to say something that would make sense, but her words were even more jumbled than her spinning head.

"Which one is it?" he demanded. "Did you want him to kiss you or not?"

Christina had no idea how she should answer. Whatever she tried to say sounded more like she was making an excuse, rather than the explanation she intended. Each attempt to tell the truth only seemed to make things worse. Tyler had every right to be furious with her. She had betrayed the trust between them, plain and simple. But that didn't mean their relationship was over.

I just have to figure out how to fix it.

"What happened between Holden and me was a mistake, regardless of how it started," she said slowly, calmly, but firmly, trying to erase the tension that threatened to overwhelm them. "It only lasted for a moment, one that I'd change if I could."

"You regret kissing Holden?"

"I *do,*" she insisted.

"Then how about what we shared in the car?" he huffed. "I suppose you wish that hadn't happened, either."

"Oh, Tyler, no!" Christina cried. "Don't ever say such a thing! I would *never* regret what happened between us!"

Suddenly panicked that things were slipping away, she reached out to take his hand in her own, but he quickly pulled away, disgusted by the thought of her touch.

Without question, she had hurt him, but now that pain was being mercilessly revisited on her tenfold.

"Then why did you do it?" Tyler asked. "I deserve to know why."

This was the question that Christina had been dreading. Not only could she not answer Tyler, but she couldn't explain it to *herself,* either.

But how can I say that to him . . . ?

Before she could offer another apology, none of which seemed to appease him, Tyler asked, "This is why you were so upset this afternoon, isn't it?"

Christina nodded.

"You should've told me." He frowned. "You should have come and told me immediately after it happened."

"Maybe you're right," she agreed, "but ever since that night, I've struggled to come to grips with what I did. I can't give you the answer you want to hear, but whatever else you might think about me, I need for you to understand that my feelings for you haven't changed, not one bit." This time, when she reached out to him Tyler didn't pull away; simply feeling the warmth of his skin gave her a glimmer of hope that this wound might eventually be healed.

"I just can't believe this happened," he

said. "My brother . . ."

"I'm so sorry," Christina replied tearfully.

"I'm . . . I'm going to need time to think about all of this . . . ," Tyler explained, letting go of her hand and slowly making his way toward the door. "But regardless of what I finally decide, after what happened to you tonight I'm still convinced that you need someone to watch over you."

"I can't ask you to do that."

Tyler smiled wistfully. "I'm not going to," he said. "I can't stay under the same roof as the two of you, not now, but my mother can care for you."

Tears began to run freely down Christina's cheeks as she watched him open the door to the hall. Light spilled over him; in that instant, she found him more handsome than ever, a thought that made her feel even worse. Just as he was about to close the door between them without a word, she spoke up.

"There's something I've been meaning to tell you all night," she said, choking back a sob.

"What's that?"

"Thank you for rescuing me. I don't even want to think about what might've happened if you hadn't been there."

"Maybe it's a good thing you didn't tell

me the truth this afternoon," he said with a humorless chuckle.

Christina smiled wistfully as she wiped away tears.

"I'm sorry that she hurt you," Tyler said with genuine concern.

"It wasn't your fault."

"But it's because of me that Annette attacked you."

"You couldn't have known it would happen."

Tyler nodded. "She was always a bit odd, but I never would've thought her capable of something like *this*."

"I'll be all right."

"Don't try to do too much and you will be," he agreed. "When you're better, we'll talk again." With a click, Tyler shut the door behind him.

Christina would have never thought it possible, but telling Tyler about what had happened between her and Holden hurt far worse than Annette's assault.

For the next couple of days, Christina stayed in the spare bedroom of the Sutters' home. The bruises on her arms and around her knee ached painfully, all blossoming into deep purples and blues. Occasionally, she would grow lightheaded, nearly faint, and needed to lie down. She slept often. Clara Sutter waited on her every need, bringing her meals, sitting down to talk, although certainly not about the strange triangle Christina found herself in with the woman's sons. Dr. Barlow stopped each day to check on Christina, examining her wounds and declaring that, while she was better, she still needed her rest. She tried to read, but looking at the pages made her head swim. Mostly, she thought about her predicament.

Neither Tyler nor Holden came to visit her.

Christina gazed out the window, watching the soft pitter-patter of raindrops against the glass, as the wind blew the treetops first one way and then the other. She wondered if the weather inside her head would forever match what was outside, overcast and miserable. Every day, from morning to midnight, she beat herself up over all that had happened. She had come to Longstock full of excitement, convinced that she would create a life in which she could take pride. But nothing had worked out as she'd hoped.

In her worst moments, she considered returning to Minnesota.

Lost deep in her melancholy, Christina jumped at the sound of a knock on her door. Glancing over at the old clock sitting on her dresser, she frowned, confused; it was still an hour before Clara usually brought lunch. A tremor of fear fluttered through Christina; after what had happened with Annette, the thought of answering a visitor at her door was much more frightening. Still, Christina knew that she was safe now.

"Come in," she said, her voice shaking more than she would have liked.

The knob turned, the door creaking slightly on its hinges when it opened. Holden stood out in the hallway. When his eyes met hers, he gave her a gentle smile that made her heart beat faster. She was relieved as well to see that Holden was unhurt. In the aftermath of her confession to Tyler, she'd been worried he might physically assault his brother in a rage of jealousy. Clearly, he'd since been ignoring his brother as much as he'd ignored her.

"I thought that you might like a little company," Holden said.

"That would be nice," she replied.

Stepping inside the room, Holden shut the door behind him, an act that made Christina a bit nervous. Just as she had done in his room, he sat on the corner of her bed and looked at her expectantly. Outside, the squall seemed to grow in intensity.

"How are you feeling?" Holden asked.

"Better," Christina replied. "Your uncle says that I just need a couple more days of rest and I should be as good as new."

"When my mother told me what happened, I couldn't believe it. I've known Annette and her family for as long as I can remember. Even though she's been in love with Tyler since we were children, I never would've thought her capable of doing something like that."

"Tyler said the same thing."

"None of us would have known," Holden explained. "I'm just glad that you weren't hurt any worse than you were." He paused a moment before adding, "I can't imagine what I would do if something happened to you."

Christina didn't know what to say. There was no use in denying that Holden possessed romantic feelings for her, not after what had happened in front of the school. But that didn't mean that she knew how to deal with them. In the end, she concluded that it was best to say nothing.

For an awkward moment, both of them were silent, staring out the window as the early summer rain was blown this way and that. Christina was upset to discover that instead of the respite she had sought, the quiet set her thoughts reeling over the things she *knew* she had to discuss with Holden.

In the days she had spent sleeping under the same roof as he was, Christina had realized that she'd never said a word to Holden about her relationship with Tyler. As far as Holden was concerned, there was nothing untoward about his pursuing her. Would he behave any differently if he knew he was competing with his *brother?* Or would Holden reject her just as firmly as Tyler had, disgusted by the fact that she'd withheld the truth?

But before she could raise the subject, Holden spoke. "I had a tremor last night," he said matter-of-factly.

Guilt raced through Christina; she'd been so worried about her own situation that she hadn't imagined he might have another reason for coming to see her. "What happened?" she asked.

"It was late, well after midnight, and I was downstairs in the living room going through some of my father's old books," he explained. "It started like they always do, sort of out of nowhere. One minute I'm fine and the next my arm starts twitching. When the book I was holding fell to the floor, I was petrified. My heart started pounding. I felt sick to my stomach. It was like everything around me suddenly turned upside down. All that I could think about was that nothing had changed . . . it was the same as always . . ."

"I'm so sorry, Holden," Christina said sympathetically. Disappointment filled her listening to his story; she'd had such hope that things were slowly but surely improving for him that she had been in denial that there could be a setback. But as rotten as she felt about it, she could only imagine Holden's frustration.

Holden sighed and then turned to look at her, smiling, and said, "But then I thought about the night we stood in front of the school. I remembered everything you demanded of me, every word. I tried to relax, to slow things down and breathe. I kept staring at my hand," he explained, holding his left hand up to the light filtering through the window, showing it to her, "and I just kept willing it to stop moving. By the time it finally cooperated, I was covered in sweat and a bit exhausted, but I did it."

"And you did it by yourself." Christina beamed.

"I did," he agreed, "but I never would have known *how* if it weren't for you. Before you entered my life, I thought that I'd always be like this, too frightened to step outside my door, never quite the man I was before Vinnie's death, but now . . . now I see that I might not have to stay this way forever."

"What are you thinking about doing?"

"Right now, I want to be able to walk down the center of Main Street, waving at everyone I know and telling them I'm still alive." He laughed, the sound so infectious that Christina joined in. "But seriously, I'd like to try carving and painting again. I used to get so much enjoyment out of creating scenes, making little people." Christina remembered the first time she'd stepped inside Holden's room and seen the figurines on display. They were beautiful, the work of a true craftsman. "Right now, anything seems possible."

"Even teaching?"

"I don't want to get my hopes up too high, but I might want to give it another try." Holden smiled. "I'd still be afraid of what would happen if I had a tremor standing in front of a classroom of children, but who knows, someday I might find the confidence."

"Your tremors might go away entirely. You might not have to worry."

"If they do, I'll have you to thank." Slowly,

Holden leaned forward, reaching out to take her hand in his. He was staring at her intently, his feelings suddenly as unmistakable as if he were whispering them in her ear.

Though there was still a fluttering in her heart, Christina knew that even something as innocent as holding his hand was a betrayal of her feelings for Tyler. It also wasn't fair to Holden. The last time she'd confessed to something, it had resulted in pain and sorrow, but now, with his thumb lightly tracing an arc across her palm, Christina knew she no longer had a choice. Slowly but firmly, she pulled her hand from his.

"What's the matter?" he asked softly. "Did I do something wrong?"

Holden's words nearly broke Christina's heart. The truth was that he'd done *nothing* wrong. He'd met someone he was attracted to, came to know her, expressed his feelings, and, if only for a moment, had them returned. Now she prepared herself to shatter the illusion she had helped create.

"No, you didn't," she said, "but I did."

Holden paused. "You're talking about the other night . . ."

Christina nodded.

"I didn't mean for what happened to

upset you," he said, his eyes searching for hers, but she would not allow them to meet, "but I don't regret what happened. I certainly didn't show up at your door so that I could kiss you. I just wanted to spend some time with you. I thought that you'd want to see that I was feeling better. But after you helped me with my tremor, once I looked you in the eye I couldn't help myself. I wanted to kiss you, consequences be damned."

"But there *were* consequences," she argued.

"For whom?"

"For me!"

"What are you talking about, Christina?" he asked, growing frustrated.

"What happened wasn't your fault," she tried to assure him, "but I shouldn't have acted as I did."

"Because you kissed me . . . ?"

"Yes."

Holden frowned. "Maybe I could have chosen a better time to show you how strongly I felt about you," he explained insistently, "but I remember what happened when our lips first touched. You kissed me back. I didn't imagine that, did I?"

"No, you didn't," Christina had to admit as tears began to well in her eyes. Desperately, she turned and looked out the window; the rain fell harder now, as if it were trying to match the tension in the room.

"Because of that, because of what all you've done for me, I've come to a decision," Holden said. "I want you to be a part of my future. I want to see where our relationship can take us. I want *you*."

Even though Christina had known that this moment was inevitable, that she'd have to tell Holden about why such a decision was so difficult to make, to finally be confronted with it nearly tore her heart in two. She could see that everything he'd said had been genuine, heartfelt, and earnest. If only she had refused his kiss, then none of this would be necessary, but she could wish all she wanted . . . nothing would change . . .

"I . . . I can't be with you, Holden . . . ," she answered him tearfully.

"Why not?"

"Because . . . because I'm involved with your brother," Christina explained. "I'm involved with Tyler."

The look that crossed Holden's face was exactly the same as the one Tyler had after she confessed in the examination room. With his eyes wide, his mouth slightly opened, and his body jolted so hard with shock that he looked unsteady, Holden was clearly dumbstruck by her words. Shame again filled Christina; she couldn't believe that she'd hurt the both of them as badly as she had. But when Holden spoke, unlike the fire and brimstone that colored Tyler's words, his voice was soft, barely a whisper.

"Are . . . are you . . . in love with him . . . ?"

Christina was stunned by his question. With everything spinning around her, there'd never been time for her to ask such a thing of herself. While Tyler had been exasperating in the beginning, she now cherished the moments they spent together, especially the day he'd shown her his bee-hives and the night they'd kissed underneath the stars.

I don't know . . .

"I never meant to deceive you," she replied. "I would've told you, had I been sure."

"But I didn't give you the chance," he finished her sentence.

Through a haze of tears, she cried, "I'm so sorry!"

"Does he . . . does Tyler know you feel this way?"

For a moment, Christina wondered if Holden wasn't trying to figure a way around the predicament she'd placed him in, but

when she looked at him and saw the resigned look in his eye she knew there was
nothing malicious about his question.

"He does. We . . . we've . . . ," but she
stopped, unable and unwilling to hurt
Holden further with the details of her
relationship with his brother.

Holden's reaction made it clear that he
understood; his shoulders slumped even
further, his expression grew even more
pained. "Did you tell him about . . . our
kiss?" he asked.

"I had to," Christina answered. "But I
kept it in too long. I only told him after he'd
rescued me from Annette. He was so upset
that I don't know if he will want anything
to do with me now."

"Tyler's stubborn to a fault," Holden said,
"but I doubt that even he's a big enough of
a fool to throw *you* away."

Holden rose from the bed and, without
another word, went to the door. Christina
desperately wanted to say something, anything that would soothe the hurt she'd so
clearly caused him, but there was nothing
that could perform such a miracle. Stopping with his hand on the knob, Holden
turned to look at her. Even though, in her
heart, she had made her choice, she knew
that he would someday make a woman

382

extremely happy.

"I'm so sorry, Holden," she said.

Smiling painfully, he replied, "Right now, I think both of us are."

Then he left Christina to her tears.

Chapter Twenty-Three

The day after she'd told Holden about her feelings for Tyler, Christina left the Sutter home and returned to her apartment. When she opened the door for the first time, a shiver of memory raced down her spine. The front room was just as it had been when Tyler had rescued her from Annette's vicious attack; a chair still lay on its side beside the shattered remains of a coffee cup; Christina was surprised to discover that, in the chaos of that night, she couldn't recall when it had been broken.

Just as she swept up the broken cup, Christina went about repairing the pieces of her life.

After thoroughly cleaning her apartment of any signs of the struggle, she did some shopping, wrote long letters to her mother and Charlotte that left out many embarrassing details, and then settled down for a good night's sleep; the next morning would be her first day back at work.

But her last thought before drifting off to sleep was a troubling one . . .

She had yet to hear one word from Tyler.

"Now where in the hell did I put that damn thing?"

Dr. Barlow stomped around his office in a huff. For the last few minutes he'd been out of sorts looking for his stethoscope, and he had proceeded to make the room an even bigger mess. Stacks of books had been toppled and then scattered. Crumpled pieces of paper had been dumped from the trash bin beside the desk. Cupboard doors were yanked open, their contents added to the chaos.

The doctor was as frenzied as his office. His hands kept rising to the top of his head, absently pulling at tufts of his white hair. When he wasn't swearing about the stethoscope, he was muttering to himself under his breath. Occasionally, he took off his glasses to pinch at the top of his nose, his eyes shut tight. He was as hard to be around as a bear awakened early from its winter of hibernation.

"Do you remember where you were the last time you saw it?" Christina asked from the safety of the doorway.

"If I knew that, I wouldn't be standing here half out of my mind, now would I?" he snapped. No sooner had the last angry world left his mouth than Dr. Barlow stopped pacing about, took a deep breath, and said, "I'm sorry that I spoke to you that way, Christina. I'm a bit out of sorts today."

"Apology accepted," she replied. "Let's just find it."

Watching the doctor as he went back to searching for his medical instrument, albeit a bit less angrily than before, Christina wondered if he was out of sorts because he'd resumed taking morphine. It pained her to even think such a thing, especially remembering how he had promised her he'd given it up, but he'd been a grouch since she'd walked in the door that morning. He'd even been curt with a couple of patients, leaving it up to her to mend things once he'd left the room.

Ever since the afternoon she'd been knocked to the ground by the strange man, Christina had worried that Dr. Barlow might fall off the wagon. It was obvious that he was stressed by their encounter. Maybe he'd found comfort with an old companion, taking the drug so that his worries would vanish. Still, she didn't dare ask, not with the mood he was in.

386

Instead, she started looking for the stethoscope. She didn't want to rummage around in the mess of books at her feet, so she began looking elsewhere: on the chair nearest the door, the top of his desk, anywhere the doctor hadn't already been. It didn't take long for her to find it; it was wadded up and stuffed into the deepest pocket of a jacket hanging from the coat tree.

"Here it is," she said, holding it out to him.

"Damn it all!" Dr. Barlow swore as he snatched it from her hand.

This time, there was no apology.

Leaving Dr. Barlow to fume in his office, Christina walked out to the empty waiting room. Callie sat behind her desk, sorting files.

"The doctor sure is in a foul mood today," Christina complained.

"It's days like this one where I'm glad I sit out here." Callie smiled, patting her desk. "Course, that doesn't mean you're not gettin' plenty of my sympathy."

"I just watched him tear apart his office looking for his stethoscope."

"Did he check his coat pocket?" Christina couldn't have held back her laughter if it was a contest with a bushel full of money as the prize. Callie joined in, chuckling along with her, knowing that she'd been right.

But even though they were laughing, Christina still couldn't help worrying about Dr. Barlow. The thought that he was abusing morphine again kept nagging at her. She'd confided her fears to Callie before . . .

"How has the doctor been since I've been gone?" she asked.

Callie rolled her eyes. "You see how grouchy he is today?" she replied. "He's been a pain in the rear end the whole time. Complainin' 'bout one thing right after another. Doesn't seem to make any difference whether it's deserved or not, he just keeps right on barkin'."

Again, Christina remembered the look in the strange man's eyes when he turned to face the doctor; for that matter, she recalled the fear Dr. Barlow had shown her immediately after the man left.

"You . . . you don't suppose he's started taking drugs again, do you?" she asked.

"No, that ain't it." Callie shook her head. "As a matter of fact, I think it's just the opposite."

"You do?"

Callie rose from her chair to sit on the edge of the desk, close to where Christina stood. She paused before she spoke, cocking her head and listening, making certain the doctor wasn't about to interrupt them.

"I had an uncle back in Alabama, my mother's brother, Earl, who had a problem with drinkin' every bit as bad as the doctor has with his drug," she began, "though he didn't come to it the same direction, took it up out of choice, not 'cause he was bein' chased by demons he wanted to escape, but it had its claws in him just the same.

"One night, Earl had been out drinkin' in the tavern where he spent almost every night. Though he's drunker than a skunk, he gets in his car and starts speedin' home. He ain't in no shape to drive, so he ain't far down the road when somethin' startles him and he crashes right into a tree. Somehow, even though his car is a complete wreck, Earl walks away without a scratch.

"The only answer Earl could come up with was that the Good Lord was giving him a chance: give up the drink or burn in hell. Well, Earl wasn't about to begin arguin' with Him, so he poured all his bottles of booze down the drain and struggled to stay sober.

"Now, most days, Earl was the sweetest man. He always had a joke or a sweet tucked away in a pocket, waitin' for one of us to come 'long so he could give it to us, but without drink in his life he turned 'bout as

389

rotten as a tomato in the summer sun. Walked round with a sour face, shoutin' at anyone unwise enough to get too close, miserable most days. Eventually, he got used to it, returned to bein' most of the good man he'd been, but it weren't an easy path to walk. The way I reckon things, Dr. Barlow's on that same road."

Christina felt the sharp sting of embarrassment listening to Callie. What she described sounded an awful lot like how Dr. Barlow had acted ever since Christina had found him in his backyard. Could it be that his grouchiness was the price he suffered through to stay off of morphine? If so, he was a far stronger man than she was giving him credit for.

"I think you might be right," she said.

"That's why we've got to be *extra* patient with him now," Callie explained. "It's clear he's strugglin' to get through this. He don't need us givin' him more grief on top of it. After all, it's like the good book says; you can't judge a man without walkin' a mile in his shoes. Whenever I imagine what he's goin' through, it makes it a lot easier to turn that other cheek."

Before Christina could respond, Dr. Barlow stalked down the hallway. Putting on his jacket, he looked at her and said curtly, "If we're going to make those appointments to the south of town, we'll need to get moving. Don't dillydally around; just grab your things and get to the car." Without waiting for a response, he turned and walked away.

Christina understood what Callie had said about being patient with him, but Dr. Barlow was making it awfully difficult.

Christina spent the rest of the afternoon gritting her teeth at every grumbled complaint, every snide comment, and every needlessly barked command Dr. Barlow hurled her way. Occasionally, a sick farm-wife or sore orchard hand would worriedly glance at Christina in disbelief of the way the doctor spoke to her, but she responded by plastering a grin on her face and weathering the storm. Regardless of how she acted, his words still stung.

Leaving the last farmstead, where Dr. Barlow had humiliated her by chastising her about how she was putting a bandage on a woman's painful, bleeding sore, Christina had had enough.

Stopping just short of the coupe, she decided that unless he revealed the reason for his grumpiness, she would rather walk home than be subjected to another abusive car ride.

"What is the matter with you today?" she asked, folding her arms over her chest and refusing to budge an inch until he answered. "You haven't had one good thing to say about my work all day."

"I have so," Dr. Barlow grunted, tossing his bag into the backseat.

"Then what was it?"

Dr. Barlow opened his mouth to speak, but no sound came out. He blinked a couple of times, trying to come up with an answer that simply wasn't there, before he sighed deeply.

"You're right," he said. "I shouldn't be treating you like I have, especially after everything you've been through, and this your first day back. I've just got a lot on my mind."

"Then why don't you tell me what it is?"

He looked back down the drive, far away from her piercing stare. "Can't this wait for another time?" he asked.

"Ever since I came to your house that afternoon," Christina said, not needing to mention what she had found, "you've told me to wait for an answer to all my questions. Doesn't there have to be a time when I get them? You can't just keep on putting it off forever."

"I told you about why I take morphine," he said defensively.

"You told me some of it," she agreed, "but we both know there were things left unsaid."

Dr. Barlow didn't answer; Christina noticed that even though he didn't agree with her, he didn't contradict her, either.

"Does this have anything to do with the man who collided with you in the street the other day?" she asked.

Without his saying a word, Dr. Barlow's reaction told Christina everything she wanted to know. His eyes flew to hers, wide open, even a bit frightened, as his mouth puckered into a tight grimace. Her assumption had been correct, her words striking their mark.

"Who is he?" she asked.

Dr. Barlow looked away, making no response.

"Did he threaten you?" Christina pressed, wanting him to open up to her.

But still she got no answer.

Christina simply could not believe the way each of the Sutter men behaved around her; getting something out of them was as difficult as pulling teeth. But eventually, both Holden and Tyler had confided in her. It was her hope that their uncle would be no different.

"I want the truth, Doctor," she insisted.

"Not here," he finally answered. "Just get in the car. I'll tell you what you want to know while we drive back to Longstock."

Christina nodded. Just as she was about to open the passenger's door, the doctor stopped her.

"Wait," he said. When she looked up, he tossed the coupe's keys across the roof and she reflexively caught them. "If I'm going to tell you these things, it'll be in both of our interests if you're driving. I'm sure you've noticed, but I'm not so good behind the wheel."

Driving the coupe back toward Longstock, Christina took each turn carefully so as not to screech the tires, checked her side mirrors to see if anyone was coming up behind them, and all the while maintained a respectable speed. In short, her driving was the opposite of the doctor's. Still, she knew that her attention wasn't focused entirely on the road.

Dr. Barlow sat beside her, one arm draped out the open window on the passenger's side. Even though he had promised to tell her what was weighing on his mind, he'd yet to say a word. Several miles had passed, and still he stared out the window, watching the countryside slide past.

Christina didn't press him; something about the way he'd spoken to her back at the farmstead led her to believe that this time would be different. A few moments later, her patience was rewarded.

"You were right to worry about that man," Dr. Barlow finally said, still looking away from her, his eyes never leaving the orchards. "Knocking a lady to the ground is the least that degenerate is capable of. Ever since that day, I've been all out of sorts."

"When he turned back to face you, he looked so . . . violent . . ."

"Dangerous is what he is. If I'd gotten a better look at him when he went past, I never would've shouted after him. Messing with Luther Rickert is about as wise as sticking your hand into a nest of vipers!"

Even the man's name, Luther Rickert, sent a shiver of unease racing down the length of Christina's spine.

"For the life of me, I still can't figure out how two fine people the likes of Christian and Celia Rickert had such a boy," he kept on. "You'd have been damn hard-pressed to find two nicer, more good-hearted folks. Why they got two sons as rotten as Luther and his brother, Donnie, only the Lord knows.

"Even when they were boys, whenever Celia brought them into the clinic you expected there to be trouble. Luther would pocket anything left lying around, some bandages or a tongue depressor, anything he could get his mitts on. Donnie went along with anything his brother did. He idolized Luther. In the end, that's probably what killed him."

"Luther's brother is dead?" Christina exclaimed.

"Yes," Dr. Barlow said, finally turning to face her. "And Luther thinks that I'm the one responsible for it."

"But why?" she asked, quickly righting the drift of the car onto the shoulder of the road. "Why would he think it was your fault?"

The doctor sighed deeply but didn't answer Christina's question.

She was just about to ask it again when he said something that surprised her. "Though it pains me to admit it, there's one thing that Luther and I have in common," he confessed.

"You're nothing like that man," she disagreed.

"In most every respect I would agree with you," he said with a faint smile. Dr. Barlow paused, as if he was weighing his words, before finally adding, "It isn't easy to say, but Luther and I are *both* addicts. We're not attracted to the *same* poison," the doctor explained. "It isn't morphine that Luther has a taste for; it's alcohol."

"Just like Archie," Christina remarked.

"The problem is that there's *nothing* likeable about Luther when he's been drinking," Dr. Barlow explained. "He was terrible enough a boozer before, but when both of his parents died in a car accident Luther wasted nearly every dime he inherited boozing. After the money was spent, next went all of his parents' belongings so he could keep getting drunk. Once all of that was gone, he turned to the one thing he was ever any good at."

"What was that?"

"Stealing," the doctor explained with a frown. "Luther would grab Donnie, toss him in the back of the car, and the two of them would drive to some town around here and rob a place in the middle of the night. They never got caught, but the sheriff started keeping a close eye on them nonetheless. Donnie must've been the one careful enough to ensure they never made too big a mistake, because Luther's mind was focused only on getting the alcohol at any cost.

"Finally, it got to the point where Luther must not have wanted to work so hard for it. Rather than drive out of Longstock and take the risk while robbing some place blind, he decided to cut to the chase and hit somewhere in town. As luck would have it, he made a choice that we'd both regret."

"The clinic." Christina understood.

"Exactly," Dr. Barlow said. "So one night about a year ago, Luther and Donnie busted out a window back in the alleyway, made their way inside, and started rummaging through the cabinets and drawers, searching for money or drugs they could sell. They didn't know that I keep everything of value locked away. To make matters worse, they weren't too quiet about breaking the glass and someone saw them. They probably hadn't been inside ten minutes before they noticed the police car cruising past the front window. I imagine Donnie had to pull Luther to the back door even then."

"They got away?"

"For a bit. Luther drove out of town like a bat from hell, the sheriff and his men right behind. Maybe he was already drunk, maybe he was worried about getting caught, maybe he was just driving too fast, but regardless of the reason, Luther drove the getaway car over a ridge and plummeted straight down into an orchard. Smashed right into an apple tree."

"And that's how Donnie died?"

"No," Dr. Barlow answered, "although I reckon it would have been better for everyone if he had."

"That's a terrible thing to say!"

"I haven't always felt this way," he replied evenly. "But what happened after the sheriff's men hauled Donnie Rickert's broken body out of that wrecked car worsened the lives of everyone involved."

"What happened?" Christina asked, though a part of her dreaded learning the answer.

"Donnie was brought back to town and taken straight to the clinic. I had just arrived, one of the deputies had come for me once the chase had ended," he explained, "and I was surveying the damage that'd been done when they hurried him through the door. Donnie was a mess, bones broken, his clothes so soaked with blood that I had no idea what color they were supposed to be, clinging to life by a thread. I tried everything I could think of, but fifteen minutes later, Donnie was gone."

"It sounds to me like you did the best you could."

He didn't answer, choosing to again look

away at the countryside.

"What?" Christina asked, a sickening feeling filling her gut. "What is it?"

Dr. Barlow sighed deeply, his shoulders drooping as his eyes grew faintly wet. "That night . . . before the sheriff's men came for me . . . I'd given myself a shot," he admitted. "It wasn't as much as the afternoon you found me, but enough for me to not exactly have my wits about me. I've thought about treating Donnie Rickert every night since, and I don't believe that the morphine affected how I cared for him, but . . . I can't say for certain . . ."

The very thing that Christina had feared might happen, that when someone desperately needed his care Dr. Barlow would be too messed up to provide it, now seemed to already have occurred. There was no satisfaction to be gained from her worries having been well-founded, only sadness.

"Luther hates you because he blames you for the death of his brother?" she wondered aloud.

Dr. Barlow nodded his agreement.

"How does he know that you'd taken morphine?"

"He doesn't," he explained. "Luther thinks that the reason Donnie died was because I was upset that they'd broken into

400

my clinic. He believes that I got my revenge by refusing to treat his brother."

"Why isn't he in jail for trying to steal from you?"

"Because he joined the Army instead."

Christina had heard about men being given such an option; the authorities would much rather have them with a gun in their hands fighting the enemy than uselessly taking up space in a prison cell.

"So his running into you the other day wasn't an accident," she said. "You think that he wants his revenge?"

"That's the way I see it."

"Aren't you afraid that he could do something violent?"

"A man like Luther doesn't know any other way."

Christina couldn't believe how matter-of-factly Dr. Barlow answered her questions. It was as if he was resigned to his fate; not knowing for certain whether his drug use had contributed to Donnie Rickert's death clearly weighed heavily on him, a sliver of guilt he couldn't remove.

"You should go to the sheriff," Christina said, shivering at the way Luther had winked at her.

"There's nothing he could do." The doctor shook his head. "All Luther's done is try to frighten me, but he hasn't broken any laws to do it. Until he does, the sheriff's hands are tied."

"But couldn't he talk to him? Try to figure out what he's up to?"

"Luther would only laugh in his face."

Unease raced across Christina's chest. She didn't like the idea of someone confronting Luther about his hatred for the doctor, but she thought even less of just doing nothing. She was about to suggest another tack when Dr. Barlow gently placed his hand on her arm.

"There's no reason for you to be frightened, my dear," he said softly. "Luther won't do *you* any harm. No, I'm afraid that he has his sights set on me and, until he finally decides he's through toying around, I'll just have to live with it. For everyone's sake," he smiled faintly, "let's hope that I do a better job and stop being such a grouch."

Christina knew that Dr. Barlow was trying to put the best face on a terrible situation, but he had done little to ease her concerns.

"After all," he mumbled, turning back to the window, "I just might deserve whatever he has in store for me."

Shocked by such a thought, Christina

remained silent, instead concentrating on the winding road before them, her fingers clenched to the steering wheel in order to keep them from shaking.

CHAPTER TWENTY-FOUR

Two days after her conversation with Dr. Barlow about Luther Rickert, Christina walked down the faint path through the woods behind the garage where Tyler worked. High above the thick canopy of trees, threatening clouds blanketed the sky. A persistent breeze rustled the branches, pushing them this way and that, and stirred the bushes beside her. The fresh scent of rain filled the afternoon. No birds chirped and no animals scurried through the brush, choosing instead to huddle somewhere safe and dry out of the coming squall.

But Christina ignored all of that, determinedly striding forward. Ever since Tyler had turned his back on her at the doctor's office following Annette Wilson's brutal attack, Christina hadn't heard a word from him. At first, she'd been willing to remain patient; after all, it was undeniably her fault that he was so upset. But now, she'd become annoyed. Even if Tyler had decided that their relationship was over, the least he could've done was say it to her face, rather than leave her wondering.

Last night, she'd called the Sutter home and asked Clara if she could speak with him; Clara's answer had been that Tyler was working in the garage and was refusing to come to the phone, even after his mother had told him who was calling. Christina had politely thanked her, then hung up the phone and fumed for the remainder of the night. She'd wakened with the determination to make him decide their future, whether he wanted to face her or not.

Trying to find him, she'd gone to the garage where he worked. When one of the other mechanics had told her that Tyler had taken the day off to care for his "precious little bugs," Christina had turned without a word and headed around the garage and into the woods. Remembering how he'd insisted on her seeing his hideaway made her flush with anger at how he was avoiding her now.

"Why does he have to be so difficult?" she muttered to herself. "I was truthful . . . I apologized."

Tyler's reluctance to speak with her was made worse by her painful, yet still necessary, talk with Holden. As hard as it had been, Christina had made her choice; though she still had no explanation for why she had kissed Holden short of her getting caught up in the moment, she had rejected his advances, choosing instead to follow her heart to Tyler. Now came the hard part of convincing him that her feelings and commitment to them was genuine. All she needed was a chance.

No matter what, he's going to hear what I have to say.

Tyler was just where she was told he would be. When Christina entered the clearing, she saw him stooped before his three bee-hives, clothed in the outlandish costume he'd pulled from his trunk and swathed in a thick column of grey, billowing smoke. He knelt close to the ground, intent as he peered inside something, his back turned to her; even if she'd been standing just before him, Christina doubted he would've noticed.

Bees flitted all around her, buzzing incessantly as they wafted among the clusters of clover that covered the ground. She wondered if they were so hard at work because the hive had been opened, as she recalled how Tyler had explained that they became confused by the smoke, or the changing weather forced them to collect pollen before the rain fell.

Mindful of where she stepped, Christina moved forward, stopping a close, yet secure, distance behind Tyler. From where she stood, she could see what kept his rapt attention. One of the hives' drawers had been pulled out and laid on the ground. With the lid off, she could see that there were nearly a dozen planks that were slid vertically into the drawer; it looked like files in a cabinet. Tyler had lifted one, examining it; thick clusters of bees clung to the honeycomb that had been intricately constructed on the sheet. Even in the drab light of the marbled clouds, Christina could see the honey glisten where it leaked through the comb. She was also shocked to see that Tyler wasn't wearing gloves, just as he'd explained.

One after the other, he lifted the sheets of comb, inspecting them. While he painstakingly worked, angry bees buzzed about his head, landing on his bare skin. It was almost certain that he was being stung, though he gave no sign of any discomfort. His movements were slow, measured, and the care he took with the bees' home was apparent.

While she watched him work, Christina

was reminded of why she'd become attracted to Tyler Sutter. Though he was brash and outspoken, sometimes painfully rude, he was also patient, meticulous, and passionate about the things he cared strongest about. He had allowed her to see the real him, the one he kept hidden out of sight, and standing there she realized that what she felt in return was undoubtedly *love.* In that instant, she knew that she would fight for their relationship, that she would try to convince him that it couldn't be easily discarded, no matter what.

Finally, when the drawer was replaced, Tyler stepped back and took off his enshrouded hat, his face sweaty. He turned to look at the sky, and that was when he noticed her.

"I never expected to see you here," he said with a faint smile.

"With the way you've avoided me, I started wondering if you wanted to see me *anywhere,*" Christina snapped back. "How long did you think I'd sit around waiting for you to show up?"

"I was going to come for you," Tyler replied.

"When?"

"Soon. I just needed time to get my head straight." Absently, he wiped a hand across his brow; Christina could see a triangle of angry, red welts as they blossomed on his skin. "I'm not sure that I have, but then again, maybe I never will . . . ," he finished ominously, his eyes holding hers coldly.

From off in the distance, a rumble of thunder rolled across the valley, heralding the storm that was about to break.

"I told you that I was sorry for what happened with Holden."

Tyler shook his head. "But those are nothing more than words. In the end, what matters is that you kissed my brother. Even after the feelings between us, you couldn't resist a chance to throw yourself into his arms."

Christina winced at his painful, unexpected words. "Are you as angry with Holden as you are at me?"

"I was," he said. "After I left my uncle's clinic, all I wanted to do was rush up those stairs, kick down his door, and beat the hell out of him. But as I walked, I realized that I couldn't blame him. Holden might have done plenty to earn my hatred, but he's not the sort who would steal a girl from anyone. In the end, I figured that he had no idea about the two of us."

"He didn't," Christina admitted.

"Because of that, I couldn't be angry with him."

"Just me."

Tyler said nothing; with the way he looked away, he didn't have to.

Thinking about it, Christina knew that, in the past, she would have been emotionally devastated by Tyler's reaction; tears would have flowed freely as she pleaded with him, practically begging for his forgiveness. But now, she was surprised to find that she was angry, almost furious, at him for holding her one transgression, a kiss that was measured in seconds, against her without even trying to understand how it could have happened.

"When we first met," she said, the words tumbling from her with a shockingly strong sense of urgency, "you sat at your mother's dinner table and said that your brother was a coward for staying in his room. But now I see that it's you who is really afraid."

"What did you say?" he asked incredulously.

"I said that you're afraid!" Christina shouted, her anger finally getting the better of her. "All it took was this one moment, one mistake that I willingly confessed to, and you're going to let it destroy everything we have between us, all without a fight. If you weren't frightened, if you didn't want to run away just like you accused Holden of doing, you'd stand your ground and do whatever it took instead of pushing me away."

"That's not what I'm doing," Tyler argued.

"Yes, it is!"

"You kissed my brother." He shook his head. "That's not something I can forgive so easily, especially without an explanation."

"I told you, I don't have one to give," she kept on, refusing to quit. "I might've done it out of pity for everything he's been through, because I was caught up in the moment, because it was the middle of the night. I have no answer, not capable of satisfying you! What matters is that I regret what happened! I told Holden the same thing! All I want is —"

"Wait," Tyler said. "Wait; you've talked to Holden about this?"

Christina nodded. "He came to my room while I was recuperating at your mother's house. I told him the same things I've told you: that what happened that night was a mistake, that I could never be with him because I've already got romantic feelings for you! I love *you,* Tyler!"

Her declaration struck them both mute. Filling the silence between them, a crack of lightning laced across the sky to the south, a brilliant flash that was almost immediately followed by a tremendous crash of thunder. Even as the first spattering of raindrops fell from the dishwater clouds, Christina refused to budge, even to blink, waiting for his response.

"Do you . . . do you mean that?" Tyler said hesitantly.

Moving a step forward, Christina took him by his hands, watching as a pair of bees floated between their faces, hesitating before disappearing over his shoulder. Breathlessly, she said, "I have never lied to you. Not about Holden and certainly not about my feelings for you."

"It's just . . . ," he trailed. "It's hard to forget . . ."

"I'm not asking you to forget," she soothed. "All I want is for you to understand and forgive. What's already happened is for the past. For both of our sakes, let's leave it there. Allowing it to threaten our future, that would be the greatest mistake. Can you do that, Tyler? Can we have a future?"

Before he could answer, the heavens opened above them. Torrents of rain pounded down on them, soaking them through. Christina was shocked by how cold the incessant rain was, instantly shivering as the droplets struck her bare skin. Before she could even think about running for shelter,

Tyler grabbed her by the hand, pulling her with him.

"Come on!" he shouted over the deluge.

The rain fell so hard and so fast that the ground beneath their feet turned almost instantly to mud. Christina struggled to stay upright, her feet sliding and treacherously slipping as she kept moving forward. Shielding her eyes from the pouring sky, she saw that Tyler was leading them to the dilapidated building leaning dangerously close to collapse in the corner of the pasture.

Panting, they raced through the open doorway. Though they had been caught under the storm for only a few seconds, Christina's clothes were completely soaked through, clinging to her goose-pimpled skin.

The inside of the building was barren; a few random pieces of old, broken furniture had been tossed against one wall, and a cot and water bucket sat in a corner. Everywhere, the smell of damp hay lingered. Rain pounded on the tin roof in a loud drumbeat.

"Wrap this around yourself."

Christina hadn't realized that she was shivering until Tyler draped a worn horse blanket across her shoulders. It didn't smell particularly fresh, but she was thankful for the warmth it provided. As her chill receded, all she could do was watch as the storm unloaded before her.

"Did you mean what you said?"

Christina turned to look at Tyler. Water ran in rivulets from his short hair, cascading down his neck. Lightning flashed outside, illuminating his face; she had never found him more handsome than she did at that moment.

"Do you really love me?" he asked, a bit more insistently.

Looking at him, Christina felt her heart flutter. Suddenly, nothing in her life seemed more certain. When she'd first met Tyler Sutter, falling in love with him had been the *furthest* thing from her mind. But somehow, by allowing her to witness who he truly was inside, to see him as he let few others see, he had caused a feeling to begin welling inside her, finally overflowing.

"I do," she said simply. "Even though you've never said that you love me."

Tenderly, Tyler leaned down, his eyes closing just before his lips found hers. Tentatively, Christina rose to meet him, enjoying the touch of his whiskers against her soft cheek. When she began to kiss him, unfamiliar sensations of passion thundered through her. Feeling Tyler's hands roam across her shoulder and then down all the way to the small of her back, pulling her tight against him, made her gasp involuntarily.

While her kiss with Holden had been momentarily pleasurable in the instants before her head cleared, Christina had no misgivings now. She was nervous but not uncomfortable, anxious but still excited. But as their kiss continued, she was surprised when Tyler gently pushed her away.

He looked at her imploringly, as if he wanted her to understand his thoughts without his giving them voice. Christina *knew* what he was thinking, but she refused to interrupt him when he told her, his voice barely heard over the roar of the unending rain against the building.

"I do love you, Christina," he said softly, melting her heart.

There was no reason for her to respond with words; instead, she kissed him again, this time more passionately than before, knowing that something special was happening.

Christina hesitated for only an instant when Tyler pulled her toward the cot. She followed, her fingers trailing lightly over the sleeve of his beekeeping outfit. She watched as he undid the zipper, pulling it to his waist, before starting to unbutton his shirt. Suddenly, as her eyes grew wider, he stopped.

"Christina, wait," he said. "Is this something that you *want* to do? I don't want you to have any regrets."

When she had stepped into the clearing only minutes earlier, Christina would never have imagined that it would lead to them making love. But from the moment Tyler's lips had touched her own, when she had heard him tell her that he loved her, she'd known where things were headed. Though she had little experience in love, especially when it came to the more physical aspects, it didn't mean that she was naïve. Allowing Tyler into her heart had made making love with him inevitable, desirable, something she anticipated.

Christina thought of all they had shared: the laughs in his mother's kitchen, Christina's listening as he admitted his troubled feelings toward Holden, the passion of their first kisses beneath the moon and thousands of stars. She remembered her incredible relief at seeing his face above her when he'd saved her from Annette's attack. She even recalled the look of shock that had darkened his face when she'd admitted kissing Holden. All that had happened to them had led here, to this old, run-down building, to this instant. Though she was undeniably nervous, she was determined not to let it show.

"There's nothing that I want more," she whispered. "Nothing . . ."

"I just want —"

Placing her finger on his lips, Christina shook her head.

Tyler understood what she was saying to him. Tentatively at first, she took over for him, resuming the undoing of his shirt's buttons as he did the same to hers; feeling his fingers brush against her chest sent shivers of pleasure racing through her. In a matter of seconds, he was peeling off her soaking wet blouse. Her skirt, shoes, and underwear soon followed it into a heap on the dirt floor. With a little assistance, he soon joined her, naked before the bed. Without shame, they looked each other up and down; Christina marveled at Tyler's taut body, the muscles of his chest, arms, and stomach clearly defined. Gently, she reached out and touched him. When her fingertips drifted through the thick hair of his chest, Tyler sucked air between his teeth, quivering. It gave Christina a thrill to have pleasured him.

But then when Tyler reached out to explore her body, she understood why he reacted in such a way. As his hand trailed across her belly and then up to cup her breasts, the sensation was so intense that it made her weak in the knees, but somehow she managed to stay upright. His thumb traced a path around her nipple and she thought that that was it, she was going to collapse, but she fell forward, thankful that Tyler was so strong.

Once her spasms had subsided, they lay down on the bed, huddling beneath the blanket. Even over the pounding rain, Christina could hear her heart beating. She raised her hands to frame his face, searching every inch of his features, tracing the faint lines around his mouth.

"How was I ever so lucky to have found you?" she asked.

"Hey, I'm the one who's supposed to ask that question," he replied, smiling.

"I don't have an answer."

"Me either."

When their lips touched yet again, Christina melted into Tyler's embrace. Feeling his body as it pressed against hers, she couldn't resist the temptation to start exploring all of the places she'd never touched before. Tracing a path down his chest, then his abdomen, and then skirting along the length of his thigh, Christina gasped when her hand touched his penis. It was both harder and larger than expected, but she knew that was a sign of his arousal at being naked beside her, so her first tentative touch became longer, more confident. With every movement, Tyler hissed and groaned into her mouth; both stoked the fires of her passion, urging her to do more.

But it was now Tyler's turn to give as good as he got. As sensitive as her nipples had been, Christina shook with unbelievable ripples of pleasure when his hand crossed her stomach and moved between her legs. Just the slightest pressure was nearly enough to make her see stars. It was almost too much, nearly painful in its way, but the last thing she wanted was for it to stop. Her excitement had stimulated her body, making it easier for him to slip around, increasing her desire for what they were about to do.

"Oh, Tyler!" she gasped.

Hungrily, she continued to kiss him. Even though there had not been many opportunities for them to become familiar with each other physically, Christina still found that things between them were never awkward; each touch was met with a perfect response, and every time they sped up or slowed down it seemed to anticipate just what the other wanted. Even now, she tempered the passion of her kisses and found him matching her, looking deep into her eyes.

"I want you," Christina said.

"Not as much as I want you." He smiled, unable to resist the tease.

Smoothly, Tyler rose above her, moving the worn blanket so that they were protected from the chill of the rain. Christina spread her legs to welcome him as he prepared to enter her.

Never in her life had Christina felt so right about anything. Right then, the confusion that had plagued her about Holden seemed miles away, something to be forgotten forever. The choice she had made between the Sutter brothers was difficult to be sure, but now she knew she'd chosen wisely. Tyler stimulated her, physically and in every other way. He was challenging, a prankster, but caring and loyal, too. Now they were to be joined in a way she'd never been before, as woman and man.

At first, when Tyler gently allowed his weight to move forward, Christina gasped as a sharp pain pierced her. She'd known to expect it, but it still caught her momentarily off-guard. Gritting her teeth, she tried not to let Tyler see the discomfort she felt, but she wasn't successful.

"Are you all right?" he asked, concerned.

Her answer was to kiss him.

Tyler moved inside of her slowly, carefully,

waiting for any reaction from her that would signal he'd gone too far. But Christina grew steadily used to the new sensation of having him inside of her. Each stroke became more pleasurable than the last. Her hands grasped his waist, her fingers digging into his flesh. Sweat began to bead on her brow and between her breasts, but the warmth was pleasurable, shared between them. Their breathing became ragged, their chests rising and falling in unison every time he pushed deeper.

Tyler began to move faster and Christina's urgency grew with every increase in speed. His mouth was against her ear, his breath hot and wet, their bodies mingled.

"I love you!" she cried, her hands running up his back and raking through the short hair on the back of his head.

Christina climbed up and up a mountain of pleasure until she finally peaked, shuddering as spasms raced through her. Desperately, she bit down on her lip in an attempt to stifle a scream, but she couldn't have hoped to keep a whimper from escaping. This time, there was no chance that Tyler could mistake the sounds she made as discomfort; instead, they energized him. His hands roamed almost pleadingly, sliding up and down her thighs before one rose to her breast, giving it a squeeze that made her gasp again.

Never could Christina have imagined that making love could feel so wonderful. She gave in to it fully, willing to let this unbelievable experience take her wherever it wished. She wanted it to last forever, for the rest of her relationship with this man to be as carefree, as passionate, and as indescribable as it was now.

She was a woman, truly and completely, with a man to share in her life.

"I . . . I can't last . . . ," he moaned.

"You don't have to, my love," she said as she kissed his neck.

Tyler's shoulders quaked, his arms growing as tight as tree trunks, and the movements of his hips became frenzied. Suddenly, it all came to a full, sudden halt. Christina felt his seed spill into her, filling her with a warmth that coursed throughout her entire body. Spent, Tyler pressed down on her, heavy, yet he was clearly not allowing his full weight to fall.

Everything was perfect, just as she had hoped for. Listening to his breathing competing with the steady rain, feeling his heart as it beat into her, knowing that no other man would ever touch her in such a way,

Christina couldn't resist a big, beaming smile.

This was what she had come to Longstock for: a new beginning, a new life complete with adventure, laughs, even some tears, but especially love.

"I love you, Christina," he breathed in her ear.

"And I love you," she answered, never wanting that moment to end.

But, for the second time, someone was watching them . . .

Chapter Twenty-Five

Stepping out of the run-down building, Christina took a deep breath of the cool evening air and looked up at the night sky. The storm that had drenched them with rain only hours earlier had moved on to the east, leaving behind a cloudless sky bejeweled with thousands of twinkling stars. Only a winking, thin sliver of the moon hung low in the west.

Christina shivered. After she and Tyler had made love, they fell asleep, their bodies entwined, each warmed by the other's bare skin beneath the worn blanket. She blinked slowly awake, content to revel in Tyler's touch for a while, before rising and putting on her still-damp clothes. There'd been no other choice; she couldn't bring herself to go outside naked, and she couldn't have taken the blanket without leaving Tyler uncovered. Even without any wind, it was still cold; she rubbed her hands up and down her arms for warmth.

What a magical day . . .

Christina still couldn't believe what'd happened and wondered if she hadn't been dreaming. She'd always felt certain this day would come, somewhere, with the right man, but never in her wildest imagination had she daydreamed it would be so perfect. Just thinking about what would come next, the future she and Tyler might build, filled her with hope and anticipation. Charlotte had found the man of her dreams, and now her little sister had done the same . . .

Walking away from where Tyler still slept, Christina was more aware than ever of the sights and sounds around her. Moths darted across the sky, searching to and fro. Crickets sang across the abandoned field. Droplets of dew clung to every blade of grass, as many as the multitude of stars above. Glancing over at the beehives, Christina wondered if the bees were sleeping as peacefully as the man who tended them.

Christina absently followed a small creek that ran heavy with rainwater, lost in her own thoughts. When she heard a twig snap somewhere behind her, causing her to jump, she had no idea how long she'd been walking. Certain she knew who was behind her, she spun around quickly, hoping to ruin

Tyler's attempt to frighten her.

But discovering who had followed her chilled Christina to the bone. It wasn't Tyler but rather the man who was responsible for knocking her to the ground, the man who mistakenly blamed Dr. Barlow for the death of his brother.

It was Luther Rickert.

"Oh," she gasped, unable to contain her surprise.

Even in the faint light of the night sky, he looked dangerous. When she'd discovered him approaching, he'd been hunched over slightly, stalking toward her, but now that she'd seen him, he straightened, though she could still see the measured tension in his wiry body. His body and clothing were wet from head to toe. He said nothing, content to stare at her, his eyes never blinking, never leaving her, full of malice.

Over Luther's shoulder, Christina could see the building where Tyler still slept. It was much farther away than she'd thought, well over a hundred feet. She hadn't realized she'd walked so far. Luther had positioned himself between her and Tyler, cutting her off from rescue. There was no chance Christina could dash past him; he'd be on top of her in an instant. Even if Tyler heard her shout, it'd take time before he could reach her, time she didn't have.

For a long moment, neither of them moved or said a word. Finally, Christina couldn't stand it any longer.

"What are you doing here?" she asked fearfully. "What do you want?"

"Sure sounded like you two were havin' a good time in there," he answered, licking his lips. "Thought I might have me a taste."

Christina didn't know what was worse, the embarrassment of Luther overhearing her and Tyler making love or her terror at his declaration that he'd like to do the same. Clearly, there was no use trying to reason with him. With him blocking her way, there was only one choice left.

"Tyler, help!" she screamed at the top of her lungs before turning and dashing into the dark woods.

Luther smiled as he watched Barlow's nurse dash off into the brush. There was something undeniably satisfying about scaring the living hell out of a woman. Though Luther had hoped to sneak up on her, he was pleased he'd have to give chase. If he was going to have his way with this high-and-mighty bitch, he might as well earn it.

"Run, whore," he muttered, "for all the good it'll do . . ."

Ever since he'd followed her into the woods, watching as she'd disappeared into the shack with Sutter, Luther had felt a stirring in his britches that was getting harder and harder to ignore. Standing in the downpour had done nothing to ease his want. That desire had nearly overwhelmed him. But if there was one thing getting off alcohol had done for him, it was to provide clarity he'd been sorely lacking. Instead of barging in on the *two* of them, pulling out the gun stuffed into his waistband, ending things the easy way, he'd waited, certain one of them would wander off alone. That patience had just been rewarded.

Luther could almost picture the agony Barlow and his nephew would feel because of what he was about to do to the girl. Though it'd be nothing compared to what he'd experienced when Donnie died, there was some satisfaction knowing they'd suffer for the rest of their miserable lives. Someday, Luther would go to Barlow's house in the middle of the night, wake the bastard, and make him listen to every gruesome detail.

Luther hadn't anticipated the bitch screaming the way she had, but what was done couldn't be changed. Sutter wouldn't be able to help, but even if he could, Luther would make him pay with his life.

Without a look back, Luther plunged into the woods after Christina.

Now it was time to play.

Tyler awoke with a start. His heart raced as he pushed back the blanket, the air cool against his bare skin. He felt as if he'd been having a dream where he'd been falling, only to awake seconds before he hit the ground. In the darkness, he struggled to get control of himself.

"I hope I didn't wake you," he said to Christina. "I must have been having one heck of a dream."

But there was no answer.

Tyler reached out for her, wondering how she'd slept through his outburst, but his hand found nothing. Feeling around, he found the edge of the cot, but Christina wasn't there.

Where in the hell is she?

Swinging his feet over the edge, Tyler shook what sleep remained from his head. As his eyes adjusted to the darkness, he saw that Christina's clothes were no longer lying beside his own. As he looked around, there was no sign of her anywhere.

Memories clawed through his head, fleeting images of what had startled him awake.

429

It was right there, just outside of his reach, brushing up against his fingertips, tantalizingly close. He'd heard something . . . a shout . . . it was a name . . . it was *his* name . . . coming from outside . . .

Panicked, Tyler threw on his clothes, not bothering to button up his shirt, before bursting out of the cabin and into the night. Everything was shrouded in darkness.

There was no sign of Christina.

Tyler knew she wasn't the sort of woman who'd leave without a word, certainly not after what they'd just done. She'd been careful enough to get up without waking him, but then something must've happened.

Straining to listen, he heard nothing but the sounds of the night. If he was wrong about hearing her shout his name, then where was she?

"Christina?" Tyler called.

There was no answer.

"Christina?" he shouted again, this time with much more urgency. "Can you hear me? Where are you?"

Still nothing.

This time, without any hesitation, he took off running.

Christina ran through the woods as fast as she could, too frightened to look back over her shoulder, certain that Luther Rickert was right behind. Branches lashed against her face, unseen in the darkness, their nettles snarling in her long hair, grabbing at her, trying to slow her down. But Christina ignored the painful cuts on her bare skin and yanked free of whatever clutched at her, desperate to escape.

Don't slow down; don't stop; just run!

When Christina had first dashed between the dark trees, she had no idea where she was headed. In those first, frantic moments, her hope had been that she'd find herself back at the garage where Tyler worked, someplace familiar. But with every passing moment, she knew she was running *away* from town and deeper into the woods.

Leaping over another swollen creek, Christina landed awkwardly, her ankle twisting beneath her, and she crashed down in a heap, her knees slamming hard onto the rocky ground. It took everything she had not to scream.

Frightened, alone, and now hurt, Christina feared she'd become too paralyzed to act, unable and unwilling to go any farther. From somewhere deep inside her, a memory rose; she was a child, lost in the woods around Lake Washington, so terrified at the thought of being chased that she ran into the woods and away from her sister, desperate and crying.

But Christina knew she was no longer that terrified little girl. She was a woman now. She'd left her home in Minnesota, become a nurse in the Army, and set out to discover what life had to offer. Standing up to Tyler's jokes, telling Holden she couldn't be with him, and pressing Dr. Barlow until he told her the truth about his morphine use, these were all the acts of an independent woman, not a child afraid of her own shadow. To quit running meant she would be left at Luther's mercy, of which she knew there was none.

She would fight, for Tyler, for their future.

From back down the path that she'd run, from somewhere close, there came the sound of rustling branches. Though her ankle and knees throbbed painfully, Christina rose and struggled forward, resilient, wanting to get away.

Christina ran up one low rise and then down another, her feet stumbling on rocks and slipping on loose pine needles, her arms pushing back one branch, then missing another that hit her nose so hard she saw stars. With her lungs burning, sweat and rainwater soaking her blouse against her skin, and a limp in her step, she suddenly burst through an opening in the woods and stopped.

Before her lay an apple orchard. Row after row of trees stood silently. Christina had the uncomfortable feeling she'd accidentally stumbled upon a graveyard. Silence hung over the orchard like a blanket. Though the scene unsettled her, she was no longer faltering through the darkened woods with no idea where she was going.

In the middle of the orchard was a barn. The building was dark in the starlight, but Christina felt a flicker of hope that it might be occupied, that there was someone who could help her. Sliding awkwardly down a short embankment, nearly falling once, she started to make her way between the trees.

From atop the small hill the barn hadn't seemed so distant, but now Christina felt as if it were getting farther and farther away. Abandoned baskets lay beside trees. A huge tractor glistened with raindrops, a chain connecting it to the tree it would soon uproot. As her eyes nervously darted from one thing to the next, all the while she was hoping she wouldn't hurt her ankle further by slipping on a fallen apple.

Finally, she neared the barn. But just as she was about to reach it, her breathing ragged and heavy, she heard Luther's voice from somewhere behind her.

"You can run all you want!" he shouted. "But it ain't gonna do you no good! I'm gonna get you, girlie!"

Christina turned to see Luther standing on top of the embankment, right where she'd been only moments before. He was only seconds behind her. Once again, panic threatened to overwhelm her, but her determination to survive proved greater. On she ran.

She had to find someone. She had to hide. She had to get away.

Luther laughed out loud. Watching the girl run away made his juices flow that much faster. He knew he shouldn't have called out to her, letting her know how close he'd come, but he hadn't been able to resist. Besides, it wasn't as if there was anything she could do to stop what was coming.

Making his way down the embankment, Luther set off after his prey with a smile on his face.

The bitch had run right where he'd hoped she would.

The beating of her heart thundered in Christina's ears as she raced toward the doors of the barn. There was no point looking behind her to see where Luther was; she was far too focused on getting to safety. No matter how frightened she was, she had to keep going.

The barn sat as dark and silent as any of the trees surrounding it. Up close, it was clear that no one was inside. Christina had hoped that, once she got closer, she'd see more buildings behind the barn occupied with orchard workers, a light in a window, but only darkness looked back. Racing to the closed double doors, she tried to pry them open with all of her might, but they refused to budge; it was only then that she noticed the padlock keeping them shut.

"No!" she cried. "Oh, no!"

Hurrying around the corner, she found a door halfway down the wall. Unfortunately, it was also locked. Circling the building, Christina could find no other way in. She was stuck outside.

What am I going to do?

Panicked and at the height of her desperation, Christina considered a series of stalls that were built against the side of the building. Tarps covered rakes, sawhorses, buckets, and a couple of ladders. Her first instinct was to hide among the tools, but she knew it'd be the first place Luther looked.

But then, at the rear of one of the stalls,

she saw that a barn window had been left partly open. If she could manage to reach it in time . . .

Forcing her way through the tools, wincing as she banged her sore knee against a wheelbarrow, Christina managed to reach the rear of the stall. The window was small, only a foot or so across, but she believed she could squeeze through. Standing on an empty apple crate, she leaped, grabbed the window's ledge, and strained with all of her might, pushing and pulling herself up and in.

Halfway through, Christina got hung up on something and could no longer move forward. She didn't know if it was a bent nail, a hook, or the window clasp, but she hung there helplessly. Desperately, she yanked forward, tugging until she heard her clothing tear. Released, she plummeted into the dark barn, landing awkwardly on her shoulder. Ignoring the pain, she rose and shut the window before sinking to the floor.

Don't make a sound, not even a whisper!

The inside of the barn was darker than the night outside; Christina couldn't see more than a few inches in front of her face. But she found it comforting in its own way; because she couldn't see a thing, it also meant nothing could see *her.* With her arms

436

huddled around her knees, she waited as quiet as a mouse.

Even as she wondered where Luther was, Christina thought about Tyler. There was little hope that he'd heard her cry and was coming after her, but she clung to it anyway. All she wanted was to be safe and sound in his arms once again. If she could just stay quiet and out of sight until dawn, maybe an orchard worker would find her.

But as soon as she had that thought, Christina heard the sound of steps just outside the main barn doors. She knew it was Luther. Her hope was that he'd take a few tugs at the locked doors before giving up and moving on, searching somewhere that she wasn't. Instead, she heard a noise that filled her with the deepest dread.

It was the clicking of a key in a lock.

Slowly, the barn doors swung open. Instinctively, Christina shrank away from the meager light, trying to move farther out of sight. Her view of the open doorway was blocked, but she heard every sound as clearly as the ringing of church bells; more footfalls were followed by the scraping of metal and finally the striking of a match. The soft glow of an oil lantern began to fill the barn.

When Luther spoke, it nearly made Christina cry out in fear.

"Come out, come out, wherever you are . . ."

CHAPTER TWENTY-SIX

Luther held the lit oil lamp high above his head as he peered into the dark depths of the barn. In the flickering light, shadows danced frantically in one spot before leaping to another. One side of the barn was lined with stalls like those normally used for horses but shallower. Benches were set up to deal with the demands of the orchard; tools reflected the lantern's light. On the other side, bales of hay were stacked at the rear of the barn.

That bitch is in here . . . I know it!

Luther had no doubt his prey was hiding inside the barn. Once he'd crossed the orchard, it hadn't taken him long to check around the building. He'd seen her prying at the doors, so since she hadn't been outside, it meant she'd found a way in.

Now it was up to him to ferret her out.

Imagining how terrified that bitch must've been when she heard his key slide into the lock made Luther's groin throb with excitement. There was no way she could've known she'd sought sanctuary in one of Amos Worthington's orchards, let alone the same one Luther had been working at for the last couple of months. Though he'd been let go because he'd gotten so drunk that he missed work, he'd pocketed a key to the equipment barn before he left. He hadn't stolen anything *while* he'd been working for Worthington, but that didn't mean Luther wouldn't do so *after* being fired.

"If you come on out now, I promise I won't be too rough with you," he lied, grinning in the lamp's light.

He wanted to draw this out, to savor it. Somewhere along the way, Luther had come to believe that the worse he made it for Barlow's nurse, the more agonizing it would be for the doctor when he found out what had happened. Oh, how Luther wished he could see that son of a bitch's face . . .

Christina cowered in the work stall, wondering what horrible fate awaited her now. Luther held up the lamp no more than thirty feet away. All it would take was for him to walk the length of the barn. In seconds, he would find her.

All the options available to her seemed as

if they would end in her being savaged at Luther's hand. Staying put seemed pointless; he'd discover her eventually. There'd been so much trouble getting *in* through the window that he'd almost certainly get to her well before she managed to escape, and even if she did, where would she go? If she tried to run past him, she'd never make it to the barn doors.

What am I to do . . . ?

As she tried to choose a course of action, Christina watched in horror as Luther made his way farther inside the barn. He swung the lamp in front of him, the light moving up one wall and then the other. It was so terrifying that she looked down at her shaking hands instead.

"I reckon a pretty girl like you wouldn't normally have the time of day for a fella like me," he growled. "But you ain't gonna be able to ignore me now."

Knowing full well what Luther's intentions were, Christina reflexively scurried backward. Even with the light of the oil lamp, the stall was swathed in darkness. She never saw the bucket of tools before she hit it, knocking it over and making such a ruckus that she might as well have stood up and shouted for Luther's attention.

Before she could register the enormity of

what'd just happened, Christina looked up to find Luther standing in the open gate to the stall. He hadn't had to do anything to find her; she'd done it all herself. The light reflected in his eyes danced maniacally, his lust apparent.

"You made that easy," he sneered.

"Stay . . . stay away from me!" she screamed. "Don't you dare come another step closer!"

"I like it when there's a little fight in a gal," Luther said calmly, setting the lamp on one of the posts that made up a corner of the stall. Her eyes were wide with horror as he pulled a gun out of the back of his pants, held it up so that she could see the light glinting off the metal, before placing it next to the lamp. "When they're like that, it usually means they ain't against things gettin' a little rough when you're rollin' round in the sack with 'em."

Slowly, patiently, Luther began to undo the buttons of his shirt. The utter hopelessness that Christina felt at the sight threatened to overwhelm her, drag her down into a sea of misery she was certain to drown in. But what could she do? Fighting back would entertain him; just letting it happen would kill her. But then, just as she was about to decide to go down scratching tooth and nail, Luther suddenly flew to the side, lifted from his feet, and crashed to the ground out of sight. In an instant, Christina knew who had come to rescue her.

It was Tyler.

When Tyler ran from the shack beside his beehives, he'd decided against taking the path that led back toward the garage and instead gone in the opposite direction. He couldn't say for certain *why* he'd done so, but something nagged at him, a feeling of worry that made him run up and down the gently sloping hills, leaping over swollen creeks.

Exiting the woods, he stood and looked out over one of Amos Worthington's orchards. Everything was clear in the starlight. What Tyler noticed wasn't Christina but a man scurrying toward the barn standing tall among the surrounding trees. Though he'd no idea who the man was or what he was doing there, Tyler felt certain he was up to no good. So instead of shouting, Tyler chose to keep quiet, dashed down the hill, and hurried after him through the orchard.

Halfway to the barn, Tyler stopped as the man flung open the huge doors and stepped inside. Tyler knew he'd have to be careful from there on out; he'd never get the drop on the stranger if he came at a full run, so he began creeping forward, darting from tree to tree. Reaching the side of the barn, he flattened himself against the outer wall and took a quick, careful look inside.

The man had lit a lantern and was turning it from side to side, as if he was looking for something. For an instant, his profile was visible to Tyler. He recognized him immediately.

What in the hell is Luther Rickert doing here? Like every resident of Longstock, Tyler knew everything about Luther: his addiction to alcohol, how he'd gotten his brother killed; he even felt pity for the man's dead parents. Tyler also knew that Luther was dangerous. If he were to confront Luther, he'd be taking his life in his own hands.

Tyler was startled by a loud bang, followed by Luther's voice, and then another; with his heart in his throat, he understood it was Christina's. For an instant he was frozen in place, shocked into indecision. For whatever reason, Luther Rickert had come to the clearing and chased Christina from the shack all the way to the barn in the middle of the orchard. When Tyler listened to Luther's words, there wasn't any question about what to do next.

Tyler's blood pulsed in his temples; his

hands clenched into fists. He crossed the distance between them in an instant, leaving the ground and barreling into Luther. Tyler struck hard but out of control, making the other man gasp before sending them both sprawling into the dirt. Even as Tyler leaped back to his feet, he was thankful for one thing; if even for just a moment, he'd gotten that bastard away from Christina.

Luther came up slowly, his hands at his ribs. He was like a wild animal, guard up, claws extended. He spat a trail of blood onto the ground.

"This ain't your fight, Sutter," he snarled.

"You made it mine the second you threatened her," Tyler shot back. "Whatever reason you had for coming after her, it isn't good enough to keep me from giving you the beating you deserve."

"Tough talk," Luther sneered. "We'll see if you can back it up."

Tyler ignored him. "Christina," he said loudly, never taking his eyes off the dangerous man in front of him. "You need to leave right now. Head to the east and you'll see the road that leads back to town. Follow it until you find help."

"I'm not leaving you," she countered.

"Don't argue with me! I won't let him get to you, but you have to go!"

"Let her stay," Luther interjected. "When I'm done with you, I'll be all worked up and ready for a woman's attention. From what I heard comin' out of that shack, she's talented that way."

Tyler's intention had been to persuade Christina to leave and then wait for Luther to make the first move, but listening to the man speak so disgustingly about their making love, he couldn't contain his rage. Rushing forward, he cocked his right hand and threw it, expecting to feel the solid collision of bone against bone, but instead he swung through the air, twisting himself like a corkscrew. For his poor effort, Luther danced to the side and punched him once in the nose before popping him in the breadbasket. The force of the second blow was enough to unbalance him and he dropped to one knee.

"Whooeee!" Luther whistled. "Looks like we're gonna have some fun!"

Tyler didn't know what stung worse, his nose or sense of pride at having given in to his impulses. Luther was no novice when it came to fighting; he might have been a drunk, but that didn't mean he didn't know how to use his fists. He'd been in more bar brawls than he could count. While Tyler was the bigger, stronger man, his lack of experience placed him at a disadvantage. If he was going to beat Luther, he was going to have be the *smarter* man.

Christina watched, terrified, as Tyler rushed at Luther, threw a punch that missed, and was then struck hard enough to drive him to one knee. She was utterly sickened by the joy Luther seemed to be taking in the fight; he was a despicable, vile man whose heart was blacker than the night outside the barn. With all her might, she willed Tyler to get up and wipe the smile from Luther's face.

The relief she'd felt when Tyler tackled Luther was enough to bring tears to her eyes. He'd now rescued her twice. Christina remembered her elation after he'd saved her from Annette. But somehow, this felt even more significant, that the fate awaiting her had been even worse than being pummeled to death with a steel pipe.

That was why when Tyler told her to run for help Christina had refused. If he was willing to fight for her life, she wouldn't abandon him. Luther was a psychopath; if they needed to face him together, so be it.

"C'mon, Sutter." Luther grinned. "You don't want to be disappointin' that gal of yours, now do you? Come get your beatin'."

But this time, Tyler refused to rise to the other man's taunt, choosing instead to wait just out of range. They circled each other like wild animals waiting for an opening. Eventually, Tyler's patience won the day; in mid-step, Luther suddenly rushed at him, his hands raised. Christina gasped, fearful that Tyler didn't have a chance to protect himself, but just before Luther reached him he took a quick step to his right, ducked his head beneath his opponent's grasp, and thundered a punch into his rib cage; the force of his blow was enough to lift Luther from the ground.

"Hit him again!" Christina shouted.

Tyler didn't need any encouragement; with Luther momentarily stunned, he bludgeoned the man in the face, cracking him on the cheekbone. With his momentum pulling him one way and his tangled feet another, Luther fell hard onto his back, dust rising from the impact, a woof of air bursting from his lungs. But before Tyler could press the attack, Luther quickly rolled to his side and got back to his feet, although a bit unsteadily.

"Well, c'mon on then," Luther growled, all of his earlier enjoyment of their brawl evaporated in an instant. "Fight me, you bastard!"

This time, Tyler was more willing to oblige him. He moved steadily forward, his hands raised in a guard, ready to finish what he'd started. The moment he was close enough to Luther, he landed another punch, snapping the man's head back.

But instead of being the only one taking punishment, Luther remained determined to deal some of his own. Dodging another blow coming straight toward his nose, Luther threw a quick left that split Tyler's lip, leaving a trickle of blood dripping down his chin.

Christina felt helpless. The men went back and forth, brawling from one side of the barn to the other, trading blows, one getting the upper hand before the other struck back, and she wrung her hands as she watched them fight.

What happens if Tyler is beaten?

Just as Christina had her fearful thought, Luther suddenly struck Tyler hard in the mouth and then rushed him, grabbing him around the midsection and brutally driving him to the ground. Faster than a snake, Luther straddled Tyler's chest and began raining down blows. Tyler did all he could to deflect them, but they started slipping through; one landed and then another. She could see he was becoming dazed; soon, he

449

wouldn't be able to defend himself. If things didn't change quickly, the fight would soon be over.

"Stop it!" she screamed. "Stop hitting him!"

Luther paid her no mind, his attention focused on beating Tyler into the ground.

Desperate, Christina looked around for something, anything, she might use to force Luther to stop his vicious attack. Lying beside her on the ground was the bucket of tools she'd accidentally knocked over, drawing Luther to her hiding spot. Screwdrivers, picks, and wrenches were everywhere, but what grabbed her attention was a hammer. Picking it up, she felt its heft in her hand, sure it would succeed where her shouts had failed.

Aiming carefully, Christina reared back and threw the hammer at Luther with all the strength she had. End over end it spun, striking him just above his elbow. It wasn't a direct hit, it seemed to surprise him more than hurt, but it was enough for Tyler to even the odds.

While Luther spun to look at Christina, his eyes full of hatred, Tyler punched upwards, striking him on the chin, hard enough to force him off his chest. Scrambling back to his feet, Tyler leaped on top of

his shocked and wounded foe, his fists flying. Their positions suddenly reversed,
Luther tried to fight back, but flailing away
with his hands did nothing to deter Tyler.
Blow after blow struck just where he intended; Luther's jaw, his cheeks, his nose
became a bloody mess. Eventually, the
man's hands dropped to his sides and his
head lolled to one side as he fell unconscious. Tyler cocked his hand to throw one
more punch, one hand lifting the man up
with a fistful of shirt, but he showed mercy,
dropping Luther's head down to the dirt
floor with a thud.

The fight was over.

Tyler had won.

Christina rushed to meet him, throwing
herself into his arms. Tears of joy streamed
down her cheeks as she held Tyler as tightly
as she could. All her worry disappeared in
an instant, replaced with a feeling of relief.

"Are you okay?" he asked. "Did he hurt
you?"

"No." She shook her head. "You came at
just the right time. I was so frightened . . . I
thought that he . . . that he . . . ," she tried
to explain, but the emotions of what had
happened overwhelmed her and she
couldn't finish.

"Shhh," Tyler soothed, running his hands though her hair, his embrace both comforting and firm. "None of that matters. All I care about is that you're safe, nothing else."

"I stepped away from you for an instant!" Christina explained, reliving those terrifying moments over again in her mind. "I wanted some air," she said, "but when I turned around, he was there! I shouted your name, but then I turned and ran —"

"Christina!" he said insistently. "Calm down! You're safe now! Stop talking and look at me!"

Tyler's words broke through the panic overwhelming Christina. She did as he told her, taking deep breaths and concentrating on the face of the man she loved; it was with a sliver of irony that she realized she'd given similar instructions to Holden. But as she gazed into Tyler's eyes, Christina saw the price he'd paid for her safety; his face was a mess of bruising, ugly welts throbbing a bright red and cuts that trickled blood.

"Oh, Tyler!" she whispered.

When Christina reached out and touched a particularly nasty mark near the corner of his mouth, barely brushing it with her fingertips, he winced and quickly turned away.

"You're hurt," she said.

"I'm fine," he disagreed. "I'm sure it looks worse than it feels."

"But you have no idea how bad it looks."

"I can see it as plain as day in your eyes."

Christina frowned. "Then you should know why I'm so worried."

Instead of arguing the point further, Tyler leaned forward and tenderly placed his lips against hers, giving her a soft kiss. The sensation of his touch filled her, reminding her of why she'd fallen in love with him, as well as why he could be so frustrating.

But after everything they'd shared that night, from the declarations of their feelings to the act of making love and the terrifying race through the woods and apple orchard, Christina knew that Tyler was the man she'd spend the rest of her years cherishing.

When their lips slowly parted, she said, "I love you, Tyler."

"And I love you."

Those simple words made her feel as if she were the luckiest woman in all of Long-stock, if not all of Wisconsin.

The feeling lasted until the moment she looked over Tyler's shoulder and discovered that, while they had embraced, Luther Rickert had disappeared.

Beneath the faint light of the stars and the

thin, slivered moon, Luther limped across the orchard and back toward the road where he'd stashed his car. With his muddled head and bruised ribs, to say nothing of his wounded pride, it was taking forever to get there. Each step was painful. It was as plain as the blood that stained his shirt he'd made one hell of a mistake.

"Damn you, Tyler Sutter," he mumbled through a busted lip.

It seemed hard to imagine now, but there was a part of Luther that had been excited when that bitch's lover had shown up; he'd never been one to shy away from a good fight. Even after Sutter managed to land a few punches, Luther had never been concerned that he could *lose*. He'd been winning! One or two more blows and Sutter would've been finished! But then things had gone to hell, and here Luther was, running away with his tail tucked between his legs.

The mistake had been going after the girl in the first place. She'd been a tempting target, especially because of her looks, but his focus on her had been misguided. The only person who deserved to feel his wrath was Barlow. Taking someone from him the way Donnie had been stolen would make the bastard suffer, but it wasn't enough.

The son of a bitch has to die!

Luther knew anything short of that wasn't good enough, not for him, and certainly not for Donnie. Once Luther made it to the car, he'd drive back into Longstock and do what needed to be done: end Samuel Barlow's life.

Luther wished he could've grabbed the gun from the stall post; he would've liked nothing more than to get hold of it and pump lead into Sutter and the goddamn nurse, but they surely would've noticed him. Luther knew he didn't need it; his hands would be more than capable weapons.

But even as he formulated his plan, Luther felt something familiar nagging at him. With all that had taken place, with the way he hurt, broken and bruised, it would be so easy to find a bottle, feel that familiar burn in his throat, and . . .

Furious at himself, Luther shook his head. *Don't be such a damn fool!*

Once he was done with Barlow, he could do whatever he wanted, consequences be damned. He could die in a hail of the sheriff's bullets, wrap his car around a tree hard enough to do the job right, or hell, he could let that nurse bash his brains in with her hammer.

Or I could go home and get so drunk I never wake up . . .

Luther knew he had to act quickly. Sutter and the nurse would call the sheriff the first chance they got.

There was still time . . .

CHAPTER TWENTY-SEVEN

Christina did her best to keep up with Tyler as he raced through the woods and back toward the garage. Before they'd left the orchard barn, she'd told him everything about Luther Rickert and Tyler's uncle, beginning with being knocked to the ground and ending with Dr. Barlow's confession that he'd been under the influence of morphine the night he'd treated Donnie Rickert's injuries.

Tyler listened closely to every word, his jaw tight. Before Christina had finished, his brow had creased with concern and he took her by the hand, pulling her toward the door.

"What do you think is going to happen?" Christina had asked.

"He's going to go after my uncle." Tyler had frowned. "I'm sure of it."

"Wouldn't Luther be more likely to leave town?" she argued. "Surely he has to know that we're going to contact the sheriff."

"I knew a couple of guys in the Navy just like Luther, too stupid to know when to quit. Once they got something in their heads, they'd never be satisfied until they'd done what they set out to do. If he went after you to get back at my uncle, now that we've stopped him from getting his misguided revenge he'll go after the source of his troubles before the law catches up with him."

"What will Luther do if he finds him?"

Tyler shook his head. "I don't want to think about it," he answered. "The only way to protect my uncle is to find him fast!"

Running down the narrow paths, dodging tree branches that suddenly appeared out of nowhere, Christina could only imagine the worry Tyler must be feeling, not to mention the physical pain. After the brutality of his fight with Luther, Tyler's body had to be aching, but he didn't allow it to slow him down or show on his face.

Christina tried her best to follow his example, but every time she stepped awkwardly on her ankle or her shoulder struck a tree limb she had to bite her lip not to cry out. She'd volunteered to remain behind, painfully aware of the hindrance she presented to their getting to Dr. Barlow in time, but Tyler refused to leave her alone after what had happened, even for an instant. Despite the discomfort, she continued on.

Her heart hoped that Tyler had been wrong about Luther's intentions, but her head was clear enough to know he was right. Luther's defeat in the barn was only a temporary setback, nothing serious enough to keep him from getting the revenge he so desperately sought; Christina knew the only thing keeping him from it was she and Tyler.

So on they ran.

Finally, they burst from the underbrush beside the garage. Longstock spread silently before them, full of families settling themselves down for sleep, unaware of the would-be murderer in their midst.

Racing to his car, Tyler leaped behind the wheel, turned the ignition, and slammed down on the accelerator. The vehicle took off like a shot; Christina scarcely had time to shut her door before the car hurtled down the road, its tires screeching on the pavement.

"I still think we should call the sheriff," she said, holding on for dear life.

"There isn't time," Tyler disagreed. "If Luther had a car stashed closer than ours, he's got a hell of a head start on us. If we take time to call the authorities, we might be too late."

"Then we should go straight to your uncle's house," Christina said, dread filling her chest.

"He won't be there. My mother said that he was coming over for dinner tonight. If we're going to keep Luther from getting to him first, that's where we'll have to look for him."

Tyler tapped the car's brakes while spinning the steering wheel to the left, skidding around the corner and onto Main Street. The tires protested, the sound so loud that Christina felt everyone in Longstock must have heard them, before steadying and roaring forward, the gas pedal jammed to the floorboard.

"What . . . what if we don't get there in time . . . ?" she asked fearfully.

Tyler didn't respond, but Christina had the feeling that, even though the speedometer was still rising, the engine straining as it worked harder and harder, he would do whatever it took never to have to answer.

Luther stood in Samuel Barlow's bedroom, scowling. The room was as pitch-black as a tomb, an observation that would've given him pleasure if it were still occupied, for when he left he intended to leave someone dead behind. But the bedroom was empty.

"That son of a bitch," he muttered in fury.

Even though every bit of him had wanted to come racing down the street, screeching to a stop at Barlow's front walk, kicking the door down before strangling the bastard with his bare hands, Luther had somehow managed to show some restraint. He'd parked a block away, made his way through the shadows, careful not to be seen, before arriving at Barlow's home. Every window had been dark, but Luther hadn't been deterred; he'd hoped that Barlow had retired early and would be easily caught unaware. Slipping the lock on the back door had been child's play. And so, holding his breath with every creak of the staircase, Luther had made his way to the bedroom, breathless with anticipation, only to find it empty.

He knew there wasn't much time; he had a lead on Barlow's nephew and the nurse, but it wouldn't be long before they caught up. But if the doctor wasn't home, where was he? There were only two choices: he was either still at his clinic or visiting his sister. Both were about the same distance away, but in opposite directions.

There'd only be time to check one.

In the scant light of the bedroom, Luther caught sight of himself in the mirror above Barlow's dresser. Though his face was shrouded in shadows, he could still see how badly Tyler Sutter had messed him up. But it was nothing compared to the loss the doctor had inflicted upon him; Donnie had died because Barlow had been angry, upset that they'd tried to steal from him. He could've saved Donnie if he'd wanted to.

For that, he has to die!

Leaving the bedroom, Luther knew just where to go.

Samuel Barlow made his way down the short walk from his sister's front door before turning at the sidewalk and heading home. Though lately life had handed him a bucketful of lemons, he'd had a wonderful evening. Ever since Holden had decided to leave his room, Clara had been beside herself with happiness. The meal she had prepared had been as delicious as it was overblown; there was so much food on the table Dr. Barlow hadn't known where to start. When Holden descended the stairs, his uncle still couldn't believe what he was seeing. But there Holden was, smiling and laughing through dinner, looking much like the same young man who'd gone off to war. Still, Dr. Barlow saw a sadness lurking behind Holden's eyes and knew exactly where it came from.

But the best part of the evening had been forgetting his troubles, if only for a little while. Ever since Luther Rickert had re-entered his life, he'd been walking around on pins and needles. Sleep was hard to come by, so he spent most nights walking restlessly around his house, jumping at every creak, seeing Luther lurking in every shadow. But when Eunice Hester died, Dr. Barlow had made a decision.

To hell with Luther Rickert . . .

Dr. Barlow had meant what he'd said to Christina; he might deserve what Luther had planned for him. He believed that his drug habit hadn't affected his treatment of Luther's brother, but he couldn't say for certain. Walking home beneath the brilliant night sky, he realized that he could never know the truth.

Just as he reached the end of the block, Dr. Barlow was startled by the sudden, frantic honking of a car's horn. Ahead of him, a car fishtailed around the corner, its headlights swerving wildly, the tires screaming as they skidded across the pavement. The roar of the car's engine filled the otherwise quiet night. It was then that he realized it was headed straight for him.

Its lights flipped on and off as the horn blared, drawing ever closer. He was so frightened by the sight of it that he froze in place. Even if he could have moved his legs, there was nowhere for him to run, and even if there were, he was in no shape to get there fast enough.

This is it! This is the end!

But just as the car swerved across the street toward him, causing him to throw up his hands and turn his head so he wouldn't see the inevitable collision, the driver surprised him by slamming on the brakes. The car bucked and shook, sliding slightly to the side as it struggled to stop. Finally opening his eyes, Dr. Barlow was shocked to see that he recognized not only the car but also both of the people getting out of it and rushing toward him.

Tyler and Christina.

Christina couldn't believe how relieved she was to find Dr. Barlow unharmed. Worrying about him had nearly made her sick, although Tyler's frantic driving had certainly done its share. Once the car had come to a complete stop, she'd pushed open the door and run to the doctor's side.

"Are you all right?" she asked him frantically.

"Other than the heart attack you nearly gave me, I'm fine," he answered.

"You haven't seen Luther Rickert tonight?" Tyler asked.

"No, I haven't," Dr. Barlow said, turning white at the mention of the name. "Why do you ask? And what happened to your face?"

Christina gave Dr. Barlow a quick rundown of what had happened since Luther surprised her in the woods. The doctor's eyes grew wide when she recounted her dash through the orchard and desperate attempt to hide in the barn. There was even a glimmer of pride in his face when she told him about how Tyler had prevented Luther from forcing himself on her.

"He was trying to get to you through her," Tyler explained.

"Why, I never!" Dr. Barlow declared. "If I'd had the slightest idea he was capable of something so low, I would've throttled him myself!"

"All that matters is you're safe," Christina answered.

"Something's not right." Tyler frowned.

"Nonsense, my boy!" the doctor disagreed. "You gave the bully a beating and he's off to lick his wounds! He's halfway to

Milwaukee by now!"

"What are you thinking?" Christina asked, ignoring Dr. Barlow's premature celebration.

"Luther might be many things, but he isn't a coward. He wouldn't have run away, not knowing whether we'd go to the sheriff."

"Then where is he?"

Before Tyler could answer, Christina heard something behind them. It began as a faint sound but quickly grew in volume and intensity. She looked down the street, back toward the Sutter home, but couldn't see anything in the dark night. Still, the noise persisted, growing.

Suddenly, her eyes were blinded by a brilliantly bright light, and it was then that Christina knew what she was seeing.

It's a car . . . and it's driving straight for us!

In the time it took her heart to beat, Christina understood what was happening. Luther was behind the wheel of the rapidly approaching car. He had come upon them as quietly and sneakily as he could, driving with his lights off for as long as possible, all to remain unseen. Now, he meant to run them all down, even if he had to drive up onto the sidewalk to do it.

There wasn't time to run or even move out of the way. Luther's plan for revenge

466

would come to pass; he would wipe out all three of them in one bloody act. As his car approached, its engine sounding like a wild beast, Christina looked over her shoulder at Tyler, wondering what their life together might've been like.

Without warning, Christina was struck hard, the force of the collision lifting her from the ground and through the night air. She crashed onto her side, the pavement unforgiving, as her breath was driven from her lungs. Just as she fell, the night was shattered by the sound of screeching metal as one car crashed into the other. The noise was deafening.

Struggling to rise, Christina couldn't believe she was still alive. The pain in her ribs was nearly overwhelming. Stars swam before her eyes, but she knew she hadn't been struck by the car.

What . . . what happened . . . ?

Dr. Barlow lay beside her, his head bleeding from where it struck the ground. Christina was stunned to find that they were in the middle of the street.

But the biggest shock of all was who was lying between them.

It was Holden.

Christina didn't know what had happened, but he'd saved both of their lives.

Unfortunately, that left one question unanswered.

Where is Tyler?

Luther coughed as he struggled to open his eyes. His mouth was filled with copper; he touched his lower lip and his fingertips were stained with blood. For a moment, he was unsure of where he was; he wondered if he weren't sitting beside Donnie, his brother's body broken and twisted by the crushed automobile.

But then Luther remembered . . .

He couldn't see anything through the cracks of the shattered windshield. The cracked radiator hissed. Everything ached, but he shut out the pain. He tried to open his door, but it wouldn't budge. He wanted to get out, to see the damage he'd caused.

I need to see them bleed . . . I need to see them die . . .

Right before impact, everything had been a blur. Though Luther was ashamed to admit it, he might've closed his eyes at the last instant. He didn't *know* if he'd hit his intended targets.

Groaning, Luther worked his way from behind the steering wheel. His already bruised ribs screamed in agony. Sliding through broken glass, he managed to get the passenger's door open. Unsteady on his feet, he held on to the open door to keep from falling on his face.

Looking at the chaos he'd caused, Luther was surprised he hadn't been hurt much worse. He'd slammed his car straight into Sutter's, hitting it almost dead-on; both hoods resembled accordions. Glass, oil, and bits of metal littered the ground.

Though his vision was still a bit hazy, Luther noticed something moving off to his right. A man crawled in the grass, slowly trying to get away, blood soaking the back of his shirt. Immediately Luther knew it was Tyler Sutter.

So where in the hell are the others?

Luther hoped Samuel Barlow and that bitch of a nurse had been crushed to a bloody pulp in the wreckage of the two cars. They'd been there seconds before impact. Surely they were dead. What mattered now was eliminating one last thorn in his side. Once Sutter was as dead as his uncle, Luther and Donnie's revenge would be complete.

"Not so tough now are you, you son of a bitch," Luther snarled.

Sutter looked up, his face a mask of blood.

Luther knew he had to act quickly; lights were already on in the houses around him.

Someone had to have called the sheriff.

"Time to finish what we started." Luther smiled, even though it made his face hurt. "And this time, there ain't no runnin' away."

Tyler saw Luther limping toward him, but there was no chance he could defend himself. His whole body was in agony, especially his left arm and down his side, right where Luther's car had hit him. Everything had happened so quickly, too fast for him to do anything. It had only been a glancing blow, but it still hurt like hell. But Tyler did his best to ignore the pain. All he could think about was Christina; even now, covered in his own blood, as he knew that Luther was going to try to kill him, his only thought was whether the woman he loved was safe.

"Ch-Christina . . . ," he coughed painfully. There was little doubt one of his ribs had been broken.

"You might as well be cryin' out for your momma, all the help that bitch is gonna be to you now." Luther smiled, his teeth black with blood. "She and that goddamn murderin' uncle of yours are gone! Both of 'em are smashed between those wrecked cars! But don't worry; I'm gonna help you join 'em!"

If Luther's words were intended to

frighten Tyler, to make him lose his resolve to keep fighting, they'd been wasted.

"You son of a bitch!" Tyler roared.

The pain that had paralyzed him only seconds before vanished in an instant, replaced by a furious anger that brought him up off the ground and launched him at the man who'd stolen Christina from him. For a moment, he managed to surprise Luther, punching him hard in the jaw, sweat and blood spraying onto the ground.

But it lasted for only an instant.

Luther punched Tyler hard in the ribs and all the pain came flooding back, overwhelming him. He screamed as he collapsed in a heap at Luther's feet. With no hesitation, Luther dropped onto his chest, nearly causing Tyler to pass out, before he started punching him again and again, relentlessly. There was nothing Tyler could do, no defense he could offer. It was only a matter of time before Luther's prediction came true and Tyler would be dead, right alongside Christina.

Christina heard Tyler scream and her blood ran cold.

Holden had just helped her from the ground, her hand still in his. She'd landed on the same shoulder she'd hurt when slipping through the window of the barn; it throbbed painfully with every beat of her heart. She could see the concern on his face, his eyes searching hers for answers to questions he'd yet to ask. Though she'd wanted to say something to express her gratitude for how Holden had saved her life, there hadn't yet been time.

"Tyler!" she shouted.

Without hesitation, Holden raced around the destroyed cars, Christina right at his heels, her heart in her throat.

What she saw sickened her; Luther straddled Tyler just as he'd done in the barn, but this time Tyler wasn't fighting back. With his back to them, Luther kept hammering away, one punch after another.

Holden sprinted toward the pair, slamming into Luther and sending the man sprawling. "Get the hell off my brother!" Holden hollered, angrier than a hornet.

Luther struggled to his knees, his eyes wide with shock. He kept blinking, as if he couldn't believe what he was seeing.

"How . . . how in the hell . . . ?"

The only thing that mattered to Christina was Tyler. Running over to him, she fell to her knees at his side, taking his twitching hand in her own. His face was a bloody mess, far worse than it had been before the crash. She was afraid to touch him, fearful that she'd somehow make things worse. Instead, she cried heavy tears, worried that he was so badly injured she would lose him forever.

But then Tyler did something that shocked her; he looked up at her and smiled so brightly that it lit up his face, blood, bruises, and all.

"I . . . I thought . . . that you were . . . ," he struggled.

"Hush, now," she told him.

Slowly, Tyler nodded, and then he lost consciousness. It was then that Christina's anger flared. She hated Luther Rickert for everything he'd done to Dr. Barlow and to her, but now she wanted him to pay even more, this time with pain of his own.

"You bastard!" she shouted at him.

"That ain't nothin' compared to what I'm gonna do to you," Luther snarled back. "I'm gonna make you wish you'd let me have my way back in the barn."

"You'll have to get through me first," Holden warned.

"That won't take but a second." Luther chuckled. "Even in the shape I'm in, takin' care of a coward should be easy."

"Come on then."

Confidently, Luther did as Holden asked,

running toward him with a shout; immediately he discovered he'd made a mistake. His first punch missed wildly; Holden ducked in a blur of motion, turning his hips and snapping off a tremendously hard blow to Luther's midsection. Christina couldn't know for certain, but it sounded as if a rib snapped. Uncontrollable screams of agony roared from Luther's mouth.

Holden didn't allow his opponent even a second to regroup. He mercilessly pummeled Luther's ribs, hitting him so hard that it lifted him from the ground. Within moments, Luther found himself as defenseless as he'd left Tyler, arms hanging limply at his sides.

Christina saw fear in his eyes and it warmed her heart.

"You'll never threaten my family again," Holden said angrily. "Remember this moment while you're rotting in jail!"

Holden measured his last blow, squaring his shoulders and putting all his weight behind the punch; it struck Luther flat against his jaw, snapping his head hard to the side. He was unconscious before he even hit the ground.

"Is . . . is it over . . . ?"

Surprised, Christina looked down to see that Tyler was again alert. His eyes were little more than slits, his breathing raspy, after his savage beating. Her love for him at that moment was so intense it nearly broke her heart.

"It is." She nodded, patting his hand.

Holden knelt down opposite her, taking Tyler's other hand in his own.

Tyler gave Holden a weak squeeze. All the anger toward his flesh and blood was gone.

"I'm . . . I'm so sorry for —"

Holden hushed him. "What's in the past has to stay there," he said. "All that matters is today."

"And tomorrow," Christina added.

Holden looked over at her. Unspoken words were shared between them; what had happened in front of the school, the kiss and the feelings that accompanied it, belonged to the past. Holden wouldn't interfere with her relationship with Tyler. Instead, he'd support it, while at the same time doing everything he could to repair the damage between him and his brother.

She'd come to Longstock to start a life, and even though she'd gotten far more than she'd bargained for, she was oh, so happy she'd come.

EPILOGUE

Longstock, Wisconsin
April 1948

Christina stood at the window and looked out into the street. The spring afternoon was perfect; brilliant sunlight warmed the newly budded leaves on the trees, the recently opened flowers, and the faces of the people walking the sidewalks, happy to be outdoors. The last resilient clumps of snow had melted only a week before; winter was finally gone for another year.

Ever since she'd come to Longstock, Christina had loved the coming of spring. To her, it signaled a new beginning, the passage from the old to the new, the opportunity for things to change.

From the moment Dr. Barlow had met her at the train station that fateful June afternoon a couple of years earlier, Christina's life seemed to have done nothing *but* change. The doctor's morphine use, Eunice

Hester's death, and Luther Rickert's violent desire for revenge each would have been hard enough to deal with on its own, but those troubles were nothing when compared to meeting Tyler and Holden Sutter.

Even now, years later, Christina easily recalled how difficult each of them had been in his own way, how Holden had shouted at her to get out of his room, followed later that night by Tyler frightening her half to death in his car. Thankfully, neither of those first impressions had proven accurate.

To think, she thought to herself, *one of those two became my husband . . .*

A little less than a year after her arrival in Longstock, Christina and Tyler had married in a simple ceremony. The church bells rang beneath a cloudless sky as they promised their lives to each other. All of Christina's family came to celebrate, making it one of the happiest days of her life. After everything that had happened to them, after how close they'd come to losing it all, in the end those struggles only made their love that much stronger.

"Staring out the window won't make them get here any faster."

Christina looked over her shoulder; Tyler leaned against the doorway to the kitchen. Even at that first dinner at his mother's house, when he'd annoyed Christina no end, she'd always considered him very handsome; if anything, he became more so with the passage of years.

"I'm excited," she said.

"You should be." He smiled as he crossed the room to her. "I reckon you've imagined what this day would be like since you were a little girl."

"In my daydreams, my husband was much better looking than you," Christina teased. "Smarter, too."

"Isn't it a shame you ended up with me."

Stepping behind her, Tyler slipped his arms around Christina's waist, resting them on her stomach. Inside, their child grew. Though Christina's pregnancy was only four months along, she'd started to feel the tiniest of flutters, the first, unmistakable signs that their son or daughter was beginning its long journey to join them. The morning Christina told Tyler about the baby, his eyes had immediately filled with tears of joy; in that moment, she'd never loved him more. Imagining him as a father, playing with their child, taking a walk to visit his beehives, telling stories that would make them all laugh, these were thoughts that made her smile.

Nestling her head against Tyler's chest,

Christina thought about all that had occurred since that first summer.

After Holden stopped Luther Rickert's brutal attack, the sheriff had thrown Luther into a jail cell, promising he'd do his best to lose the key. Eventually, Luther found himself standing before a jury, which came to nearly the same conclusion; he was sentenced to thirty years in prison. Though Luther burst into laughter at the verdict, he'd be an old man before he was again a free man. Because of all the damage he'd caused to the Sutter family, Christina thought Luther should have been locked up much longer. Many long weeks had passed before Tyler grew healthy enough to get back on his feet, and his body had scars that would never fully heal. Still, with the passage of time, Christina found that she thought less and less about Luther, and she wasn't the only one who did.

Once Luther was behind bars, Dr. Barlow succeeded in letting go of his feelings of guilt about the night Donnie Rickert died. He'd never explained his reasons, but Christina believed he'd decided to worry about the present, instead of a past he could never change. But that wasn't the only demon he'd escaped; from the day Christina found him under the influence of morphine in his yard, the doctor never took it again. Just like Callie explained, it took some time for him to stop being such a grouch, but eventually those difficult times passed. Dr. Barlow cared about Longstock and the people who came to him for help and dispensed care and wit in equal doses. Christina was proud to continue serving as his nurse, though she lamented that his driving hadn't improved a lick.

The other member of the clinic's staff had also had plenty of changes in her life. Callie had spent many long years trying to get Abraham to sing. Together, she and Christina had brainstormed dozens of ideas, only to see them end in failure, one after the other. But then something miraculous happened. After years of unsuccessfully trying, Callie became pregnant, giving birth to a baby girl, Gwendolyn. One day, about a month after she was born, Callie stood in the hallway and listened to Abraham sing to his child, a surprise so wondrous that it sent tears streaming down his wife's cheeks.

"He sounded just like an angel," she'd told Christina.

But the biggest change belonged to Holden. After what he'd done that fateful night, pushing Christina and his uncle out of the way of Luther's car and then protecting his brother from the beating that followed, Holden was hailed by all of Longstock as a hero. Though at first he was reluctant to accept such praise, Holden slowly began to spend more and more time out in public. Soon, all of the qualities Christina had believed were still buried deep inside him began to be reasserted; he was charming, funny, and a confident, handsome man. While he still suffered an occasional tremor, he refused to allow it to embarrass him; Christina was convinced that one day the tremors would disappear altogether.

Once Holden started taking steps to return to his old life, it only seemed natural he'd turn his attention back to teaching. Christina remembered how passionate he'd been about standing before a classroom and helping children learn, about shaping young minds. Therefore, she wasn't the least bit surprised when he'd told her he was going to enroll in teaching college.

And so, last fall, Holden had packed up his things and headed off for Madison on the GI Bill, hoping he could finally make his lifelong dream a reality. Tyler found it hilariously ironic that Clara had cried as Holden drove off; for what seemed like forever she'd wanted nothing more than for her son to leave his room, but now that he was gone she wanted him back.

The relationship between Holden and Tyler continued to get better. During the long weeks Tyler spent recovering from Luther's beating, Holden was there every day, often talking with his brother well into the night. They kept at whatever grievances they had until they were worked through. Now the two were back to their boyhood friendship, thick as thieves.

Still, every once in a while, Christina looked up to find Holden staring at her. He'd look away quickly and act as if nothing had happened, but she knew he thought about what might've been. But Christina had made her choice; nothing could ever change her mind.

"Do you think Holden will make it home in time?" she asked.

"The last I talked to him, he said wild horses couldn't keep him away," Tyler answered. "I think he knows what we're announcing."

"Did you tell him?!" Christina swatted her husband.

"I didn't!" he protested.

"You better not have or you're going to start sleeping at the garage!"

Just before Easter, Tyler's boss had announced that he was retiring to Florida and asked if Tyler would be interested in buying the business. With Christina's blessing, he'd agreed. Along with the house they'd purchased near the river, they'd begun putting down roots, building a life that would sustain them, their child, and their future. Still, when Christina drove down Main Street she couldn't help but look up at her old apartment, remembering the good times as well as the bad.

Once Annette Wilson was released from jail, her father sent her far away, never to be seen in Longstock again. No one knew where she'd gone, although rumor said she was living with an aunt in Massachusetts. Occasionally, Christina dreamed about the night Annette had attacked her, and awakened covered in cold sweat. Whenever it happened, she moved closer to Tyler, remembering how he'd rescued her and knowing she had no reason to be afraid.

Christina looked up as Tyler started laughing.

"What's so funny?" she asked.

"You're missing it," he replied, nodding his head out the window.

Out in the driveway a car had stopped, and delightedly Christina recognized their visitors.

The first person who stepped out was her

older sister, Charlotte, her hair still just as blond and curly as ever. Zipping past her and hurtling out into the yard, tired from being cooped up for too long, was her six-year old son, Clint. The boy hadn't made it very far before a sharp whistle stopped whatever mischief he had in mind before it even started. Charlotte's husband, Owen, slid out from behind the wheel and got out of the car; he laughed as he tipped his cowboy hat back.

Just then, the rear doors opened and Christina saw her parents. Rachel and Mason Tucker both looked older than the last time Christina had seen them; her father looked especially tired, though it was to be expected after the long drive all the way from Minnesota.

They'd all come to Longstock because she'd asked them to; Charlotte and Owen had traveled from Oklahoma, stopping first to pick up Christina's parents. They were there to see the life she'd built, to eat and laugh and be a family. They were also there to hear about the baby she and Tyler had just discovered they were to have, a secret that had been agonizingly difficult to keep. Her excitement for their arrival had been endless. But now that she'd seen them all, she had butterflies in her stomach.

Just then, Charlotte and Christina's mother looked up at the house and saw Christina and Tyler standing in the window. Both of the women began waving, smiling as brightly as the sun; all of Christina's nervousness vanished in an instant.

"They look pretty happy to see you," Tyler said. "Just imagine how they're going to react when you tell them the big news."

Christina smiled; she could hardly wait.

ABOUT THE AUTHOR

National bestselling and award-winning author of thirty-eight romances that often feature the exciting backdrop of the Old West, **Dorothy Garlock** is one of America's — and the world's — favorite novelists. Her books, all enthusiastically reviewed, now total more than eight million copies in print with translations in 15 languages. She lives in Clear Lake, Iowa.